of STORM & SEA

a nautical adventure anthology

# of Storm & Sea

stl
PRESS

This is a work of fiction. Names, characters, places, and events are either products of the author's imagination or are used fictitiously. Any resemblance to actual persons, either dead or living, events, or places is completely coincidental.

Published by Sky's the Limit Press:
www.skysthelimitpress.wixsite.com/home

Printed in the United States of America
ISBN: 979-8-9953683-0-4

Table of Contents

The Song of the Vessel in Love with the Sea by Anna Huet

A Sea of Stories by Norah Case

The Ghost Ship by Bree Pembrook

To Follow His Plan by Michaela Bush

Fate of the Glowblooded by Rose Everille

Weather the Storm by Emma Rose Thrasher

Sunset's Watch by Lilly Tanis

My Coworker Met the Dragon King by Linyang Zhang

Once Upon a Stormy Sea by M.C. Kennedy

The Storm's Surrender by Jessica B. Brown

The Vitalis by Jennifer G. Satnic

And Neither Can Floods Drown It by Grace King-Matchett

Shattered Shells by Molly McTernan

Introduction
Grace A. Johnson

The first thing that comes to mind when I think of this anthology is *time*.

The long time it's taken us to bring it to life.

The amount of time and effort that each author and editor and designer put into this collection.

The time it takes to shape and form a story, like the tides shape and form the earth.

In every time and every season, there are delays and interruptions and waits, as much as there are fast tracks and highways with 75mph speed limits.

The last four years since I published my last novel and have begun building this press and organizing this anthology have been full of those long, slow, laborious moments. It's been a bit of a culture shock in comparison to how quickly I used to work and how much time I once had on my hands. As difficult and sometimes depressing as it has been, it's also been a valuable lesson in the things that truly matter. Not getting as much done as fast as you possible can, but enjoying the journey (as cliche as it sounds). Not throwing things together or generating them with the touch of a button, but honing your skills and fostering real, human creativity.

We live in a world where instant gratification, high quantity, 2-day shipping, and automatic generation is valued over experience, memory, creativity, quality, and excellence. The things that defined a life well lived are considered inconveniences. Nature, adventure, introspection, the ocean, summertime, friendship, love—somehow these just aren't as great as cat videos or AI photos of ourselves in sparkly holiday dresses.

This anthology challenges that. It invites us to stand before the open sea and dream again, like little kids as we strained our eyes to see if we could catch a glimpse of the other end of the world from our place on the beach. It invites us to go on adventures, experience new things, make a new friend, fight for what you love, become who you were always meant to be, find meaning in your life—even when you've hit the bottom of the ocean.

That's just one of the many things I love about this collection. And I hope that, if you take the time, you'll discover something meaningful and new (or long forgotten) in these stories too. May you be reminded that life is beautiful. Life is a gift from a God who fashioned it with time and intention, who fashioned *you* with love and care. May you never forget that *you* are beautiful and full of rich, uncharted meaning and purpose.

O Lord, how manifold are your works!
In wisdom have you made them all;
the earth is full of your creatures.
Here is the sea, great and wide,
which teems with creatures innumerable,
living things both small and great.
There go the ships,
and Leviathan, which you formed to play in it.

Psalm 104: 24-26

The Song of the Vessel in Love with the Sea

Anna Huet

The song of the vessel in love with the sea,
A tale told to all who are drawn to the waves,
Lost to the ocean that let her roam free.

Upon her first voyage, the ship so naive
Did fall for the ocean, and for it create
The song of the vessel in love with the sea.

She knew of her folly, but helpless was she,
Awed by its power and charmed by its grace,
Lost to the ocean that let her roam free.

Over the waters and 'neath the sky's reach
She chased the horizon and sang all her days
The song of the vessel in love with the sea.

Heartsick the longer she wandered the sea,
Cruelly impartial, her lover's embrace,
Lost to the ocean that let her roam free.

Though long ago lost to the bottomless deep,
They say can be heard through the mist and the haze
The song of the vessel in love with the sea,
Lost to the ocean that let her roam free.

About Anna Huet

Anna Huet grew up with a fondness for stories, drawn to the adventure and hope found in fantasy. With her first poem published at the age of 12, she's since had varying degrees of success with her poems, short stories, skits, and short films; she especially enjoys writing poems with fantastical elements, stories that challenge the reader's perspective, and themes that uphold biblical truth. Anna is 21 years old and grew up in Adel, Iowa; she currently lives in Louisiana as a full-time member of the US Air Force, and takes online classes toward a Creative Writing degree. Anna hopes to eventually publish her own novel or anthology.

A Sea of Stories

Norah Case

For the Guild, which helped me find my writing wings.

Chapter 1

My powerful wing-fins split the water as I cut through it, moving beneath the turquoise shroud like a phantom. Schools of fish and other sea creatures parted before me, darting away from my lithe shape. It was as if even their dull brains recognized me and forced them to give me the respect I was due.

I was the Dragon of the East, and the seas and everything in them were mine to command.

Shafts of moonlight penetrated the water as I drifted just below the surface. Occasionally, one the silvery beams would ignite the blue-purple galaxies that made up my scales. I did a short flip, admiring the way I gleamed.

A nudge on my flank drew me out of my glorying. Mahala, my first mate, had swum over to remind me of the purpose for this late-night swim. Up ahead, a dark shape loomed in the water. It was a four-masted ship, making for the Empty Islands. It sat heavy in the waves, like a portly old man drooping in his armchair. That meant its hold was full of treasure, waiting for my crew and I to liberate it.

Mahala flashed her blue-green scales to catch my attention again. She dipped her head towards me, azure eyes wide and eagerly begging for the signal to begin.

I blinked at her, signaling that I had seen her question, then lifted my head out of the water. The ship drowsed before me, illuminated only by a few lanterns. There were no cries of alarm or hurried footsteps on deck; they had no idea we lurked just beneath their feet.

Sinking back down, I nodded to Mahala. It was time. She flashed a draconian smile, and then let out a soft hum that vibrated through the water, ordering the rest of the crew to advance.

I swam away from the ship, and then twisted in a graceful arc back towards it, gathering speed. Mahala fell into a similar pattern on one side of me, and one of my other sailors, Hatison, on the other. Together, we rammed into the ship.

It floundered on the waves. I rebounded—nearly colliding with Mahala in the process—and shook myself, trying to reorient my body. Even though I had a fairly large shape for a Hybri, the ship was still twenty times my size and bone-versus-wood was not a comfortable combination.

Over the hiss of foaming water in my ears, I caught the sound of shouts from the ship, accompanied by the ringing of a bell. Good. All hands would be racing for the deck, meaning that any riches in the hold would be easy for us to plunder.

I blinked the water from my eyes, waiting for the next assault. If the crew followed my directions, they would wait until most of the crew was above deck before rocking it again. This way, we eliminated as much of the opposition as possible.

It was somewhat of a toss-up as to whether or not they would obey me. I was young, having taken the helm only two years before. It had been just before my fifteen birthday, the day my father had gone to the Deeps and bequeathed his empire to me. It was my duty to uphold it. To help it remain the strongest pirate enterprise Arkron's seas had ever known. He had been the Lord of the Deep, and I was his daughter, his heir. The Dragon of the East. I would conquer the waves and then the very sun that rose from him.

But to do that, I would need an obedient crew.

Mercifully, the prospect of a hearty plunder seemed to have inclined them towards listening today. The ship floundered again as it was struck from the other side. Sailors tripped off the deck and into the water, where Hatison drifted, waiting to ensure that they wouldn't climb back aboard.

I rallied myself and swam towards the ship again, Mahala at my side. We collided with the wood, making the ship rock again. I swam back, shaking my head. If only my Hybri form had been a whale or some heavier creature! Capsizing ships wouldn't be such a headache-inducing routine with a thicker skull.

I abandoned the ungrateful thoughts as soon as they came. My form was a gift. I fluttered my wings, pushing the water around me. Not only were they suited for the ocean, they were strong enough to carry me into the sky. Not many Hybri shape-shifters could claim that they had mastered water *and* air. Tipping ships might be hard in my body, but I wouldn't trade the sky for anything.

The ship righted itself again, but it was riding low in the waves. As I watched, it descended further. Good. That meant it had taken on more water than they could pump out.

I swung my head about, searching for Malhala. She was swimming towards the ship again, preparing for another assault. I recalled her with a low grumble.

She hesitated, looking back at me.

I rumbled again, fluttering my wings. *Come on,* I thought. *Come on. If you listen to me, the rest of them will.*

She twisted in a graceful arc and swam back to me. She cocked her frilled head to the side, awaiting orders.

If only my dragon form could smile like my human form could. I nodded, and jabbed a talon towards the ship's side.

Her lips peeled back in a semblance of a smile, and

she twisted away from me. She chirped, and the sound carried through the water like an off-key flute.

Our crewmate, Tekla, swam around the stern of the ship. Like Mahala, he had a heavier form and was equipped with a tail that ended in a spiked ball. Perfect for smashing things. He leveled it against the side of the ship, hammering an opening into the hold. As the wood gave, water gushed into the ship, along with Mahala, Tekla, and several other crewmates.

I coiled myself to join them, but a harpoon whizzed past my ear. If it hadn't been slowed by the water, I would have found myself with a new earring.

The ship's crew had realized that it wasn't a rogue swell attacking them, and was fighting back in a last-ditch effort to save themselves. Leaving Malhala and the others to care for the treasure, I surged upward, out of the water. It took a moment, but my wings adjusted from liquid to air as I shot into the sky. I spiraled around the mast, knocking a sailor from the crow's nest before he could fire an arrow at me, and then dove back onto the deck.

My claws scraped the wood as I swung my angular head around, snarling. The sailors scrambled away, aiming harpoons and arrows at me. I lashed out with my thin tail, tripping some and smacking the weapons away from others.

One sailor brandished a sword at me. Sweat ran in streams down his face, and he was panting. His lips were parted, and behind them I could see his clenched teeth.

I laughed. Above the water, my voice could function once again. "You don't want to do that. I will spare you, if you leave now."

He charged, swinging his sword as he screamed prayers and curses in the same breath.

I caught him in my jaws, feeling flesh and bone yield

to my teeth, and tossed him overboard.

His companions pressed further away. I bared my teeth, daring them to approach. However, the deck was sinking, nearly level with the water now. Their attention had turned to evacuation.

I sat back on my haunches, watching them scramble to their rowboats. I had ordered the crew to let them escape. Someone had to carry the story of our exploits to the rest of the world. Besides, they had nothing of value, and I was not one to waste lives wantonly. It irked the crew—some of them believed that we should make a clean job of it, killing everyone. But my father had taught me that mercy could be its own treasure. Having someone in your debt could prove useful later, and a wise pirate did not waste resources.

"Captain." Mahala's head appeared over the railing. "We are nearly finished."

I uncoiled my tail from around my legs and splashed back into the water. "Good. Did you leave anything for me?"

"Of course, Captain." She tipped her head towards the jagged tear in the ship's side.

"Excellent. Herd everyone back to the *Hoard*. I'll be right behind you."

She sank back under the water without another word. I followed, though I veered into the opening. I trusted my crew to collect everything of value, but all the same, I loved the thrill of recovering something for myself.

I emerged in a mostly underwater hold. A few lanterns dangled from the ceiling, flickering as they valiantly attempted to remain burning. The room was littered with evidence of my crew's work–smashed boxes, splintered shelves, a few bodies of men and women floating atop the water. The final item was a small chest, still untouched by the water. The body of a woman drifted just beneath it. Her colorful dress ballooned around her like a toppled circus tent. I gently brushed her aside, taking heed not to catch myself on the sword in her hand. I swept the chest into the water with my tail, caught it in my talons, and dove into the ocean once more.

Mahala and my five other Hybri crewmates were ahead of me, spiraling and twisting about in the water as they celebrated a successful pillaging. All of them were dragon Hybri like myself, with iridescent scales that gleamed a rainbow of colors. Their crates and chests hung heavily in their claws, threatening to drag them to the Deeps. In the haste to escape the sinking ship, I hadn't noticed that my crate felt lighter than it should. I peered down at it. It was still tightly sealed, so nothing was leaking out...

I cursed inwardly. Had I just grabbed someone's worthless luggage of personal items? It wouldn't be the first time it had happened, but all the same, I prided myself in being able to distinguish between worthless items and treasure by their weight and their smell. But in my haste, I hadn't taken the time to check for either of those.

Growling, I dove toward the sea floor. I would break open the chest and see what it contained. If it was something precious, like fine linens or silk, I could easily get it to the surface and dry it out before it could be ruined. But if it was indeed rubbish, it would be better to leave it rather than have it take up space in our hold.

An outcropping of jagged rocks on a sea shelf loomed up before me. Coiling my hind legs, I swung the chest against the outcropping with as much force as I could muster.

Thanks to the resistance of the water, it took several tries. Finally, a ribbon of cloth drifted from it, followed by a bigger bundle. I shook my head in disgust. It looked like it was just clothes, or cheap fabric. I turned to rejoin my crew.

Then a flash of something pale made me whip back around and squint at the bundle. There it was again—a tiny, waving fist.

What the Deeps!? I snatched the bundle in my claws—gently this time, so that the tiny creature was settled safely in the center of my talons. Then I surged upward and rocketed through the surface, frantically pounding my wings. How much water could a baby take on before it drowned? What about the water pressure? Even in my massive shape, it bore down on me like a shipload of stone. Who in their right mind would lock a baby in a *treasure chest* when pirates were attacking?! Yes, there usually were casualties when we commandeered shipments, but if we discovered children on a ship, we made a point of leaving it alone. It was an unspoken rule of the sea, one that my father had adhered to, and one that I forced my crew to follow as well.

I circled the *Hoard's* mast and settled onto the deck, shaking off my draconian form. My senses dulled as human Cassia Lockheart emerged from the scales and wings of Hybri Cassia Lockheart. Sweeping my long, dripping hair out of my face, I pulled the child up to face me and ripped the damp, strangling cloths away from it. It wiggled in my hands, whimpering. Weren't babies supposed to cry? I turned it around and patted it on the back, then patted it a little harder. Heaving, the child vomited a lungful of seawater all over the deck. This was followed by a piercing wail. I drew the thing closer to me, trying to quiet it. At least, that was what you were supposed to do, right? I knew nothing of small children. I had lived my whole life on the sea. My story was one of cutlasses and escapades. Not bottles and babies. I was the Dragon of the East, striving to maintain my father's empire.

"Captain?" Human once more, Mahala ran towards me. Her human figure was as graceful as her Hybri one. Her olive skin gleamed in the sun, and her curly hair bounced against her cheeks. Its ends were blue-green, a hint at her characteristics in her Hybri form. She managed her duality perfectly, while I felt much more comfortable in my dragon shape. I was more awkward as a human, with my mane of perpetually tangled auburn hair, lanky legs, and explosion of freckles across my face and shoulders from a childhood spent in the sun. Across my cheekbones were ridges of purple and blue scales, my external Hybri characteristic while human. "Captain?" Mahala tried again, tipping her head to the side. "Are you all right?"

Her question drew the attention of our fellows, in various stages of transforming, as well as the human crew, buzzing about on the rigging and the deck as they tended to the ship and cataloged the spoils. All motion ground to a halt as I revealed the child. It huddled against my chest, whimpering.

Mahala recoiled. "What is *that*?"

"A baby," I said, slowly rising to my feet. "It—he—" I guessed from the blue color of his sodden blanket "—was in the trunk I recovered."

As if her own disgust compelled her to take a closer look, Mahala leaned close again, her nose wrinkled. "Captain, I insist that you throw this thing overboard." She waved towards the horizon, where the mast of the ship we had sunk slipped beneath the waves. "Where he can rest with his parents." Her hand closed over the child's shoulder. "He does not belong in our world."

The baby fussed, and some instinct made me pull back, shielding him with my arms. "Says who? Perhaps we found him for a reason." My father had always maintained that there were no coincidences in a world such as ours. When stories intersected, it was for a purpose. Perhaps the child hid a great power, or would be useful to me later. "He could have a place with us here."

She snorted. "Captain. *Cassia*." Her switch to my real name made me flush. Her tone made it sound like I was a silly child playing dress up. Young or not, I was still her captain, and the cutlass at my side was sharp. "You think that you could raise him to be a sort of successor for this?" She waved her hand around the *Hoard*. "He is not even Hybri!"

"No," I admitted, glancing down at the child's pale body. It showed no signs of externalities that would mark him as a shape-shifter. "Still, I found him for a reason. He survived the water for a reason! We will keep him, and see how his story plays out with us."

Mahala scowled. "He survived because you swam up so quickly! There is no predestination involved here, Cassia. Just chance. You don't have time to take care of a baby. *We* don't have time to take care of a baby! Sure, you think he's cute now, but just wait until he fills that diaper! Or drools on you!"

"I don't think he's cute." I eyed the wriggling bundle again. "Actually, I think he's quite hideous. But this enterprise does *not* harm children. It is the *one* rule of the sea! If you truly protest his presence, we can leave him at the next port we visit." There, a compromise. Would that be enough to sate her? I raised my voice to ensure the rest of the crew—who were pretending not to listen—heard. "As the captain, this is my final word. The child stays."

Mahala shook her head, a disbelieving look on her face. "This is not in the best interests of our enterprise, Cassia. Even leaving him somewhere would draw unwanted attention. And distract you! Every time we'd make port, you would want to check on him. Remember the kitten you insisted on saving last year? We almost got captured in Port

Azure because you tried to find it again!" Her eyes flashed, and before I could argue, she raised her hands into the air. "As the first mate, I invoke my right to put the captain's decision to the vote."

There was a collective gasp from the crew, and I clutched the child so tightly that he began to cry. Mahala flung a finger at me. "In this matter, I fear that Captain Cassia Lockheart has proven that she is too immature to make the correct decision. I vote for the child to be cast off."

There were surprised murmurs throughout the crew, though only a few hands went up. Good. I still had some allies.

Mahala's eyes darted around, counting the hands. Scowling, she lowered hers, and in the same motion, drew her cutlass and leveled it against my neck.

I narrowed my eyes at her. "How *dare* you. My father would have had your head for this." I glanced towards the rest of the crew, hoping that one of them would step in and wrestle her cutlass from her. However, none of them stirred. Some of my pride in them for not voting with Mahala trickled away. They hadn't advocated for the death of the baby, but they weren't moving to help me.

"Luckily, your father is no longer captain, and you won't remain one for much longer if you carry on like this." Her gaze softened. "The *Hoard*, us...this is your destiny. You are the Dragon of the East. Your story is only just beginning."

I thought of the feeling of the water flowing past me, of the power of cutting through the waves. Of seeing sailors cower beneath my roar. Yes. I was the Dragon of the East. Not a nursemaid. I wanted to follow the path my father had laid for me. It was lined with several codes, the foremost of which was that loyalty to your crew came before all. If you wanted them to be loyal to you, you had to be loyal to them first.

I peeled the child from my chest. His eyes opened for the first time, staring at me. He looked like an insulted kitten, fresh from an unwanted bath. But when he grinned, his toothless smile somehow cut me more than a set of fangs could.

Fresh doubt flooded me, as if I was a ship that we were trying to sink. This was the world I wanted to inhabit, the story that I had promised to write. This, this was my crew, the motley group of people I had been tasked with turning into a legendary force. Like my father's crew had been. Losing them over a baby? It seemed like this should be an easy choice.

Mahala snatched him from my arms and held him away from her as she carried him towards the rail. Like he was something rotten. The crew parted to let her through, but I tagged after her. "Mahala, *stop*."

With a huff, she turned. "What now?"

"We should name him," I said, thinking quickly. "It's a sacrilege to send him to the Deeps unnamed."

"We're pirates. That doesn't matter to us." She was perilously close to the rail now.

I stepped forward and grabbed her by the shoulder. "Am I or am I not the captain?" I shouted. The baby began to cry. "You will obey!"

Mahala leaned closer, eyes narrowed. "Or what? The crew is on my side in this." She lowered her voice. "And you know that you would be unable to lead them without me. I have the most experience."

"I could manage," I spat.

Mahala smirked, but before she could send another barb in my direction, the baby snatched one of her blue-green-black curls and yanked on it. Mahala roared and made to fling him away, but I caught him, hugging his little body against me while I drew my cutlass. "Mahala Seawood, I hereby charge you with mutiny and—"

A blow between my shoulders knocked my breath away and sent me into a roll, trying to get away from this new adversary and avoid simultaneously squishing the baby. When I stumbled to my feet, gasping, I found Mahala, and Hatison —who had been the one to strike me—aiming their weapons at me. The other Hybri had drawn their blades but stood aside, watching to see how this played out. My eyes met Tekla's pleadingly, but he looked down, studying the hilt of his cutlass.

I stepped towards the rail, clutching the baby, so overwhelmed with shock that all I could do was hold him close. "Why?" I whispered. "I'm the Dragon of the East. I am your captain."

The corner of Mahala's lips twisted into a grim smile. "Perhaps it is time for the sun to set on your reign. You're weak, Cassia. A mere child, trying to fill your father's boots. There are bigger prizes we could go after, but you keep us here, attacking little ships. And now, this." She gestured to the baby in my arms. "You want to keep this child like it's another stray cat, without even considering what the lasting implications could be. No. You cannot be our captain any longer."

My lip curled at the hungry gleam in her eye. She had been waiting for an opportunity like this. A chance to use my age and beliefs to unseat me. "Then who will take the helm? You?"

She smiled. "Yes." She sprang. The other Hybri followed her, swinging their weapons or crouching to shift into their other forms. With the panic twisting through me like mead on a cold night, it was easy to call up my Hybri. I exploded from their midst in my draconian form, a screeching roar tearing from my throat. Below, I heard answering caws as some of the Hybri launched after me.

But I was lighter than them, and faster. I soared over a cloudbank, tightening my talon around the baby, and peered over my wings to see the *Hoard* slip out of view, along with everything and everyone I had ever known.

Chapter 2

The rising sun crystallized the water, making it seem as if the waves had become diamonds and one could run across them, into whatever world waited on the other side of that glowing orb. Standing in the back door of my shop, I scrubbed the heel of my hand over the scales on my cheekbones as I watched it, mesmerized. It called to me—the waves, the power—as alluring and deadly as a siren's song. I wanted to go back there, but I couldn't. I shouldn't. That domain had belonged to Captain Cassia Lockheart, the Dragon of the East. A deadly, destructive child who had wreaked havoc on the seas. A monster, who had thought little of anyone but herself.

Cassia Lockheart, humble bookseller, was trying to be different. Trying, and often failing. I jerked away from the sight and ducked into the kitchen of my lighthouse-turned-bookstore. In my opinion, the squat structure could hardly be called a lighthouse, though the lamp that still sat atop it, now full of cobwebs from decades of disuse. After being replaced by a *proper* lighthouse, the place had sat vacant until ten years ago, when I had claimed it as my new home.

In the kitchen, wide windows still looked out on the sea and allowed the sunlight in, but with the glass filtering it, its song of the waves was not as tempting. Like how cotton or wax stuffed in one's ears could help block a siren's tune.

I popped open a small tin of concealer, mixed to match my skin tone, and began to spread it over the scales on my cheeks. First, however, I had to dust the shed ones away. This had been a constant problem ever since I left the water. My external characteristics got irritable, especially when my alternate form begged particularly hard to be released. The makeup was cold and sticky, and I shuddered as I spread it over my scales. In order to maintain the new life I built here, I forced myself to suffer through it.

A chime from the front of the building made me jump, nearly dropping my brush. A customer, already? "Luka!" I shouted.

No response. His bed had been empty when I rose, so I knew he couldn't be asleep. Where had the blasted boy gotten off to? Scowling, I snapped the tin shut and hurried into the shop.

Entering the bookseller's trade had been an ambitious venture when Luka and I had arrived in the Eastern Islands ten years ago. At the time, I had not yet given up my youthful hunger for some measure of notoriety, and noticing that the island of Tahella didn't have a hub for newly published works and news from the mainland, I had thrown myself into the trade with reckless vigor. Somehow, after many failures and missteps, our lighthouse had become a staple for this commodity in the Eastern Islands. It had been slow going at first, and there were often lean seasons, but Luka and I had gradually generated a faithful clientele.

Like Mrs. Rosewood, who stood patiently at the counter, holding an addition of today's news leaflet. "Good morning, dear!" she crowed, waving it at me. "Where is your lovely son today?"

I accepted her orbs and dropped them into the till. "He's not my son." Mahala's concern that keeping Luka would result in lasting implications for me hadn't been unwarranted. Most people assumed that he was my son, even though we had no physical similarities. Though the story certainly softened people towards me, a small part of my pride rebelled against the idea that the compromising of my honor had landed me on Tahella with a six-month-old baby in tow.

Mrs. Rosewood leaned over and patted my hand. "It's all right, dear. We all make mistakes in our youth, and yours has grown into quite the blessing."

We all make mistakes in our youth. I stared at her hand, wrinkled from a lifetime of holding others. Her husband had gone to sea and never returned, having been slaughtered by pirates.

Likely slaughtered by me and my crew.

Until coming to Tahella, I hadn't realized that there was another side to the stories I had always told myself about my crew's exploits. These stories ended in tears and broken families, as well as a loss of a livelihood for many. The dramatic stories I had told myself about the Dragon of the East's reign of terror were scary tales to them, with the main character a monster, a beast to be feared and hated.

And now that monster lived among them, undeserving of the kindness they showed her. "If he were a blessing, he would be here," I grumbled, jerking my hand away from hers. "Enjoy the news. I'm sure it'll be the same rehashing of politics and advertisements for someone's lost dog or hand-knitted socks that are too big for anyone to wear."

She tittered. "Perhaps you should have gone into the fortune-telling business, Miss Cassia!"

"But I didn't, and I'm a bookseller now. Good day." I ducked into the back room and proceeded to trip over a box of new books waiting to be shelved. Spitting out a few colorful curses that might have stymied Mrs. Rosewood's unending smile, I tried to catch myself on one of the shelves. I realized too late that I had grabbed our current 'problem shelf', an unsteady collection of wood and nails we hadn't been able to afford to replace yet. Amid a fresh wave of curses, I tumbled to the ground, and the shelf clattered atop me, trapping me against the floor like the bars of a cell.

"Cassia!" Luka charged into the room, a piece of candy in his hand and a worried look on his face.

"There you are! Where have you been?!"

"Delivering the books to the school, like you asked me to yesterday." He stuck the candy between his teeth to drag the shelf off me.

Oh, right. Free of the shelf, I sat up, nursing my new bruises while Luka bent over me. He'd had a growth spurt in recent months, but was still a head shorter than me. His hair was black and curly, and his eyes were a brilliant, sea-foam blue. Whenever I met them, my heart erupted with a strange combination of love and guilt.

"Are you okay?" he asked around the candy, wiping his sticky hands on his trousers.

"I'm fine." I hauled myself to my feet. "I wasn't paying attention to where I was going."

"We need to do something about that shelf," he said, pulling the half-disintegrated stick from his mouth. "I can see if there is any scrap wood down by the docks. We might be able to prop it up so it's level."

"I doubt even that would have stopped it from tipping over if I had grabbed it in a last-ditch attempt to stop myself from falling."

He grinned. "Probably not." The smile slid from his face, and he reached up to touch the scales on my cheek. "Did you not put your makeup on today?"

My hand flew to my face, and I struggled past him to the mirror in the hall. The concealer had clumped up and was oozing from the scaly ridges on my cheeks, as it did when I didn't spread it properly. Had I forgotten to blend it in before going to help Mrs. Rosewood?!

What if she noticed? Was she now gossiping to her

friends about it? How long would it take for rumors to spread?

Luka's face appeared in the mirror next to mine, and he grabbed my hand to press the final, untouched bit of candy into it. "Cassia, I'm sure it's fine. They already know you're kind of strange. If she saw the scales, she probably thought it was just paint or something."

I couldn't share his optimism. The townspeople couldn't know what I was. What I had done. I was trying so hard to write a new story for myself, and him. The Dragon of the East had been a murderer, trying to carry on a legacy of horror. My father had taught me his codes, of course, but in the end they had been designed with the intention of keeping his empire stable. He must be writhing in his watery grave to know that his policy of mercy had caused me to forfeit my inheritance.

Don't think about that, I told myself as I hurried down the hall to the kitchen. *It's over now. It's all over now. I know I'm a monster, and I'm paying for my sins in being here. By taking care of Luka and living a different life.*

Luka followed me into the kitchen, watching as I frantically opened the tin and began blending more concealer over my scales. "Maybe you should stop covering them."

I snorted, plunging my brush into a dish of water to clean it. "And let them realize a monster has been living among them for ten years?"

"You're not a monster." He leaned against my stooped form, resting his chin on my back. Picking up the candy I had placed on the counter, he offered it to me again. "Here, it's mango flavored. Your favorite."

"I don't want your candy, Luka."

He caught my hand and forced me to take it. "But I want you to have it." Smiling, he stood on tip-toe to kiss my cheek before skipping out the back door.

"Don't forget we have to pick up a shipment at the docks this afternoon!" I called after him. My hand curled around the orange-and-red-candy. A good person would have insisted that he keep it, but then again, I wasn't a good person. I was a land-locked monster who had once pillaged more than candy from other people. So I thrust it into my mouth and marched back into the shop, forcing myself to taste the guilt along with the sweetness of the mango.

Chapter 3

The ship was late. Luka and I sat at the docks for hours, fanning each other with the large leaves of a nearby sandstem tree to stave off the midday heat. More than once, I tried to send Luka home to get him out of the sun, threatening that he'd end up with freckles like mine if he didn't find shade. However, he pointed out that I wouldn't be able to carry the crate by myself. Perhaps in my Hybri form I could have, but obviously that wasn't an option now. I hadn't transformed since my early days here. It was a part of my self-imposed sentence: I must remain a fragile human.

Begrudgingly, I ceased my nagging, and we sat together, watching the sun sink lower and lower into the sea. With Luka beside me, its pull was less strong, its song less seductive. He was an anchor, tethering me to this new life. Even though he had upended all I had ever known, forcing me to question my deepest held beliefs, I loved him dearly. If confronted with the choice of saving him again and returning to my former place, the answer would be easy. He had kept me from committing more hideous crimes as I aged upon the waves. He had helped me realize that there could be a life outside of my father's legacy.

I had been right. He had come to me for a reason, to save me and my potential victims from myself.

I was pulled from my thoughts as he leapt to his feet and pointed to the horizon. "They're here! Oh...Silent Star Sea."

Normally, I would have scolded him for the curse, but my attention was currently on keeping myself from spitting ones far more vulgar.

The ship limped towards us, shunted along by its

single remaining sail. Its fellows lay in heaps of timber on the deck, and it rode low in the water, suggesting that it was taking on more as it dragged itself towards port.

"Maybe it ran into a storm," Luka whispered.

I shook my head. As the unfortunate vessel drew nearer, I could make out the long scrapes on its side, and the patched hole that had been blasted through the boards. I knew what—*who*—had caused such damage.

Bells rang as the ship's plight was realized by the harbormaster. The dock filled with deckhands and warehouse workers, all waiting to receive the ship and give aid to whoever was left alive. As it drifted to the wharf, lines were thrown down to anchor it to the dock. Luka and I pressed against a stack of crates, close enough to observe the commotion, but far enough away that we wouldn't be underfoot.

"I don't think we're going to get our shipment," Luka said.

"It doesn't matter." I watched as several covered stretchers were lowered from the ship's deck. A bloodied man was helped down and led to sit on some lumber near us. I sidled closer, listening as he babbled to the local healer, who was checking him over.

"They came outta nowhere!" he cried. "Great, hulkin' sea monsters, jumpin' out of the sea and onta our deck...tore holes in us and took the masts down...all for a few chests of fine silk we had..."

Revulsion rose in my throat like hot bile. I grabbed Luka's hand and started up the dock. I had taught my old crew how to pillage like that; I was responsible for those still forms on the stretchers, for that sailor's pain...

The harbormaster stopped us before we could get any further. "Miss Lockheart?"

"Yes," I replied, squeezing Luka's hand tighter.

He consulted the sheet in his hand—the ship's manifest. "It says you were expecting cargo off this vessel."

"Yes, a crate of books. But it seems that someone received them before I did."

"Actually, no." He gestured to several sodden crates being stacked on the dock. "They took most of the cargo, but not your books. Apparently they haven't been versed in the philosophy of 'stories being one of man's greatest treasures'."

"Apparently not." I stepped over to the crate that was embossed with our shop's name. Scratched into the side of it was a crude symbol, one that sent chills down my spine: the morning star, encircled by a dragon's finned tail. My tail. So my old crew hadn't bothered with creating a new mark for themselves after ousting me. I swallowed hard. Was this some sort of message for me? I assumed that after ten years, they had figured out where I lived. But since I had made no attempt to reclaim my helm, they had left me alone, probably to laugh at how low I had sunken: a shopkeeper with a ten-year-old the town assumed was my son out of wedlock. But I couldn't be certain. Occasionally we had scratched our symbol into the crates we left behind, so chances were this was just a coincidence. But this time when I glanced towards the sea, no longer did it seem so tempting; rather, the waves seemed to be a perfect camouflage for a hidden enemy, set on destroying me and Luka.

For the first time in years, I allowed my Hybri senses to unfurl. They came awake eagerly, yearning for freedom. With discipline borne from ten years of practice, I reined it in, forcing the shifting to be channeled to my senses rather than my physique. I used them to scan for anything unusual. However, I detected nothing but the tang of the sea and the usual combination of tar, wood, and canvas of the docks. Hints of familiar scents emanated off the crippled ship, further proof that my crew had done this. However, the water had diluted the smells, as if they were nothing but fading bruises from a fight.

There was no imminent threat. But all the same, I wanted to get back to the lighthouse.

"Thank you," I said to the harbormaster, and picked up one side of the crate. Luka grabbed the other, and together we hauled it down the docks and up the street to the lighthouse. We got it inside as the sun fully slipped beneath the horizon. Too worn to unpack it, I merely pried the lid off to ensure that there were no unpleasant surprises lurking within. The books I had ordered were stacked neatly inside. Some of the ones that rested against the sides of the crate were damp, but otherwise it seemed that the majority of the cargo was untouched.

After a quick supper, Luka and I bundled ourselves upstairs to our rooms. The second level of the squat lighthouse was split into a communal room, two bedrooms, and a washroom. Normally we would hunker in the common room and read to each other for an hour, but tonight I sent Luka off to prepare for bed immediately. In the washroom, I scrubbed the makeup off my face. My scales emerged from beneath it, like buried treasure in the sand.

After seeing the destruction my crew had caused, I felt disgusted at myself for how I had pined for the sea just that morning. Shaking my head, I swung into my bedroom—only to find Luka already there, clutching a volume of fae tales we had been working through.

"Not tonight," I said, nudging him out of the way so that I could crash face-first into my pillow.

"Aw, Cassia," he pleaded, "just half a story?" He lay down beside me, wedging his body up against mine in the way that he had as a very small child. "I want to hear about

Princess Avaleia and how she and her brother fought to free their island from the pirate queen Captain Yarrow."

Pirate queen. I rolled over and stared at the ceiling. "It's the same story we've read dozens of times. The princess or prince defeats the pirate or the dragon or whatever evil thing is threatening their kingdom. They celebrate and go on to defeat other antagonists while the bad guy disappears, either dead or left to rot away in a cell."

Luka propped himself up onto his elbow. "What's the matter?"

"Nothing."

"Liar. You're using your 'I'm pretending not to be mad' voice, which means that you're really *very* mad." His face fell. "Did I do something?"

My bitter thoughts stilled for a moment, and I pulled him close, nuzzling his hair. "No. Of course not." He was my brilliant ray of sunshine, cutting through my dismal thoughts.

"Then why are you so sad?"

I frowned. "What makes you think I'm sad?"

He shrugged, tracing the scales on my cheeks. "You can only be angry if you're sad first."

I shut my eyes, catching his fingers to pull to my lips to kiss. I had never fully explained to him who I had been before adopting him and starting our life here. He only knew that I had spent my life on the sea, and about my Hybri ability, which he was under strict orders never to divulge and had thus far obeyed. But perhaps it was time for him to know more, especially if my crew was prowling closer to Tahella.

"You know those pirates and dragons that the princess always defeats?" I whispered. "I used to be one of them." I opened my eyes to find his round and wide, whether with horror or wonder, I wasn't sure.

"Wow," he breathed. "You were a pirate? With your

Hybri?! That's...wow!" The delight in his voice was dangerous; I had to set this story straight before his imagination carried him off.

"It's not something to be proud of," I scolded. "I did horrible things, Luka. There's a reason the princess or the prince in those stories always win—because in the end, people like me have to pay for what we've done."

His face grew somber. "Is that why you're here? This is your prison?"

I hesitated. I had chosen this, chosen him over my crew and birthright, and never, ever did I want him to feel that it was begrudgingly done. "Sort of. You know how I love the sea, but I can't go back to it? That's my punishment."

He lay quietly for a moment, thinking it over. "But you're not like them. The pirates in the stories, I mean. You're...*good*. You love me, and you're a good shopkeeper, and you're fair to our customers, not like some of the others I see in the market. Maybe you were bad when you were younger, but you're different now."

"I'm not," I said. "I'm still a monster, and I always will be. So if you see that I'm sad, it's a good thing. It means I'm suffering for what I've done, and that's good."

He scrunched up his nose. "Cassia, I know I'm only ten, but that makes no sense."

I sighed and sat up, shooing him off the bed. "I pray that you never have to understand it. Off to bed with you."

"But we still haven't had a story yet," he protested.

"You heard part of mine."

"Not much of it," he complained.

"Good night, Luka," I said, pulling the coverlet over myself. "We'll read a story tomorrow night."

Chapter 4

The next morning, the sea did not call to me. Heavy clouds hid the sun from view, and the water did not sparkle like diamonds; it frothed and roiled like it was a witch's potion.

Luka shut one of the cabinets with a bang, which jolted my hand, causing me to draw a line of concealer across my jaw. "Sorry," he said, offering me a rag to wipe it up with. "We're out of food."

I raised an eyebrow at him. "Are we really out of food, or are we out of the food *you* like to eat?"

He ducked his head. "A little of both?"

Frowning, I stooped to inspect our cupboards. Luka was partially correct; there was still a little food left in the cupboards, but it was the sort that wasn't best consumed alone, like raw flour and dried rice. I sighed, straightening.

"I had planned to go to the market after we brought the shipment home yesterday...but obviously we didn't get around to that." I glanced at the timekeeper on the wall. We had an hour before we were supposed to open the shop. "All right," I said, and grabbed our basket off the table, "we'll do a quick market run. Hopefully we'll make it back before it rains."

"Does that mean we can have scones for breakfast?" Luka asked, following me out the back door and around the side of the lighthouse to the street.

I chuckled. "Yes, it means scones for breakfast."

Despite the early hour, Tahella's market was already buzzing with activity. I gave Luka a few orbs and sent him in the direction of the baker's, while I haggled over produce and other things we needed to refill our pantry. I might not steal anymore, but I wasn't going to pay six orbs for three apples that had visible bruises.

Adjusting my now-heavier basket on my arm, I strolled up the street, slowly amassing stores that would hopefully last Luka and I several weeks—if I could convince him to eat the greens before they went bad.

I stopped at a stall tucked between two of the larger shops to inspect their collection of citrus fruits. The owner was in an intense discussion with another customer, a sailor by the looks of her garb. "I don't supply ships," she was saying. "My crop isn't large enough."

"Really?" Idly, the sailor picked up one of her fruits, rolling it between her fingers. "These seem like good oranges, full of vitamins to keep the scurvy away. I'm surprised you don't sell enough to finance a larger operation."

"Well, thank you," the owner said, anxiously smoothing her hair back, "but it's just me and my daughter, and between the two of us this is all we can manage."

The sailor grunted. Out of the corner of my eye, I saw a fruit slip into her pocket, and risked another glance at her. She wore a long, dark blue coat, and a three-cornered hat. Her hair hung in many braids, which bounced against her back and slid off her shoulders. Their ends were blue-green.

Shock rooted me in place until she turned towards me. Quickly, I pretended to study the wares of the shop next to me. Perhaps Mahala had thought I was just another stupid landlubber, intimidated by her appearance. Perhaps she hadn't scented me with so many people around.

But her Hybri was still strong and active from frequent use; it would sense me soon. Fleeing would only draw her attention. For now, I was a cornered rat hiding under a bed, waiting for the cat to move so that I could escape.

I sensed movement behind me, and a moment later, Mahala sauntered past. I breathed out a soft sigh, only to choke as she swung up to the display stand I stood at, to examine the necklaces hanging there.

"Mere trinkets," she sniffed. "These fools know nothing of true treasure."

Saying nothing, I bobbed my head and dropped my hand from the string of beads I had been fingering. I risked a glance at her face; her features were still hard, and her eyes cold. There was a new scar cutting across one eye, and another along the side of her jaw.

A splatter of something on the back of my neck made me start and wheel about, half expecting to find one of my other crewmates leering at me. However, it was only rain; the heavy skies had opened up at last. The shopkeeper bolted out to drag her wares inside, shooing us away. I stumbled for the awning of a nearby tavern, trying to reach for my Hybri to see if she was following me and to find Luka. Skittering to a stop beneath the awning, I pressed close against one of its support posts and tried to catch my breath. I scanned the market for Mahala, trying to locate her figure among the ones scrambling for somewhere dry. I leaned out, trying to see in the other direction down the street—and yelped when I discovered her lounging against the other side of my post.

She raised an eyebrow at me. In her hand was the orange she had stolen from the stall; her knife was out, carefully peeling the skin from it.

"It would have been polite of you to at least say *hello*, Cassia." She split a segment from the fruit and popped it into her mouth.

"I don't owe you anything." I clutched my basket against myself. It would be little protection if she came at me with her Hybri, but if she tried to stick me with the knife, hopefully the vegetables would take the brunt of it.

"You owe me your life," she remarked, freeing

another slice and sticking it into her mouth.

I laughed. "My life? You took *everything* from me."

"You chose to leave. And I didn't come after you. I could have hunted you down and killed you when you escaped ten years ago. We knew you had made it to these islands. We could have killed you, but I've let you live."

"Then why are you here now?" I demanded, hugging the basket so hard that the wood cut into my arms.

She shrugged. "More happenstance than anything. We needed some supplies."

"I saw what you did to the merchant ship."

"Ah." She seemed pleased that I had brought it up. "A fine bit of work, wasn't it?"

"You let her make it to port."

"Indeed. It was Tahella's turn to receive the message the other islands and ports in the Sea of Jewels have. The sea belongs to us. To use it, they will have to pay tribute." She offered me a piece of the orange, but I refused it. Placing it in her own mouth, she continued, "So no, I didn't come here to disrupt your pastoral lifestyle. But I'm glad I ran into you." Again, she tried to give me a piece of the fruit, and again, I ignored the gesture. "You've taken to covering up your externalities, I see."

"They remind me of too much." That, and I didn't need Luka and I to draw any more attention than we already did.

She nodded. "I saw you, yesterday morning. At your back door, watching the sea. You miss it, don't you?"

I clenched my jaw, refusing to answer. Mahala waggled her knife at me. "I can feel your Hybri. It wants out. It wants to stretch its wings. Look at yourself. You hide your scales, but you still dress like one of us." She indicated my trousers and tunic, a stark contrast to the dresses and skirts of the other women around us. "You're poised. I'd wager you'd jump back onto a ship if the opportunity arose."

"Is that what this is?" I demanded. "An invitation to rejoin my own crew?"

She shrugged again and tossed the orange peel into the street. "Of sorts. We have our sights on a big catch for tomorrow, just off the coast here. At sundown. Your help would be valuable."

"You aren't worried that I'd convince the crew to munity and restore their rightful captain to her place?"

She laughed. "Oh, Cassia. You've changed in ten years, but some things are the same. You're still terribly naive." Her eyes flashed. "And you're still too weak to challenge me. The crew is mine, and they know it. Together, we are the Dragon of the Jewels. One body, one feared beast to rule the waves. And with you, we could be even stronger." She held out the final piece of orange to me.

A desperate part of me wanted to snatch it from her hand, throw the basket aside, and run with her to the sea. My words to Luka last night rose to mind: I was a pirate and a monster. People like Mahala and I didn't change. We would be defeated in the end; the Creator was just in that way. And if that was so, then why didn't I spend what time I had left living the story I had always told about myself? Why didn't I go back and be the villain I claimed to be?

My fingers twitched towards the orange. However, a new voice startled me from my thoughts, forcing my hand back to my side.

"Cassia!" A drenched Luka ducked under the awning and held up a paper-wrapped bundle. "I kept them dry," he said, eagerly unwrapping the scones. "They had your favorite, redberry and lavender..." he trailed off as his gaze slid from me to Mahala. "Um, hello. Who are you?"

"An old friend of your..." she glanced at me. "What *are* you to him, exactly?"

Luka looked between us, baffled, and then stepped closer to me. "She's my Cassia."

My Cassia. Somehow, the way he said it made it sound even grander than the title *Dragon of the East.* I dropped my free arm around his shoulders, hugging him close. "And he's my Luka. Thank you for the offer, Captain. But my answer is no."

She raised an eyebrow at me. "As you wish. But should you change your mind, we won't be hard to find." She offered Luka the final piece of the orange. He took it, and she melted into the rain.

"Was she...from your past?" he asked, looking up at me.

I nodded, setting the basket down at my feet to give my arms a rest. The tension was slowly draining out of my body, leaving me as exhausted as if I had just taken Mahala on fist-for fist.

He looked down at the fruit in his hand. "She wanted you to go with her?"

"Not really. She was just reminding me of all the bad things we did. Remember what I told you last night. She's not been defeated yet, but she will be." The rain was beginning to let up, so I picked up the basket again and beckoned him out onto the street.

"You weren't really defeated," he said, falling into step beside me.

"I will be, I'm sure. C'mon, I want to eat that scone you brought me."

He shook his head, bafflement written once more over his face. I noticed that he didn't eat Mahala's fruit, but tossed it into the gutter and wiped his hand on his shirt.

Chapter 5

It took a full day for my nerves to settle. However, as I stood in the kitchen making a cup of chai late the next morning, I heaved a sigh of relief. It was over. I had made my final decision to remain here, and I was at peace with it. It felt as if I had been sailing through a hurricane and finally reached the other side.

That is, I thought I had reached the other side until Luka burst into the kitchen, waving a leaflet in the air. "Cassia! A royal crier ship docked at port this morning, and these are all over the market!" He thrust the paper at me.

I grabbed it out of his hands and smoothed it on the counter to read: *The people of Tahella are encouraged to make ready for a visit from Her Majesty Queen Vellara Evenstar of the Fourth Kingdom, as she tours the Eastern Islands to celebrate her daughter, Princess Corana Evenstar's engagement to Lord Lucas Stonefeather.*

Luka hopped up to sit on the counter next to me. "We might get to see the queen!"

"Maybe." I chewed my lip, unease stirring within me. If the queen was sailing for Tahella, and her crier ship had arrived this morning, that meant that the queen's ship itself would arrive this evening...possibly just after sunset.

Mahala had said that a 'big catch' would be theirs by sundown tonight.

Horror coursed through me as the pieces fell into place. Would she really be so foolish as to attack the queen's ship?

But yes, she would. And it wasn't out of foolishness; it was a calculated move that would seal her and her crew's place as rulers of the sea.

Dazed, I dropped the leaflet and drifted out of the kitchen door. Luka followed, asking what was wrong and if I was all right, but he had only become a noise in the background, like a chirping bird. My unseeing eyes were latched onto the diamond-studded ocean as I sat sank onto the edge of our dock and dipped my feet to the water. If Mahala went through with this, all of Arkron would be thrown into chaos, not just the Sea of Jewels and its islands. She would emerge as an unshakeable power, the new Lady of the Deep. Luka sat close beside me, finally silent as he waited for me to speak.

His steady presence drew me back to myself. I whispered, "My old friend—from the market—is going to attack the queen's ship."

Luka's eyes grew huge. "Will she kill her?"

"I don't know. The queen's ship will be laden with riches, which is what she'll be after. But since it's the queen..."

"Should we warn the crier ship?" Luka asked. "Maybe it can sail back and warn them to turn around!"

I shook my head. "It wouldn't make it in time. And even then, Mahala and the crew would still be able to scent it. They probably already have, and are just biding their time. They'll want to do it in sight of the islands, as a demonstration."

"There's really nothing we can do to stop it?" Luka kicked the water.

My hand landed onto his thigh to still him. "No." I couldn't intervene. That would mean revealing myself and tasting the power I had forgone for ten years. One sip of it, and I wasn't certain I'd be able to pull myself back. I'd sink back into my pirating lifestyle as surely as a stone plunging to the bottom of the ocean.

Luka peered into my face, brows drawn tightly, sea-foam eyes calculating. "But she was your friend, and that was your crew. Wouldn't they listen to you if you told them to stop? I would!"

I couldn't resist a short, mirthless laugh as I hugged him. "It's much different out there. Remember what I told you? People like me don't change. We have to be defeated."

He wiggled out from under my arm and stood, spinning around to face me. "I've been thinking about that. And I don't think it's that simple. Maybe in those stories it was, but those stories aren't real life." The sea breeze ruffled his hair, and for a moment, I had a vision of him standing at the helm of a ship, commanding a crew and taming the waves. He would make an excellent captain someday, if his story led him to the sea. "The pirates in the stories *chose* to stay bad. But you chose to not be a pirate anymore, for me. In our story, that doesn't make you the bad guy any more. So why do you keep telling yourself that you are?"

"Because I *am*, Luka. This is the story written for me."

He tipped his head to the side. "But you're not the one weaving it, are you? The Creator does that, and maybe the story he wants to tell about you is different from the one you want to tell about yourself." Once more, he looked out across the waves, and then back at me. "Sorry. I didn't mean to be disrespectful."

"You weren't," I murmured.

"I'll go finish my chores," he said, ducking his head and turning to skitter up the steps.

"I'll be up to the shop in a minute," I replied, slowly pulling my feet out of the water. They met the dry air with a protest, and all of my being heaved with longing to dive in and return to the world that I had banished myself from.

But could I do that without being a pirate? Could I

do it as Luka's Cassia, a different person, living a different story than the one I had years ago? My attention shifted to the city, bustling with preparations for the queen's arrival. All those hundreds of people, a sea of stories which the Creator oversaw and wove together into the grand tapestry of his Story. If he was vast and powerful enough to maintain all of those strands, then perhaps there *was* room in his Story for mine to turn about, for a pirate to become a hero, and make amends for her past.

Glancing at the sun's apex overhead, I drew in a breath and exhaled. Then I turned and hurried to the lighthouse. Luka was helping a customer in the shop; on impulse, I caught him and pressed a kiss to the top of his head. "No matter what, I'm so very glad our stories collided."

His smile was as brilliant, as guiding as this lighthouse might have been once upon a time. I imprinted the memory in my mind, and held it above my twisting thoughts as I sorted through my budding ideas. He was my lodestone, keeping me on the right path. As I helped customers, tidied and closed the shop, and then made dinner, I kept one eye on the timekeeper hung above the door. With every sweep of its arm, the queen's ship sailed closer to Mahala's ambush.

And my thoughts spiraled closer to a solution. A dangerous one that might destroy my new life, and Luka's. But it was the right thing to do, and I couldn't sit here, complacent.

The Dragon of the East did not leave challenges unanswered. Neither did Cassia Lockheart, bookseller.

"Are we going to go down to the docks to watch for the queen's ship?" Luka asked around a mouthful of biscuits and thin gravy.

"You can if you want," I replied, stooping over the water basin to scrub the makeup from my scales. "I have some things to attend to here."

I could sense his gaze on my back. I glanced over my shoulder at him, and smiled. "I promise I'll have time to read our book with you tonight."

He took his time sopping up his gravy with his biscuit and eating it. Finally, he said, "Actually, I think I'd rather hear one of your stories tonight."

"It's a deal," I promised, peering at myself in the hall mirror. I hoped the flaking scales on my cheeks weren't an indication of my Hybri's state.

I would find out soon enough.

The sun was dipping dangerously close to the water as Luka departed for the docks, lantern in hand. I watched him go, and then retreated to our own dock. This time, I waded into the waves and knelt in the soft, wet sand.

And there, for the first time, I offered my story to the Creator to change as he saw fit. I was the Dragon of the East, or I *had* been. But tonight, I would go to the sea as something else. Luka's Cassia, and perhaps the queen's savior, whatever he chose. I only knew that I would stop telling myself the story of my failures, stop letting it distract me from the new directions I could take.

Then, I released my Hybri. After being pent up for ten years, pulling it out was like dragging a tangled wad of seaweed off a fishnet. I bit back a cry, unwilling to alert the neighbors that their bookseller was in the process of turning herself inside out. I fell onto all fours, inhaling water into my snout. The burn made my eyes smart, and I tossed my head, snorting it out. My limbs gave way, and I flopped into the water, expecting it to close over my head. Instead, my chin banged against the sand, and I snorted another nose full of sea water. Wonderful. I jerked my head back, shaking it away. Droplets flew from the small fronds that framed my head. I paddled into the deeper water and twisted into a tight loop, taking stock of my body.

It was larger than it had been during my pirating days. I stretched my wings wide, discovering that they were several feet longer than they had been before. I twisted my tail towards my face and flicked open its fins, admiring how they had grown from small fans to wings a quarter of the size of the ones on my back. My coloration was different as well; I was still a swirling combination of purple and blue, but rather than the undertone of these scales being dark, it had faded to a shimmering white. Hybri didn't usually change color or shape as they aged, and I wasn't certain how to account for the new look. It was as if I had been re-formed. A new look for a new chapter in my story.

I glanced toward the sky, where the first stars had begun to shine. *Thank you,* I thought to the one that had made them. *I will follow this new course wherever you direct it.*

With Luka's smile held against me like a coal to keep my heart warm, I scented the queen's ship. It was emerging over the horizon—and just behind it was the reek of the *Hoard* and my old crew, converging around it. I poised my wing-fins and surged into the water, into the setting sun.

Chapter 6

The water muffled the sound of battle as I swam upon the queen's ship. As I drew close, I began to dodge wood, cannonballs, and other detritus from the ship. When I surfaced, several of the other Hybri scattered, startled by my huge form appearing out of the murky water. I twisted up to Tekla, who, on the outside, had changed little over the years.

I slapped him with my tail. "Where is Mahala?" I shouted, over the blast of cannon fire from the ship.

His jaw slackened, revealing his rows of sharp teeth. "Captain Cassia?"

I sent a wave of water into his face with a sweep of my tail. "Where is Mahala?"

He jerked his chin upward. "On deck."

I hooked my talons into the wood, preparing to haul myself up, but Tekla swatted me gently with his tail, drawing my attention back to him. "Cassia," he said, "You have to know I never wanted that baby to die. There are still those of us who respect you as heir."

"If that's true," I snapped, "then help me end this."

I didn't wait to see what he did. I hauled myself upward, but instead of leaping onto the deck, I used the motion as momentum to launch me into the sky.

The wind kissed my face, as if welcoming me home. I spiraled upward, circling the mast to alight atop the mainmast. Fresh screams heralded my arrival. I craned my head down through the sails and located Mahala, in her human form. She stood in front of a trio of people, her cutlass leveled at them. They were dressed in simple traveling garb, but the crowns on their heads told me that this was the queen, her daughter, and her daughter's fiancé. Mahala hadn't noticed me yet; she was too drunk on her success to pay attention to her surroundings.

I rallied all the air in my powerful lungs and *ROARED.*

The blast rocked the ship, and I could feel it carrying across the waves to envelop Tahella. Mahala spun, eyes large as she found me in the rigging. My massive wings spread wide as I arced my neck, and bellowed, "*I am Captain Cassia Lockheart, the Dragon of the East and daughter of the Lord of the Deep. I am the rightful captain of the* Hoard, *and I am here to challenge you, Mahala Seawood, for possession of my kingdom and my crew.*"

She bared her teeth, but spread her arms in welcome. "Cassia! So you have decided to join us after all!"

I leapt from the mast, landing on the deck in front of her. The ship dipped beneath my weight. "You heard me," I growled. "Leave this ship, and return my birthright so I might make this right."

"Your birthright? You forfeited it when you chose that urchin over us!" She dropped her cutlass against the queen's throat, drawing a thin line of blood. The princess whimpered and pressed close to her mother. "You expect me to believe that you want it back now?" She grinned suddenly. "But it is only natural, I suppose. You are a pirate, and always will be."

"No." I bared my fangs. "My story started with piracy. But it will not end with it, nor will the queen's."

Mahala's lips thinned. "Then it will end in death."

She transformed instantly, lunging for my throat. I slapped her away with one of my wing-fins and launched onto the mast once more, trying to gain sky. Mahala's Hybri was heavier, ill-suited for flight. If I could get her into the sky, I would have the advantage. Lunging after me, she sank her teeth into the secondary wing-fins on my back, which sat just behind my weight-baring wings. I roared, my tail reflexively slapping her away. I sprang for the stars above, but she caught my tail in her talons and jerked me down. It set both of us off balance, and we toppled into the sea in a ball of tearing teeth and claws. The water slowed our fall; I desperately twisted away from her. My fighting skills were out of practice, but she was in her prime. Her hunger for revenge and power fueled her strength. She snatched me by the throat and threw me against the side of the ship; I felt some of the small spikes on my back break at the impact.

She leaned in close, jaws stained crimson from where she had taken bites out of my legs, back, and chest. "This is over, Cassia," she rasped. "This crew, this kingdom—the sea and the land—will be mine."

I growled at her, and as she darted for my neck, I sunk my lower talons into her belly. With a roar, she jerked away and I pulled myself into the air, catching a breeze and riding it into the sky.

Raging, Mahala leapt out of the waves after me. I banked, spinning about to face her, and caught her mid dive. My talons latched around her throat. We seemed to fall back through the stars before landing hard on the ship's deck. Our combined weight made the wood squeal and the timbers buckle. We plunged through the boards, into the cabins below. Shards of wood tore at my scales and pierced my wings, while the crack and pop of breaking wood echoed on my ear like exploding gunpowder. Mahala was beneath me, pinned with my talons splayed over her chest.

"Yield," I shouted. "I don't want to kill you, Mahala. I'm not a monster anymore. Yield and you will live."

"Never." She swung her tail at me.

Oh, Deeps. I had forgotten to account for her tail.

While mine had fins to help me in flight, hers was narrowed to a point, with sharp spines that worked as an effective barb. I had seen it at work on many unfortunate sailors, and now it stabbed into me, tearing through scale and muscle and bone. Agony shook a roar from me. It was over. There was little chance of me recovering from a wound like this.

Luka's smile blasted through me like another blow, but this one gave power to my weakening limbs. Something jolted inside me, some new sort of power that I had never felt as the Dragon of the East, flowing from my core and up my throat to erupt in a brilliant blast of energy that slammed into Mahala's chest.

Her tail went limp as life drained from her.

Few Hybri dragons could summon fire. We mostly relied on our teeth and claws to fight, but here, somehow, I had summoned fire, enough to end this fight. I staggered away from her as she morphed into her human form, splayed on the broken boards. Gagging on the sooty taste in my mouth, I shook off my Hybri and buckled as the overwhelming pain crashed into me. I staggered to Mahala's side and took her in my arms, staring down into her slack face. "I'm sorry," I rasped. "I'm so sorry."

The ship was coming to life around us: the queen, the princess, and what sailors were left alive peered down into the hole, while several of the Hybri from the *Hoard* slipped over the side—in their human shapes—and approached.

Tekla pulled off his hat to me and murmured, "Captain."

The other Hybri did likewise, with varying degrees of reluctance. Hatison ripped his off and stomped on it, but Tekla stilled him with a glare.

I nodded, acknowledging his words. Tossing my head, I tried to clear it enough to reach for the remains of my plan. Sweat and blood mixed on my cheeks, and I doubled over with another wave of pain. Though I fought to focus, my thoughts were only centered on Luka; I had to get back to Luka to tell him goodbye...

Tekla knelt in front of me, wringing out his dripping ponytail as his eyes skated over Mahala's body. "You have bested her in combat," he said. "And you have summoned fire. You are the Dragon of the East, and our rightful captain."

I clutched Mahala close, trying to gather some strength. They weren't going to enjoy having me as captain for the few moments I planned to hold the title. I would bring an end to this once and for all. "Tekla," I whispered. "My first act as captain is to order you to save who you can from this wreck. Ferry them to the island, and after, await the queen's judgment."

"Judgment?!" He gestured towards the water. "The *Hoard* is right there, Captain! There's still time to get away!"

I mustered all my pain into a glare and snarled, "Am I or am I not your captain?!"

He ducked his head. "You are."

I released Mahala and arranged her hands on her stomach, coughing back the blood that rose in my throat. Trembling, I rose to my feet. "Help me to the deck, please."

Obediently, he offered me his arm. We climbed out of the wreckage, and I turned to face the queen, and bowed as best as I could. "Your Majesty," I croaked. "These seas are yours and yours alone to rule. I hope that you will forgive us for our ways and allow us to try to make amends so that our stories...might not end in bloodshed." I let go of Tekla, trying to hold to some shred of my dignity by standing upright. However, another wave of pain quickly humbled me, and I had to gasp for breath before I could continue. "We will ferry your people and tow your ship to Tahella, and our ship, the

Hoard, shall be yours if you wish to continue your tour." I gestured to Tekla. "If I become—indisposed—he will see to it that the crew follows my mandate." I shot Tekla a warning look. "And if he does not, you may install whomever you think would make a wise captain to see you through your voyage."

The queen was middle-aged, her face imprinted with many lines, from various sources: laughter, scowling, smiling, and frowning. Today it was pressed into shock as it took in the carnage, and then pity as it turned to me. "So you are the daughter of the Lord of the Deep, who made my reign so difficult," she said. "And yet you have chosen a different story than his." She smiled. "How incredible."

"Only by the Creator's mercy," I whispered, reaching for Tekla's arm again. However, he had moved to direct some of the other Hybri as they tried to stabilize the queen's ship, and my hand only swept through empty air. The motion put me off balance. Staggering, I searched for the rail behind me, only to find that it had gone missing also.

My flailing body sent me over the edge along with the queen's cry. The water closed in around me, warm, welcoming. Luka's face flickered through my mind, and I pressed his smile close against me as I sank. I had promised him a story, and perhaps I had given him one that he would spread across the Eastern Islands and to all of Arkron, if the Creator willed it.

So I gave myself over to the waves and let the darkness take me.

Chapter 7

Though it is often harsh to the living, the sea is incredibly gentle to the dead. The waves carry the body to its final resting place as tenderly as a mother laying her child into its cradle. The water rinses away blood and filth, preparing the corpse to return to the Deeps where it was formed.

I had been born in the ocean, and it seemed fitting that I die there. I was dimly aware of being carried by the current, of resurfacing occasionally and gasping for breath as my body instinctively tried to save me.

After a time, my knees struck a sandy bottom and the ocean laid me to rest at last. I rolled onto my side and pried my eyes open. I recognized this small shoal, near the lighthouse's dock. So the Creator had seen fit to return me to Tahella. Gathering a fistful of sand, I squeezed it, surprised by how grateful I was to be back on this rock.

The world dimmed around me again; I sighed and laid my head on the damp sand, feeling the water nudge me gently. Vaguely, I thought I heard Luka's voice shout "Cassia!" But perhaps it was just my mind teasing me in a last-ditch effort to remain alert.

Or not. There was a loud splash nearby, and suddenly there were hands on my cheeks, turning my head towards the moon. Luka's face eclipsed it, his face a mask of alarm. Bloody water dripped from his arms as he propped me up. "You kept your promise," he said. "To tell me a story tonight."

My whole body protested at the effort of just shaking my head. "I'm sorry," I murmured. "Can't...can't..."

His face blurred out of focus, but his warm breath grazed my cheek as he kissed it. "It's okay. You already did, and I can't wait for you to tell it to me again."

He faded away along with the protest on my lips. All that remained within me seemed to be the sound of waves breaking on the shore, over and over again, trying to pull me out to sea. I wanted to let go, let them have me, but a small spark within me held tightly to Luka's words. *I can't wait for you to tell it to me again.*

I clutched it with all my might like it was a life preserver thrown from a ship, until a gentle voice said, "Let go, dear. It's all right now."

It didn't sound mighty in the way I had expected the Creator's voice to sound. Frowning, I clutched harder, only for a hand to land on my shoulder. "You're all right," a voice soothed.

My eyes flew open as reality came flooding back. I flew up with a gasp, only for it to change to a snarl as pain rocketed through every inch of my body. My hand was wrapped around Mrs. Rosewood's wrist. The grip couldn't be pleasant, but she remained beside me, trying to calm me. I released her, my attention sliding to my exposed torso instead, which was swaddled in several layers of bandages.

"I was changing them when you stirred." Mrs. Rosewood reached to refasten my robe over them. "I can give you an elixir for the pain if it becomes too much to bear."

"Why are you here?" I rasped.

She gestured to the corner of my room—for indeed, somehow I was back in my bed in the squat lighthouse—where Luka was curled in a nest of blankets. "He had the good sense to come and get me," she said, drawing the coverlet back over me.

"Luka?" I said.

At the sound of his name, he stirred, stretched, and opened his eyes. As soon as they fell upon me, he sprang to his feet and raced to my side. The feeling of his arms around me was sweeter than that of the ocean enveloping me. With what strength I had, I held him close, pressing my lips against every part of him within my reach.

"Mrs. Rosewood is a healer," he said, drawing back to hold my hands. "I knew she could help you."

I settled back against my pillows. "She has." I cast a grateful look in the woman's direction. "I didn't know you were so skilled."

"Yes." Opening a jar of salve, she picked a dollop of it up on her finger and spread it over the scales on my cheeks. "You should have come to me sooner about this. Covering these with makeup has done you no favors."

"I have to hide them," I said, wrinkling my nose at the sharp scent of the salve.

"You don't have to anymore." Mrs. Rosewood set the salve down on my nightstand. "The entire island is searching for the Dragon of the East. The queen wishes to honor you for your service to the Fourth Kingdom."

I shot her a horrified look. "Do they know I'm alive?"

Luka laid a hand on my shoulder. "We haven't told them. I thought you would want to decide whether or not to reveal yourself."

I shut my eyes. Once, I had dreamed of the Dragon of the East being known throughout Arkron. I had wanted it to be on the lips of every person who looked at the sea. But that had been years ago. And it wasn't what I wanted anymore. "Is everything okay?" I asked. "Did the *Hoard* submit to the queen?"

"It did," Luka said. "There was some fuss, but the queen's guard was able to subdue it. She and the crew are under the queen's command now, and the Hybri have a chance to work off their sentences as sailors for the Fourth Kingdom."

"Good. Then the Dragon of the East is dead." I opened my eyes to meet Luka's. "Let's keep her that way."

He smiled and squeezed my hand. I glanced at Mrs. Rosewood. "Can I trust you to be discreet?"

She raised a hand. "Perhaps contrary to a ship's surgeon, us landlubber healers have something called healer-patient confidentiality. As far as your nosey customers know, you took a tumble down the steps to your dock and need some time to recover."

I grimaced. "A tumble is putting it mildly."

"Agreed. Which is why I'm trusting this boy to make sure you stay in bed." She draped her shawl over her shoulders, transforming back into the meddlesome customer that had occasionally got on my nerves. "Now, if you'll excuse me, I need to refill some of my medicines, after which I plan to help myself to your selection of gardening books." She trotted out of the room, basket dangling from her arm.

Luka climbed up onto the bed and nestled down beside me. I tucked my head against his, content to just lay here for a moment, me and the best treasure I had ever pirated.

However, like all boys his age, Luka was reluctant to stay still for so long, and reached over me to pull a book from my night table. "You've put me off long enough," he said, setting it in my lap. "Read, please?"

"Put you off? I've been unconscious!"

"Yes, how dare you." There was a note of good-intentioned sarcasm in his voice. I poked him in the ribs and was rewarded with a shrill giggle. He snuggled closer to me, his breath warm on my neck like it had been when he was a baby, laying on my chest after a feeding. "You said that the Dragon of the East was dead, but I don't think that's true. You're still alive, after all."

I opened the book in my lap and thumbed to the place where we had left off in what seemed like a different life. "I didn't mean she was literally dead," I corrected. "Someday, she might have to come back." I pulled the marker from between the pages. "But for now, she's starting a different chapter in her story."

Acknowledgments

Writing the acknowledgments is always my favorite part of the publishing process. Putting a story out into the world is never a solo act, and I'm so very grateful to all the people who have had a hand in helping *A Sea of Stories* reach readers. Anna, thank you for your enthusiasm and feedback on the early drafts of this story—I love that we get to be published together! Grace, thank you for putting together this anthology and walking through the publication process with us. My family, thank you for everything you do on a daily basis that has let my dream of becoming an author a reality. Jesus, thank you for everything.

About Norah Case

Norah Case has been a student of storytelling since her early teens. Her goal is to write stories that encourage readers to remember who they are: sons and daughters of the King. She is the author of *Weave the Worlds*, a YA science fantasy novel coming in 2026, and her short stories have appeared in several anthologies. When she's not writing, Norah can be found reading, watching Star Wars, playing Minecraft, and sampling chai lattes. She lives in a river valley in central Iowa with her family and a posse of cats. You can find her on Instagram at @storyweavers_jargon.

The Ghost Ship

Bree Pembrook

Chapter 1

"A ghost ship, Miss Marina," the fisherman says, gutting another smelly tuna. "A ghost ship like a pirate ship of old that drifts across the water soundlessly, pale as the moon. I've seen it with my own eyes. 'Twas a starless night, and the sight sent chills into my heart."

I am so intent on listening to his tale that I hardly notice the stench of the fisherman and his catch. I glance at Caspian, who brushes his sun-bleached hair out of his eyes and shoots me an excited grin.

This elderly man is the tenth to speak of a ghost ship just in Fajardo, Puerto Rico's marina, alone. It seems that everyone in the village knows of it, and all swear that they have seen the apparition themselves. It's a mystery, and mysteries are what I like best.

"Do you think whoever or whatever is on the ship is dangerous?" I rub my finger up and down the buttonless side of the recorder in my hand.

"I don't know." The fisherman holds out a fish to Caspian. "Buy a fish, ma'am? Sir? Only thirty pesos."

Caspian pulls some bills from his pocket and takes the meat from the Puerto Rican's outstretched hand. Buying it is the least we can do in exchange for his information, and anyway, I love seafood and have been told that I cook it to perfection.

That's a good thing since every fisherman we've spoken to has sold us at least one fish.

We thank him, turn from the man and his boatload of fish, and stroll through the growing early morning crowds on the dock. I can't resist the spring in my step. We have our next adventure, I'm sure of it.

And boy, will it be a blockbuster. Our next podcast episode and website story is sure to garner many, many listens. Bermuda Triangle? Ghost ship? Ghost ship *in* the Bermuda Triangle? What could be better?

"Another one?" our photographer Florian asks, camera poised and at the ready, as always.

"Yep. I think we've got a story." Caspian can't hold back the smile that creeps onto his face. "I'll drive."

A grin tugs at the corner of my mouth. "Um... I don't know about that. You're easily distracted. Remember last time with the—"

"Marina! We do not speak of the narwhal encounter," Florian interrupts, and I slap a hand over my mouth and try to keep from chuckling at the memory. I still can't understand how he managed to get so distracted we somehow ended up face-to-face with a narwhal while in our RV. Our previous RV, that is.

As we begin our walk back to the RV-turned-adventure-headquarters, a sea breeze picks up, wonderfully cool on my sunburns and through my honey-blonde hair, still tinted pink at the ends from my most recent lost bet.

Once Caspian and I make it in, Florian climbs behind the wheel and the vehicle roars to life.

"Where to, Marina?" Florian asks.

Caspian answers for me as he stuffs the fish into the chock-full fridge. "The boathouse. We're getting out there as soon as possible. I've been dying for another adventure; I can't wait another minute!"

Sharing the exact same sentiments, I don't mind that Caspian interjected. Being the children of a world-famous explorer and treasure hunter means that we twins have adventure in our blood.

Florian, on the other hand... Well, he only tags along

on our dangerous ventures because the pay is too good to pass up.

While Florian drives, Caspian and I pack all the gear and other necessities for an expedition.

"Mics?" I certainly don't want to forget those again. Having a story for a podcast but being unable to record it defeats the purpose of a voyage.

"I got 'em. You have the cooler loaded?"

"Yep." That important detail had been forgotten on one occasion as well. The result of such a mistake was a cranky brother and a snappy photographer.

Everything small enough is tossed haphazardly into a huge duffel bag, which Caspian sets on the rolling cooler beside the door.

Finally, after a debate about whether toothbrushes were really necessary to pack—I won because I had experienced Caspian's morning breath firsthand many times over our twenty two years as twins and pulled the big sister (if only by a few minutes) card to avoid that catastrophe again—we were ready. I can't wait to get out on the ocean again and in my favorite yacht.

"Almost there, guys," Florian calls from the front of the vehicle.

I kneel on the couch and look out the window watching the buildings crawl by. Tourists and locals alike crowd the streets, making travel slower than usual. Pressing my cheek to the glass, I look farther down the road, over the heads of the pedestrians. We're nearly to the smaller, private dock that houses our boat.

I can't help but do a little excited dance. I know from experience that the call of adventure can never be ignored. After all, I inherited the daring and venturesome personality that dictates where my wanderlust feet take me from my father, and Caspian shares the trait. Florian isn't allowed to call the shots unless it's an emergency and both I and Caspian are incapacitated, so there are no worries about us turning back in a voyage due to seasickness or some terrible excuse.

I turn to Caspian. "What's your take on the idea of ghosts? Could the ship really be a ghost ship, or is there something natural that makes it seem like a specter?"

Caspian shrugs and gives a noncommittal grunt without turning to me. He's fiddling with something, but I can't see what. Standing, I peer over his shoulder.

"What are you doing with Florian's camera?" I whisper urgently as I bend over and snatch it from him.

"Just taking a couple of pictures." He shrugs again, but he has a mischievous look in his eye.

A brief look shows there's no permanent damage to the camera from Caspian's usually rough handling. Letting out a sigh of relief, I wipe the smudged lens on the edge of my shirt. "How many pictures did you take? Twenty? You know how protective Florian is of his cameras, Caspian. He hates it when you take pictures with his camera. If I didn't know any better, I'd say you were just trying to bother him."

Caspian's grin tells me that that's exactly what he was doing. "You've gotta admit, it isn't that hard to do. All you have to do is snap a pic. And it's kind of funny when he gets all red like a tomato."

I decide to ignore my aggravating little brother, glancing at Florian to make sure he hears none of this. He's parking our oversized vehicle.

"We're here. Prepare to disembark." Florian kills the engine and slips out of the RV.

Caspian and I gather all of our gear and follow Florian's example. My heart rate picks up when I see our ride at the end of the dock, bobbing in the waves like the buoys farther out, waiting for us to float away. I tug the rolling cooler over a bump and onto the floating dock behind Caspian. Florian is grabbing his camera bags from the RV while Caspian and I bring everything else.

At the end of the dock, Caspian pulls the boat closer to the dock and its fenders prevent the yacht from colliding with the barnacled wood of the pier. He steps on and sets his luggage on the deck. I hand him my own bags and then heft the cooler into his waiting hands. He arranges our heavier luggage to balance the boat before heading to the captain's spot.

I board and Florian hands me his camera bags, moaning about how bad it would be to drop them in the water and warning me to be very, very careful. The boat roars to life. After loosing the ropes that held us to the dock and giving the craft a shove, Florian jumps on board, and we're off. Florian leans out and pulls the fenders into the vessel.

As land fades from view, I feel like a bird released from her cage. The sea is the place for me. It's wild, untameable, and majorly unexplored. Just the kind of adventure I need.

Caspian whoops as we get far enough away from the other boats to speed up. "Let it begin!"

Chapter 2

"Good boating weather today," Caspian calls over the engine's noise. "Smooth sailing as far as the eye can see."

I kneel in the prow and let the wind blow my hair out behind me. The water is crystal clear below, and fish are visible swimming deep down. It's all so beautiful, I almost think it had to be made by someone greater than a big bang.

I cringe as I realize I'm starting to sound religious.

Tearing my attention from the thought, I glance to where Florian sits inside the cabin, already looking seasick and miserable.

"Just think about payday, Flor," I remind him.

He rolls his eyes and smirks. "If we survive this, I'll gratefully accept my upcoming paycheck, as well as that long-expected *raise* you've been promising, Marina. I'm getting too old for this job."

"You're only twenty."

"Exactly. Much too old for this."

"No drama," Caspian chimes in.

All Florian does is roll his eyes again as he returns his attention to checking the camera battery. I look back out to my beloved ocean, admiring the clearness of the water and the blue emptiness of the sky. I lean my chin on the cool railing, and my eyelids droop. Water travel always makes me drowsy. I blink hard. I can't sleep now. I need to keep my eyes open for the mysterious ship straight out of the 1600s.

The messy load from a seagull plops onto the railing dangerously near my head, and I'm forced to move from my comfortable position and keep from falling into the temptation of sleep. I cross the deck to sit beside Florian on the cooler.

Florian doesn't acknowledge my presence, his face

buried in his hands as he suppresses nausea and a camera sitting discarded in his lap.

Grabbing my thermos of pre-made coffee, I take a sip. Florian sighs dramatically, and I attempt sarcasm, though I'm not as skilled in the art as he is. "We must pay you really well for you to risk sea sickness for cash on payday." I give Florian a playful poke with my elbow.

He groans through his hands. "You just knotted my insides with your bony elbow. I think I'm going to be sick. Sick*er*, I mean."

I can't help but give him another light nudge, just because. He gives a dramatic moan and glares at me over his fingertips.

I snicker but leave him in peace. After a few quick mouthfuls of coffee, I head up to visit Caspian. Climbing the ladder is my least favorite part. I scale it quickly, not wanting to be hanging over the water for too long. I scramble to the top deck and fall into one of two built-in chairs behind Caspian's.

"How goes it, Cas?" I ask, staring out at the mesmerizing waves.

"A little choppier than it was earlier, but good. Making great time, though to where we have yet to discern. Keep your eyes open."

"Will do, Captain." I pull a pair of binoculars out of the pocket on the back of Caspian's seat and hold them to my eyes. I'm confused by the blackness I see. Everything is dark. Ah, silly me. Lens caps. I pull them off, tuck them in my pocket, and swivel them back and forth, taking in the horizon. A tiny gray cloud in the distance catches my eye.

I nudge Caspian's shoulder. "Storm, ten o'clock."

He looks where I direct. "Very far away, and the wind's blowing it the other direction. We should be fine."

The wind shifts.

Ten minutes of smooth sailing later, raindrops are falling. They're steadily growing heavier and thicker. Caspian slows the boat to a safe speed and tells me to pull up the canvas tent arrangement he built for this situation. I do so. The makeshift roof shields Caspian and I from most of the rain, but I can't see well now. I take the binoculars and climb carefully and slowly down the slippery ladder, ducking into the cabin where Florian is sifting through pictures on a camera. I pass him and exit onto the deck, grabbing my thermos and chugging the warmth into my core. All too soon the small container is emptied and the cold invades my limbs again. Raising the binoculars to my eyes again, I scan the horizon. I can barely see past the raindrops smudging the lenses, but I catch a glimpse of a big, distant... something. The big something is moving. It looks like a giant white ghost on the horizon, but not particularly a ghost ship. But what else could it be? The rain makes it look ethereal.

"Caspian!" I yell, though I doubt he can hear me through the storm. "Nine o'clock!"

A growl emanates from the cabin. I tear my gaze from the whitish thing and enter the calm dryness of the cabin, sitting next to Flor. He's scowling at the screen and his finger has stopped pressing the button to flip through photos.

I can guess what picture he's found. "Caspian's glamor shot?"

Florian gives a dry laugh. "It's not Caspian's vanity I'm worried about currently." He points at the corner of the picture.

In the photo, behind Caspian's grinning head, all of our walkie-talkies sit on the shelf of the RV.

"We're so smart."

Why, oh why do we always forget *something*? There's

no cell service out here, so our phones are useless. But I've just sighted something on the water—we can't turn back now. "We'll be fine. I just spotted an unidentified formation in the distance. We can't go back for them." I shrug. "It's just a little boating trip. What could happen?"

As soon as I say those three words the weight of doom seems to settle upon our vessel. The rain pounds a little harder and the wind blows a little stronger. Florian's unamused look isn't helping me stay confident.

"We can't!" I say one more time, but it's mostly to reassure myself that we will have no need to radio back for help.

But since when do we have emergency-free trips?

I shake the thought away. We'll be fine.

Florian might quit his job, but that's happened before, and he always comes back... Yes. We'll be fine.

There's a thud from the pilot's deck above, and the boat accelerates once more. Caspian probably wants me to get back out there with the binoculars. I sigh and, too soaked already to bother with a jacket, head onto the deck.

I nearly drop the binoculars when I see how close the wind has brought the ship. It's very obvious that it's a schooner, even though it's still only the size of my palm, and the wind is bringing it closer by the second.

I whip around and fling the cabin door open. "Florian! Camera. Now."

Florian looks very pale and sickly as he slips his camera strap around his neck and reluctantly joins me in the deluge. He grabs an umbrella by the door and hands it to me, and I open it to hold it above him and his camera while we both try to stay upright in the wind and with the rocking boat beneath our feet.

I point at the thing we need photographed, and

Florian goes a shade whiter when he sees the schooner. Still, he raises his camera obediently. The shutter clicks six or seven times before he lowers the device. "That's the ship alright."

"Ghost ship."

"Ghosts aren't real."

"How do you know?"

"Only crazy people like you believe in ghosts."

I scoff, my eyes never leaving the ship. "I never said I believe in ghosts."

"You never denied it either."

I don't answer. Caspian still has the boat moving very fast, despite the growing swells, and it's worrying me. Going this fast on these choppy waters isn't safe. I tear my gaze from the ever-nearing ship—so close now that I can make out small forms on the deck, surrounding a big, strange contraption—and wave up to the top deck to get Caspian's attention. I can't see through the rain to be sure his eyes are on me, but I motion for him to slow down anyway.

Nothing happens.

My crazy brother is going to get us killed. We're going so fast and breaking over so many huge waves, Florian and I can hardly keep our footing. We're both holding the rail for dear life and my palms are so sweaty and the rail so wet that holding on barely does me any good.

Something isn't right. Caspian's a bit crazy sometimes but not crazy enough to do something this risky. He needs to slow down. At the rate we're going, we'll come in contact with the ghost ship in minutes.

I move through the cabin and to the ladder on the back. The idea of climbing it makes me queasy, but I have to. Tossing the binoculars onto the cooler, I grip the wet bars. I go up as quickly as I can without falling, terrified of the cold, roiling waters beneath me. Scrambling up onto the top deck, I let out a sigh of relief.

My sigh becomes a sharp intake of breath when I see Caspain slumped in his seat. I rush to his side, pulling his limp foot off of the gas pedal before my limbs stiffen and I forget how to breathe. "Florian!"

Florian's head appears at the top of the ladder as the boat slows, his face still pale. "What's wrong?"

"It's Caspian."

Florian hoists himself up and comes to my side, dripping water across the already wet floor. "What—?" He brushes Caspian's unruly hair from his forehead, revealing a large, bruised lump. A jagged cut runs across it, and blood trickles steadily down. "He's been knocked out by something."

"By what? How?" I want to grab Florian's shoulders and shake answers out of him.

"I don't know. There's nothing he could have possibly hit his head on, anywhere—"

Florian stops mid-sentence and stares open-mouthed past my head and through the windshield.

I follow his gaze.

The ship is bigger than I had imagined, coming closer and closer to our now immobile boat, but my attention is caught by the hole in the windshield. It's big enough for me to stick my fist through, though I'm not going to risk trying to do so with the jagged edges of glass around the opening. Spiderwebs of cracks weave through the rest of the glass. I don't know how I couldn't see it from below...

I turn to see Florian searching for something. "What is it, Flor? What happened?"

Florian lifts a rock off of the floor and mutters something.

"Is it the ghosts?" The foolish words slip out, though I'm quite sure I don't believe in ghosts.

"It's not the ghosts. It's the crew on that ship. They are very much alive and in a bad mood."

Chapter 3

Florian half-drags Caspian from the pilot's seat, settling him gently on the floor against the wall. He drops behind the wheel.

This isn't good. "You don't know how to drive one of these!"

"Guess I'll have to learn quickly because those *people* cannot catch us."

I sit down on the floor beside Caspian just in time for the crazed photographer to get the boat in motion.

Suddenly, there's the sound of breaking glass, and Florian dives from the chair, narrowly escaping a rock identical to the other. The boat's engine is idling, and we're bobbing helplessly on the waves. Our only capable boat captain is incapacitated and flying rocks are a hazard to whomever sits behind the wheel.

Our boat is jerked forward and I topple over. I pull myself to my feet and nearly scream when I see what's happening on the deck below.

The ghost ship is hardly ten feet from the prow of our boat, and grappling hooks are scratching Caspian's nice paint job like claws. Several strong ropes, woven together like a spiderweb, connect the hooks to the ghost ship, and my stomach sinks when I realize we can't escape. The most terrifying part is the people climbing onto our boat, though. They are all shapes and sizes, and most of them look like they came straight out of *Treasure Island.*

"Ow." Florian pries my hand off of his arm. I didn't realize I was digging my fingers into him, let alone holding onto him in the first place.

"What do we do?" I'm having trouble keeping my

voice level. This is nothing like any adventure we'd been on before, and it's making this whole trip seem like a terrible idea. "This should not be happening! There are no more old-timey pirates around here! Or at least there shouldn't be. It's the twenty-first century, not the seventeenth!" I've never panicked before, not even during the narwhal encounter, and the idea of not being levelheaded makes me sweat even more and dig my fingers further into the arm I'd subconsciously grabbed again.

"Marina. Let go of my arm."

I yank my hands back. They seem to have a mind of their own. A mind set on gripping Florian's forearm. "Well. You still haven't answered my question. What do we do?"

A very hairy head appears at the top of the ladder. A knife is clenched between the burly man's teeth.

"Surrender. It seems like a good option, seeing as we're both unarmed and far outnumbered. I think after this I'll demand a pay raise, for real this time." He puts his hands up, and I do the same.

The man pulls himself onto the deck. He's so huge his head brushes the canopy. Rainwater drips from his long dreadlocks and messy beard. His eyes are a steely gray that analyze me, deciding whether or not I'm a threat.

I can't help but sidestep behind Florian.

"Some explorer you are. Can't handle a giant, armed-literally-to-the-teeth, tattooed man in a pirate costume?"

For obvious reasons, Florian's sarcasm isn't very funny to me.

The big pirate glares at me and Flor for a moment before removing the knife from his mouth and sliding it into a scabbard that looks tiny beside his sheathed cutlass.

His mouth remains a thin line, but he gives a short bow and I blink. Aren't cutthroat pirates supposed to be...

cutthroat?

"Good day."

I can't help but gasp. This one has manners, too. This is getting weirder and weirder. I'm curious enough about everything to be brave and speak. Curiosity—and maybe a little caffeine, an irresistible lip loosener for me—is overtaking my fear.

"I have so many questions." I start blabbering. "Who are you? Why are you... pirate-y? What is this, cosplay gone overboard? Why did you throw a rock at my brother but now are acting like a perfect gentleman? Do you guys have mood swings and anger issues or something? What on Earth are you doing here? Tell me everything!"

Florian's elbow reminds me that I'm demanding answers from a huge, armed pirate.

Caffeine was a bad idea.

"I'm sure Captain Meeri can answer your questions. She does with every curious captive we collect. I shall insist that you step this way, or must I use more persuasive means of making you move?" The giant motions for Florian and I to move toward the ladder.

I can't get my feet to move, thinking of the pirates that no doubt wait in the cabin below. Florian grabs my wrist and pulls me into motion while the pirate slings Caspian over his shoulder as though he weighs no more than a sack of potatoes.

I know for a fact that he weighs much more than potatoes. This guy's strength is terrifying, and I want to make him put Caspian down. If he so wished, he could snap my brother's neck with one huge hand.

Florian lets go of my wrist to climb down the ladder. It's all I can do to keep my caffeine and adrenaline-fueled fists from flying into the gentleman pirate's face and free my brother from his clutches.

Instead, I lower myself down the slippery ladder and focus on the sound of rain hitting me, the water, the deck... and the pirates that have swarmed our boat.

Nope, thinking of the rain isn't helping.

When I reach the bottom and enter the dry cabin, there are four pirates waiting. And one of them is a girl who I assume is Captain Meeri. I stand beside Florian and study the woman since the other three in the room are just your average hairy and scary pirates.

Captain Meeri, on the other hand, has golden blonde hair held back by a crimson scarf, and it's silky smooth, no dreads in sight. I assume she possesses a hairbrush, unlike the men of her crew. She stands at the same height or a little taller than the men beside her, only dwarfed by the giant who has maneuvered down the ladder with Caspian. When I look at Meeri's face, her blue eyes are softer and warmer than the icy cold I was expecting.

"Goededag, latest captives. Join me on the *Houten Zeemeermin* and I'll explain everything to you. Captives are always full of questions, let me tell you. I have had much practice giving answers. But we must be underway, so, after you." Her mesmerizing Dutch-accented voice stops and she steps to the side. With one hand, she gestures for us to follow two of the three pirates onto the stormy deck.

Florian mutters about wanting to bring his cameras as we exit. More pirates meet us. One catches my eye, another lady pirate. She's balancing on two ropes of the spider web connecting the ships and reaches down to help me over the churning water below.

I suddenly feel as seasick as Florian, the contents of my stomach matching the stormy sea I'm about to climb over. I step back and collide with the barrel chest of the giant holding Caspian. He smells like fish and saltwater. I step forward again to give him his space and save my nostrils. I can only imagine what Caspian is suffering, even in his unconscious state.

He moves around me, Caspian still flung over his shoulder, and climbs the ropes one-handed, sending my heart flying to my throat. Once he reaches the top and is level with the huge ghost ship's deck, he hands Caspian off to another large pirate, nearly identical to himself, and climbs back down. He's a very fast climber for his size and is soon standing directly in front of me.

"If you would like, miss, I can carry you up the way I carried your brother. Same for you, sir." He glances at the extremely pale Florian.

Florian's eyes widen, but as I expect, he clutches his camera to his chest and moves toward the rope. He'll never let anyone carry him in such an undignified way.

I might though. "If you wouldn't mind."

I suddenly find myself slung over his shoulder. The fish smell is overpowering, and it's not particularly comfortable. His hard shoulder digs into my stomach.

It becomes even more uncomfortable as he climbs the ropes and all I can see are the pirate's feet, balanced on thin ropes, and the roiling waters below. We pass Florian, who's going very, very slowly to keep his camera strap from slipping over his head.

If I knew how to force myself to faint, I would do so now. It would be better than screaming, I think. Screaming would require inhaling large lungfuls of Stinky-Guy's fishy clothes.

I settle for balling my fists in the grimy, soaking-wet material of his shirt and trusting him to not drop me into the sea.

Lucky Caspian's unconscious for his trip.

After what seems an eternity, I'm passed off to the mirror image of the giant and set on my own two feet on the deck of the ghost ship. Or the *Houten*... whatever Meeri called it.

I look up from my soggy tennis shoes and give a muffled cry of panic. Pirates, everywhere. There are even a few above me, walking along the yards and climbing across the rigging, managing the huge canvas sails. Beside me stands the contraption I noticed earlier and a basket of stones beside it. The device is no doubt what flung the rock so far and hard that it broke through the windshield and knocked my brother out. A pirate sits atop it, tossing a stone between his hands and giving me a pleasant but still unnerving smile. He looks just like the pirates in the movies, eye patch and all. The one thing that doesn't match is the gentlemanly air about him. That doesn't change the fact that he's a pirate in a pirate-free sea.

I pinch myself once more just to be sure I'm not having a nightmare.

I wince. My skin burns where I tried to wake myself. This is all very much real.

Surrounded by pirates, I stand awkwardly on deck until Florian finally makes it up the ropes and onto the deck, his face as white as a sheet. "That... was terrifying." He tries wiping water from his camera with his damp sleeve in vain. "And look at my poor camera. I had to leave all three of my other ones behind, too! How terrible is that?"

The lady pirate that had been standing on the ropes walks by with something in her hands. "Flor, isn't that your camera?"

Florian's jaw drops. "That—that's mine! Marina, that's mine! They're taking my precious cameras!"

"I dare you to try and stop them."

"That's not even funny." Florian crosses his arms and glares at the camera-holder's back.

Pirates are coming aboard bearing their bounty: our things. I feel almost as irritated as Florian when I see my empty floral print thermos carried by.

Someone clears their throat. I look around to find whoever did it, but no one is near, and no one seems to notice the three new people on board.

Only when I look down do I see the throat-clearer. Before me stands a very short pirate, hardly up to my elbow, his legs crossed as he leans casually on a sword almost as tall as himself. "Your boat's been cleared, so we're going to move out now. Follow me to the cabin, ma'am. Captain Meeri will meet you and your mates there soon. Your brother's already there"

With one last glance at Caspian's poor boat, bobbing in the storm and empty of all passengers, I follow the man. I hear the crew haul in the grapples, and Caspian's boat, our one escape, is set adrift in the ocean.

No way out now. Might as well make the most of it, even if we are trapped and never record another podcast episode. "Florian, if your camera is still working, keep it out of sight and keep snapping pictures."

Chapter 4

The chair I'm sitting in is comfortable, but my surroundings are most definitely not. It's exactly how one would imagine a captain's cabin: the diamond-paned window looking over the sea, a table covered with maps, and a crimson-curtained bed. Rainwater drips from my pants cuffs and soaks into the thick carpet underfoot.

The short pirate is standing beside the door, presumably guarding, though there is nowhere for us to run in the first place. He's still leaning on his sword, and its sharp tip scrapes a divot into the rough planks.

We sit in silence, waiting for Captain Meeri. Caspian is laying on the sofa across from Florian and me, still out cold.

The pirate scratches his clean-shaven chin, his eyes never leaving their place on the wall.

He sure is taking his job seriously.

The door latch creaks and the short pirate steps aside as the door swings open, permitting entrance to Captain Meeri. She's carrying a pitcher full of water.

Meeri dumps the pitcher's contents over my brother's head. His arms jerk and his eyes squeeze shut before his hand flies up to swipe the liquid from his face with a groan. The dried blood on his forehead is moistened and mingles with the water running in rivulets off of his face. Leaning across the gap between us, I gently scrub off the remainder of the blood with the blanket thrown over the back of the sofa and wipe water from his face.

Captain Meeri sighs. "You could have asked for a towel instead of using my favorite blanket, *ondeugend.*"

I mutter an apology and drop the damp corner of the blanket.

Caspian's eyes are wide as he examines his surroundings. "What in the... Where am I?" His eyes land on Captain Meeri and her pirate-y clothes. "Who are you?" When he doesn't get an answer, his eyes move to the short pirate. "Who are *you*? That's a big letter opener, mister. Don't use it on my sister, or I'll knock your block off."

The little pirate rolls his eyes but otherwise doesn't move.

He turns his attention back to Meeri. "I demand an explanation, Miss Larp. Where am I, who are you, and what are we doing here in this... swaying log cabin? And why on Earth was I asleep, and why does my head hurt? And," his voice becomes more serious, "where's my boat?" He scoots up on the sofa and crosses his arms, glaring at Captain Meeri as if boring into her to chisel out answers.

Florian and I turn our eyes to her to triple the effect.

Captain Meeri is unfazed by our inquiring gazes as she drops into a chair and snaps her fingers. The pirate by the door leans his sword against the wall and steps toward a little fireplace, removing a steaming tea kettle and pouring the boiling water into a white teapot. He drops a sachet of mint leaves into the pot and sets it on a tray with four matching teacups and bowls of sugar and cream. He swiftly places it on the coffee table between Meeri and us.

Meeri folds her hands and rests them on her crossed legs. "Help yourself to some tea before you begin interrogating me. I promise you, it's not poisoned. Sergio grows the best mint leaves ever tasted."

I feel my eyebrow quirk. "On a ship? You grow mint on a ship in the middle of the ocean?"

"Oh, no, back on the island."

Island? "There are no islands here."

"You are mistaken. *Kromme Berg* Island is no more

than a day's worth of good weather sailing from here. It's been in my family for generations."

What? *What?* There aren't any islands in this area. Or there shouldn't be. "There aren't any islands here..." I repeat in a daze.

Meeri grunts. "There is one and always has been. We've lived there for hundreds of years."

Caspian seems to have his wits about him compared to me and Florian, who's silently listening with his mouth open. Caspian sits up higher. "If you've been there for hundreds of years, why are there not so many of you?"

"Of course, there's more of us. As I already said, an island full."

Caspian raises his eyebrow. "How big of an island? This is a bunch of baloney, I'm sure. You're trying to scare us into submission, aren't you?"

"I'm quite serious. Why would I need to scare you? You have nowhere to go, and we have no qualms against you. We're merely doing our job."

Caspian falls silent. It seems that Meeri won't have as many questions to answer as she thought she would unless Florian or I speak up.

I'm sure not going to. I'm too stunned to hear any more of this malarkey and be able to comprehend it.

"If that is all your questions, I now have a simple one." She pours herself a cup of tea and takes a sip before setting the cup aside and pulling a leather-bound journal into her lap. Opening it to the middle, she pulls a quill from the inkwell, tapping the excess off the tip.

I crane my neck to see what's in the book and read a bunch of upside-down names. Is it a log of all these pirate's murder victims?

"It's not a ledger of bodies buried, just so you know,"

Meeri says as though she can read my thoughts. "What are your names?"

Silence.

Florian breaks the awkward quiet. "Florian, Marina, and that guy with the bump on his head is Caspian."

Meeri puts down our names in a swirling script that matches the previous entries. "Thank you very much. Now, Sergio will escort you to the guest's lounge and answer any further questions. I would love to answer them myself, but I have work to see to. Enjoy the trip, friends." Meeri sets aside the book and quill to stand, bow, and glide away, leaving us to imagine what horrible fate might await us.

Sergio clicks his tongue and removes the tray of unused teacups. "You're missing out, young folk. There really is nothing better than my tea, if I say so myself."

"Well, look who's so puffed up for his size," grumbles Caspian.

I elbow him but he hardly notices. Caspian stands shakily, nearly falling as his foot catches on the edge of the rug. I stand with him.

"I heard your snide little comment, young man. I may be short, but at least I have the capability to be logical and form legible sentences. I don't think Longshanks here has enough brains in his head to even tell us how the weather is up there." Sergio smirks.

Caspian scoffs. "Watch it, Buster. I'd make a joke about your height right now, but I'm afraid it would go over your head. You look up to me, admit it."

I glare at my brother who's acting like he and this little pirate have been best pals their whole lives, but he doesn't notice. Once he gets caught up in banter, there's no turning back.

"Only in the literal sense. I'd rather have a role model

that is capable of doing things without hitting his head on every doorway and being an impertinent and stubborn young man." Sergio shoulders his sword and motions for us to follow him out the door and onto the stormy deck. The sky is darkening, and a glance at my watch tells me that it's grown late.

Caspian huffs, but a sharper elbow jab to his side keeps him from responding. I change the subject as we follow Sergio. "If you pirates are as peaceful as you say you are, what's with the weapons? And you threw rocks at my brother!"

"We are peaceful, yes, but some of our captives have not been. These 'letter openers' are merely for self-defense. About the rocks... we need to get boats to stop moving somehow. But those little ships with no masts are hard to disable. No masts to knock down and most of the ships are too small to put a cannonball through without completely destroying the ship. So, to stop the windless ships, we have found out we must disable the captain."

I suppose that makes sense.

Sergio opens a trapdoor in the deck and motions for us to climb down the ladder. Caspian goes first, and I follow, soon finding myself almost getting my hands stepped on by Florian. As we descend, it grows darker and darker. Once my feet hit the bottom, it's so dim I can barely see Caspian's form. I move out of the way of Florian's feet as he joins us on this deck. Sergio scrambles down the ladder faster than any of us and resumes his lead position. He pulls a candle seemingly out of nowhere and lights it with a match from his pocket.

It seems this little Sergio is ready for anything. Soon he and the faint light of the candle are leading us through the hold, past crates and barrels that smell of salt and fish. He comes to a stop before a door and swings it open, revealing a well-lit room. We follow him.

I'm surprised. The "guest lounge" is actually a lounge. There's a thick rug similar to the one that adorned the Captain's cabin, and two sofas sit along the walls. Lanterns hang at intervals from the ceiling, letting out sufficient light despite the lack of portholes. They swing with the motion of the storm-tossed ship.

If it weren't for the knowledge that we have no way of getting home, I might enjoy this whole captive thing.

Caspian seems to be thinking the same thing, and he trundles over to the couch and drops onto it. "I'll be napping if anyone needs me. My head is killing me."

He's really taking this whole captive thing in stride. Maybe I should follow his example.

Nope. Florian's taken the other sofa. I'll have to settle for...

Something catches my eye. Hidden in the shadowy corner of the room there's a queen size, four-poster bed. Am I lucky that those two didn't see it?

"The wind is in our favor, my friends." Sergio sets the candle on a table beside the door. "Sleep, and when morning comes, you will see our beautiful Kromme Berg."

I scramble to the bed in the corner as Sergio closes the door behind him. The lock clicks, but I don't care. I'm so exhausted from this extremely unusual adventure. I kick off my soggy sneakers and crawl under the quilt, drifting off as soon as my head connects with the pillow, hardly noticing the rocking of the ship.

Chapter 5

I'm jerked from dreams of pirates and buried treasure by a rough finger poking my arm. Where am I? Caspian's fingers don't feel like carrots wrapped in sandpaper. I open bleary eyes. The room is dimly lit, and my tiredness makes it seem darker. The room sways, rocking. I can't wrap my tired brain around how it's moving. A short man with unruly black hair is jabbing my upper arm with a meaty pointer finger.

Who on Earth...?

Everything floods back. The ghost ship that I'm currently in, the crazy pirate people, Caspian's injury.

Caspian's injury! I should probably check on that, even though I have no medical experience.

Surely I have no reason to be worried. A little bump on the head can't be that bad, right?

My wandering thoughts are jerked back to the present when Sergio speaks. "Do you wish to get your first glimpse of our fair island?"

I reluctantly shove the quilt off and glance around, hoping my brother is still in the room. I don't trust a crazy, well-mannered pirate I just met even if he is more polite—to me, at least—than anyone I've ever met.

Much to my relief, Caspian is sitting on the couch, his hair ruffled from his ritual nighttime tossing and turning. One of the huge pirates from yesterday stands before my brother, wrapping a strip of white cloth around Caspian's head, concealing the ugly bump. My bleary-eyed brother is staring at the wall, eyes having trouble staying open.

I shift my focus from Caspian to Sergio. "Where's Florian?"

Sergio chuckles. "The lubber regained his tongue

early this morning. He's in Meeri's cabin, demanding his loot back. Something he called cameras... We've never seen any device of this type, but we have people who can figure out how they work. They might not get a chance to investigate if your friend gets his way, though."

Maybe I can help Flor a little. "I bet he can strike up a deal. He'll tell you how they work, and you'll give him some back."

Sergio's mouth quirks into a half-smile. "I'll talk to the captain. Now you need to get yourself up onto deck. We're almost to the Lighthouse."

The short pirate walks toward Caspian and the big doctor, leaving me to wonder what he's talking about.

I swing my legs—still damp—over the edge of the bed, setting my bare feet on the rough wood deck. The idea of replacing my wet shoes on my feet does not appeal to me so I forgo them. The giant pirate finishes tying off Caspian's bandage and follows Sergio out the door, closing it behind them. The motion beneath my feet has decreased, so I guess the storm has died down. I pad across the floor to Caspian's side. He's leaning his head against the wall, eyes closed, arms thrown across the back of the sofa. I nudge his hand and he opens his eyes.

"If my head didn't hurt so much, I'd be convinced this is all just a weird Alice in Wonderland dream."

All I can do is hum in agreement. "Did you hear Florian's up there demanding his cameras back?"

Caspian snickers. "Good ol' Flor." He puts his hands over his face and groans. "It hurts to laugh. Don't talk about our camera-protective friend, it's too funny."

I chuckle and reach out my hand to help my brother to his feet. He grips the arm of the couch to keep his tipping self steady once his feet are under him.

The blow to the head must've been worse than I thought. My big sister instincts flare within me, and I want to whack the nearest pirate upside the head. We didn't even have anything valuable for them to steal, but they decided to give my brother a concussion, abandon our one way home, and kidnap us.

Not exactly the adventure Caspian and I were imagining.

Although... we might as well make the most of it. "We need to start interviewing these pirates and taking notes. You know, if we get back to land, this would be a good story."

I pause and feel each of my jeans pockets. My microphone is still jutting from my back pocket. How I managed to sleep with it there I'll never know. "I still have my mic, we can do it."

"Whatever you say, boss. How much battery is on it?"

I didn't even think about that. I look at the little screen and sigh in relief when I see that there is still almost one hundred percent battery. "We've got a couple days worth."

"Now we'll just need to hope Florian's cameras have that much juice."

I nod and throw Caspian's arm across my shoulders. "Let's go make sure he hasn't gone into a protective rage to retrieve his cameras. And see that lighthouse they were talking about."

Caspian and I move toward the door, which I assume is unlocked, my brother leaning heavily on me. We make our way through the dark store room, and I let Caspian slowly climb the ladder before me. I cringe every time his foot slips, but he catches himself each time. When he pushes the trapdoor open, wonderful sunshine falls on me. Definitely no storm clouds near. I scramble up the ladder and on deck. The salty sea air is cold, but the warm rays of the sun drive away the chill. There are pirates working all around, but somehow I feel semi-comfortable.

One night aboard a pirate ship, and I'm getting used to them? I must be crazy. I notice that I'm not affected by the rocking of the ground beneath me, either. How odd.

I help Caspian to the rail as a little wind blows my pink-tipped hair. Land is in sight, very close, though I'm no seaman and can't tell exactly how far. The island is one jungle-covered mountain, though its slopes don't seem to be too steep. It's mostly green foliage, but buildings rise from the trees in several places and the shore is rocky with sand bars at random intervals. As we draw nearer, a huge gray structure on a peninsula of stone jutting out from the island catches my eye.

Ah. That must be the lighthouse.

The building is a tall, weathered, stone building of an unusually curved shape that stands nearly as high as the ghost ship's masts. The lower half is obviously a residence, and the thinner tower rising from it ends in a small, glass-enclosed room. A few panes are broken, matching the worn and battered look of the rest of the structure. I can barely see the unlit brazier and reflecting mirror within when the sun catches them.

I direct my attention past the lighthouse and nearly fall over the railing.

Not far from this rocky outcropping is a village straight from 1700s Europe. The Baroque architecture is apparent even at this distance, and it's a mixture of styles from several different countries. Tiny people move between the structures, and I can pick out horses and wagons as well.

Captain Meeri isn't a lunatic after all.

Well... that's still to be decided, actually. Maybe I

have time for a short interview before we arrive at the port near the village.

I sidestep, momentarily forgetting the brother leaning on me in my haste to find Meeri. He staggers after me, eyes flying open. I mumble a quick apology as I half-drag him toward the captain's cabin.

Is this how I should be treating a guy who probably has a concussion?

Eh, he's Cas. He'll survive. I mean, this is my twin brother who had at least one major injury every year until we were eighteen! His big toe alone has been broken more times than all my bones combined.

And that's a lot.

I stop outside the cabin door and make sure no pirates see us enter. I'd rather not get run through for trespassing. When no one is looking, I barge through the door, heaving Caspian with me.

"You have a deal, Captain." Florian shakes Meeri's hand as we burst inside.

It seems my idea has worked. Meeri, her hair twisted into a rope braid and wearing a skirt instead of pants today, strides over to a huge chest at the foot of her bed and reaches into it. Her hand comes back out with one of Florian's two camera cases. She hands it over to our cameraman, who takes it and clutches it to his chest.

"They won't last long without more of your contained lightning anyway." Meeri looks up and notices us. "Good morning, friends. Can I help you?"

I nod, settling my half-awake brother onto the couch. "I've got more questions." I put my hands behind my back and subtly slip the microphone from my pocket, flipping the switch on. I sit beside Caspian and nestle the microphone between me and the arm of the sofa. "Can you briefly explain the history of the island? And the people? And how do you all speak English? And why you're so polite? And—"

"Yes, yes, I will tell all. Though it will have to be the short version, as we will reach the port in half a glass." Meeri settles on the armchair she had occupied yesterday and Florian drops into another seat, flinging the case open to inspect his precious cameras.

Sergio appears out of nowhere with a tray of teacups. Once he's settled it on the coffee table, I pour myself some, which earns a small smile from the man.

Meeri pours herself some, crosses her legs and adjusts her dark navy skirt. "My ancestor, Captain Daan, and his crew found the island almost three hundred years ago. They had just raided the coast of Puerto Rico when his vessel was caught in a storm. They wound up on Kromme Berg, and we, the descendants of the crew, are still there today. We've been raiding passing ships since then. Daan invented the stone-throwing machine, though when the flying ships started coming through, someone else strengthened it to be able to reach."

I suppose this all is plausible. I adjust the recorder beside my leg. "So how do you explain the courteousness? What will you do with us on the island?"

"We are polite because our mothers taught us to be, of course. There is no need to be harsh to captives, thus we are not. And we'd rather not scare them into an unusable state."

Unusable state? What in tarnation does that mean?

Oh, no. Surely not. "What exactly do you mean by that?"

"Why, unusable meaning unsellable, of course. No one wants a slave that's paralyzed by fear because of mistreatment."

Chapter 6

Oh, my great goodness gracious. My hand finds Caspian's arm and squeezes. "But... that's... that's *horrible!* You sell your captives into slavery? Amelia Earhart was a slave for the rest of her life after vanishing?" I feel lightheaded. I take a slow sip of mint tea, but it threatens to evacuate as soon as it touches my tastebuds.

"Oh, it's not as bad as you imagine, think of it more as a hired help position. You will be treated well. The people of Kromme Berg have the same code of conduct as I do on my ship."

I can't stifle the disbelieving noise that sounds like a cross between a shriek and a crying pig. "That doesn't justify that you're selling human beings! This is illegal!"

Meeri gave a disarmingly nonchalant shrug. "Not here. We are not under the authority of your people and have our own laws. Slavery is perfectly fine."

I look to my brother for help, but his eyes are closed and his chest is rising and falling rhythmically. How can my brother sleep at a time like this? Frantically, I turn to Florian. He's paler than a full moon and his camera is slipping from his clutches. A moment later it clatters to the floor.

I run through the situation in my head. Obviously, we can't escape, not now; there are too many pirates. All I can do now is gather more information. Cas, Flor, and I can figure out what to do later. I take a few deep breaths before glaring at Meeri. "How do you justify these actions?"

Meeri releases an irritated sigh. "Honestly, Miss Marina, slavery is a step up from what Daan would do. He'd just slaughter everyone aboard! We now are humane, letting our captives live."

"Humane, huh? So selling people like cattle is better than killing them? Taking them against their will? You don't actually care about people like us. I bet you only do it for extra profit." I lean back and cross my shaking arms. It's all I can do not to react in a wild way, either screaming and running away or punching the captain's nose in.

"Sergio," Meeri suddenly says, summoning the pirate from his place in the corner, "return our guests to their room, and lock the door, please. I think they don't wish to stay with us, though they must." Meeri waves her hand and Sergio moves forward.

Florian jumps to his feet, narrowly missing stepping on his camera. "You aren't taking me anywhere!" He swings his fists in the air with the finesse of a flapping chicken.

With a sigh, Sergio hefts his sword from its resting place on his shoulder. "I will use persuasion if I must, sir," he grunts.

Florian's fire leaves him and his balled hands drop to his sides. He scoops up the camera he had dropped and returns it to its case, clicking it shut.

Sergio nods before turning his eyes to meet mine. "Miss, if you would please assist your brother to his feet."

Abandoning my untouched tea, I stand and pull on my sleeping brother's hand.

As expected, he doesn't budge, his eyelids fluttering and a small moan escaping his lips. My brows furrow and my stomach churns as I bend over him, gently lifting the crisp white bandage around his head. It looks normal. Not that I know what a goose egg of such enormity should look like.

"I need help. Caspian's not well." *No thanks to you dunces,* I silently add.

Sergio sighs again and pokes his head out the door. "Aadan!"

The dreadlocked giant—or maybe his look-alike—ducks into the cabin. I have to stifle a laugh seeing this Aadan next to Sergio, despite the direness of the situation. We're going to be sold, and I'm snickering at kidnapper height differences?

Aadan inspects Caspian's head before scooping him up. "He'll be fine. He's just exhausted from his injury and loss of blood. He needs rest."

I wonder if this man's outrageous amount of hair has addled his brains. Surely it isn't as simple as that.

The giant heads for the door, and Florian and I fall in step behind him, Sergio taking up the rear with his sword in hand. I throw one last scowl over my shoulder at the captain.

We are led back down to the lounge prison, which suddenly feels more like a prison than it had last night. A few of the lanterns have gone out, their candles spent, casting the room into an eerie twilight. I stalk over to the bed and sit down stiffly, ignoring the tray on the table that is piled with rolls, breakfast brought in while we were above deck.

Aadan settles Caspian onto the couch and takes his wrist. "Normal." He straightens, his superior height causing his head to collide with a hanging lantern. He reaches up to steady it as Sergio closes the door and leans his sword against it.

Florian crosses his arms tightly and drops onto the mattress beside me. We both pin scowls on the pirates, though I'm pretty sure Florian's is scarier than mine. Our dear underpaid photographer can be menacing if he so wishes.

My scowl falters when I realize that the pirate duo isn't leaving.

Florian voices my thoughts. "Aren't you going to obey your precious captain and lock us up, you demented skunk's behinds?" His voice drips with contempt.

The corner of Sergio's mouth quirks upward as he comes to stand before us. "Keep your trap buttoned, good sir, and save yourself a world of trouble. Aadan, can you wake Caspian safely?"

Aadan bends over my brother and gives him a vigorous shake that makes his head wag side to side.

Oh, saltwater taffy. He's going to snap Caspian's neck at that rate. I twist my hands in the quilt nervously.

Caspian's eyes open slowly. He groans and puts a hand to his head. Looking up into Aadan's face, he mutters "Five more minutes" and lets his eyes fall shut again.

"Not right now, young man." Aadan gives Caspian one more shake. "You'll want to hear what Sergio has to say."

"And what could the little sea rat have to say to such lowly slaves as us?" Florian asks bitterly.

"If you want to get back to your own land, I recommend you listen up."

My eyes jerk from my lap to Sergio's face. I move to sit beside Caspian, whose eyes are wide open now. "What are you talking about?"

"Listen closely. Aadan and I have been formulating this plan for months, and it seems you three are the lucky captives to become the first escapees. When we walk out of the room, you need to prop the door open, but not noticeably. We will distract the crew while you escape. Our comrades have arranged a fully stocked sailboat for you—you know how to pilot a sailboat, right?"

Caspian starts to nod but switches to answering vocally as he puts a hand to his bandaged head. "Yes, I know how. I won't be able to, though, due to my battle injuries. So there goes your bright idea, shorty. Do you have a plan B, or do you even know your alphabet?"

It seems Caspian's goose egg hasn't affected his

tongue. Unconscious one minute and being sarcastic the next.

Sergio scoffs. "I am fluent in three different languages, spoken and written, but that is beside the point. You will have to make do with the sailboat because it is all we can provide."

Caspian huffs and lets his eyelids slide shut. "How do we even know this isn't a trap? Why are you helping us in the first place?"

My thoughts exactly.

"Meeri's slaving doesn't sit well with us and goes against our beliefs. She uses the slaves in the Bible to justify kidnapping, because Israelites of those days had slaves, right? However, that form of slavery is different. Most of those slaves sold themselves to pay off debts, and slaves were to be treated well. It's an entirely different story when someone kidnaps people and sells them for their own personal gain. She thinks what she's doing is biblical, but it isn't in the least."

So these people are Christians. How quaint. There is no God, and if there is, he certainly doesn't care about his people. Although... I suddenly can't shake the nagging voice that has appeared in the back of my mind, telling me otherwise. Where did this prodding come from? My lack of faith has never bothered me before.

"So?" Caspian says, interrupting my thoughts.

"So, we're helping as many people as we can escape to freedom. Will you accept God's providence, or will you not trust us and stay?"

Well, that doesn't sound right. "So you're claiming to be God since it's your ship you're offering us?" I cross my arms and raise my eyebrow.

"Of course not," Aadan says, "we are only being used by God to give you the opportunity you need. We are assisting your escape... and giving you something worthwhile to think about on your voyage."

Unfortunately, giving me something to think about is working. The little voice in my mind is still there, shocking me with its persistence. Is it Sergio's fault?

Caspian opens his mouth, probably to spew another question, but Sergio stops him. "We don't have time for your blabbermouthing, young man, so if you don't mind letting us know if you'll take our offer or not before my and Aadan's time down here becomes suspicious?"

With a huff, Caspian crosses his arms. "Fine, we'll accept your sailboat."

Sergio gives a short nod. "Remember, prop it open."

I rise and hurry to the door, pulling a forgotten binocular lens cap out of my pocket. I stand, my back pressed to the wall just in case anyone is outside, as Sergio and Aadan open the door and exit. As the door falls shut, I slide the lens cap between the door and the doorjamb, keeping the door open a quarter of an inch. Hopefully, the dimness of the store room will disguise the difference.

I listen as the pair's footsteps fade until I know they are safely away. I move to Caspian's side, contemplating the sanity of our decision to trust these people.

Caspian reaches for his head again, this time yanking the bandage off and dropping it in his lap. He fiddles with it, twisting it around his fingers.

Florian absently taps his fingers on his camera case, the drumming noise the only thing breaking the silence other than water lapping against the hull of the ship.

This situation is impossible. Maybe I went crazy and am imagining things. I'm batty, that's what it is. There are no pirates, we aren't going to be sold, and there aren't crazy Jesus freak pirates trying to save us.

Definitely not.

"So..." Florian sighs, stopping his tapping fingers and interlacing them to keep them still, "did they ever tell us when to run?"

So much for that plan if we can mess it up by timing it wrong. Timing is not this group's strong suit. "As a matter of fact, they didn't."

One of Caspian's eyes cracks open. "Uh, guys—"

"I can't believe it! That was just a trick to get our hopes up." Florian throws his hands in the air.

"Guys—"

"Flor, calm down, you should have expected to be duped."

"Hey—"

"Are you calling me gullible, Marina? Because it sounds like you're calling me gullible." Florian's arms cross and he stares at me with an eyebrow raised.

"No! Of course not!"

"Guys!"

Florian and I both turn our gazes to Caspian. Caspian scoots up higher in his seat.

"Read the instructions, for crying out loud." He holds his bandage out to me.

I take it. Sure enough, on the inward facing side right next to the bloodstain from Caspian's bump, there's small, neat handwriting.

"Oh. Sixty seconds left. Guess we ought to get ready."

Chapter 7

I rip the pillowcase from one of the bed's pillows and put my cloth-wrapped mic in the bottom, burying it with all the breakfast rolls. I knot the opening and hand the bundle to Caspian, who takes it as though it weighs a ton.

Florian dramatically tears a strip from the sheet on the bed, forming it into a strap for his camera case. He hooks it on his shoulder. "I'm ready now. As long as it means a pay raise. Or at least hazard pay, because I'm going to demand hazard pay from now on."

I don't blame him, but I don't think he can convince Caspian to give him a raise either.

"Are we ready?" Caspian asks.

"Hold on," I say, "Florian, take some pictures. You haven't taken much, you've been too busy battling Meeri for the rest of your stuff."

Florian puts his hands to the camera he's been wearing as a necklace since being taken. Caspian and I wait by the door as Florian snaps photos of the room from different angles.

Thirteen different angles.

Florian just keeps going, muttering about lighting, fiddling with buttons on the device.

"I think that's enough, Flor. Let's get going."

"You can't rush this, Marina." Florian snaps one last photo. "It's got a special technique to it. You see—"

"Save the photography lecture for later," Caspian interrupts. "Let's go."

Caspian musters his strength and stands, taking semi-steady steps toward the door. I can tell he's still tipsy, and the swaying ship isn't helping his lack of balance. I stand beside him just in case. Florian is behind us.

Caspian glances over his shoulder at Florian before placing his hand on the door latch. "Ready?"

Flor and I nod in unison. As Caspian pushes the door open, there's a thump on deck.

I think Sergio and Aadan's plan has been put in motion, which means we're at port. Sounds like a very distracting distraction.

Florian and I follow Caspian through the dark storage room and up the ladder. Caspian shoves the pillowcase at me then slowly climbs the ladder, stopping at the top and pushing the hatch open a fraction.

"What do you see?"

"Every hand on deck is at the rail. Now's our chance. Follow me."

Caspian shoves the hatch open, careful not to let it slam, and climbs out. As I climb the ladder after him I can't help but think of how proud I am of Caspian for pushing through his pain to help us escape.

Once Florian and I are both on deck, I glance at the horde of pirates on the port side. Recalling the bandage-written instructions, I look to the starboard side. Sure enough, the gangplank is leaning against the rail. Caspian and Flor quietly raise it and settle it in position. We walk down it, Caspian not the only slow one in this case, as the waving of the water below makes me and Caspian dizzy too. Once my feet hit the dock, I nearly fall. It's so still.

"Marina! Come on!"

I look up from my feet. Tied alongside the pier several dozen feet away, closer to shore, is a good sized sailboat, and I'm surprised to see that it's just like one you'd see in any other marina. It was probably stolen from some poor soul who is now—or was—a slave. Caspian is already climbing aboard, and Florian is halfway to it.

I start toward them, but someone grabs me from behind.

"Where are you going, little miss? I'm afraid I can't let you leave."

I crane my neck to see who is holding my arms. It's the other lady pirate from the ship. How did she catch me?

"Let go! Caspian! Florian! Help!" I struggle, but the woman has a surprisingly strong grip. She jerks me backwards a step.

"You're not going anywhere, I'm afraid. Let's go get someone to grab your friends, yes?" The woman's thick Scottish accent combined with my swirling mind blurs her words together.

"Caspian!"

Panic overtakes me when I realize that they can't hear me over the wind and waves, which have picked up. I struggle harder and will the woman not to call for assistance, hoping desperately that no pirates on the ship could hear me calling for my brother. She starts dragging me backwards, inland. In my head, I find myself begging some higher power —perhaps Sergio and Aadan's God—to please, please let me escape and reach my brother.

A burst of adrenaline floods my limbs and I decide that sometimes a girl's gotta do what a girl's gotta do. I twist until I grab the pirate's arms, then push myself from her grip. I tighten my grip on the pillowcase and make a dash for it as the pirate releases an ear-piercing whistle. I speed as much as possible without tripping on the uneven planks. Footsteps thud on the dock behind me, growing closer despite my efforts to get away.

Florian looks up finally in time to see me barreling toward him. I jump into the boat and land on top of him.

He groans and shoves me off. "Caspian, we need to get out of here, Marina attracted too much attention with her blindingly white teeth." He gets to his feet and frees the boat from the dock.

The lady pirate and two other pirates summoned by her whistle are rapidly nearing the boat. Florian shoves us off with his foot.

Caspian is messing with various ropes and cranks and, by pulling and winding them, somehow unfurls the sail. "The wind's in our favor. Brace yourselves."

I grab the railing just in time for the wind to catch the sail and shoot us forward. Our sailboat's prow bounces off of a rowboat, making the boat unusable, and we move toward the open ocean. In a matter of moments we'll pass the *Houten Zeemermin*, and the entire crew will see us. Will they pursue?

I'm about to find out. We round the prow of the ship and suddenly all eyes are on us. Surveying the crowd, I see a soaking wet Sergio, clutching his arm. He gives us a nod, as does Aadan behind him.

Guilt floods me when I realize what this man we'd only known for a couple hours had done to ensure our escape. I make eye contact and nod back to Aadan and Sergio, who glance upwards as one final prompting for me to remember their God.

Up on the crowded deck, Meeri pushes through the crowd and to the rail. She stares at us as we go by for a moment before calling out. "*Je verrast me, gefeliciteerd*. I will let you go, but I will never forget." She tips her hat at us.

I can't help but grin. We bested her—with a little help from her own crew, but we wouldn't tell her that—and she has acknowledged that.

Florian snaps a photo of this momentous occasion, and Caspian yells, "*Sayonara* suckers!"

We sail farther out to sea, leaving the nightmare behind. Only once the *Houten Zeemermin* has faded from sight do I dare relax and inspect the contents of the storage compartment.

Fully stocked. There are five loaves of bread, two jugs of fresh water, and a small keg of salted meat, as well as a leather-bound book with "Holy Bible" emblazoned across the front in gold print.

Of course, that's what they'd call "fully stocked". These crazy pirates are really pushing their faith on us. On top of one keg sits a tricorn cap, a few dyed ostrich plumes protruding from the band. On the brim sits a note. *A feather in your cap, safe voyage you'll have.* I wonder what suspicious old coot added this hat to the stock. Or maybe it was Sergio. He seems like he could be a suspicious old coot.

I take the hat and set the stuffed pillowcase in its place. Rising to my feet, I move toward Caspian. I come up behind my hardworking twin and drop the hat on his head. "Thanks for coming through, brother. Sergio would tell you the superstition behind this hat right about now."

Caspian momentarily frees his hands from the wheel to remove the hat from his head. "You dropped it right on the grand canyon in my head, but what's the superstition?"

"He left a note saying 'a feather in your cap, safe voyage you'll have.'"

"Then you or Florian better wear it, because I'm about to pass out if I don't hand the wheel to you. Take it."

"But I don't know how—"

Caspian pulls me in front of him and places my hands on the smooth metal of the giant wheel. "I'll let you know if and when you need to adjust. Just keep us going this direction. I trust you."

"Why not Florian?"

"He only knows how to use cameras."

"I heard that," Florian calls from where he sits sifting through photos at the prow of the ship.

"I know," Caspian calls back.

Florian huffs and returns to his camera.

"I trust you, Marina. You're my twin, thus you have the same amount of brains as me, thus I can trust you."

"How worrying that I only have your paltry amount of brains."

"Har har. Just do what I say."

"Yes, Captain."

"Now that's a real insult."

I chuckle and readjust my grip. Excitement wells within me. We're going home.

I just hope Caspian knows the way.

An hour later I'm still gripping the wheel. Caspian is sitting half asleep where he can man the sails without moving. I keep the ship pointing the right way, if my compass readings are correct. Florian's about to nod off as well.

I suppose it's just me and my thoughts. And that obnoxious prodding that has made residence in the back of my head. I give in and think about what Sergio said. For some reason it makes sense. I'd never thought Christian beliefs could make sense.

A thought I've never had comes to mind. What if the Christians believe the right thing and I'm wrong? What if I'm just too stubborn to accept Jesus' free gift of salvation his followers are always blabbing about?

The idea freezes my heart. I could be dooming myself to eternal death just because of my stubborn disbelief.

That mean old Sergio. Now I'm going to have inner conflict all the way home.

This is going to be a long ride.

Then the Bible in the storage compartment catches my eye. I kick Florian into consciousness, hand the wheel off to him after giving him short instructions on how to keep it going the right direction, grab the book, settle on the floor, and read.

I read until it's too dark to read more.

Epilogue

I sit down at my desk in our precious, very-much-missed RV adventure headquarters. It's good to be back after a long day and a half on a sailboat with nothing but dried meat and rolls to eat. In the living room, Florian is editing photos, and in the bedroom, Caspian writes a blog post. Here at my desk, I'm about to record this week's podcast, a plate of blessed real food beside my equipment, ready to be ravenously ingested after recording. All three of us work on the same story: our Bermuda pirate encounter.

I adjust my headphones then flick on the microphone. Once I know it's recording, I begin.

"For years, the Bermuda Triangle has had an aura of mystery around it. What is the reason behind all the disappearances? As of today, Caspian, Florian, and I know exactly what has claimed dozens upon dozens of boats and aircrafts." I find my hand resting on the leather cover of a book, still smelling of salty sea air and still working the seed of a new idea—perhaps a new faith—into my soul. "My name is Marina Galleon, and today I'll tell you a tale of buccaneers and boldness, of storm and sea..."

About Bree Pembrook

Bree Pembrook is the alias of a teenaged, plot-bunny-farming hobbit who writes in just about every genre there is. She sports a long list of unusual things she's done in the name of writing research, spouts off random facts about random things at random times, and still holds out hope that there are dragons and wardrobes that lead to other worlds. She has an irrational fear of heights, but isn't afraid to defend her faith and she hoards books and chocolate like a dragon hoards gold and jewels. Follow her crazy antics on her blog, laughsandliterature.wordpress.com.

To Follow His Plan

Michaela Bush

Cresting the damp wood ramp, I
Paused, looked up, and you
Met my gaze as you took my
Hand. My breath stole away as I
Dove into the ocean blue of your
Eyes, and mesmerized, I was swept
Aloft. The ramp fell to the abyss, the ship's
Hustle and bustle slipped softly to nothing
And you quirked a grin and a brow.
Ruddy-faced, sharp-jawed, and curly-haired, you
Said, "I've been waiting for the day we meet."

Deep familiarity sparked alive in my
Chest and danced in the air as I
Looked deeper into your
Gaze, and suddenly, I knew you—
Somehow, somewhere, in my dreams,
Perchance. I knew you, and you me.
But how? "How did you know?" was all I could
Say, and you chuckled, stepping close
And with the snap of fingers...

Now we were standing in the midst
Of the sea. Upheld by—something, I
Glanced around first in surprise, then terror, but you
Shook your head and caught my eye.
"Look at me. Not around you.
Just at me."
But a storm roiled on the horizon, and
Didn't you see that? The world I tried
To escape, the terrors pushing me to sneak
Aboard the ship that disappeared into thin air—
The promise of an unknown kingdom, anonymity—

"I know," you said softly, knowingly.
"You do?" I asked dumbly. Waves swept
Around you and I, but never touched,
My green gown never splotched wet,
It all foamed and writhed in the deep.
Wind tousled your hair, whipping mine
Into a frenzy, twisting light curls around my
Face, blinding me...
You tucked the locks away and
With tenderness, you said, "Dream and you
Will see too. Let Your Savior guide you
Through the storm, and we'll meet one day—
In the midst of the storm is where peace is found.
Follow the path set before you, and you
Shall find me in the seas."

The waves slammed beneath me, and I wobbled—
Fell forward and clung to your linen shirt.
Suddenly dawn awakened as the thunder roared
Nearer in this little world, and understanding
Finally wrapped around my heart.
"The dreams I saw as a child," I whispered,
Eyes wide open,
Seeing this dear stranger anew, my
Heart leapt up in surprise. But the wind grew
Stronger, and I tore my eyes away again.
"Don't look at the storm," you said, pleading
This time. I wanted to ask why, but I stumbled and
Suddenly a wave roared in, slamming me away from you.

And I was crushed beneath roiling waters
Battered beneath their weight, tossed to and fro
And when I pushed to the surface, faces of the men who

hunted me
Were waiting with blade and dagger on dry land
Waiting to make me theirs—
I opened my mouth to scream for the father who sold me to them—
Then to cry for the one who stood before me moments ago—
But water rushed in and—

I flew awake on hard cobblestone and I
Gasped, heart mimicking the thunder from my
Dream. My hands still reached out for you.
But you were a dream. Again.
I've seen you a thousand times in slumber, and yet you
Never appeared before my eyes.
I collapsed against the stone wall behind me
And breathed.
"Do not be tossed to and fro with doubts," I murmured,
The verse from my dreams when we were mere babes
When the stranger with ocean-eyes first appeared.
Speaking little messages, riddles, promises from a Holy Book
Father never let me touch.
And then the cry rose in predawn dark:
"Boarding!"

I rushed to gather myself, tucking through alleys and twisting roads
Hiding from prowling eyes and toothless bandits
Seeking to find me. I darted into the mass of
Men and women crushing aboard the ship set for a foreign land
And prayed to slip in with nary a boarding cost.
Almost there! The damp ramp met portside and my skirt—
It caught on a splinter—

I gave it a hefty yank and tumbled forward—
A hand reached out to catch my elbow and I
Paused, looked up and—*you*
Met my gaze as you took my hand.
My breath stole away as I met the
Ocean blue of you...and you grinned.
"There's a storm coming, miss..." A mischievous
Glint appeared in your gaze. "Are you prepared?"
I paused, thought back on the dreams.
I met your stare levelly and beamed. "Yes."

About Michaela Bush

Michaela Bush is a Christian author, editor, and entrepreneur. She graduated Magna Cum Laude in 2019 from Clarion University of Pennsylvania, where she earned a B.A. in English and a minor in Psychology. She has enjoyed writing from an early age, and mostly writes Christian fantasy and romance. When she isn't working or creating her next story, she enjoys spending time with her family, horseback riding, playing violin, and spending time at church. Follow her @tangledupinwriting.

The Fate of the Glowblooded

Rose Everille

For AJ and Daniel. Thank you for loving this story as much as I do, and for helping me figure out that the dragons are in fact "Fisherian-Runaway, bioluminescent-microbe symbiosis, mosasaur-relative peacock whale dragons" and teaching me that whales have hair.

Laikal perched on the mainmast yard high above the ship. The wind ripped through his loose shirt, letting it flutter around him. The sound mirrored the flapping of the sails. The sea beneath him stretched to the horizon, the pattern of the waves like woven cloth. The air swirled thick with salt from the sea and tar from the ropes, and he wished he could absorb every sense. He wanted to feel like this forever.

He glanced at Aranél, who tried to tie up the sails on the opposite side of the mast. The stream of muttered complaints was a sure sign of that. Aranél disliked balancing high in the mast of the lurching ship more than most.

Laikal didn't mind, though maybe that was because the chore had not yet gotten old to him. This was the first season he was old enough to join his father, the captain, aboard the *Erynnes*, a dragon-hunting schooner. He had dreamed of this day since he was a child. He used to sit on the piers and stare at the red sun dripping into the water. It had called to him, so faint he could barely hear it. He wanted nothing more than to follow it into the shimmering mirror of the sea.

"Stop loitering and get on with it," Aranél snapped.

Laikal jerked himself out of his reverie. "You're so nice to me today," he said, tightening one of the final ropes to hold the shortened sails up. He glanced past the mast.

Although Aranél was only about four years Laikal's

senior, the scars through his lip and eyebrow made him seem older and twisted his expression to be even more surly. The scars were thin as twine and jagged as snaking seaweed along the hard edges of his face. They glowed a soft aquamarine, a usual effect of working with processing dragons. The dragons' Glow, a radiant substance between their scales, would often settle in open cuts of those who hunted them, leaving an otherworldly glow a lifetime after it had healed. The gold and turquoise beads he'd braided into his dark hair caught the light as the wind roared past them, whipping his braid like the telltale on the sails.

Aranél loosened his grip on the yard and leaned over to grab the shroud, the rope net spanning from mast to deck. The ship lurched sideways as it hit the top of a wave and Aranél held on again, white-knuckled.

"Glowblood's fangs," he swore under his breath.

Laikal laughed, though he'd also been startled. "You reused that one. Do you need new ones? Glowblood's scales, Glowblood's claws. Oh, what about Glowblood's nose?"

Aranél didn't reply, but Laikal imagined him gritting his teeth as he let go and started to climb down the shrouds.

Laikal scrambled along the rope strung beneath the beam to the shrouds on his side. He wasn't sure if there was anything exceptional about Glowbloods' noses, but neither did anyone else. They'd been nothing but a threat and had been exterminated a few generations ago. Laikal shuddered as he thought of the grotesque illustrations that showed something vaguely humanoid with scales, fangs, and the dragons' glow.

Laikal paused, one hand on the shroud. The sea reached to the horizon, an endless expanse of darkness. It was as though he and his shipmates were the only ones alive, and the rest of the world was swallowed by the tide.

The rippling silk of the sea was broken by a spray of white, off to port. Laikal's eyes widened and he leaned out, one hand caught on the shroud still. He balanced there, feeling the wind's tug. A moment later, in the same spot, a ripple of glowing aquamarine appeared. A delicate dorsal fin, fine as fabric, crested atop a dragon.

Laikal's heart jumped into his mouth, and he yelped in excitement. He'd been waiting for this moment his whole life.

"Did you fall and break your neck?" Aranél's voice soared to Laikal from halfway down the shroud.

"Spray to port!" Laikal called. His voice shot into the heights, a laugh carrying through it.

Aranél heard him and picked it up, calling down to the ship. His usually uninterested tone brightened. Soon it echoed from the deck like a trumpet of victory, interspersed by commands from the captain and the three mates.

Laikal grabbed onto the thick ropes, clinging to them like a spider to a wall. He kept his eyes on the dragon, as it appeared and vanished into the velvety waves. The wind whipped tears into his eyes and breath into the sails.

Laikal clambered down, his feet finding the rests as naturally as walking down stairs.

The deck swarmed like an ants' nest someone had stepped on. They had to get aboard the boats before the dragon dived deep again.

As Laikal swung onto the deck, the ship tilted beneath him, sending him skidding along the deck. He lost his balance and fell on his rear. A wave of laughter spread through the sailors as the deck righted again, the first mate's laugh carrying above the others. Cheeks burning, Laikal grinned. It wasn't the first time this had happened and it wouldn't be the last.

Someone reached out a hand and helped him up. It was the first mate, Sildonus.

"Thanks," Laikal started, and Sildonus nodded, still laughing.

He was young for a first mate, though much older than Laikal and Aranél. His hair and beard were golden, and his nose had once been broken. Despite his cheerful nature, he tolerated no disobedience, and if any sailor put someone in danger, Sildonus was scathingly harsh.

"Laikal!"

His father called from the stern, and Laikal scrambled along the deck, weaving between the frantic activity around him. His father had his spyglass in hand, turned toward the distant dragon.

"Yes, sir," Laikal said, breathless.

His father's hair was rough and brown as unraveled rope, and his beard rippled like waves, the silver streaks like seacaps. His clothing was orderly, if you excused the windswept look that was a part of his profession. His undyed shirt was rolled up past his elbows, exposing the dragon tattoo that twisted around his arm. Laikal had gazed at that dragon so often that he had it memorized. It was a male dragon, the crest of dorsal fins fluttery as wings of a bird. The mouth was open, exposing small sharp teeth in its leaf-shaped face. The front fins were large and bat-like. The entire tattoo was done in dragon Glow, radiating aquamarine even from under his shirt. Laikal could barely see the outline of the dragon's tail wrapping around his upper arm.

His face was rugged and looked older than it was from many years at sea. Upon first glance, people might assume he and Laikal were related by blood, but the differences were there. Laikal's skin was lighter, though heavily freckled, his hair black instead of brown, his build and features more delicate. Laikal rarely thought about the fact that he was a foundling. He'd never been left in doubt that this was his father.

"Did you spot that dragon?" the captain asked.

Laikal straightened. Even if it was his father, aboard this was also his captain.

"Yes, sir," Laikal said.

"Well done," his father said, as blunt in his compliments as in his rebukes. He peered through the spyglass again. "Seems a fine-sized male."

Males were easy to distinguish by their large decorative crests. Females were smaller and duller.

Laikal grinned wide enough to split his face. He bounced on the balls of his feet. "Can I go along to see them catch it?"

His father lowered the spyglass with a jerk and glared at him. "Absolutely not."

Laikal's face fell. "But I saw it first—"

His father scowled. "I know. There's plenty of time to die by a dragon once you're grown. You're staying aboard."

Laikal gritted his teeth, his heart falling down to his feet. Here he was again, held back like a child. He was old enough to be here, wasn't he?

"Do you understand me?" his father asked, his voice low and stern.

Laikal's gaze dropped to the rough planks of the deck."Yes, Captain Dad, sir."

His father smiled and ruffled his hair. Laikal smiled again, though the excitement was bittered. His whole life he had dreamed of seeing a dragon, and here he was, watching at a distance again.

Laikal dug his nails into the palms of his hands and bit his lip to hide the disappointment. Why did growing up have to take so long? He was tired of being held back when he knew he could do more. He just wanted to belong and do his part, like Aranél and the other sailors.

"You can watch from aloft," the captain conceded.

Laikal resisted the urge to sigh. That would not have gone down well.

Nodding, he started back to the shrouds again. He didn't want to be up there all by himself, watching everyone else in the most exciting part of their daily lives. The usual activity aboard the ship was deathly dull in comparison—days filled with nothing but errands, working on the sails, and lookout duty.

And now he was relegated back to watching.

One of the sailors pushed him out of the way, none too gently. Laikal hastily stepped back until he stood against the cabin. Staying out of the way was one of the main parts of his job. The rest was making himself useful. He couldn't fulfill the second part, so he'd stick to the first.

Laikal watched wistfully as the last few orders were fulfilled. The sailors crowded by the bulwarks, ready to board the boats as soon as they were loosed.

The captain passed him to address the third mate. He couldn't see Laikal through the crowd of others. Laikal edged closer to the throng of sailors.

Aranél stood nearest Laikal but didn't notice him. The sailor fidgeted with the beads in his braid. This was Aranél's first voyage as a foremast sailor instead of a cabin boy, and his first time joining the hunt. Laikal wouldn't even be the only new person aboard. He edged closer to the bulwark and the nearest boat. He could make it aboard in the chaos that would come soon. Nobody would notice he was missing until it was too late to turn back.

"Ready?" The captain's voice boomed across the

deck. Laikal jumped. He was always shocked by the difference between his father's regular voice and his captain voice.

He'd hear that in full when he got back. His father would be seething because he'd disobeyed a direct command. It was worth it to see the hunt and be part of it.

"Ready, captain," the mates replied. The impatient murmur from the sailors grew louder.

Laikal took his chance and edged closer to the nearest group. He'd only have a few seconds, and he'd need to make use of the tumult to get on board.

"Lower away!" The captain ordered. The ropes whirled around the sheaves, dropping the boats in the water below. They landed with a hollow splash. Aranél followed the others, vaulting over the bulwark and jumping to the boat below. Laikal did the same, not allowing himself to think. His landing rocked the boat, and he dropped into a crouch.

"Places, hurry!" the commander of the boat barked. It was the first mate, Sildonus.

The sailors scrambled to reach the oars, the confusion increasing. Someone pushed Laikal aside. He scrambled to get to the bow of the boat, as far from Sildonus as possible. It might delay his discovery enough to get away from the ship.

"Go, go! Don't let the others get there first," Sildonus urged, his voice harder than Laikal had ever heard it.

Laikal grabbed onto the edge of the boat as it plunged into motion. Lacy white spray parted on either side of the bow as it cut through the waves. Laikal could only see the backs of the others behind him as they rowed. Aranél was far from him, near the stern where Sildonus and the harpooner stood.

They had been talking but now Sildonus turned back to the others. His gaze flitted over them, making sure everything was in order. Laikal tried to duck behind one of the rowers but Sildonus had already seen him.

"I'd throw you overboard if it wouldn't slow us down," he yelled, voice cutting. "Stay out of the way."

Laikal tried to vanish. Maybe he hadn't thought this through well. Squirming, he kept quiet.

Sildonus turned his attention back to steering and shouting instructions. The noise was somehow even more than on the ship.

The harpooner, Nahatal, crossed between the rowers to the bow and crouched next to Laikal.

He was so tall that Laikal still had to look up to him. He wore his dark curly hair twisted back in patterns adorned by the same golden and turquoise beads Aranél used. A glowing blue tattoo shone through the back of his shirt, barely appearing from his collar. It shone bright against his dark skin.

"You're absolutely not supposed to be here," he said, his voice hushed so it almost vanished between the rushing of the waves and Sildonus' yelling.

Laikal nodded sheepishly.

"You will have to explain to the captain why you're endangering yourself and everyone here, and he won't be pleased."

Despite how quiet his words were, they cut deep. Laikal flinched. But surely that was an exaggeration. He couldn't have put anyone in that much danger. They were going to ignore him anyway.

"When this starts, go back to the stern and stay there. If the dragon attacks, you might be out of the way. Do you understand?" he asked. His voice was so intense that Laikal squirmed and looked down.

"Yes, sir."

"Good. You will be listening from now on, since the first mate doesn't have time to babysit. Neither will I as soon as this starts, so you're going to pipe down and, for the love of the Glowbloods' graves, don't get in the way."

Laikal nodded, studying the floor planks.

"Bit late for regrets," Nahatal said wryly. He unsettled Laikal. Nahatal spoke as little as Aranél, but lacked the spite, though he had that same intensity.

He rose and stared out over the water, his posture straight as a mast. He seemed unfazed by the swaying of the boat.

Laikal had thought he'd managed to tune out Sildonus' loud instructions, but he still started as the first mate called, "Nahatal! Where's that cursed dragon?"

"I'm looking, sir." Nahatal barely raised his voice, but it easily carried.

A wave hit the boat from the side and salt water splashed over the edge, soaking Laikal and the sailors on that side, testified by a chorus of curses. Laikal blinked away the stinging spray.

"Help look," Nahatal instructed.

Laikal obeyed, squinting against the sun's glare and the monotony of the waves.

The repetitiveness numbed his mind and made it easy to skim. On the other hand, any small change stood out.

"What are we looking for?" Laikal hissed.

Nahatal gestured over the water in a wide arc. "Spray. It's regular as clockwork. Look for dorsal fins since it's a male. Sometimes you'll only see a long line of broken water. That can be enough."

Laikal searched for what he'd described, hoping he'd understood correctly.

A fine line like Nahatal had described appeared to

their port side. It loomed closer than Laikal had thought. He almost cried out but caught himself in time. He grabbed Nahatal's sleeve and tugged on it. Nahatal shook him off and glared down at him in a mixture of confusion and irritation.

Laikal pointed at the dorsal fin breaching the surface. It shone clear as stained glass, bright green as the turquoise beads Aranél wore. It glittered with thread-like patterns of glowing blue, pulsing a slow, visible heartbeat.

"Portside!" Nahatal shouted. Laikal almost sprang upright in surprise but gripped the edge of the boat instead, leaning closer. The fin was several lengths away but still closer than he'd ever been to a living dragon.

Nahatal grabbed him by the collar and tugged him away from where he'd been leaning out.

"For the love of the Dragon King. I understand why Aranél is always so irritated," he muttered.

Nahatal waved in a wide gesture to portside so the boat on starboard would join them.

"Now you get back and stay back." Nahatal pushed Laikal ahead of him towards the stern. Laikal didn't protest but stared at the dragon alongside, mesmerized. He couldn't look away. Was this what he had been looking for those nights the sea called to him?

The huge fin unfurled like a sail. It rippled, the fine edges lined with glowing threads.

Nahatal pushed Laikal down beside the steering oar, next to Sildonus. He grabbed one of his harpoons and strode between the rowers, the rope tied to the harpoon trailing behind him.

The sharp point of the harpoon and the wide, strong haft made Laikal's heart ache. It felt odd, as though his whole chest throbbed. He had seen the parts of dead dragons and had never been squeamish. Why would he feel that way now?

They were alongside the dragon now, far enough that they would not be pulverized if it rose. They drove it like a dolphin drove a school of fish. Had the dragon realized it yet?

The boat shuddered, mirroring the uneasy tingle trickling down Laikal's spine. Nahatal balanced, steadying his stance before the throw. Some part of Laikal wanted to call out to him to stop, but the words stuck in his throat.

In a hard, aimed arc, Nahatal threw the harpoon into the dragon's flank. Laikal's heart wrung like an old rag. He shrank, wrapping his arms around his knees.

"Back, back," Sildonus shouted. The ship backed away from the dragon precipitously.

That's when he heard the dragon's roar for the first time.

He had heard stories, but nothing could have prepared him for the deep, sobbing bass that vibrated in his bones and echoed through the wood of the boat. Laikal covered his ears and shrank even deeper into himself, trying to block out the feeling that found an echo chamber in his chest.

Maybe the salt he tasted wasn't seaspray. He wouldn't cry, not when he had chosen to come along.

The boat jerked as though picked up by a giant hand, then whirled forward, pulled by the harpoon inside the dragon. The rowers grabbed their oars. One or two laughed or whooped in excitement. How could they?

They were dragged along after the dragon, further and further from the ship, from the safety he had known, with no way to steer or slow down.

Time was nothing more than a blur of yelling and salt water and the desperate fear that every moment would be his last. Every time he opened his eyes there was nothing but people, noise, the violence of being battered against the waves, and the trail of blood in the water.

Why was everything about the hunt so hard and ugly? The creature had been so graceful, and now it was reduced to nothing more than a frenzied beast desperately trying to escape its doom.

The spray lessened as the dragon slowed. Sildonus' orders strung together.

"Nahatal, back here," Sildonus shouted.

Laikal looked up. He shook as he gripped his arms around his knees. Sildonus and Nahatal switched places, the boat swaying under their steps, and the first mate readied the steel spear.

How did they know where to strike the dragon? How could something like that be mortal, to be slain with nothing more than a sharp piece of steel?

He flinched as the dragon let out another shuddering roar, this one weaker than the last. Its swan song, the final cry for help that would never arrive.

The dragon tried to swim away, exhaling a spray of blood, but its motions weakened. It drifted to the surface and turned in the water. The corpse towered above them, many times larger than the boat. Its skin shone the color of a stormy sea. For the first time, Laikal could see the patterns traced across the dragon's body. They no longer throbbed with the strong, steady pulse of a heartbeat. Rather, they flickered and sparked blue like he was used to seeing Glow do. Broad swathes of Glow etched into the dragon's skin, nestled beneath the scales. The patterns formed swirls, triangles, diamonds, and even patterns that looked like four-pointed stars. Its front fins were almost as big as the whole boat. They were delicate as the finest shirt.

Blood dripped down the dragon's face from its blowhole, staining the Glow. Laikal couldn't look away from its face. Crests and spikes framed it, intricate yet huge.

"Well done, we got him!" Sildonus called, and was answered by a tired cheer. Nahatal lit a flare and sent it off into the sky. The bright light left an arc of blood red in its wake.

Laikal was still shaking, couldn't seem to stop, even as the others relaxed and started talking. Now all they had to do was wait for the ship to come pick them up.

He peered past the other rowers to find Aranél, seeking some kind of comfort.

Aranél leaned back on his elbows, head tilted back, eyes closed. His hair stuck to the sweat on his face, but he didn't frown as hard as usual. Maybe he was too tired.

"How'd you like your first hunt?" Sildonus asked, shoving Laikal playfully.

Laikal tried to smile but couldn't manage it. That ache hadn't left his chest.

Sildonus laughed. "You're awfully pale. Not worth sneaking out for?"

Laikal shook his head. "Is it always—like that?"

Sildonus frowned and rubbed his hands together. They were bloodstained from the spear.

"Like what?" he asked, as though he couldn't see the horror of what had happened.

"So—bloody? Is it always that hurt? With the roar?" Laikal said, struggling to express the full scope of the violence he had never thought existed. He'd loved everything about the life he was destined for; the sailing, the work, the people. Now, this was all it was about, and it was *horrible.*

Sildonus laughed, harsh and careless.

"Of course it is. We're hunting them, not playing with them."

Perhaps he noticed how upset Laikal was because he

thumped him on the shoulder again. It was more pain than comfort. "Buck up kid, you get used to it quick."

Laikal didn't want to get used to it. He didn't want the bloody work to feel normal.

As Sildonus strode to the other side of the boat, Laikal understood why nobody disobeyed him. Sildonus had made himself at home in the violence that came with their life, and he would turn it upon anyone he thought deserving.

He joined Nahatal in the bow, observing the dragon.

Natahal pointed out traits of the dragon, and Sildonus nodded as they judged how much it would bring up in oil, Glow, and bones.

Laikal finally stretched out, no longer clutching his legs to his chest. His heartbeat had slowed back to normal, but he still felt shaken.

He sensed someone's gaze and looked around. It was Aranél glaring at him.

It was so familiar that Laikal managed a sheepish grin. He crossed to get closer to Aranél, drawing the attention of the other sailors in the process. They hadn't paid attention to him before in the flurry of action.

Several laughed.

"Decided to join us, Laikal?" one of the sailors asked. Laikal nodded, managing to keep up the smile. The usual banter put him at ease.

The sailor tried to hide his laughter but was doing a poor job.

"I'm sure I heard the Captain tell you to stay on board. Might want to stay here instead, the dragons are more merciful than the captain."

Laikal couldn't help but see the truth in that statement.

Aranél grabbed him by the back of the neck like a cat

and pulled him closer. Laikal yelped indignantly. Aranél was still stronger. Laikal stumbled over and someone complained about them rocking the boat.

"What do you think you're doing here?" Aranél hissed.

Aranél shook him again before letting go. Laikal rubbed the back of his neck and glared back at Aranél.

"Why are you scolding me too? It was the first mate, then the harpooner, and soon the captain, and now you too," Laikal counted on his fingers. "That's four whole scoldings for one thing I did wrong. That's too many."

"Impeccable logic," someone commented behind him. Aranél glared at whoever had said it, then back at Laikal. He was even angrier than usual.

"You should get one for every person you endangered, and that's a whole lot more than four."

Laikal glared back at him. He was already upset and this made things worse. Besides, his neck really did hurt.

His gaze caught on the dragon floating behind Aranél. The sailors who had been watching their bickering turned back to their conversations. Laikal asked, in a hushed tone, "What did you think of the hunt?"

It was Aranél's first hunt too. Had it been as awful to him as to Laikal?

Aranél shrugged, eyes closed again, face tilted to the sunlight. "Tiring. I want to go to the ship and take a nap. You wouldn't know, you were doing nothing the entire time."

Laikal rolled his eyes but didn't argue.

"I didn't think it would be so...ugly. It's so bloody and you heard the way it roared. I didn't think about it much."

Aranél had opened his eyes and was looking at Laikal. He was scowling less now, more contemplative than angry. "I've seen worse in my life, brainless. This was just an animal, not even a person."

Laikal shook his head. "It shouldn't be like this."

Aranél sighed and closed his eyes again. "It isn't something we can change."

Laikal still frowned, but Aranél was clearly done arguing.

Someone behind them called out. "There's the *Errynes*!"

Laikal turned, and sure enough, the white speck of the sail was growing before the horizon. They just had to wait a bit longer.

"Better start rehearsing that apology," Aranél said, without opening his eyes.

Laikal had finished memorizing the third format of apologies when the *Errynes* arrived beside them and threw down a rope ladder. The ship loomed far above, dwarfing the dragon.

When Laikal unobtrusively tried to slink to the back of the boat, Sildonus grabbed him by the collar before he got the chance.

"Youngest first, get it out of the way so the captain doesn't have to worry about you," he said.

Laikal tried to squirm out of his grip but it wasn't working. With a sigh, he clambered up the ladder. Someone grabbed him by the arm as soon as he reached the top.

"Are you deaf or just stupid?" his dad said, his voice more ominous than the crash of breakers. "What did I tell you to do?"

All the apologies fled him, leaving him tongue-tied. He would only make this worse. The Captain shook him by the arm, and Laikal answered quickly, "Stay on board—I'm sorry, I shouldn't have gone, sir."

"Glowing right you shouldn't have," the captain

thundered. "You could have died, people could have died because of you and more than that, I told you not to."

He punctured these last words with another hard shake.

"Yes, sir," Laikal said, keeping his eyes down. He hunched his shoulders, doing his best to look as contrite as possible. Sometimes it worked. Often, it didn't.

The others were coming on board behind him. The captain still glared at him. In hindsight, it hadn't been worth it. His father had known that.

"I'll settle on consequences for this later. Get out of the way and don't pull something like that again," the captain said. He finally let go of Laikal and turned to Sildonus, still scowling.

Laikal didn't have to hear that twice. He hurried to the other side of the ship, out of the captain's line of sight. He sat down against the cabin and let out a breath of relief. That had gone better than he'd feared. The captain would have time to cool down before he decided on a punishment, so it would be fine.

Laikal stretched and yawned. The sun was warm against this side of the ship, and the wind had calmed, so the waves swayed the boat instead of throwing it. He hadn't realized how tired he was. There would be another frenzy of heavy work when they'd start processing the dragon, but for now, he had a few minutes off.

He peered around the corner to see what was going on on deck.

The ship was in as much chaos as it had been before they had gone after the dragon. There was a lot of processing to do before they could store the parts. Several sailors perched in the rigging, silhouettes against the blue sky, like the birds that settled on the stays while they rested in port.

They dragged oversized pulleys after them, securing them from the mast. The thick ropes hung from them trailed along the deck. They were thicker than Laikal's wrist, strong enough to haul the dragon's corpse up.

The sailors from both boats had returned and spread around the deck, following the orders of the second and third mate. The ones who had been on Laikal's boat called playful insults to the others about how they'd been too slow. The competition always fueled them, and this was a side effect.

They chained the dragon to the side of the ship, set up the cutting platform above it, and started the work of cutting it apart. The dragon was mature but not exceptionally large, so it wouldn't take longer than a day to process it completely.

Laikal leaned over the bulwark, trying to get a look at the dragon. He had accidentally ended up next to Nahatal, who pushed him away from the edge. Craning his neck, he couldn't see more than a glimpse of the dragon's prone corpse.

"If you thought killing it was gory, you'd best back off for this part," Nahatal warned, nodding for Laikal to follow him. They headed towards one of the temporary tables set up by the mast.

"I'll show you how to cut the Glow off the fins," he said. "It's the safest job, even if it involves knives."

One of the sailors passed them the first piece of the dorsal crest they had cut off. Laikal winced at the blood leaking from the severed end while Nahatal didn't even blink as he laid the piece on the table.

He drew the knife he carried at his belt and demonstrated how to cut the strips of Glow. Tossing them into a barrel with seawater, he explained that the organisms would drain into the water, producing the Glow concentrate that was generally sold.

He gestured for Laikal to try. "Remember, you're on a ship, it moves around. You have to work slow or you'll injure yourself with that knife."

Laikal nodded. He had experience with that. Knives slipped easily.

Around them, the greater work of cutting the huge slabs of blubber and skin into chunks started. Laikal found himself hoping a wave would wash overboard and rinse away the blood and Glow covering the deck. If it didn't, he'd be the one cleaning it off.

He tentatively grabbed hold of a chunk of the dorsal fin. The dragon's skin wasn't smooth like a whale's, or barbed like a shark. Instead, it was covered in fine scales. He drew the short knife he carried at his belt, more a tool than a weapon. Laikal cautiously cut around one of the patterns. The Glow leaked out from beneath the scales, onto the table.

Gradually, the work got easier as he disconnected it from the slain dragon.

It wasn't too tiring, but there was an endless amount. Besides the Glow under the scales, there were also small pockets of it, hung from the edge of the fin like tiny lanterns. He was focusing on cutting one free when his knife slipped, cutting a gash in the side of his hand. He yelped and dropped the knife.

Nahatal glanced up sharply.

"Take a finger off?" he asked dryly.

Laikal shook his head, showing him the gash. The Glow on his knife had leached into the cut; blue Glow and blood mixed in the wound.

Nahatal dismissed the cut. It was shallow and fairly small.

"Finish that piece of fin and go clean it. Put on a

bandage if it doesn't stop bleeding. Congratulations on your first blue scar."

Laikal picked up his knife and continued with the piece of fin.

He understood now why glowing scars were so common. Nahatal himself had plenty of small ones all over his hands, probably from incidents like this.

Tossing another glowing piece into the barrel, Laikal started cutting the next strip. His focus was interrupted as he realized there was something on his hand near the cut. It looked like bumps, maybe an odd rash.

Laikal put down his knife and wiped away the blood leaking from the cut. There were definitely bumps on his hand, and they were spreading, fast enough to see new ones appearing.

"Can someone be allergic to dragon?" he asked Nahatal.

"I don't think so. Less talking more working," Nahatal said, without looking up. He probably thought Laikal was asking idle questions to slack on work.

Laikal hesitated. The rash spread beneath his sleeve. It wasn't red, so it was probably okay. Still, he couldn't ignore the tingling sensation spreading up his arm so easily. He had never gotten Glow in a cut before. Maybe this was normal.

"I never realized Glow tingles so much. Getting tattoos with it must hurt." Laikal picked up the knife again. He couldn't distract himself from the fact that something was wrong.

"It's not so bad," Nahatal said, the same edge of impatience to his voice. He clearly wanted Laikal to stop interrupting him.

Laikal bit his lip. The rash had reached his shoulder. It was like a fever, his skin hot and cold at once, goosebumps chasing up and down his arm. He picked up the knife and tried to make another cut but froze as he looked down at his left hand and forearm.

His hand and arm were traced with glowing patterns, throbbing with his heartbeat.

"Nahatal," he said, his voice shooting up in alarm. "Can you look at this?"

Nahatal sighed impatiently and stuck his knife into the table with a solid thud. "I told you, it's just a little cut. You've had worse—"

He saw Laikal's arm and froze, eyes widening.

"When did that happen?" he asked, breathless.

"Just now," Laikal said, panic leaching into his voice. The tingle spread over the rest of his body, faster and faster. As he watched, delicate glowing patterns grew down his other arm, like a rope twining down the mast. It was a soft, sparkling blue, glittering in the light like the sun upon the sea. It would have been beautiful, if it hadn't been etched in his skin.

He frantically rubbed his arm across the front of his shirt, but the patterns didn't budge. They stayed there, quietly throbbing. The dragon's blood on the front of his shirt now stained his arm too.

"Has this ever happened before?" Nahatal asked.

Laikal didn't like the edge of panic in Nahatal's voice. "Of course not," he said, anxiety cutting into his throat. "What's happening?"

Instead of reaching to help him, Nahatal took a step back, his eyes still wide. He grabbed his knife off the table, pulling it out of the wood.

Why was he doing that? What was going on?

Laikal looked around. He needed his dad to tell him it was nothing and to stop making a fuss.

Nahatal was ahead of him.

"Captain? I think you need to have a look at this," he said.

Laikal spun to where his dad stood supervising the cutting up of the dragon.

His sleeves were rolled up, arms crossed, exposing the dragon tattoo on his right arm. He was frowning, apparently still aggravated at Laikal.

He hurried to them, but stopped in his tracks when he saw Laikal's arms. "What—"

"I got Glow in a cut—the ship lurched. I'm sorry, sir, I was really trying to be careful," Laikal stammered, his words gushing out too quickly.

"That's not supposed to happen," his father said. He didn't come closer but eyed his son warily. Laikal had never seen that directed at him before.

"What is it? Why is this happening?" Laikal asked. He couldn't hide the panic in his voice anymore. It was hard to be brave when you had no idea if you were dying.

Both Nahatal and his father stayed silent, but they exchanged looks, their expressions shifting from confusion to worry.

Laikal looked from one to the other.

The other sailors had noticed the fuss. Work fell silent, and those with hands free edged closer to see what it was all about.

Sildonus crossed towards them, standing behind the captain. Unlike the others, he didn't look shocked. An instant scowl overtook his face. He stepped back, his lip curled in disgust.

"Glowblood's fangs, he's one of *them*."

"One of what?" Laikal asked.

"A Glowblood," the captain said, his voice breathless.

"I can't be, they don't exist anymore, they were all

hunted..." Laikal's voice caught in his throat as he realized what he was saying. The Glowbloods had been hunted down and murdered like the dragons because they were a threat to the humans. The dragon's wild death-song still rang in his chest.

Blood covered the deck, covered his shirt, covered the other sailors' hands. Nahatal was in it up to his rolled shirtsleeves, their edges stained red. Nahatal carried the knife in his right hand, low but ready. There was a reason he'd grabbed it before he had backed away from Laikal. They all carried knives.

If he was a Glowblood, that violence he had never known existed would turn against him.

"How do you know?" Laikal asked, breathless. "Why do you think I am?"

Nahatal gestured to the patterns that now spanned his entire body. Laikal had even felt the burn on his cheeks and ears.

"The Glowbloods are documented to have had 'patterns like unto a dragon'. There's a legend that it would manifest after they got Glow in their blood. It's what they used to summon the other dragons."

It was why the Glowbloods had been hunted. They had used the dragons against humans and had been deemed too dangerous to exist.

"But I can't do that," Laikal protested.

"You don't know. Anything could happen," Nahatal said. His voice was more distant than ever, with the same touch of wariness.

Laikal shook his head. He was sure he couldn't, though he wasn't about to try in case he could. Oh no, then maybe he could if he did try. Nothing made sense.

His patterns flashed, the light rippling like waves. He

had no idea why this was happening.

He wasn't any stronger than he had been. If they decided to harm him, there was nothing he could do about it. Not only was the world unsafe, but he was weak. If anyone decided to hurt him, he was helpless.

Surely his father wouldn't let that happen. Laikal looked towards him, silently pleading for help, for reassurance. His father stood with his arms crossed. He wouldn't even look at Laikal.

"Now what do we do?" Nahatal asked.

"We do as someone hopefully did to its parents. Get rid of it," Sildonus said, without hesitation.

It was as though someone had stabbed him in the neck, cutting off his words. Laikal had always thought his parents had left him in the village because they wanted him to be found. He had comforted himself with the thought that perhaps they were poor, perhaps unmarried, but that they still wanted the best for him.

Now he faced the truth. They had been in danger of being killed for what they were, and they knew that if they kept him, he would be too. They had given him a chance, and it had lasted fourteen years. But now that was over.

He looked back at his father who looked at the ground, but shook his head, decidedly.

"We're not killing him," he said, coldly.

Not "Laikal," not "my son." Perhaps he had been abandoned a second time.

By this time, a sizable crowd had formed around them. The sailors gaped at Laikal or stared in disgust or fear. He hated seeing their expressions and backed away until his back hit the table.

Nahatal frowned and Sildonus scowled.

"We can't ignore what happened. He's a Glowblood.

His presence endangers everyone aboard this ship. They attract and control dragons. We spent more than a generation ridding ourselves of them, and now you want to keep it around?" Sildonus said.

Laikal scanned the crowd, desperate for sympathy or even any indication that they still saw him for what he was. He was just Laikal. He didn't feel any different. Why were they treating him so differently now?

He found Aranél, near the back. He frowned like always, and his gaze was fixed on the captain, not Laikal.

"We're not killing him, and we can't do anything else until we reach port. We'll turn for port right away and make a decision what to do there." The captain finally looked up. His expression was set, merciless.

Nahatal's frown deepened, and he tilted his head, uncertain.

"But—" Sildonus started.

The captain spun on him. "That was an order, not an option," he thundered, his voice loud enough that Sildonus and Laikal both flinched.

He turned to the sailors, his expression stormy. "I didn't tell any of you you could stop, back to what you were doing!"

They scattered like a school of fish when you throw a rock into the water. Aranél went without looking back at Laikal. Only Nahatal stayed behind.

"Make yourself scarce," the captain snapped at Laikal.

Laikal looked around, a futile search for somewhere without people. They were below deck and above. He didn't dare go to the cabin, and the sailors would come down to the forehold at night.

Taking his last option, he scrambled up the shrouds,

trembling so hard he worried he'd fall into the sea below. The ship no longer safely carried him; it too betrayed him as it bucked and shuddered beneath his grip.

Laikal didn't stop until he'd reached the first platform. He clung to the mast, trying to still the throbbing of his heart and the way his breaths hitched. Maybe he should cry. Maybe that was one way of proving himself human. Dragons didn't cry, did they? The memory of the dragon's final roar seemed to course through him and he shuddered again. They did.

His patterns flashed bright and frantic. He tentatively reached out and touched his cheek. The skin was no longer smooth; it felt like the small, soft lizards he had picked up when he was a child. He raised his arm and stared at it with a mixture of horror and wonder. It had the same scales, only larger. Edged beneath them lay the Glow, sparkling in the light.

He tried to control the flashing, but he had no idea how. It was like trying to move his ears. People could do it but how did you think of moving something you had never moved before? How did you control the glow if you couldn't even tell where it was? The patterns kept changing ever so slightly, as though they were words traced across his skin in a language he couldn't read.

He ran his tongue across his teeth, half worrying they would no longer be human either. His canines were a little longer perhaps, a little sharper, but that was it. He had definitely felt something change about his ears. He reached up and checked them. They had always been more pointed than the average person's, but he had thought this was nothing more than an odd quirk. Some people were just like that. Now, they were much longer and even more pointed, the edges frilled.

Laikal turned his hand over. The palm was still the same as it had ever been, unmarked by any patterns, while the back of his hand bore a four-pointed star.

He turned his hand over and over, flipping between human and dragon.

Sniffing, he wiped his nose. The hushed scatterings of sound on deck had evened out, like the wind settling after a storm. He leaned his head against the mast. A few strands of his curls fell in front of his eyes, some of them glowing. Apparently that was another permanent fixture. There was nothing he could do except try to disappear. It was the only safety he could find from his former friends. He was not one of them, but their prey.

The next few days passed in a miserable blur. The captain didn't even look his way, and the other sailors avoided him like the plague as much as they could aboard ship. Laikal didn't make it hard for them. Every time he saw the disgust and hatred on one of their faces, something inside him died.

It had started raining early on the third night. Perhaps it was a good thing, to wash away the blood left on deck after processing the dragon. The sailors had finished storing the parts in barrels beneath deck.

Laikal shivered. He was already soaked through. His patterns throbbed a slow, flickering beat he still hadn't gotten used to. The light shimmering through his shirt lit up the night like a lantern.

He stared over the frothing, seething sea. The ship rocked with the higher winds and waves, wind tearing through his clothes. He sneezed. He had to find somewhere out of the rain.

He would try the galley. The past few days, he'd stolen food when the others weren't around. The cook tacitly allowed it. It meant he could stay away during mealtimes and that caused less trouble for everyone.

Maybe the cook had left the door unlocked, even though everything was supposed to be tied down and locked for the night. He had done so on the previous nights. It felt all wrong to be sneaking around the ship that used to feel like home. He was expected to be as scarce as the few rats, and if it was up to the sailors, he would meet the same end, killed and tossed overboard for the sharks.

Laikal attempted to pull the heavy door open. It didn't budge. He tried again, then pushed for good measure. It had never been a pushing door. He rested his forehead against it, silently admitting defeat. This too was locked.

He sat down against the door, wrapped his arms around his legs and rested his chin on his knees. The rain beat down on him. He was so cold he'd already gone numb. His mind drifted to unwanted places. To his hammock in the foremast with the others—where it was cramped and dim, but still dry and warm. To dry clothes and a night's sleep that wasn't interrupted by waking from the cold or being thrown against something by the jolting of the ship.

He sneezed again and bit his tongue as his chin thudded against his knees. Tears welled in his eyes. He was alone, wet, and cold. Maybe they should have killed him and gotten it over with. At least it would have been finished quickly.

Maybe they would take pity on him if he tried the forehold.

He got up, knees stiff and achy from the cold. He padded across the deck, the rough planks slick with water. Another wash of seawater spilled over his bare feet and around his ankles.

He crossed the deck to the small, warm strip of light that shone beneath the door to the forehold, the opposite of his blue Glow. Pausing in front of it, he gripped the heavy steel handle. He'd have to hurry or he'd let in the rain.

He strained at the weight of the door as he pulled it open. It gave way before him, letting in the darkness, the streaming rain, and the cold blue light shining off him.

The door was closed behind him as quickly as he had opened it, but there was no dimming the Glow that flung drops of light off him.

The forehold where the sailors slept was warm, though stuffy. It was a small price to pay. Only the light from a single lamp by the door illuminated the rows of hammocks strung across the hold. Laikal's was right beneath Aranél's, by the door. It was no more than two steps from him. Aranél's hammock hung slack, as did several others. They were on watch.

The quiet was broken only by the sound of breathing, the creaking of the ship, and the rush of waves against the hull. The few sounds seemed louder than ever, the silence thick as the warmth.

Laikal tentatively took a step forward, testing if he was allowed here, if he was still one of them.

The boot struck him solidly on the shoulder, confirming everything he feared. It wasn't a merciful throw. It had been aimed at his head and missed.

Laikal scrambled back, into the relative safety of the entryway, halfway up the stairs again.

He paused once he was out of reach of grabbing hands and thrown objects. He looked over his shoulder. He had seen street dogs flee when children threw stones at them. It probably felt like this.

A dark silhouette sat up in one of the hammocks near the door. He lit up in the blue of Laikal's glow, features hard and forbidding.

It was Yichar, one of the younger sailors. He'd often tagged along with Aranél and Laikal. He was Aranél's opposite, with short, light brown hair that always looked windblown and a ready smile for everyone. When he'd first come aboard, Yichar had been the one who answered Laikal's questions and showed him the ropes both literally and figuratively. Aranél was too bad-tempered, the others too busy. Yichar never snapped at him, never dismissed him, always found a way to help.

And now he was staring at Laikal as though he was less than human, with that cold disgust that couldn't even be called hatred. Hatred was something personal, something you had to strive and work for, something that acknowledged the object of your hatred as somehow deserving of it. This disgust was the same he would have had for a mangy rabid dog. There was no sympathy, no memory of the days they had shared. Laikal was just something dangerous and foul to drive out.

Yichar reached below his hammock for something, probably the second boot. He held it poised and stared Laikal down, no leeway visible in his expression, poorly lit as it was.

Laikal ran up the stairs and pushed open the hatch.

The cold and rain blasted in, the warmth from inside making it feel even colder in comparison.

He shut the door behind him, a barrier between him and them. He wasn't strong enough to open it again.

The rain beat down on him, pooling in his heart like it did on the floor. Another wave washed over the deck. He shuddered, biting the inside of his mouth to keep from crying. He'd forgotten about the new sharpness of his canines and bit himself harder than he'd meant. Now the tears really were coming.

Trying to gather himself, he sniffled, knowing he needed to find somewhere to spend the night. Soon enough it would be light and he'd be dry.

Laikal crossed the deck to where some of the tied-down crates stood. The gap between them looked wide enough to wedge himself in. It would be as wet and cold as everywhere else, but at least he didn't run the risk of being washed overboard in his sleep.

If it wasn't for the glowing, he would have been hidden. He closed his eyes tight, watching his eyelids light up red against the flares of light. He hated the glowing. It didn't let him sleep without interruption, didn't let him sneak into places where he was supposed to be, didn't let him live.

He leaned against the crate and tried not to think. The wind howled and the strong waves tried to fling him away into the cold, dark depths. He must have drifted off to sleep because he woke up with a start at what he guessed had been the lurch of the ship over an unusually high wave. He opened his eyes and instantly realized what it actually was. His Glow seemed to have gone berserk. It flared out in circles like a pebble dropped into a pool, faster and faster, patterns blending together, bouncing off each other, spinning and flickering.

Something was wrong, very wrong. He had no idea what his patterns meant but he also knew it was a bad idea to stay curled up in a corner if something strange was happening to his dragonness.

He slowly rose. He couldn't have slept much. The night was still dark, rain gushing out of the sky. He tried to blink the sleep from his eyes. His patterns hadn't slowed.

He squinted, trying to peer through the darkness.

Something darker than the night loomed between the crates, blocking his only escape route. His back was to the cabin, the tall crates on either side.

Laikal's light flashed off the gleams of metal.

Earrings, belt buckles, shoe buckles, and a long knife held in a hand.

He stumbled backward, instincts faster than his mind. Someone had finally decided to dispose of the problem before more unrest was created.

Laikal stared at the knife as though it was the stars and would point his way out of the situation. Was it the captain? The same knife Father had used to teach him how to carve from the dragon teeth? He had made a clumsy sailboat, the edges rough and blocky. His father had worn it around his neck beneath his shirt but had probably thrown it away by now.

The man took a step forward into Laikal's glow, which illuminated the attacker's face.

He had known Sildonus wanted him dead but not that Sildonus would go against the captain's orders to do so.

A thud came from Laikal's right. He didn't dare take his eyes off the knife, but he tensed. Were more people attacking him? He was as weak as he had ever been, and the sharper teeth wouldn't do much.

He tried to straighten his shoulders, but his knees were shaking. Sildonus' face showed that same distant disgust he'd seen in Yichar, though there was something else. Triumph that he had been right, that he knew what was best for the crew, and that he would bring it to pass. Laikal was a small price to pay for his pride.

Laikal backed up until he was pressed against the rough wood of the cabin.

His last few seconds and he couldn't think of anything besides the fact that he was wet and cold, and that Aranél hadn't looked back, and that the place where Yichar had hit him with the boot still hurt.

A dark figure dropped from the sky. Laikal pressed

himself even further back against the wood, expecting the hot throb of a knife between his ribs. Perhaps it was appropriate if he died by being speared.

"I believe this isn't the captain's orders," an indifferent, familiar voice said. Aranél never could sound like he cared about anything.

"The captain is wrong. I'm trying to keep everyone safe and alive, unlike him."

Aranél didn't get out of the way. He rested his elbows against the crates, hands curling around the tops. His position was easy, but completely blocked Laikal out of sight. The only way for Sildonus to reach Laikal was to move Aranél, and Aranél wasn't about to move.

"I'm sorry, sir, but we're all under the captain's orders, whether we like it or not."

Laikal tried to peer around Aranél, but the effect was similar to moving a lamp out from behind a curtain. Sildonus glared at him and Laikal ducked away again, hiding himself behind Aranél.

"I will take my orders from the captain, sir," Aranél repeated.

Sildonus took a step forward, knife still gripped in his hand.

"And I will remind you, sir, that there are others on watch within earshot, and they will respond to me," Aranél said, the respect vanishing from his tone.

Sildonus turned and disappeared into the darkness, away from the glow of Laikal's light. His footsteps were hard as his expression had been.

Laikal let out a shuddering breath. "Thank you—"

"Shut up," Aranél snapped, pulling off his coat. He tossed it at Laikal, who caught it before it landed in the water. The outside was drenched, but it was thick and the inside was still warm and dry. It swallowed him when he put it on. He turned up the collar and buttoned it.

The long sleeves and thick fabric quenched his glow, leaving only the glow from his hair and face visible. It made it hard to see Aranél, who started off into the darkness again. Laikal followed.

"You can't do that and leave me again," he protested.

"I won't," Aranél said, briefly.

That appeased Laikal. He sat down by the edge of the crates, still in their shelter. He pulled his knees up beneath the coat, trying to keep every part of him warm.

Leaning against the crate, Aranél crossed his arms against the wind. Strands of hair clung to his face and his braid was drenched.

Laikal buried his face deeper into the collar.

"Why are you helping me?" he asked. "Nobody else will. Not Nahatal, not Yichar."

Aranél sighed as though Laikal was asking silly questions.

"You're still Laikal, and unfortunately I'm stuck as your babysitter since your dad isn't here."

He shoved Laikal's shoulder. Huddled up as he was, he lost his balance and toppled over. He spluttered, and Aranél snorted in amusement.

Laikal righted himself laboriously, wiggling to get upright again. He scowled at Aranél, but he was looking away again.

"Try to get some sleep. I'll take an extra watch so Sildonus doesn't come back tonight. You're on your own tomorrow. I'm not going through two nights of this for your measly self."

Laikal tried to snort in contempt, but it was lost in the rumbling of the waves.

He settled against the corner of the cabin and the chest. Cradled by the warm coat and the knowledge that Aranél was there for him, he drifted off.

By the time he woke, it was light and Aranél was gone, without his coat. He must have been soaking and cold after his night in the rain but he hadn't said a word before he left.

The day itself seemed lighter. People still glared at him, and he still skulked across the ship, but he wasn't completely alone anymore. Even if Aranél didn't spare him a glance, he was still on his side.

The next dragon came only one day later. They were still far out at sea, even if they had been sailing towards the nearest port.

Laikal crouched on top of one of the chests he'd been hiding behind a few days ago on the night that Aranél had found him. The weather had thankfully cleared up.

On one hand, he felt the doom of a port slipping ever closer, with whatever unknown fate awaited him. On the other, the situation was less hopeless now that he was no longer alone. He would face whatever came to him, no matter how unfair it was.

He might have been one of the first to hear the thin cry, barely carrying through the air from far above.

"Dragon to starboard! He's coming right at us!"

The call lacked the usual triumph. It only had fear.

The captain hurried across the deck to starboard, spyglass in hand. He stood at the railing, feet spread to keep his balance on the bounding ship.

He didn't call for them to take to the boats, and relief poured through Laikal. He couldn't stand another slaughter, especially now.

Laikal stood, not caring that he would be in clear

view of the others.

The fine white line in the water headed towards them. A large fin rose, far larger than any shark, glowing with flickering patterns.

It was as though a soft, indistinguishable voice spoke to him, inside his mind, like he'd read something without realizing it. He couldn't form the feelings into words, but it was pain, and anger, and bitterness, and more than anything, justice.

Laikal winced, the emotions a physical touch. His patterns shifted, morphing into something different, the rhythm of the flashes changing, a variation on his heartbeat.

If he could see the dorsal fin from this far away, it was huge. It was heading straight for them, at the speed of a predator, not prey.

Sildonus ran up to the captain, scrambling to keep his balance as the ship bucked.

"Captain, it's coming for us," he gasped, out of breath. Instead of the fear Laikal expected, his tone was that of someone who had announced the truth long ago and hadn't been believed.

Sildonus turned and stared directly at Laikal, his eyebrows drawing over his eyes. He pointed, and Laikal dodged away from the accusing finger, sharp as a harpoon.

"The Glowblood summoned them; I told you this would happen," he said.

Laikal ducked away, dropping behind the crate. He didn't want to make himself a bigger target than needed. If he had summoned the dragon, wouldn't he have known it was coming? Wouldn't he have been aware of summoning an entire dragon?

He tried to mentally yell at the dragon to go away, a reverse summoning, if you will. He peeked out from behind the chest. It was still coming at them. Clearly that wasn't the solution.

There was nothing he could do but hide from the others' wrath and watch it play out. That might end with them all eaten or drowned.

The dragon was getting closer fast. The dorsal fin grew out of the sea, appearing and disappearing with the waves.

"Captain, are we supposed to head to the boats?" Nahatal asked, stopping next to the captain.

He hesitated, glancing out towards the sea.

"Not yet. If the ship sinks it will be safer, but otherwise we're far more vulnerable. If it comes to it, I will give the order. Do not go before that."

"It's changing course!" the lookout shouted. Laikal stood on tiptoe. It was true. The dragon, now close enough that the patterns were distinguishable, had veered aft, swerving around the ship.

"It's not attacking us?" Sildonus asked, disbelief ringing in his voice.

The captain shrugged, shoulders stiff with apprehension.

He called to the sailors to let out as much sail as possible and directed the course away from the dragon. They were the hunters chased by their prey.

The ship leapt forward into the waves. Laikal crashed against the crate he'd been standing against. His shoulder throbbed.

He couldn't hear the voice anymore, though he had heard a whisper when he'd looked at the dragon.

"It's on our other side now," the lookout shouted.

The dragon was swimming circles around its prey. As fast as the *Errynes* could travel, the dragon was always faster.

Laikal had seen that powerful tail and the huge front fins, sweeping through the water like wings.

It was toying with them. If it tired, it could simply crash into the ship or destroy it in a hundred other ways.

Laikal didn't care what happened to him anymore, he had to fix this. He wouldn't let them get hurt if he could help. He squeezed out from the crates and ran to the bulwark. The sailors scattered like a wave breaking on the shoreline.

He peered into the depths where he had seen the dragon.

He caught a glimpse of the flashing patterns and instantly, the words resonated in his mind.

"You destroy, so you will be destroyed."

The words were blurred and uncertain, as though heard across a great distance. It wasn't like he had heard something, more as though he had read it, and it appeared in his own inner voice.

The next instant, a bone-shattering sound split the air. It was another roar. This one wasn't out of fear or pain; it was anger, justice, revenge. It was hard and raw, and the entire ship vibrated with it. The bulwarks beneath his hands shuddered and seemed to withdraw.

Laikal closed his eyes and concentrated. He had tried before, and there was no way to think his patterns in a certain direction. However, he had noticed they changed with his emotions and heartbeat. Right now, they flashed faster, because his heart was racing. He could only hear the dragon if he could see it, so it must be the same for the dragon.

"You, get away from there!" someone yelled. They grabbed at his collar, about to throw him back. He dodged away just in time. The dragon was nearby— it rose to the surface, lights flashing words that escaped him.

He let out a burst of emotion, as concentrated as he

could make it. It was panic, a cry for help. It was the emotion he could amplify most easily. His patterns burst into light, like they had when Sildonus attacked him.

The dragon rose closer to the surface, its dorsal fin lighting up like a stained glass window against the sunlight. The patterns rippled, hesitating, as though it was uncertain what it had heard.

Someone grabbed at him again and this time caught him by the back of his shirt.

He had to get out of here and find a way to communicate with the dragon.

The two problems combined into one solution. He drew the knife at his belt and sliced his shirt open down the front, cutting away from himself. The pressure of the grip released as he wriggled out of the loose linen shirt. The patterns across his arms and torso were no longer dimmed by the shirt and flashed bright. He shoved the knife back into the sheath. Before anyone realized what was happening, he vaulted the bulwark and dove into the black ocean beneath, far too close to the angry dragon.

The water hit him like a blow. They were north because of the summer migration, and it could be felt in the icy water.

The darkness enveloped him from all sides, and he resisted the urge to gasp. Thrashing, he tried to right himself. As he did, his limbs left trailing paths of light. He was as visible in the dark water as he had been in the dark cabin of the ship. If the dragon was hostile, it would find him immediately. But he had more urgent things to deal with, like air.

He was a strong swimmer, and he'd swum in open sea before. Still, he never got used to the endless void stretching to all sides and the inevitable dangers lurking within.

He kicked up, away from the ship, towards the light. He pushed through the weight of the water, up to the surface.

He burst from the world of quiet and darkness into air, light, and shouting.

He gave in to the temptation and looked over his shoulder, still trying to draw in as deep a breath as he could. His father stood at the bulwark, his expression stricken. Though whether it was at the seemingly inevitable loss of his ship or at Laikal's rash move, he didn't know.

It didn't matter, because Sildonus stood right next to him, his face flushed with rage. He pointed at Laikal with a ferocity that didn't bode well.

Laikal took the cue and a deep breath and dove under again, looking for a different source of light. He closed his eyes and tried to send out another signal for help. His communications were rough, like someone who could only shape a few words to shout.

He didn't have long. His breath still ran out; apparently that wasn't a Glowblood gift.

Opening his eyes to make sure he wasn't accidentally swimming underneath the boat, he found himself an arm's length from the dragon's head.

His patterns flashed, then stayed bright as his mind went blank.

The dragon's head dwarfed Laikal. Huge patterns spread over it, swirling across the front of the face, along the jaw, around the eyes, and tipping the spikes along the top of its head, leading into the torso.

Laikal hovered near the eye of the creature, and it peered at him, more with curiosity than with malice. The eye was larger than his fist and blue with Glow.

The dragon's skin blended into the sea around it. The scales were far rougher than Laikal's own. A four-pointed star dropped from beneath the Dragon's eye like a tear.

The patterns rippled like light across water as the Dragon turned its head to see him better. Laikal read the patterns without thinking about it.

"What are you? I did not think I would find Dragon-lit here."

Laikal struggled for words. He hadn't managed to express anything more specific than the equivalent of a rock thrown into the water. How was he supposed to form words?

He tried to think one word at a time, stammering like a child. "I'm—Glowblood—"

His patterns flashed, halting, uncertain.

The dragon's patterns rippled, the fins twitching. "That is what the humans call those of your kind they kill. You are Dragon-lit, a survivor."

Laikal shook his head. He hadn't survived much of anything. Except that his crew had tried to kill him and treated him more like a monster than a person. Maybe that counted.

The dragon read his hesitation and circled around him. His tail rippled behind him, almost meeting his head again, encircling the boy.

Laikal floundered. The tightness on his chest became heavier. He exhaled, and bubbles drifted upwards, lit around the edges by their combined light. His and the dragon's.

He needed air. His muscles were heavy, tired with the constant kicking and the cold. He burst out of the water.

He didn't stop to listen to the shouting. He shook the hair out of his eyes, droplets of water and glow dancing all around him. He took a deep breath and arced through the water, diving down again, to the dragon who was waiting for him.

"Hold on to me," the dragon flashed.

Laikal hesitated. The fear of dragons ran deep but the realization that he couldn't keep swimming was stronger.

He swam forward and gripped the crests behind the dragon's head. The skin was hard, the scales so much larger than his own tiny, supple ones.

He forced himself to relax and rest in the water alongside the dragon.

"Why are you here?" The words came easier this time as he strung them together.

The dragon's Glow rippled away from him, hard and flashing shortly. "They destroy our kind. They will be destroyed in turn."

There was a pause, a lull in the pattern.

"Why didn't they kill you yet?" the dragon asked.

Laikal's patterns flashed involuntarily, a quick outburst of fear and uncertainty.

"They wanted to, didn't they?" The dragon asked.

He nodded, and his patterns flashed agreement.

"You can come with me. I know places where there are other Dragon-lit. You will be safe there."

Laikal stalled. A place where he would be one of many, instead of a monster. A place where he didn't have to worry about his family turning on him.

A place where he wouldn't know a soul, where nobody knew his life or his loves. A place where he would never truly belong. He'd never see his mother again. He wouldn't even be able to tell his father goodbye or to thank Aranél for saving him.

What would become of them if he agreed?

"You destroy so you will be destroyed." The words echoed in his mind. Did they deserve punishment for how they had treated him?

Didn't he deserve the same fate? He had helped kill a

dragon. He had sighted it and called to the others. The dragon's death was his fault as much as anyone's.

As much as they had threatened him, others had saved him. His father had stalled to give him time, Aranél had saved him, and so many others hadn't harmed him even though they had the chance. They didn't deserve to die.

He would not inflict the violence he had experienced upon others.

"I can't leave my family," he flashed. "Please spare them, for my sake."

"They wanted to kill you," the dragon retaliated.

"They saved me from those who did. I need them."

The dragon flashed slower this time, the same hesitance as earlier. Then another flash, more final than the last. He had come to a decision.

"You are Dragon-lit. You have the wisdom of both our kinds. I will spare them, but if they are ever seen hunting our kind again, their lives will be forfeit. If you ever need us, call for us."

Laikal's flashes sputtered. "I don't know how," he admitted.

The dragon's patterns rippled, soft and fleeting as silk. It sounded like a laugh."Place your hand on my Glow."

Laikal pressed his palm against a patch of Glow. Energy rippled between them. It was hot and cold all at once, like when his Glow had first appeared.

When he took his hand away, his handprint stayed engraved in the dragon's Glow, dark scales now showing beneath it. Laikal jerked his hand back in surprise, scared he'd hurt him. His palm was covered in Glow, embedded into his skin. A pattern was traced out in the middle, a collection of swirls and stars. When he watched it, a name appeared. "Astrakrasis." Who would have known dragons had names?

Another ripple of laughter from Astrakrasis. "We are of one heart. I will come when you call, or I will send others. You will not be alone among strangers. Fare well, Laikal, Dragon-lit."

Laikal nodded and let go of Astrakrasis. Lungs burning, he kicked to the surface. His muscles ached from the exertion, but it was the good kind of tired.

He gasped for breath as air flooded his lungs. He had stayed under too long. He inhaled a mouthful of water and coughed, which did not mix well with staying afloat. His eyes watered from the salt and Astrakrasis' bright light. He floundered, then kicked towards the ship blindly. If they chose not to let him aboard, he might drown before Astrakrasis could save him. The dragon's presence hovered beneath him like a shadow.

"Laikal!" It was Aranél, and the relief in his voice was more emotion than Laikal had ever heard from him before.

Laikal couldn't call back as he was too busy trying to stay afloat.

"Head for the stern," Aranél called.

Laikal tried. Kicking through the thick, cold water of the ocean was almost more than he could manage.

After what seemed like an eternity, his hand hit hard, rough wood.

A rope ladder swung from the side of the ship beside him. He grabbed it and pulled himself out of the water. Usually, he would bound up the ladder as though it were a staircase, but not today.

He pushed himself over the bulwark, intending to flop on the deck. If someone wanted to stab him he couldn't stop them anyway.

Instead, he stumbled into someone's arms. He didn't even have to look, he'd recognize his father blind. He was here, and his arms were wrapped around Laikal, despite the fact that Laikal was dripping wet and glowed like a flare. For so long, his father had barely even looked in his direction, and now he was here, and Laikal was safe.

Laikal buried his head in his father's shoulder and finally let the lonely, terrified tears escape. He'd thought it would just be a few tears, but before he knew it he was sobbing, all the terror and relief releasing at once in painful waves.

His father's arms were tight around him, one hand on his dripping, glowing hair.

"Shhh, it's okay." His voice was as gentle as it used to be when Laikal fell and skinned his knee.

It made Laikal cry harder. His father didn't hate him, didn't see him as a threat or a monster, and wouldn't let anyone hurt him.

Gradually, his sobs died down until he was sniffling. He still trembled, partially from the cold, partially from shock.

His father let him go but kept him close, one hand around his shoulders. Laikal hovered in the safety he'd found again.

Most of the crew had gathered, chatter flying between them, voices confused and hurried as they tried to figure out what had happened, what would happen next, and what they were supposed to do about it.

Aranél wasn't in the crowd. He waited beside them, tense and ready for anything.

There was a clear line drawn on the deck between them and the rest of the crew. They stayed well away from Laikal.

Taking a deep breath, Laikal tried to steady himself. He had to keep them safe.

"I have a message from the dragon. He wanted to sink the ship to punish us for hunting dragons, but I convinced him to spare you if we never hunt dragons again."

This sparked a reaction. Instant protests and murmurs popped up from all sides.

"This is our trade." "We don't have anything else we can do." "How do we know you aren't lying anyway?"

That last one hurt. Laikal pushed the thick tangles of hair out of his face. "I think I can show you that I can talk to it, but you'll have to trust me."

"Trust you?" Sildonus scoffed. He stood nearer than the others, arms crossed.

Laikal edged closer to the bulwark and leaned over the edge, searching for Astrakrasis below. The dragon's patterns flashed in anticipation and perhaps anxiety.

He called the dragon's name and instantly read his name flashed back.

"I'll ask him to blow," Laikal said.

"They don't believe me; could you please blow?" he silently added to Astrakrasis.

That same ripple of amusement spanned across Astrakrasis as he exhaled, blowing a cloud of mist and droplets into the air. Laikal had not taken the wind into account, and the water blew onto the deck, soaking them all. There were a few outcries of indignation, but Laikal was sure he heard Aranél laughing.

Laikal shook the water out of his eyes and turned back to them.

"Please believe me." His voice cracked.

"You were the one who endangered us in the first place." Sildonus stepped forward.

Laikal shook his head, the water droplets flying around him like a halo. "I'm not—the dragon didn't even know I was here."

Aranél stepped forward, between Laikal and Sildonus.

"I don't care if you're right, I won't obey you after what you tried the other night," Aranél said, blunt as usual.

A murmur of indignation spread through the crowd around them, a few people shooting glares at Aranél, others looking over at Sildonus in confusion.

The captain looked up with a start.

Aranél turned back to the captain, the defiance disappearing from his expression. "Captain, the other night while I was on watch, I caught Sildonus threatening Laikal, planning to kill him against your orders."

The captain's gaze fixed on Sildonus, so flinty it made even him flinch.

Sildonus straightened. "He's lying, and nobody can prove he isn't. It's my word against his."

Laikal took a step forward.

"He's not lying," he said, his voice shooting up in indignation.

The captain hesitated and cast another look around. "Is there anyone who was awake and witnessed what happened?"

A long silence followed, thick as the water beneath them.

Someone pushed through the crowd and edged forward. Laikal recognized his messy light brown hair. It was Yichar, looking as if he'd rather be anywhere else.

"I was awake that night. I woke up because Laikal tried to enter the hold. I—prevented him from doing so. I was scared—" Yichar admitted, his eyes dropping to the deck.

Aranél muttered something about how at least he had the decency to admit what a pig he was. Laikal elbowed him, and Aranél glared.

"I felt guilty later. I went up to the deck to see where he was, and I saw them over by the crates. Laikal was against the back, and Sildonus was between him and the exit. He was holding a knife."

Sildonus' head snapped around, eyes wide with shock. "How could you even see anything? You say this was the middle of the night," he retorted.

Yichar frowned and Aranél laughed.

"Laikal glows, I'd think you would remember that," Aranél said, mockingly.

Sildonus' face clouded, anger rushing to fill the void surprise left. "He's the one endangering everyone here, and the captain refuses to do anything about it."

Nahatal stepped forward, scowling likewise. "It's not your place to question the captain, even if you are first mate. Laikal hasn't done anything wrong. He just saved us."

The chatter started up again, the tone arguing, louder than before.

"Enough!" the captain shouted. The sound stilled, and the captain stepped onto one of the crates so he was more clearly visible.

"Sildonus, you have confessed your guilt and you have two witnesses testifying against you. You have forfeited your position as first mate on the basis of disobedience, insurrection, and attempted murder. You will be expected to leave the ship at the next port and will not be able to reapply for this position."

Sildonus sputtered but couldn't argue.

The captain turned to the rest of the crew."Laikal is a Glowblood—"

"Dragon-lit," Laikal interjected, quietly.

"—Dragon-lit, but he has no intention of harming

us. More than being a—Dragon-lit, he is also my son and a member of this crew, and I expect him to be protected and treated as such. Any violation hereof will be punished. If you wish to leave the crew on this basis you are free to do so at the next port."

There was no protesting, merely a soft murmur. Laikal spotted a few of them nodding in agreement, Nahatal among them.

"I shall see how we work out the future of this ship, but I plan to heed the dragon's warning. Now, back to what you were doing," The captain said, stepping off the crate.

The crew scattered, some of them still talking quietly amongst themselves. That would take a while to clear up, but Laikal didn't expect any serious trouble. The ship soon settled into its familiar, deceptively quiet hum.

Many of them still wouldn't see him the same way and wouldn't befriend him. Not everyone would accept him, and his existence was still a matter of contention. That wasn't what he cared about. There would always be a few loyal people who would stay by his side and protect him. His father, Aranél. Maybe even Nahatal.

The captain turned to Laikal and Aranél, the only ones still left by the bulwark.

"Thanks for taking care of Laikal, son," the captain said to Aranél.

Aranél made some vaguely complaining comment under his breath, which was as close as a 'you're welcome' anyone could expect of him.

Laikal pushed his head into his father's shoulder. The captain ruffled his wet hair.

Laikal winced as Aranél's balled up coat hit him in the head.

"Put on a coat, it's much too cold for this," Aranél

said.

Laikal obeyed. He'd have to fix his shirt once it had dried.

In the distance, spray rose like a geyser. The waters stirred, a wave pushing to all sides, and Astrakrasis appeared, arcing through the air, fins extended like wings as he breached. His patterns flashed.

"Farewell, Dragon-lit, until we meet again."

Laikal flashed back, the light shining out of his coat.

"What did it say?" Aranél asked.

Laikal grinned as the wind blurred between them. Everyone he cared about was safe, and they didn't see him any differently. He would never be forced into the violence that was the world. Even if it was everywhere, there was safety too.

"It said you should be nicer to me."

Laikal's patterns rippled as he laughed and ducked away from Aranél trying to smack him on the head. He belonged here, even if it wasn't in the way he expected. Not everyone would see him as a part of the crew, and not everyone would accept him, but he had people who would, no matter what happened. Perhaps one day the world would be more favorable to Dragon-lit. Perhaps when he was grown up, he would go with Astrakrasis to where the other Dragon-lit were. That could wait. He had plenty of time.

About Rose Everille

Rose Everille is a comic design student by day and a writer of Christian fiction by night. She lives on a small farm surrounded by books, art materials, and far too many pets. She has written an unpublished fantasy trilogy, multiple short stories of varying genres, and is currently wandering through a hopeful post-dystopian standalone. She enjoys wielding a longsword, a paintbrush, or a pen.

You can find her on Goodreads, Pinterest, or Instagram with the username Rose Everille.

Weather the Storm

Emma Rose Thrasher

To my future husband.

Prologue

The night was black, the waves were cold, and the girl was alone.

She'd left her father's house when she heard the news. How could she have stayed? Her mother had called after her, but she'd ignored her and kept going. There was nothing for her there now, nothing but pain, shame, and loneliness.

Her wandering feet took her up the familiar path to the cliff where she and Anshel—oh, Anshel!—had spent many happy hours. The sea wind blew, bringing with it the scent of salt like tears.

She blinked, hard, then knelt by the cliff's edge. Anshel had left her. Anshel had betrayed her. Anshel wouldn't be there to sit with her on the cliffside and stare at the clouds and dream of the life they'd live when they were married.

He was gone.

Her hands shook. She reached up and tugged at her braids, pulling out the strands she'd carefully pinned that morning. Braids were for betrothed or married women, and that was something she'd never be, not again.

Soon, her hair was loose, and she ran her fingers through it, feeling the tangles separate. *How could he do this to me? I loved him. I told him I was true to him. But he was a liar all along.* She bit her lip and tasted blood but felt no pain.

What would they do to him if he came back? Would he be exiled? Probably—nobody wanted to live in the same town as a traitor. He would deserve it. He'd brought her so high just to throw her down.

Whatever was done to Anshel, it wouldn't heal her, that was certain. Everyone in the village had heard by now. Now everyone knew—knew that she had been so unloveable that even the man who said he loved her most had changed his mind and cast her away like a piece of dirt.

The girl hardened herself. There was only one option left. She couldn't stay here, but the sea was always a friend to the forsaken.

So she stood, walked to the edge of the cliffside, and fell.

Chapter 1

Anya breathed in slowly, savoring the scent of the salty air and the feel of the sunlight on her hands. It was no wonder Father had loved the sea so much. It rumbled softly in the distance, present and constant like the stars sailors used to navigate.

Right now, she needed something constant to remind her that even though much was about to change, some things would stay the same no matter what.

Anya's thoughts were interrupted by footsteps. "Anya," Mother said softly, "are you nearly ready?"

Anya glanced back at Mother. "I've got the dress on," she said, hardly able to believe the words. "Would you help me with my hair?" Her hair hung loose down her back, even though she'd worn it up ever since that night on the dock with Lev. She'd taken it out one last time before the wedding, and Mother was far more skilled with braiding.

Mother stood for a moment longer with her hand on the doorway, long enough that Anya almost repeated the question. But eventually, she mustered a smile and said, "Of course. Sit down, I'll get the comb."

Anya did. Soon Mother began combing through Anya's dark hair, and Anya closed her eyes and listened to the even sound of brushing.

"How do you feel?" Mother asked at last.

Anya smiled. "I feel happy. Nervous, but I suppose that's normal."

"I'm glad." Mother hummed a tune and pulled Anya's hair back. "It is. Zaveta once told me, 'let yourself feel the fear and you will remember the joy.'"

"How do *you* feel?" Anya asked.

Mother paused a long time before answering.

"Happy for you."

Anya wondered if, like herself, Mother's happiness was mixed with something she couldn't quite place. For so long, their family had been just the two of them. Now...

"Lev is a good man," Mother continued. "He'll take care of you, and me too, when I'm older and need taking care of. I only wish Evron was here to see you wed."

Why did hearing Father's name always strike Anya mute?

She swallowed. "He really is a good man. He's so dutiful and caring, and he works so hard. I'm just glad I get to spend the rest of my life with him, us helping each other."

"You certainly have a lot to look forward to." Mother's voice was cheery; Anya wondered how hard she worked to make it that way. "How's he doing in all of this, do you know?"

"Fine, I think," Anya said. "He's been worried, though. The king has asked him to investigate the recent disappearances, and he hasn't been making much progress." She couldn't keep the note of pride from her voice. Lev was a trusted man despite his youth; he was probably the youngest man in Paskayt to ever hold the position of elder. Still, he had more worries than other men his age.

Mother clicked her tongue as she wound the braids around Anya's head and began pinning them up. "On his wedding day, too. He shouldn't have to think about such things today."

Anya frowned. "He doesn't want to, Mother. It's just that the king needs his help, and he wants to do what's best for Paskayt. It's not as if he can ask all the problems to please stop so he can have a peaceful wedding." Once they were married, things would settle down, at least—they'd have a day or two of quiet, and Lev had said they'd go out sailing in his new boat, the one with the sunburst flag.

Mother didn't comment on this. "Well, the times certainly are strange. Fishermen disappearing without a trace, storms getting worse—even the people seem to be changing, and not for the better. Did you hear about the girl from Arudyne? Oh, what was her name..." She tapped her fingers against her other hand. "Fenya, that's it. She was betrothed, but when they found out he'd been unfaithful, the poor girl couldn't cope with it and drowned herself."

Anya swallowed. "Oh." The village of Arudyne wasn't far from Paskayt, and Fenya was a familiar name—if Anya recalled correctly, they'd met once briefly at the midsummer festival. How could such a thing have happened to her?

"But I'm sorry for bringing it up," Mother said, shaking her head. "Today should be a happy day. Here, your hair's done. Take a look."

Anya accepted the looking glass her mother handed to her. Her hair was in neat braids pinned up about her head, more intricate than Anya had ever managed to do herself.

"It's odd," she said, handing the mirror back. "I always saw you and the other women with their hair up, but for years I never thought it could be me." *I never thought anyone would love me like Lev does.* Her eyes felt heavy; she blinked, and her eyelashes were wet.

Mother put a hand on her shoulder. "Oh, Anya, dear girl. I never wanted to think about this day. Perhaps it was cowardly, but I didn't want to lose you."

The tears were harder to hold back now. All her life, she had imagined her future as a simple one: she'd stay with her mother and try to provide for her, keeping out of the way and trying to be content. But now everything was changing.

The change was for the better, and she wouldn't give it up for an instant—but it was still hard to think about what she was leaving behind.

"You aren't losing me," she said, trying to be cheerful. "I'll just be on the other side of town. And you'll visit me, won't you, Mother?"

"Of course I will, Anya," Mother said. She walked over to the window and looked out, silent.

Music drifted in from outside. Anya stood, touching her hair lightly. "It's time," she said, breaking the silence. "I should go."

"Yes," Mother agreed.

Neither of them moved for a moment. Then Anya stepped to her mother and hugged her tight and quick—something she hadn't done in years—then, before she could hesitate, turned away and walked out of her home for the last time.

***

Lev whirled Anya around, weaving in between the rows of dancers on either side. The dance was quick, one involving simple but fast-paced steps and a *lot* of twirling.

Just as they reached the end of the line, the song ended with a flourish. Anya and Lev's eyes were locked on each other, and her head spun from more than just the dance.

Lev smiled at her—one of his brief, subdued smiles that always felt like a secret shared between the two of them—and then turned to the other dancers and guests. "That concludes today's festivities," he announced. "My wife and I are very grateful for your presence."

Anya leaned on Lev's strong arm, relishing the sound of those words. *My wife. That's me.* It felt too strange to be true—but, she supposed, she would have a long time with him to get used to it.

As the people dispersed, Lev and Anya were at the center of it all, thanking people for coming and accepting congratulations. Anya herself felt radiant, like she could finally be at peace. Lev was a good man—he was well-respected in the community, and he noticed her. He saw her work even when nobody else did. And he cared about it, too—he didn't take her work for granted, but he thanked her and often helped her when he could.

The wedding guests finally dwindled away, and the musicians packed up their instruments. Only a few women remained, taking down the linen hangings and flower garlands that had decorated the city square. Anya felt the urge to help, but it would be unthinkable for the bride to work on her own wedding day, so she looked up at her new husband instead.

Lev's hair was the color of wet sand but much less orderly—he hated cutting it, so he would let it grow out long and crop it short every so often. For the wedding, he had done his absolute best to smooth it into a semblance of order, but the dancing had thrown all of his efforts to the wind. It brought a surge of joy to her heart. *My love with his wonderful messy hair.*

Lev noticed her gaze and glanced at her. "How do you feel?"

Anya giggled. "A little tired, but happy. What do we do now?"

"We'll go home." Lev's voice was decisive. "The house is all ready for us. I made sure of that this morning. It's sturdy; I think it would weather a storm just fine. And then we'll go sailing."

"Our home." Anya turned the words over in her mind. A home that would weather a storm—something everyone needed, in more ways than one.

"Imagine," Lev said, a smile lighting up his face.

"We'll live in that house for years, decades, even. And maybe there'll be a child—"

"Or more than one," Anya jumped in, caught up in Lev's excitement.

"Or more than one! We'll build a life, Anya, and we get to start today."

She leaned her head onto his shoulder. "It's wonderful," she said, and it was true—it was the most wonderful thing she could dare to imagine. "Let's go."

Lev offered her his arm, but before they could leave the village square, a man ran up to them. "Lev!" he called out. "Wait a moment!"

Anya stiffened, but Lev stopped walking and raised a hand in greeting. "Rurik! What brings you?"

Rurik, a tall man with dark hair and a scraggly beard, approached them. "Congratulations," he said, nodding to Anya.

Anya smiled, but suddenly the tightness in her stomach, which had disappeared during the dance, was back. Why did Rurik seem so uneasy?

"Lev," Rurik began. "Paskayt is in danger. The tides, the storms, the disappearances—the situation is critical, and we simply can't stay here any longer."

Anya's mouth went dry. They had to leave Paskayt? The danger was that bad?

"I... didn't realize it had gotten so serious." Lev's forehead was furrowed, and his eyes flicked to Anya before he looked back to Rurik. "But we've discussed this before. What do you need to talk about?"

Rurik sighed. "We have to do something, and fast. The king wants to send out an expedition to find somewhere to resettle, perhaps an island, where there's food and safety."

"A good idea. Who does he want to send? Eriks or

Ivan, maybe? They need a bit more experience, but they'd do fine."

Rurik hesitated. "He wants you."

Anya's grip on Lev's hand tightened instinctively, and she sucked in a short breath. They were taking him away from her? But—but they'd just married. Surely Lev would refuse.

Lev glanced at her again for just a heartbeat. "Rurik." His voice was low.

Rurik lifted his hands. "Lev, he tried all the others already."

Lev looked up at the sky then down at the ground, then finally met Rurik's eyes again. "If the king commands it, I'll go, but are you *sure* there's no one else?"

Anya's heart skipped a beat. What?

"There's no one," Rurik rubbed the back of his head as if embarrassed. "No one who can lead. I know it's not a good time, what with..." He shrugged and nodded to Anya without looking at her. "But this could be the only way Paskayt can survive. We need you. I'm sorry."

"No, that's all right. I'll do it," Lev said, his voice growing more resolved. "Tell the king I'll gather a group and leave in the morning."

Rurik breathed out a heavy sigh. "Thank you. And, congratulations again."

Anya couldn't manage a smile in response. Lev was leaving her? They hadn't been married for more than an hour and already he was leaving her?

As soon as Rurik was gone, she dropped Lev's hand. "You're going with him?" she asked in a voice more high-pitched than she had intended.

Lev raised his hands in defense. "I'm sorry, Anya. But this could be our only hope to find a safe home, and I can't ignore a request from the king."

Anya bit her lip. "But—" She faltered. "But why can't the king send someone else? You've already done so much. If you talk to him, I'm sure he'd be willing—"

"It's not enough," Lev cut in. "We don't know what's happening to the ocean. You heard what Rurik said. The tides are changing, and at this rate, we'll be swept away before midmonth, maybe even earlier. We have to act soon before the community is threatened further."

He was avoiding the question. "But we're only just married. What will people say?"

Lev looked back at her, altogether too calm for the situation. "Anya. You have to learn to make sacrifices for the greater good. It's my duty to help, and I can't change that. I love you, but I can't let anything stand in the way of doing the right thing."

"So the right thing is to leave your *wife* and go off to sea, just to find a new homeland that may not even exist?" Anya burst out. "How is that the right thing?"

Lev's face hardened. "Why are you making this so difficult? I have to do this. I thought you would understand."

Anya bit her tongue. He *didn't* have to do this. Wasn't she more important to him than the king was?

It felt like she was losing him, just after she'd finally found someone to love her and shelter her. It felt like the only happiness she'd ever had was slipping away before her very eyes.

"You said our house would weather the storm," she finally said, feeling numb.

"It will. But today I have to care about the houses of others."

Let them care about themselves, Anya almost snapped, but held herself back. She shouldn't be callous. This was who

Lev was—he would lay himself down in the service of others, even if they wouldn't do half as much for him if their positions were reversed. If Lev had a chance to save them, he would take it, no matter the cost to himself.

Or, apparently, to his wife.

There was one last chance. She stepped forward and took his hand with both of hers. "Then let me come with you. I don't want to be separated so soon."

It was sincere, but not sincerely taken. Lev laughed. "I don't think the king would think much of that."

And why not? But the thought of braving the ocean, the malevolent, seething mass of water where anything might happen and rarely happened for good, filled her with dread and made her almost glad that Lev refused. Almost.

She dulled her heart and looked away from her love. "Fine. Do what you have to."

Behind her, Lev sighed. "Anya, don't be angry. I thought you would react better than this."

"Better than what, exactly?"

"Better than—oh, I don't know." He gestured vaguely with both of his hands. "You're making this far worse than it needs to be. I'll only be gone a few weeks."

"You don't know that." Anya clenched her skirt in her hands. "If the ocean is more dangerous now, you might *never* come back." Just like Father hadn't come back, all those years ago.

"It's a risk I have to take."

"If you take it, I have to take it too."

Lev frowned. "And you're not willing?"

No. Not for you. The words were on her lips, but she couldn't say them. She knew what would happen if she did—Lev's face would change, his eyebrows lower in that look he sometimes got whenever someone didn't do their job properly or failed to keep their word. He didn't mean to be cruel, but she didn't want to disappoint him.

So instead she bit her tongue and said nothing, not trusting her voice. He was going, and there was nothing she could do about it. No matter what she tried, she would lose him.

In silence, they walked from the square to the cottage. Anya took deep breaths, trying not to let the tears out and spoil the day even more.

Their house was sturdy, but soon, she would live in it alone.

Chapter 2

Lev left early the next morning. He said goodbye to Anya, but she couldn't bring herself to anything more than terse conversation. She had to keep herself hidden, safe. If she let her true feelings through, she would fall apart.

And now, Anya sat with the windows in her new house shuttered to block out the light, wondering what on earth to do with herself.

She stood and began to pace. Everything in the house bore marks of Lev—from the floorboards he'd so carefully cut and sanded to the chest she knew contained the clothes he hadn't brought with him. It was so clear that he belonged here, and without him, the house felt like a person missing half their soul.

Footsteps thumped outside on the rocky pathway. "Anya!" Mother's voice called. "Are you home?"

Anya backed away from the window and sat down quietly. Maybe Mother would go away. Part of her wanted so badly to open the door and let her in, but she couldn't imagine talking to anyone right now. Better to be left alone.

Mother's knocks persisted. *I'm not home. Please go away.* Anya gritted her teeth to keep from crying. Why did she have to stay here? Why couldn't she have gone with Lev instead of remaining behind in the dying land of Paskayt? Then, at least, she wouldn't be alone.

Eventually Mother stopped knocking, and she went away. Anya breathed out a sigh of relief. If she wasn't home, nobody could bother her. Nobody would come with their words of sympathy that stung like burning coals.

Sympathy wasn't what she needed. What she needed was Lev back. His work was important, that much was certain.

The danger was real. But there was hardly anything she could do about it.

Eventually, Anya stood up and brushed off her skirt. The rays of sunlight arced through the window, lighting up the motes of dust in the air. Her head spun, reminding her that she hadn't eaten anything since a hurried breakfast that morning. She had sat there for hours.

This was ridiculous. Anya set her teeth. Just because Lev was gone didn't mean she had to mope around like a lonesome girl with no sense. She was a grown woman who had work to do.

So she busied herself around the house. She tidied the floor and arranged the furniture, and then she swept it. Then she grabbed the wooden bucket to go to the well and get some water to wash the floorboards.

When she pulled the bucket up, it was empty.

Anya stared. What had happened to the well? She hadn't heard anything about it drying up. Perhaps she'd ask the elders about it later—for now, she had enough fresh water to drink, and the floors could wait.

The beach was nearby, and she turned her eyes to the horizon for a moment. The view of the ocean was beautiful, but movement caught her attention from the corner of her eye—a figure walking on the beach, though Anya couldn't make out its features in the fading twilight. Or was it the twilight? Her eyes wouldn't focus. And the figure seemed indistinct, like it was made of shifting shadows and smoke and not a real person at all.

The figure wavered, then disappeared.

Anya stifled a scream. What was that? Surely she'd imagined it—people didn't just disappear into thin air—but it was undeniable that the figure *had* been there, and now it wasn't.

She realized her hands were shaking. The bucket slipped from her fingers and fell with a clatter to the ground. She didn't pick it up, but walked forward, finding her way through the dunes to the beach. Surely she was imagining it. No one would be there. Or if there was, they'd just walked away without her noticing.

Anya had almost convinced herself of this when she reached the ocean shore and saw a man's body lying on the sand.

Well, there was no shadowy figure. Cautiously, Anya approached. "Hello? Are you all right?"

He made no response. Anya's heart pounded. *He's unconscious,* she told herself. *Just wake him up.* She shook his arm.

The man's arm was still and cold as ice. She faltered. Then, shaking, she reached out to tip his face toward her.

His face was pale and the eyes were lifeless.

He was dead.

Anya screamed and shoved the man—the corpse—away from her. The horror made her skin crawl, and the coldness of his skin lingered on her hands. A dead man. How had it happened?

Think, Anya, think. You can't leave him here. Her skin crawled. She was probably in danger right as she spoke from whatever—or whoever—had killed him. *Raise the alarm. Quick.*

So she ran, nearly tripping over the hem of her skirt in her haste. "Help!" she screamed. "Help!"

Her voice felt weak, but it was enough. The villagers came running out of their houses and gathered around her. The faces were familiar—Raizel, Nalman, Katya, Naemi, her neighbors since she was born—but the darkness of the evening combined with her shock made them seem shadowy and accusing. She shrank back.

"What's the matter?" Nalman demanded, staring at her.

Anya swallowed. " I—there's..." She swayed on her feet, head light.

Raizel grabbed her arm and held her steady. The girl was strong despite her small size. "Whoa, Anya, I've got you! Don't fall."

Anya gasped for breath, leaning on Raizel's arm gratefully. "Thank you. There's—there's a dead man on the beach."

Gasps came from the small crowd that had gathered. It was no wonder; Anya hadn't believed it until she'd felt the man's body herself. Tragedy had seemed distant and unreal until it was brought near—now, it was visceral and close. She held herself stiffly to keep herself from fainting again.

"What did you see?" Nalmon pressed.

Anya shook her head. "I don't know exactly. I thought I saw a person standing over him, but when I got closer, it was just his body lying there." And cold as ice.

"Well, let's go, not stay here gawking!" shouted Teive, one of the older grizzled fishermen. He stomped down the path, brushing past Anya and Raizel. The others followed suit.

Raizel looked at Anya doubtfully. "You look worn out. Do you want to go with them, or...?"

Anya shook her head. "No, but I should. I was the one who saw—" She choked on the words. The man was *dead*. She was the only witness.

Oh, why wasn't Lev here? She needed him.

Raizel walked with her down to the beach. The crowd had gathered, and a few were kneeling beside the man's body.

"It's Moshe Minikson." Teive looked up, face grim.

"I knew he was dead ever since he didn't come back last week. Didn't I tell you?"

"But what killed him?" shouted someone from the back of the crowd.

"It must have been the storm," Teive said. He pointed down the beach to a pile of splintered wood that Anya hadn't noticed earlier. It was barely recognizable as a boat. "He was shipwrecked."

Shipwreck? But what about the figure?

Nalman stepped forward and gestured to Moshe's neck. "A storm wouldn't leave marks like that. He was murdered."

The word set off an eruption of arguments and shouts. Anya shrank back, but the same questions tugged at her mind. There hadn't been a storm. Moshe was a good sailor. And what about the figure?

"Silence!" Rurik shouted. His deep voice cut through the chaos, and the people quieted. He raised his hands. "We cannot be certain about anything yet. We will investigate. And until we can find out who was responsible, I would urge you not to assume the worst—in times such as these, we need to be unified, not constantly worrying about backstabbers."

His suggestion was met with mixed reactions from the crowd. Some of the men—Teive especially—nodded along, but some began to mutter amongst themselves, probably voicing the same concerns as the ones in Anya's mind.

But all at once, the murmuring quieted. Anya looked around to see the old woman Zaveta pushing through the crowd to come up to Moshe. The people parted to let her pass, and she knelt down beside the body, examining his face. Anya didn't know how she looked at the body so calmly—she herself was avoiding looking at it as much as possible—but

Zaveta was wise and hardy.

The old woman straightened up, and her wrinkled face was grave. "This was not the work of a storm, or even a common murderer. This was the work of a legend that I wish had remained forgotten."

The silence stretched on for a moment. Rurik cleared his throat, head inclined toward the old woman. "A legend, Zaveta?"

"Yes, a legend. The legend of the Rusalki." Zaveta turned to look out toward the ocean. "You know them. Spirits, evil ones, that seek to destroy men in a misguided attempt at revenge. They have taken Moshe and they will soon take us."

Anya shivered. The Rusalki? She had heard stories when she was young, but not many. Most of the stories contradicted each other, but they all agreed on one thing: the Rusalki were evil, and yet they had not troubled Paskayt for centuries.

"No!" someone shouted. "The Rusalki are a myth. They can't hurt us more than a fairy can!"

Zaveta frowned. "Simply because one story is false does not make all of them lies. The Rusalki are real, and they are threatening us as we speak. We must act, and quickly."

There was a long silence, broken only by whispers. The villagers' faces were shadowed in the fading light. Some were amused and perhaps annoyed—they didn't believe in legends. Others feigned amusement to hide their fear. Anya had never believed in the Rusalki, but after seeing a shadowy figure disappear into thin air, she was beginning to consider impossible explanations.

Rurik stared at the corpse's face, then gathered himself. "We'll see him buried directly," he said firmly. "That'll be the end of it. I'll need some of you to help dig."

The crowd began to disperse. Anya stood for a moment, trying to make sense of what had happened. Rurik seemed confident, but likely he knew people needed direction if they were to avoid chaos. He probably didn't know what was going on any more than the rest of them did. Lev had used similar tactics on occasion.

But one person knew. Anya glanced back and saw Zaveta trudging off in the direction of the village. She stepped quickly to catch up with her. "Zaveta, what are they?"

"What are what?" Zaveta's wrinkles deepened.

"The Rusalki. How do you know it was them? And are we in danger?" Anya slowed her pace—despite the old woman's authoritative bearing, she was quite short.

Thunder rumbled over the ocean. Zaveta took Anya's arm. "This is not the place to speak of such things. Come back to my house. Dark things shouldn't be left to the darkness to discuss."

It began to rain. Anya ducked her head, but Zaveta only hurried through the streets toward her house. It was nearly too dark to see, so Anya was glad when they reached the hut and saw the light streaming through the windows.

Chapter 3

The kettle whistled as it sat over the fire. Zaveta bustled around the kitchen, and Anya tried fruitlessly to get the image of the dead man's face out of her mind.

She had grown up familiar with death. Sailing was dangerous work, and Father's trading always made them fear he wouldn't come back—and one day, he hadn't. Anya was familiar with the emptiness that came when a loved one went away forever. But seeing Moshe's face had shocked her. This time, she had actually touched him—felt the coldness, his body devoid of life. She shuddered and clenched her fingers in a fist to get rid of the memory.

At last, Zaveta sat down with a clay cup in each hand and handed one to Anya. "So tell me," she said, fixing Anya with her piercing eyes, "what did you see tonight?"

Anya shivered and told Zaveta everything, from the dried-up well to the shadowy figure on the beach, all the way until she found Moshe dead. It had happened so quickly. Something was wrong, and terribly so.

Zaveta took Anya's hand and held it tightly in her own wrinkled one. "You've had a very difficult evening, dear," she said in her creaky voice. "Just take a breath and drink your tea for a moment. The Rusalki will wait."

Anya swallowed. "Will they?"

"They won't, but thinking about them won't do you any good just yet." Zaveta's eyes twinkled. "Go on, drink the tea."

Anya sipped from the warm cup but barely tasted it. "Zaveta, won't you tell me what they are? There must be something we can do."

Zaveta stared into the fire. "I do not know that there

is. The Rusalki are old creatures, Anya. Some have been alive for decades, centuries. It is hard to contend with an evil so well-established."

"How do you know it was them?"

"You said you saw the figure, didn't you?" Zaveta looked at Anya intently. "And that she vanished?"

"She? Yes."

Zaveta nodded. "I don't *know* she was a Rusalka. But if you know you saw someone, I know I believe you. People have seen stranger things that have turned out to be true, and you are not one to lie about something so important."

"I thought it could have been Moshe that I saw," Anya said, looking down. "And that he died right there in front of me. I thought I was imagining it all."

Zaveta shook her head. "Anya, I doubt you were imagining it. You saw her when you were calm, before you had seen the body. This is the simplest explanation, evil as it is."

Anya's chest was still tight, but Zaveta's calm presence gave her comfort. Zaveta believed her and understood what was going on. Maybe—just maybe—things weren't as desperately out of control as they seemed.

Zaveta stared at the fire. "The Rusalki are spirits. The stories say they are the cursed souls of young women who died because of love."

"They died for love?" Anya asked. "Why would that lead to a curse?"

The old woman shook her head. "Not for love—*because* of love. Not all love stories are as happy as yours, Anya. You have a good man, but many are not so fortunate."

Anya bit her tongue. Yes, Lev was a good man—yes, he was perfect, just like everyone thought. And yet he'd left her and acted like her love meant nothing. If that was a happy love story, a dead tree could be the strongest in the land.

"The Rusalki were young women with lovers who betrayed them. They chose to escape the lives they hated rather than try to forgive and rebuild, and they did so in a terrible way." Zaveta picked up the poker and nudged the wood on the fire, sending up a cascade of sparks. "Now, they wander the ocean, seeking men on whom to enact revenge in the stead of those who wronged them. Moshe was one."

Anya stared at the fire, watching the smoke twist up into the air. "They kill them," she said softly.

"Yes." Zaveta's voice was solemn.

So the figure she had seen on the beach was a Rusalka. "What do they look like?"

"Young women who wear their hair loose and have dresses of the ocean, according to my grandmother. And before you ask, I don't know what that means—I've never seen one myself."

The description was vague, but perhaps that matched the elusive appearance of the woman she'd seen. She gripped her cup tightly. "What does it mean for us if the Rusalki are coming back?"

"I don't know, dear. Not fully. But if the king tries to find a solution, it won't work unless he addresses the real problem. And it means none of us are safe at sea, nor perhaps on land. The ocean is no longer our friend."

The ocean wasn't safe. *Lev!* What if he ended up like Moshe? What if his body was the next she found?

Outside, thunder rumbled. The rain pounded down and filled the cabin with an oppressive feeling of solitude. Usually, Anya loved the rain, but now, when Lev was out on the ocean and might never come back, she couldn't bear the sound of it. She tried to keep back the tears, but a few slipped out.

Zaveta took her hand. "Anya, he may still come back."

"How do you know?" Anya wanted to believe Zaveta, wanted it so, so much—but she couldn't.

"Because," she said simply. "He loves you. Love is a strange thing, my dear, and when you've seen as much of it as I have you might understand that a little bit more. The Rusalki are born from a lack of love, but the presence of love is far more powerful than its absence."

Anya stared at her in confusion. What on earth did that mean? Was Zaveta just trying to distract her to cheer her up?

Zaveta sighed, as if she knew the skepticism Anya felt. "You know, I've watched you grow up. I've seen how you and your mother reacted to Evron's death. No, I'm not accusing you," she said, holding up a hand to forestall Anya's instinctive reaction. "Your mother did admirably, all things considered. But I know, and I've wanted to tell you for a long time, that hiding away isn't the proper response to heartbreak, and she hid herself away. You both did."

Anya bit her tongue. Hiding away—she hadn't hidden away. She'd been seven. She'd barely known what it *meant* that Father wasn't coming home anymore.

But as she thought of the past years and how she'd lived them, she began to see the truth of Zaveta's words. She'd always been a fearful child. She'd feared losing Mother, she'd feared being seen and shamed, and above all, she'd feared never finding someone to love her.

She pushed the thoughts away. Her fears were completely reasonable, and Zaveta didn't have to condemn her because of them. Zaveta hadn't lived the life Anya had. She didn't know the same pain.

"But," Zaveta continued, "love is strong, though you

may not see it yet. If it has the strength to turn a maiden into a monster, it has the power to do the reverse as well."

"Lev left me." Anya's face was hard, and the tears were drying on her cheeks. "I told him not to go. I *begged* him, Zaveta. If he'd only listened to me, he wouldn't be in danger now. But he is."

"Then he needs your love now more than ever."

Thunder crashed outside. The fire popped. Anya closed her eyes. Did she love Lev still? She hated to ask the question, but she couldn't avoid it anymore. She was angry. At the same time, she was afraid for him, terrified, and she badly wanted him to come back. Did that count as love?

"Everyone always leaves me," she whispered. "I don't see how love can be strong if it never lasts."

Zaveta swirled the tea in her cup. "It's true that people can hurt you. No one is perfect. People always hurt each other, and sometimes the ones they love most are the ones they hurt the most. But then, you and I do that, too. I've hurt people when I never intended to, and sometimes I intended to very much."

"Then what's the point of loving at all?" Anya couldn't keep the despair from her voice.

"Well," Zaveta said thoughtfully, "pain shouldn't be the end of love. Oftentimes it is, but people can respond differently to hurt." She looked up and stared at the ceiling. "Some people hide away. Some people fight back and defend themselves. Some people run. And some people try to move on, rebuild, and forgive. Only the people who do the last know how to truly love."

Anya thought of how she'd behaved that day. She had hidden herself from everyone, even her mother. But rebuilding, forgiving—she hadn't felt able to do anything but hide.

"I don't know," she said finally. "I can't see how to move on when he's not here. It's not as if you can rebuild a house when half the boards are missing. And I don't know what that has to do with the Rusalki, anyway."

"More than you imagine. But perhaps it can wait for tomorrow. Decisions made at night are often regretted in the morning." Zaveta creaked to her feet and took Anya's cup. "I'll get some more tea. Sit and think for a while."

Anya felt young and helpless again, but she did as Zaveta suggested. Thunder echoed across the island. The storm raged outside, but the storm in her heart seemed so much more out of control.

Chapter 4

Anya was woken by a harsh banging on the door. She stirred, briefly disoriented, before realizing she was still in Zaveta's cottage.

The banging came again. "Everyone to the square!" a man's voice shouted. "The king's summoned us!"

Zaveta roused herself from the chair next to Anya, grumbling. "No need to be so loud." She rubbing her neck.

Anya stood and helped Zaveta up. "I'm sorry to impose," she said, feeling out of place. She must have fallen asleep in her chair without meaning to.

Zaveta waved a hand, trudging toward the door. "Nothing to apologize for. I kept you up talking all night. Now, shall we see what all the fuss is about?"

The two women left the house. Outside, the village was in confusion. The rain had stopped, but debris littered the streets. Ankle-deep puddles lay on either side of the road, which Anya guided Zaveta to avoid. Several buildings had lost shingles. The storm had brought casualties.

When they reached the square, Anya and Zaveta took their places in the crowd and waited. There was tension in the air; the sounds of whispering and talking was unusually subdued. Anya let out a trembling breath, unable to relax.

After what seemed a small eternity, King Haskel stepped up onto the crate and waited for silence. Anya stared at him, trying to push down the tangled mess of emotions coursing through her. He wasn't a bad king. He'd always kept the peace in Paskayt and made sure everyone was provided for. He had a kind heart—in theory. But he'd sent Lev to his death.

King Haskel raised his hands to address the people.

"No doubt," he began, "you have heard rumors about our present situation. The wells have dried up and the fish have stopped coming, not to mention the disappearances. And the tides... if they continue to grow, we will be washed away. Paskayt is no longer safe." He paused, as if gathering strength for what he was about to say. "We have to evacuate. Inland."

There was a stunned silence. To Anya, the news was a blow. Inland? Once they got past the river, the land turned to a desert. There was no soil to grow food in, and the river didn't have enough fish to sustain the whole population. The move would be devastating.

Teive stepped forward. "We can't go inland. We'll die."

"We'll die if we stay here," King Haskel said. He spread his hands. "By going inland, we have a chance of survival, at least. The river will give us water. We will adapt to what we must."

Zaveta clutched at Anya's arm. "This is not the solution," she whispered in Anya's ear. "You must tell him. Convince him that there is no safety by the river; the Rusalki will find us there too. We must leave behind the water entirely or face them head-on."

Anya's heart dropped. "But if we leave the water we'll die! The river's our only hope."

"It is a false hope." Zaveta shook her head.

"Why can't we stay?" someone shouted. "We'll dig new wells. We can survive."

Anya shrank back as her countrymen began to argue. The chaos grew louder by the second. "Zaveta, what do we do?"

Zaveta only shook her head, and Anya felt more helpless than ever.

Rurik stepped up and banged the gong with a

hammer. It reverberated through the square, cutting through the noise. "Silence!" he roared. "Listen to what the king has to say!"

The crowd quieted, but the mutterings remained. They were clearly displeased, and Anya couldn't blame them.

King Haskel's thin beard wavered in the breeze. "Would you rather live in a land that is dying, unable to bring back food and water for your families? If we leave, at least, we will have a chance. We will work hard. We will unite. We will find a way to survive." He tapped his fist into the palm of his hand to emphasize the point. "Going inland is not one option of many. It is our *only* option. You can choose to come with us and start a new life, or you can stay here and try to scrape by on rainfall and foraged leaves. But we will only survive if we act together."

Anya half expected everyone to start shouting again, but instead, they were silent. Despite their resistance, they knew the king was right. They had to leave. There was no future left in Paskayt, not while the Rusalki still threatened them. And Anya couldn't see a way of stopping them.

"We leave in the evening hours," King Haskel said. "Meet in the square. Take only what you must." The words were final. There was no going back for them anymore.

Silently, the people dispersed. Zaveta let go of Anya's arm and marched up to the king, but Anya didn't have the heart to follow. So the king would use Lev as a last effort to save their people, then give up and abandon him when hardship came. It felt in that instant like her heart was hollow and alone, like she was a wrung-out rag or a torn sail hanging lifeless above the bow.

Zaveta's hand motions grew more animated as she talked with the king. Haskel looked down with respect at the elderly woman, but behind the respect was a settled stubbornness. He would not listen. He was like Lev—when he made up his mind, there was little anyone could do to change it. Zaveta may as well have been talking to a stone.

"Anya!"

Anya turned to see Mother making her way through the crowd toward her. She lifted a hand to wave, but Mother reached her and wrapped her in a hug before she finished.

When Mother moved to let go, Anya clung to her for an instant longer before stepping back. "Mother," she said desperately, "what am I going to do?"

"What do you mean?" Mother said. "It's a difficult situation, but we'll work it out—"

"Lev's not here. He's out on the ocean, the king sent him away. He might never find us after we're gone, and there's no way he'd be back by this evening." Anya clenched a trembling hand into a fist. "I can't leave without him."

Mother's face went blank for an instant, then was covered over with a look of studied concern. "But you can't stay here. Come with me, I'll take care of you."

Anya knew she couldn't stay. And it would be so much easier to go with Mother. She would grieve for Lev, but who would blame her? She could return to her old life, her old ways, fit into her old place in the village. How could she do otherwise? But the thought of losing him—the thought of him being murdered by vicious water-spirits who only lived to destroy—of never seeing his face again or hearing his laugh—

Her hurt seemed to hardly matter now. She pressed her lips together to keep from crying.

Mother took her hand and held it tightly. "Anya, if he comes back, he will find us. The king would leave a note or map to where we've gone. If you leave, he'll find you again."

Perhaps. But Mother didn't know about the Rusalki. And even if by some miracle Lev and his men survived, they would never find the new inland settlement. He would never return on his own.

The easy path couldn't be the right one if it led her away from him. She squared her shoulders. "We'd better start preparing to leave. I should get back to the house."

Mother nodded. "I'll see you in the evening. We'll get through this together, Anya. Don't worry." Giving her one last look, she turned and walked out of the square.

Immediately, Anya turned to look for Zaveta, but the old woman stormed through the square with a scowl and walked right up to her. "What are you standing there for?" she demanded. "We're leaving in only a few hours. Our fool king won't listen to reason."

"Zaveta, I'm not leaving. Lev's going to die. You know it's true. I have to find him, but I don't know how." Anya felt tears run down her cheeks but refused to hide her face. Hopelessness couldn't overwhelm her—there had to be a chance. But it seemed so small.

Zaveta put a hand on Anya's arm. "Oh, Anya," she said, far more gently than she had been moments earlier. "Dear girl, there's no need to lose hope just yet."

Anya looked down at her. "Why? How?"

"Do you remember last night, when I told you that love has a strange power?"

"Yes." Proverbs and metaphors, hadn't it been?

Zaveta grabbed Anya's hand and shook it. "Then *use* it! The Rusalki use their love for evil, but they should not be the only ones to use it at all. If you truly love Lev, use that power for good."

Anya stared at her, brow furrowed. What could Zaveta possibly mean? How could Anya use her power when she couldn't understand what kind of power it was?

Then in that instant, she felt something inside her

heart—a tugging, a strange pull out towards the sea, a *direction*.

Was that it? Did she understand? But the ocean was dangerous. Wouldn't she too be taken by the Rusalki? Anya's heart shrank at the thought. Even if Zaveta was right, and even if Lev was still alive, she would never reach him safely.

I'll die if I go.

But he would die if she didn't.

He hurt me. He doesn't deserve it.

But what kind of a thought was that? Of *course* he hurt her. She had hurt him too. That didn't mean their love had ended forever.

Maybe love wasn't meant to keep her safe and happy all the rest of her life. Maybe, instead, it hurt. It was dangerous. It meant sacrificing yourself—your worries, your wants, your insecurities—for another person's good.

And maybe, that love could act as a compass drawing her to him.

Anya nearly laughed aloud. She looked at Zaveta. "I think I understand. Goodbye, and thank you."

Zaveta seemed to know exactly what Anya meant. She grabbed Anya in a hug. "May the wind speed you on your journey."

Tears slid down her cheeks again, but this time, they weren't from despair. They were from the strong conviction inside her that pushed her forward. She *would* save Lev. If she had to, she would die doing it.

And if he was alive, she would find him again.

Chapter 5

Anya dashed down the rocky path to her house. There was no time to lose.

Bursting through the door, she grabbed a cloth bag and threw some food and other supplies she'd need for the journey into it. What if Lev was starving? Or hurt? She'd need to be prepared.

She threw the bag over her shoulder and ran for the boats. No one would stop her. Everyone was at the square or in their own houses; no one would miss a single boat.

As she ran down the path, Raizel stepped out of the boathouse with a sack over her shoulder. "Anya! Where are you going? The square's the other way. Here, let's walk together."

Anya skidded to a stop and bit her lip. How could she tell Raizel? "I... I'm not going with you."

Raizel furrowed her eyebrows, but slowly, understanding dawned. "You're going to the boats instead. But why?"

"Lev," she said simply. "He's out on the ocean. I have to try and save him."

Raizel opened her mouth, then closed it again. "You—Anya, you know how dangerous the ocean is right now! There's another storm brewing, just look at the clouds."

Anya glanced at the sky, and her heart sank at the unnaturally dark storm clouds that hovered over the horizon. Another storm? Now, when it wasn't the season for it? But she set her jaw. "I have to try."

Raizel stared at her, then grabbed Anya into a hug. "Don't die, please. Come back safely."

"I'll try." Anya held her friend tightly. "You be safe,

too." She let go and met Raizel's eyes. "You'll tell my mother where I've gone, won't you? I wish I could tell her goodbye, but there's just no time."

Raizel laughed even through her tears. "Of course I will. But how will you even find him? You don't know where he's gone."

Anya thought of the strange pull she'd felt earlier. "I think I can feel him," she said, almost more to herself than Raizel. "I can find him, Raizel. I don't understand it, but I know I can."

"That doesn't make much sense, but I believe you. May the winds guide you, Anya." She grabbed Anya's hand and held it tightly, then let go and left for the square.

Anya watched her go, and her heart ached. But she was the only one who could do this. She would find Lev, and she would rescue him, or at least she would die trying.

She searched through the boats until she found the one that belonged to Lev's father, Kir. Hopefully Kir wouldn't mind her borrowing it. It was well-made and sturdy, and the sail was a pale canvas that looked strong enough to withstand any ocean gale—and hopefully it would, because at that very moment, thunder rumbled in the distance.

Our house will weather the storm, even if I have to hold it together with my bare hands, she thought fiercely.

She threw her bag into the hold and pulled the boat out, untying the rope that held it to the dock. Soon, the boat was drifting on the water. Anya hoisted the sail and caught the wind, and she drifted out to sea. Her heart pounded furiously, and she readied herself for the coming storm. She would not turn back. She would *not*. She would save Lev whatever the cost.

The clouds darkened, and the storm hit.

Rain pelted onto the deck like arrows. Anya held up a

hand to shelter her face enough to see—but the wind was worse than the rain, and it tossed the boat around like a child's toy. She held tight to the mast and barely avoided being flung out into the water.

The sunlight was blocked by the clouds; the sky looked dark as night. Anya's grip on the mast slipped. For one heartrending second, she fell—but she stumbled against the edge of the boat and caught hold of a rope.

Dashing the water out of her eyes, she gripped the rope like a lifeline. If she didn't do something, she'd be thrown out of the boat like a rag doll. Straining her muscles, she pulled herself over to the mast and threw the rope around it, then knotted the other end to her waist and pulled it tight. There—she was as secure as she could make herself.

Crack. Lightning. Around her, the storm raged. Anya could see nothing but the torrential rain pelting her and the boat, the dark clouds, and the huge waves that lifted her up with every swell.

But as she watched, she began to see strange shapes—figures leaping like dolphins out of the water, shadowy and indistinct. They looked as if they were dancing a strange and vicious dance, like leaping fish trying to fly. Anya watched them and wondered why she did not feel afraid.

She set her face toward the prow of the boat and closed her eyes. The stormy waves tossed her, but she held to the mast and simply felt. Where was Lev?

Faintly—oh, so faintly—she thought she felt a beating heart.

Her eyes snapped open and she pulled the rope to turn the sailboat to the right. The strong gusts of wind pushed the boat around, and it tipped dangerously, but Anya angled the boat into the waves and sped onward. The movement sent Anya into the path of several of the figures.

They leapt toward the boat, and Anya threw herself back to avoid them—but they dove into the ocean instead.

Soon, the storm slackened. Every so often, Anya paused and listened for the sound of the heartbeat. It seemed to be leading her on like a pole star; she navigated by it, steering the small sailboat to find the one she knew was calling to her. Nothing mattered anymore but finding him. There was nothing but her, him, and the ocean—and the figures that had gathered behind Anya, following her from a distance.

They never stopped her. They only watched. And she ignored them as well, as there was no reason to pay them attention if they would not hurt her. She didn't understand her own certainty, but she knew she was in no danger.

The boat sped onward. Anya's arms ached from steering, but she refused to slacken her grip. She closed her eyes and listened for the heartbeats. For a moment, they didn't come—but there they were again, albeit weak. They felt close.

Through the fog, she saw a looming structure up ahead with jagged edges. As the boat grew nearer, the image clarified into a natural spire of rock. *Land!* Was this it?

Her hands shook from effort and fear. She pulled the ropes and angled the sails to bring her to the island. When the boat was close enough to the shore, she tossed the anchor overboard and pulled at it, then cautiously stepped out and made her way to the shore.

The island was dark, as if it was twilight. Anya stared at the sky. Surely it wasn't night yet? She couldn't believe that she'd sailed all day—it had been only a few hours at most, and it was morning when she'd left. No, this darkness was unnatural.

Heartbeats came from the right. She jogged across the sand, and her wet skirt flapped around her knees. Unease grew in her. It was dark, but also cold, far too cold for midsummer. What had happened here?

Along the beach lay driftwood and debris. Anya paused to examine a pile of broken planks. They were sanded and had clearly been crafted with care before they had broken upon the shore. A corner of blue fabric caught her eye. She pulled it out, then gasped.

The flag bore a sunburst. It was his boat.

Anya tucked the flag into her belt and stared around, heart pounding. "Lev?" she called. "Lev? Are you here?"

There was no answer. *He may be unconscious. Nothing to worry about. You'll just have to find him.* She walked along the shore again, checking each pile of debris for any sign of Lev or his crew. The wreckage was jagged and difficult to see.

She had nearly given up hope when she saw him.

He was lying on the shore next to a pile of broken planks. He wasn't moving, and his face was turned away from her. As soon as Anya saw him, she raced to his side and knelt down on the sand. "Lev! Lev, are you hurt? I've found you, oh, I can't believe I actually found you. Zaveta was right, I wish you could have heard her. Everything will be all right... now..."

She trailed off. Fear had seized her. Cautiously, she reached out and touched his head, tipping it towards her.

His face was empty and his skin was cold.

No.

She choked. He couldn't be—he wasn't—she was misunderstanding. This was all wrong.

Lev's face was an ashen gray. His beard was encrusted with sand, and his face was expressionless. His eyes were open, but glassy, and they were as empty as Moshe's had been. Dimly, Anya noticed there were no marks on his neck. So the Rusalki had not strangled him, at least.

That was when her heart broke. She grabbed his shirt and bent down, hot tears streaming down her face. He was dead. Lev was dead. She'd come all this way—she'd found him against all odds—she'd sailed through the storm—but none of it had mattered.

Then, footsteps sounded behind her.

Chapter 6

Anya froze. None of Lev's companions had survived, had they? She hadn't seen them, but if Lev was gone, surely all of them had perished too.

The footsteps came again. Anya couldn't bring herself to turn around. Somehow, she already knew what—who—it was. She closed her eyes and bent her head downward, gripping Lev's shirt as if it would bring him back to her.

"Why do you weep?" The voice was whispery and seemed to come from the sand all around her, like the ocean waves crashing on the shore.

Anya knew what it was, but she didn't care that she was probably in mortal danger. "Because I love him." Her voice shook. *Don't you understand love?* But of course it didn't. It only existed because it didn't.

The creature hissed. "He hurt you. I saw. I saw everything. How you cried and you wept for him when he left, how he barely felt guilt, how he pretended that he had done nothing to hurt you. You owe him nothing."

It wasn't as simple as that. "I don't want him to die."

There was silence. The wind whistled through the air, and the sounds of thunder crashed in the distance, sounding far away. The sand crusted onto Lev's body was grainy beneath Anya's fingertips. Death was a thief. It had stolen her happiness right after she'd realized its true value.

Shuddering, Anya gathered her courage, then turned around to see who was speaking.

She was a girl: a young woman, just past adulthood. Her skin was unnaturally pale, and her loose hair was thick and clumped together like seaweed. She wore a white dress of torn and dirtied fabric that had clearly once been beautiful before all traces of its intricate embroidery and weaving were lost to the waves.

Anya's heart broke a little more. How could this girl have been reduced to such a state of inhumanity?

"How did you come here?" the Rusalka asked.

"I sailed."

"There was a storm."

"I was safe."

The Rusalka bared her teeth. "I know. We kept you safe. *I* kept you safe. I wanted you to see."

Anya's fist clenched around Lev's shirt. See what? The dead body of her husband?

"I thought you would be happy," the Rusalka continued. "He did not love you."

"How would you know that?" Anya's anger spilled into her voice. "You don't know him. You haven't seen him."

"I have seen enough." The Rusalka's voice was contemptuous. "I saw how he promised his heart to you and took it away as soon as he pleased. I saw how you promised your heart to him and found that he did not care enough to stay."

Anya felt cold, both inside and out. "That's not what he did. He made a mistake. I know he loves me."

The Rusalka watched her with an unmoving face, almost statuesque in its stillness. Her features were delicate and finely shaped. She might have been beautiful if it had not been for the inhumanity of her form. Even still, something about her seemed familiar.

Then it clicked. "You're Fenya," she said, voice barely above a whisper. "You died, didn't you?"

The Rusalka recoiled and didn't respond.

Anya pressed on. "I met you once, do you remember?

We were at the summer festival in Arudyne only a year ago. I saw you dancing with Anshel."

The girl hissed, and suddenly she was right in front of Anya, leaning close to her face. "Anshel died. Anshel left me. He paid the price."

Anya didn't flinch. The girl seemed vulnerable, like a freshly-caught fish on the deck of a fishing boat, floundering around for home but never seeming to find it. She had the same helplessness in her face, a dead expression Anya knew only too well. What was Fenya looking for?

"You don't know what it is to love," Anya said aloud.

Fenya's eyes narrowed into slits. "No one knows love. Love is false."

Anya shook her head. "Not always. Not—not for me. Please, Fenya, what Anshel did was wrong. He hurt you so badly. But not every man is like that. Lev isn't." *Wasn't.*

Fenya took a step backward. "Lev still holds your heart. How could you give your heart to someone who can't hold it as he should?"

Anya looked down at Lev's face and tried to imagine he was merely sleeping. "No one can hold another person's heart. Not without breaking it at least a little. But we can love them anyway, because we have to." *We'd been married less than a day before we started breaking each other's hearts. But even still...*

Fenya stared at her. Anya saw the marks on her face, layers of tears and dirt washed over with ocean water that hadn't quite made her clean. She said nothing.

Anya's hands were shaking. She looked down at Lev. "Please," she whispered, "I lost him twice. I can't bear to see you tear the world apart."

Fenya tilted her head. "You know that he is alive."

She hadn't. And yet she had. She shook her head and closed her eyes. His heart was beating, but it was growing weaker by the minute.

"He is. But not for long." Fenya stepped forward, and Anya couldn't tell if she was menacing or timid. "I have taken him. It is what I must do."

"What you *must* do?" Anya bit her lip. No one *needed* to murder and kill.

"It is my purpose." The voice was flat, almost regretful. "I have but one life. My sisters and I, we live by taking those who hurt us and any like them. If we do not, we pass away ourselves."

Anya felt cold. So it didn't matter that he was still alive, because Fenya was killing him as they spoke.

A thump sounded against the sand. Anya looked up to see Fenya kneeling in front of her, staring at Lev. "How can you love him?" she whispered.

In that moment, Anya saw her. Not the Rusalka, warped by anger and a strange magic into something terrible, but the woman—betrayed, hurting, confused, and in need of a friend.

"Because I know him," Anya said simply. "And I love him."

Fenya shook her head. "I don't understand."

Anya searched for the right words, but she didn't know if there were any. How could she explain it? What would explaining do?

Fenya bowed her head, looking smaller than ever on the beach. "I wish I understood. But I can't." She raised her head and looked at Lev again. "If I don't fulfill my purpose, I die."

Anya felt the words like a knife in her heart.

"It is all that keeps me in this world," Fenya continued. "I must. But..." She reached out a hand toward Lev's pale unmoving body. "You have real love, somehow. I cannot take it away from you."

Hope sprung alive inside of Anya. What did she mean? Could she really—?

Fenya touched Lev's chest lightly with her fingertips. She closed her eyes, breathing out a sigh, and then shuddered as if she'd been struck. Her skin, already colorless, seemed to turn a shade of gray. But she didn't pull away from Lev.

Anya watched as Fenya began to tremble, starting with her hand, then her entire body. Her eyes were closed and her face was twisted in an expression of pain.

Then—slowly—she began to dissolve. First, her fingertips began to flake away into sea foam, which the wind carried off into the ocean. Soon, her whole body was gone.

Anya stared at the place where Fenya had been, feeling a strange sense of loss. Even though the Rusalka had been her enemy, she grieved. The girl had died—not once, but twice—without ever knowing the true peace that Anya had felt.

Then, Lev stirred beneath her hand.

Chapter 7

Anya's hands were trembling. She looked down at Lev, hardly daring to believe her eyes. His face was still pale, but a new note of color bloomed in his cheeks. Anya pressed her hand to his neck to check his heartbeat, and it was steady and stronger than before.

Lev stirred, moving restlessly like he was awakening from a long sickness. He mumbled something, then was seized with a coughing fit.

Anya gripped Lev's hand, pressing it to her forehead. "You're alive," she whispered. "You're alive, you're alive, you're alive."

Lev was barely awake, but his face had regained its color, and he looked as healthy as he ever had back home. He tried to sit up, but he collapsed back down again, breathing hard.

Anya was laughing and crying at the same time. "Stay still, you've only just come back to life. You need to rest."

Lev stared up at her, and the wonder on his face made him more beautiful than she'd ever seen him. He tried to speak, then cleared his throat and tried again. "Anya? How did you—how did you get here?"

Anya nearly laughed. How could she explain it to him? She'd sound like she'd gone mad. "I heard you, somehow," she said. "I followed you to the island. And the Rusalki helped." If *helped* was the correct word. But Fenya had saved Lev in the end, so she supposed she couldn't be too angry.

"The what?"

Anya shook her head. "It doesn't matter. What happened to you?"

"I don't remember. I—there was a storm, and there were people in the ocean, there were *people*, Anya, and I don't remember what happened but I know they were dangerous and about to kill us—"

"Shh, I know." Anya rubbed his forehead like she was soothing a child. "It's all right now. You're alive, and the danger's gone, and we're together again."

Lev rested for a moment, then pushed himself up into a seated position. He wavered, and Anya reached out to steady him. He leaned on her hand. "I'm sorry," he whispered. "I shouldn't have left. I shouldn't have been angry at you."

Anya only smiled. "I'm sorry too. I shouldn't have reacted the way I did in the first place. But I love you, Lev, and I don't intend to lose you again. Not if we can help it. We'll stay together, and we'll build our life together, just as we wanted." Dreams, but good ones. And she knew now that it would take effort to build them, but she was willing to work.

Lev didn't say anything for a moment, only stared at her face with that awe-filled expression. "I never should have left you. We underestimated the danger; I should have stayed on land and protected you and everyone instead of—"

"Lev," Anya interrupted. Her eyes were filled with tears, happy ones. "It's over. We're safe. You don't need to make up for anything, I only want both of us to be safe together."

Lev touched her hand, searching for words. "I don't understand how this happened, but you are the most wonderful thing in my life, and I am so grateful for you."

Anya held him tight, happier than words could express. "I love you too," she whispered.

The storm was over, and they were both still there.

***

Apparently, Fenya's sacrifice had extended to the rest of the crew, because Lev and Anya found them stirring on the beach. Lev's boat was broken beyond repair, but the other could still sail, and with Anya's small sailboat they found Paskayt without trouble. The village was deserted, but after a short trip inland, they found the people of Paskayt mostly unharmed and ready to listen to solutions. Inland had not been kind to them.

King Haskel was surprised to see Lev alive. Anya had to bite her tongue to keep herself from angry words—but while the king listened to Anya and Lev's story with astonishment and skepticism, he was grateful to hear that the ocean was safe again.

The threat of the Rusalki was gone, but Paskayt still bore the wounds of their attack. The storms had made the land unstable, and the wells were still dry. It would be many years before they could live there again. The people mourned, but Lev's journey hadn't been completely fruitless—against all odds, he had found an island that would serve as a homeland for their people.

And so, Anya and Lev began building their new life together on new ground.

Together, they felled and prepared the timber for their house. They helped raise the village and provide for those who needed it. They became leaders in a community that greatly needed their help.

And after a few months, Anya learned that their family of two was about to grow.

The child was born a year after Anya found Lev alive on the beach. She was a healthy, happy child, with hair like the sand and eyes like the ocean. Her parents named her Fenya. They hoped their daughter would grow to have a better life than her namesake, and they wished to give the fallen girl another chance. They had never forgotten Fenya's sacrifice.

And so, the pages turned in Anya's life. The sea winds blew, the sun shined, and gradually, the chapter closed. But she didn't mourn. After all, she had Lev. She had little Fenya. They were safe, and they were together. That was what mattered.

She would love them, and she would fail, and she would ask forgiveness and try again. They would move on and grow—together.

And in the end, that would be enough.

Acknowledgements

To those who have shaped my writing: Brett Harris, Jaquelle Crowe Ferris, Josiah DeGraaf, and all the other instructors at the Young Writer's Workshop, thank you for providing high-quality craft and business training for writers. Dr. Sarah Huffines, thank you for helping me find my own voice. Emma Sloan, thank you for your wonderful feedback, and (more importantly) for your faithful friendship.

To those who have shaped my life: Proverbs 27:17 says, "Iron sharpens iron, and one man sharpens another." If I were to list out the friends who have taught me to love, the acknowledgements would be as long as the story.

To the one who shapes the seas: Thank you, Lord, for loving us enough to die, and for raising us with you to walk in newness of life.

About Emma Rose Thrasher

Emma Rose Thrasher was named after Emma Woodhouse and Rosie Cotton, so she was practically destined to become a book nerd. She was a member of the Young Writers Workshop for four years, where she learned the skills to pursue writing as a sustainable career. Now, she studies writing and music at Covenant College and learns about high-quality Christian art. She loves tea, fresh bread, and deep conversations about theology.

Sunset's Watch

Lilly Tanis

The sun's last rays kiss the cliff
Who stands as an enduring wall
Upon whose base waves continually swish.

He reaches out with his beckoning rays
To clothe her with colours glorious
Her jagged edges become beautiful displays.

The barnacles and their many friends
Clinging, glued, to her steadfast feet
Won't be swept away by the waves' mischievous bends.

Swells play at her sparkling feet,
In awe at her garments of every colour,
Hoping to bring higher their smoothing reach.

The winds blow through her crevices,
Boasting to the waves below,
In sleepy, soft music, of their loftier reaches.

The gulls above cry at her beauty.
She shelters them in her hollows
Where they are safe from storms most ghastly.

Atop her, wild grasses grace her head
Vibrant green sprinkled with blossoms
With bright hues of pink, white, violet, and red.

A lass sits atop this awesome sight
Upon the bed of soft wild grasses
Her senses drinking it all in with delight.

She is dressed in commoners' garments
A white apron over pastel blue skirts
Under whose hem peep her delicate slippers.

Leaning against an aged tree's embrace
Her fingers caress the delicate flowers
With heels softly tapping against the cliff's hard face.

The sun's disappearing golden beams,
As they seep into her exposed skin,
Conflict with soft updrafts of the ocean's cold breeze.

Her eyes close as she breathes in deeply.
The scents of salty sea and mossy bark
Mix with the delicate scent of the blooms sweetly.

The sounds of the gulls as they cry
Mix with the rumble of riotous waves
And the grasses as they whisper and sleepily sigh.

Hidden beyond the knoll behind her,
Deep. Gentle. Loving. A voice calls.
Soon up the grassy ridge emerges the caller.

Wearing shirt checked with red and black
Neatly tucked into his work-worn trousers.
With curly tousled hair rebelling under his cap.

At his sight, a smile lights the lass' face
As she brushes at wisps of corn-silk hair
That over the long day have come out of place.

He comes and sits beside her.
Watching the sunset above the sea
Her head comes to rest upon his solid shoulder.

About Lilly Tanis

Lilly has moved from place to place during her life but currently resides on Canada's Eastern shore in the beautiful Nova Scotia. She sat down one day and wrote a poem and hasn't stopped since. She loves the way poems paint word pictures of the things she sees and experiences in life. She seeks to reflect her Saviour and bring glory to God through her writings. In her free time you'll find her walking the local beaches, writing a new piece of poetry, drinking copious amounts of tea and coffee, and reading (debatably) too many books. You can contact her at lyricallillys@gmail.com.

My Coworker Met the Dragon King

Linyang Zhang

It had been twelve days since Ren Guang had walked into the sea.

Everyone thought that his body would resurface, but nothing had been found. It was like he had been swept away, leaving only his shoes and socks to get soaked by the tide on the shore. Disappeared into thin air, to who knew where. Carried off into the sky, or dragged beneath the waters...

Lu Fei had gone down to the beach to see if there were any footprints, whether that be going into the waters or out of them, but there were none, only sand and stones and the never-ceasing waves that crashed over them. He watched the mist over the horizon, the salt spray staining his suit, and when the first rays of sun broke through the gray, he turned around and left, feeling slightly more lonely than before.

It wasn't like they had been friends or anything. No, they were coworkers, and Ren Guang had always been friendly to him. Lu Fei wouldn't have considered them anything beyond casual acquaintances or work buddies, but truth be told, there was no one else he had been close with. If you could call this close.

"Staring at the ocean won't bring him back," his grandmother had said on the third day he had gone out there. "He's gone to see the Dragon King."

"Dragon King?" Lu Fei hadn't thought about that story since he was a little kid. "He's not real, grandmother."

"How do you know? Have you ever been to the bottom of the ocean before?"

"No..." And he'd rather not.

The work day passed in usual dreariness, although the air was much more somber than it had been before. Everyone's workload had increased now that Ren Guang was gone, and there was no one to distract Lu Fei from everything he had to do. The click of his mouse, the sounds of his keyboard, all the words on the documents blurring together into the paper... Until there was nothing left but white, a tiring white, the white of the ceiling or the floor or the walls of his room, the white of the flowers that lined Ren Guang's desk, the white of the sea foam—

Lu Fei jerked awake, out of breath, and found himself sitting at his desk, his cursor blinking on the page that he had been filling out. Why the sea? Why did that come up in his mind's eye again? Surely he had been staring at it too much, and now it possessed his mind. The crashing of the waves filled his ears, and it wouldn't stop...

He stood and stretched, deciding it was high time for a break. Everything was getting to him.

As he walked past Ren Guang's cubicle he couldn't help but wonder when they were going to clear out his stuff and put in someone new. HR was usually pretty quick with these matters. But it was like they weren't quite sure that he was completely gone yet, that there was still hope that he would come back, because he hadn't put in his two weeks' notice. But the flowers, wilting, were a distraction, and whoever was to take his cube next would be haunted by the scent of funeral flowers for the rest of his time here, which probably wouldn't be long. Who would want to work here anyway? Not Ren Guang, apparently. And certainly not Lu Fei himself.

He poured himself a little plastic cup of water from the water cooler, and paused to look at the fish tank the company kept in the hallway. At the sight of him, the little creatures all darted into their hiding places, and when Lu Fei tapped the glass, there was no response. He figured as much. Not even the animals liked him. And then Ren Guang crossed his mind again, and at the thought of his smile Lu Fei's heart twisted within him.

Not even friends. Why did he care? He tossed the crumpled plastic cup into the wastebasket nearby, missing, but he didn't bother to pick it up before heading back to his desk.

The office was so quiet, without him...

By the time he clocked out it was already dark. Nine thirty-one, and he debated on getting dinner. The thought of cooking when he got home seemed exhausting, and he had almost convinced himself that he wasn't hungry until he passed a lit ramen place, and his stomach growled. Eh, whatever. He could afford to splurge a bit.

"The usual, sir?" the chef asked, and Lu Fei nodded. He was the only customer right now, but it was no wonder. This town was small and rural, barely making up anything for the province of the city it was part of. A good deal of people knew each other, and knew him, too, since he had grown up here. Living with the constant crashing of the waves in his ears...

The chef set his noodles in front of him, and Lu Fei broke open his chopsticks and blew lightly on the food. For some reason the steam carried the salty spray of the sea with it tonight, but Lu Fei didn't question it, and instead began eating his meal without tasting it. He accidentally burned the roof of his mouth with the soup but didn't stop, the tears welling up in his eyes the only indication of his pain. Stop crying, he scolded himself. You're only going to make the soup more salty. So he wiped his eyes and pretended that it had never happened.

After he finished Lu Fei didn't quite feel like returning home yet, so he stopped by the rocks on the side of the sea again. Standing on one of them, he thought he could see the lights of the lighthouse in the distance, and the waves seemed all the more louder. What a lonely place to die in, he thought to himself, and he wondered what it must have been like for Ren Guang when he had left. Was it all dark like this, with the crying of the gulls that couldn't sleep? Or was it sunset, all colors calm and beautiful, and he could enjoy a last view of the world before he sank into the depths of the sea?

Seized with sudden recklessness, Lu Fei climbed down the rocks onto the sand, abandoning his briefcase and shoes and socks by the side. Rolling up his pant legs, he stepped down, the waves washing over his feet. The biting cold of the water didn't feel too bad on this humid summer's night. Lu Fei tore off his jacket and tossed it with the rest of his belongings, and waded further in. The sea, it was alive, it was calling him, playing with him, talking to him in tongues he didn't understand, and all he could do was—

It stopped. Everything stopped, and it was quiet, save for the ringing in his ears. Lu Fei stood there, unsure of what he had been doing, the waves still wrapping around his ankles like the tall grass on a field. What was he doing here? He had been looking for Ren Guang, had he not? He was going to look for Ren Guang, he was going to find him, and then—

The ringing faded, and Lu Fei shivered, so he waded back to shore and picked up his things. On the way home, sandy footprints all along the road.

The next day he overslept, and decided that he would rather take one of his sick days than go back to that hell and be reprimanded. After he was fully awake he dressed, in a jacket and a pair of jeans and worn sneakers that he hadn't worn since college, and he felt strange, his mood lighter. Maybe today wouldn't be too bad after all. He was still full from the noodles last night, so he went outside to an overcast sky and a dreary wind that whistled through the trees near his home, the leaves shuddering.

He remembered he had bumped into Ren Guang

outside on a day just like this a few years ago, when he had just started work at the company. He had gone to the bookstore and was looking in the comics aisle for the latest volume of his favorite series, when Ren Guang had called out his name. Mortified, he looked up, but Ren Guang had only laughed and said that he greatly enjoyed that series as well.

"My favorite is this one." Ren Guang had pointed out another comic's cover to him. "You should give it a try sometime! I think you'd really like it."

The bookstore was still open, right? Lu Fei soon found himself standing before it, the wind chime hanging over the door dinging in the wind. He pushed the door open and stepped in. The familiar smell of books swept over him, but they had rearranged the shelves. He remembered coming here as a kid with his mother, first to look at the picture books, then to purchase textbooks for school, and then as a teenager exploring depressing novels, and finally, when he hated reading pages of black words printed on white, he had found comics, and comics had remained his solace.

After sifting through the comics section, he found the book that Ren Guang had recommended to him. He took it out and sat on the floor to read, sandwiched between the shelves. It was a little weird and quite dreary, not at all what Lu Fei would expect someone like Ren Guang to read. As far as he could tell there was only one volume of it in the store, so when he finished it there was nothing more to read, and he felt a little more empty inside. It was about a group of students who had made a promise to see the ocean together, but due to life and circumstances, that would never happen. But the ocean was right there, Lu Fei thought. It was right outside the window. So he put the book back where it belonged, although its cover was significantly more creased, and left the shop without buying anything.

The outside was still cloudy, but it seemed a little more bright. Hands in pockets, Lu Fei found himself walking that familiar path down to the ocean. He had never paid much attention to it growing up until he had gone to college somewhere far away, and then he had realized the absence of it and how much it haunted him—the quiet in his ears, the lack of the fishy smell, and nothing open and broad and exciting to look out the window to. And so when he graduated he came right back here, to his hometown.

Ren Guang wasn't from here, was he? Most kids in this town, once they grew up, went to work in the city. How much more exciting, how many more prospects there were out there! But Ren Guang, he had come here instead. And what was that he had said?

He couldn't remember. And Lu Fei felt ashamed of himself. There was only the last line of the comic, echoing through his mind:

"It doesn't really matter anyway, not anymore."

Yeah, of course it didn't matter. Ren Guang was dead and gone and Lu Fei was all alone again, just as usual. Nothing had changed, and nothing ever would, and he could only live this life until it was done with him, after he had been long done with it himself.

He climbed onto one of the boulders and stood there, looking across the horizon. Something glinting, shining... Was that the sun? No, it couldn't be, it was already midday, and...

The waves were growing larger and larger, and Lu Fei felt a sense of dread and excitement fill his stomach. And then one, larger than he had ever seen, rose up before him. His foot slipped on a rock, and he stumbled, and—

The water was cold, it was dark, and Lu Fei thrashed around, trying to find the surface. Not like this, not on his day off! But the waves were too strong, and he was sinking deeper, deeper down into the depths of the ocean...

Oh...maybe this wasn't so bad. And right before he blacked out, he wondered if Ren Guang had felt the same.

When he came to, he was lying on a cold marble floor. When he tried to look around, immediately he was grabbed under his arms and hauled to his feet by two guards, dressed in armor that looked like it had come out of his history books and holding equally ancient weapons that looked lethally sharp. A four-pronged fork, a double-ended axe...

"Finally awake, human? Come with us, we have no time to spare."

"W-what is this place?" Lu Fei asked, but he was given no reply. For a moment he thought that he had died and gone to Hell, but this made no sense to be Hell. It seemed like they were in some sort of palace, and outside the windows, he could still see the murky waters. Was that a cloud of fish swimming by? Just how deep were they?

"O Great Dragon King! We have found a human trespassing outside the palace!"

Lu Fei was thrown roughly to his knees. Before him on a throne sat a man in silk azure robes. A long tail covered with scales peeked through the fabric and curved down the steps, the end twitching. Was this the Dragon King from all those myths he had been told when he was little? But that was impossible, none of it was real—

"Stand down." The Dragon King motioned the guards to step back. "Human, what are you doing here?"

Lu Fei's mind blanked, and he could only think to say one thing. "I'm here looking for my friend Ren Guang! He disappeared two weeks ago, and he was last seen near the ocean!"

"Another human?" The king tilted his head. "What

makes you think that he has come here?"

"My-my grandmother said so..." Lu Fei bowed his head closer to the floor, feeling very foolish and very scared. "Would Your Majesty have seen him, by any chance?"

"What would your grandmother know about our underwater affairs?" The Dragon King gave a laugh. "Maybe she's lying to you."

"I mean...she just...says things, sometimes. I didn't believe her, but now I see I was wrong..."

"About my existence?" But the Dragon King did not seem upset. "We do have humans wander in, from time to time. Back then, during the floods, so many were swept away... If you are looking for your friend, it is possible that we have him here. But what are you going to do with him once you find him?"

"B-bring him back..." And Lu Fei's voice was almost too quiet for himself to hear.

God, what was he going on about? Friends? Finding him? Trying to explain his case to this dragon, of all things? Surely he had gone mad. They weren't friends and never were, Ren Guang was long dead, and dragons didn't exist! But all of this felt very real regardless, and Lu Fei hated how his arms and legs were trembling.

"Guards, take the human to the cells and lock him up for the time being, until we figure out what to do with him."

The shrimp guards took him down to a small stone cell that wasn't any warmer than above, and in Lu Fei's pain and confusion he could only lie there, wishing for sleep. Could he try to escape? But when they had passed by the entrance he saw the waters, and knew that if he tried, he would surely drown. All of this, and for what? He wasn't really trying to find Ren Guang; this had all been just a stupid mistake. But now that he was here...

Maybe, just maybe, Ren Guang was actually here, and not dead. Just like his grandmother had said.

After his eyes had adjusted to the underwater lighting, he noticed that his cell was connected to several others, and there was someone lying there, seemingly asleep. Upon closer inspection, yes, it was Ren Guang, his work clothes dirty, his hair unkempt, his shoes and socks missing. And Lu Fei felt a bit of excitement twitch at his heart. Something he hadn't felt in so long...

Ren Guang must have felt his gaze on him, for he yawned and rubbed his eyes. Opening them, he turned his head and looked over at Lu Fei. A grin broke onto his face.

"Well, well, well, if it isn't Coworker Lu! Seems like you've got yourself wound up in the same predicament as I!"

"So you're okay?" Lu Fei tried to hide his trembling hands by pressing them against his legs. "You've been gone for quite a while now."

"Do the guys at work miss me yet?" Ren Guang's grin did not fade, and Lu Fei was reminded of a schoolboy.

"I think they held a whole funeral for you and everything. We all have extra work to do now, because you didn't have a replacement."

Ren Guang waved his hand. "Surely not a funeral. I specifically asked for none. It's so expensive, and besides, none of my family are here."

"Maybe I misremembered. But there are a lot of flowers on your desk."

"So they do miss me." Ren Guang chuckled. "Probably because of the work, though. I'm sorry about that for you, Lu Fei."

"It's okay," Lu Fei wanted to say. "It's fine. Everything is fine. But why doesn't this feel real?"

Instead he asked, "So what is this place?"

"It's the palace of the Dragon King, of course! Just kind of wandered in a few days ago, and they thought to lock me up in this cell. Can't leave, either." Ren Guang finished with a sigh. "It's not too bad, I guess. Kind of cold."

"What did you want to see the Dragon King for?"

"Pardon?"

"Did you really come here by accident? Surely you came here with a request?"

Ren Guang laughed. "You're confusing me, Lu Fei. I'm not sure what you're talking about."

"I guess...never mind." No, Lu Fei couldn't bring himself to say that either. To say that Ren Guang didn't seem like the type to wander into the ocean for nothing, to come across the Dragon King's palace by pure chance, to disappear without a reason...

"So what's up with you? How have you been doing?"

"I read the comic you recommended me," Lu Fei replied, pushing all his true feelings from the past two weeks away. "It was...interesting."

"You still remember that?" And once more, Ren Guang's response was accompanied by a light laugh. "I'm glad you picked it up, though. Now I have someone I can talk about it with!" But he brought no more up about it.

"Do you think that we can escape?"

"It's impossible with one person, but I think with you here, we can make it."

There it was, Ren Guang's positivity that Lu Fei so remembered. Perhaps one of the reasons why he had taken notice of him was because he stood out so much among his coworkers, like a single sunflower in a field. But Lu Fei wasn't sure where that positivity stemmed from or if it was real at all.

"Do you know what they're going to do with us?"

"Not sure." Ren Guang stretched and lay back down.

"But they seem to be in no hurry to get rid of us, so I wouldn't stress about it. You seem tired, Lu Fei. Is it work?"

"Maybe. I guess."

"Then maybe this is a much needed vacation for you! You just got here, so let me worry about the way out. I think you should rest."

It was like Lu Fei had gone on vacation to a tropical island only to find that he would be sharing a room with Ren Guang. Ren Guang would be splayed out on one of the beds, laughing at the coincidence, apologizing for the inconvenience, and was this maybe a company-paid group vacation that they didn't know about? Come sit down, have a drink, maybe go walk along the beach later. The waves will be nice. I promise you'll enjoy yourself.

Lu Fei closed his eyes, wondering if this itself was a dream. When he opened them, would he be at the desk in his office, a bunch of gibberish on the screen before him?

Ren Guang said something else, but the ringing in his ears had started up again, so Lu Fei tried to forget that he had said anything, so that those unheard words would not plague him in his sleep.

Why had he started work at that company in the first place? He could hardly remember. It wasn't like it had been his dream job or anything; no, it had been the first job to offer him a position after weeks and weeks of applying, and somehow, he had found himself stuck there.

He hadn't even gotten into university for what he wanted; his scores were far too low. And why had that been? He hadn't possessed any particular motivation to study; there wasn't anywhere he wanted to go, nothing he wanted to do...

No, that wasn't true. Once, he had had dreams, but he had forgotten them by now, after years of lonely corporate gray. Once, he had felt more alive than he had in recent years, and he could remember as a kid riding his bicycle down the town roads, and ditching it so that he could run across the sand towards the ocean.

The ocean again...

What was that that Ren Guang had said? "I came here to live a quiet life, to live in a house with a view of the ocean." And when had this been? A memory resurfaced, the two of them, sitting on the rocks near the water, watching the sunset. According to Ren Guang, they were missing the sunset every day because of their work hours, so they should go and take their break on the beach, so that they weren't wasting their days away. When they had gone back, they had tracked sand on the carpet, and received a talking-to from their supervisor. But Ren Guang gave Lu Fei a wink, and their supervisor's words no longer cut to his heart.

No, they weren't friends. Just coworkers, friendlier than usual.

When Lu Fei woke, he half-expected to be lying in his own bed, but he was still in the cold stone cell. He looked for Ren Guang, and the man was there still, looking out of a window at the underwater scenery. Lu Fei wondered what to say to him, but he seemed so peaceful, content, staring out at the blue, that he didn't want to disturb whatever idyllic thoughts Ren Guang was dreaming.

"You're awake?" It was Ren Guang who spoke first, and Lu Fei sat up awkwardly, joints stiff.

"You have any idea how to get out of here?"

"Yeah." Ren Guang wore a satisfied smile. "Almost done with the plan. Just need to put it into words."

"The Dragon King wishes to see you." One of the shrimp guards opened the cell door and grabbed hold of Lu Fei. "Come now, make haste."

Ren Guang gave him a thumbs up before Lu Fei was

completely out of view, but it didn't make him feel any better.

The Dragon King's tail twitched as Lu Fei was hauled before him, slapping the marble this way and that in a manner that suggested he was bored. Lu Fei hesitated to raise his eyes to meet the King's gaze, and found himself staring at those long dark-blue nails that the dragon held close to his face, his sharp eyes holding an icy gaze as he eyed Lu Fei from between his fingers.

"So you are a human, yes? How much do you know about that other human there?"

"How much...?" Lu Fei tried to pull his mind out of the fog, all the confusion that he drifted in, day-to-day, for however long as he could remember. "Why do you ask, Your Majesty?"

"Do you know what a soul orb is?"

"No, I've never heard of it."

"Well, see, that's the strange thing about humans. You each have one, and back in the day, why, they were the most attractive thing to creatures like us, all bright and shining. Do you know why the demons desired to eat those considered blessed and holy? Because they could live forever, if they consumed their soul orb. Not many know about it, but that is the real reason."

"So...you want to eat me?"

"Pfft, no. Humans these days, your soul orbs have grown small and dark and dirty, as if covered with ash. No one wants to eat them anymore, and we all live a long time anyways, so what's the point? See..." He stuck his clawed hand into Lu Fei's chest before he could stop him, and pulled out what looked like a large black marble resting in glowing yellow light. Lu Fei gasped, feeling as if all the warmth had been sucked from him at once, and he tried to speak, but choked on his own breath. "Compared to him, yours is something like trash, just like the rest of you humans. But that human back there..." And the Dragon King's eyes glittered, as he plunged the soul orb back into Lu Fei's chest. "That human's soul orb is perhaps one of the most perfect ones I have seen in my entire lifetime."

"So you wish to eat Ren Guang?" Lu Fei still hadn't recovered from seeing his own soul ripped from him.

"If I wanted to eat him, I would have done so already, no? See here, I simply wish to extract his soul orb, and look at it, and show it to the heavens, for I am sure that they have never seen such a fine specimen. And then, afterwards, I suppose I can eat it, or I can give it to one who has served me best."

"And what about Ren Guang? Will he...will he die?"

The Dragon King gave a small laugh, and leaned forward. "Human, I am asking you for your help. For when that human walked into the ocean, his soul orb shattered, and I need you to piece it back together again."

"I'm not sure I understand..."

"It is very rare to see a soul orb shattered, and usually, I don't think any of us would heed that fact. But your friend, his soul orb is so perfect, so priceless, I think it is a great loss not to repair it. When it shattered, its pieces were scattered throughout his memories, and only a human has access to another human's memories, to put the pieces back together again. So I have been keeping him here, in hopes that someone else would come by, and I could ask them to piece his soul orb together..."

Lu Fei pretended like he understood, trying to sort out his thoughts between the cold pain in his knees and the hard smoothness of the floor tiles beneath his palms. "And if I...if I do this for you, will you let us both go?"

The Dragon King's expression seemed cold, almost

cruel. "Well, by then, I'll have no use for either of you anymore, no?"

Lu Fei bit his lip. There was no way of telling what sort of benefit he would gain or lose from this, not when dealing with mystical creatures, whose thoughts and plans were much more lofty and other-worldly-centered than a mere human's. Ren Guang had said that he had a plan, but Lu Fei had no idea what it was, nor how feasible it was, and besides, he wasn't sure if he had any choice to say no...

"How will I access his memories, O King?"

The Dragon King waved a clawed hand, and a floating, glowing door appeared beside him. "Just step through."

Lu Fei was hauled to his feet by the guards, his knees aching, and they cut the ropes around his wrists. "And...how will I find these soul orb fragments?"

The Dragon King's gaze was unreadable. "You'll know when you find it. Don't worry."

Lu Fei was pushed towards the door, and, finding himself with no other choice, he opened it.

It was a hot summer's day. He was standing on a dirt path by a small shop, and cicadas and other bugs screamed in the bushes nearby. There was a small creek on the other side of the path, hidden by tall reeds, and he blinked in the all-too-bright sunlight, already feeling the prickle of sweat roll down the back of his neck.

One of Ren Guang's memories? So much more vivid than his own...

A couple of small children were running up the path behind him, and Lu Fei quickly stepped aside. One boy tripped and fell, clouds of dust billowing up from the dirt, but the other children had gone too far to notice or hear his cry. Lu Fei bent down next to him to see if he was okay.

"Are you all right? Does it hurt anywhere?"

The boy sniffed, and looked up at Lu Fei, eyes watery. "I'm okay, it's just..."

Lu Fei winced, seeing the blood starting to seep through the scrapes on his hands and knees. He patted the dust from the boy's hair and clothes and helped him up. "Come on, let's find you some water."

The owner of the small shop had some water, ice, and bandages, and after Lu Fei patched the boy up he bought them each an ice pop. The two of them sat on the front step of the shop, enjoying the large box fan that ran behind them.

"Ren Guang," the boy sniffed. "Thank you for the ice cream, mister."

"No problem." So this was a memory from Ren Guang's childhood, eh? How was he supposed to find the orb from here? "Where were you kids running off to?"

"Off to the ravine... The bigger kids said that there was a huge frog that had never seen before living there."

Lu Fei recalled distant memories of his own childhood, and various failed attempts at trying to catch fish out of the sea. "What do you think they'll do with it?"

"I don't know, but now I'm not even gonna be able to see it, since they're all so fast..."

Lu Fei finished his ice pop and pocketed the stick. "I could take you, if you want. You'd just have to tell me which way to go."

"Really, mister?" Ren Guang stared up at him, eyes filled with excitement.

"Yep." Lu Fei bent down, holding out his hands. "Just hop on my back. We'll be there before you know it."

The hike was a bit more steep than Lu Fei had expected, but they got there in less than ten minutes, him all covered with sweat and out of breath. Ren Guang slid off and ran to where the other kids were gathered, their feet and hands covered with mud. Lu Fei stood at a distance, until Ren Guang ran back and tugged at his hand.

"You should come see too, mister! He's reallllyyyy big!"

The expression on his face Lu Fei recognized, he had seen it twice before. Once, he had seen it when Ren Guang was giving a presentation, and apparently they had made double the amount of sales over the past month; the other, Ren Guang had found an abandoned puppy outside near the office, and was holding him when Lu Fei passed by.

Lu Fei let himself be tugged along, and crouched down along with the other kids to observe one of the largest bullfrogs he had ever seen. His skin crawled a little, but it was cool. The animal met eyes with him before letting out a loud croak, and a shining something floated out from its mouth into the air.

Lu Fei caught it with his hands, and just as he realized it was one of the soul orb pieces, the scene melted away around him, being replaced by another.

A teenage Ren Guang was sitting in an empty classroom, the warm afternoon sunlight seeping in and a light breeze rustling the white curtains over the windows. He was dressed in his winter uniform, although Lu Fei could see that the weather was clearly warmer outside. Ren Guang didn't seem to notice him, too busy staring out of the window, and Lu Fei moved closer to see his Chinese textbook and a pencil with its tip broken off lying before him.

A couple of boys burst into the classroom, out of breath, but Ren Guang barely looked up. As the boys went through their desks for some books and supplies one of them said:

"Still here, Classmate Ren?"

“Yeah.” Ren Guang gave a small shrug, a slight smile lining his face.

“I don’t think anyone’s going to care if you go. What is it you were supposed to write again? How many times?”

“Nothing much.” Ren Guang moved to put his textbook away, and Lu Fei saw several pieces of paper sticking out from it, scrawled with some unintelligible sentences beginning with “I will not”. “It’s okay, thank you. I’ll just go home when I feel like it. I don’t think Teacher Wu is really going to care either.”

“Yeah, aren’t you usually a good student? He likes you; I don’t think you should worry about it.”

Ren Guang gave the boys a half smile. “Thank you, Classmate Wang. I’ll see you two tomorrow.”

The boys left, and Lu Fei was left alone with the boy, who sighed and put his feet up on the desk, leaning back in his chair. There was a sense of discouragement and tiredness lining his face, and he flipped his textbook open again, the sheets of paper falling into his lap.

I will not stare out of the window during class.

Huh? What an odd thing to be punished for. Lu Fei was about to open his mouth and comment so when suddenly Ren Guang tore the papers apart in a fit of violence that Lu Fei had not seen before, again and again, until he opened his hands and only tiny scraps of white remained, floating down to the floor like some miniature angel’s wings.

Ren Guang got up, slinging his backpack over his shoulder, and shoved his chair over, so that it clattered to the ground. Lu Fei jumped to avoid it, but it merely passed through him, like he was nothing but a ghost.

Outside, Ren Guang got on his bicycle, and Lu Fei followed, although Ren Guang quickly disappeared out of sight. The school was located on a hill, and, especially with the bicycle, Lu Fei knew that he wouldn't be able to catch up. He watched Ren Guang stop by a convenience store, the very one from the last memory, and come out with a dripping ice pop in his mouth. Mounting on his bike, he went on his way again.

When Lu Fei finally caught up, Ren Guang sat inside his room at an old and worn keyboard. He plunked out a couple notes but ended up slamming the keys in frustration. Then he froze and touched the instrument softly, whispering about how sorry he was. Then he got up and left the room, to ride his bicycle again.

Lu Fei was starting to wonder how he was ever going to find the fragment if his memory was so big, and he was getting extremely out of breath trying to follow Ren Guang. If he could interact with him, maybe he could ask him to slow down or find out what the purpose of this memory was.

After a long trek of looking and trying to follow his gut feeling, Lu Fei found Ren Guang sitting beneath a tree near the fields with a drink and a comic book, the back of his hands scraped as if he had fallen off his bicycle earlier. He looked up as Lu Fei approached, his expression wary.

"What do you want?"

"Um." Lu Fei hadn't thought this far. "Mind if I take a seat?"

Ren Guang shrugged, and returned to his book. "Suit yourself."

Lu Fei sat down, his legs and back aching, glad for the moment of rest. "What are you reading?"

Ren Guang showed him the cover, and Lu Fei recognized it as one that he had seen in bookstores when he was younger. Fairly popular, although he had never really gotten into it.

"What are you doing out here, mister?"

"What do you mean?"

"I mean, shouldn't you be at work or something? And I haven't seen you around here before."

Lu Fei shrugged. "I'm just wandering. Trying to enjoy a day off."

A pause. Ren Guang stared at the pages, clearly not reading them. "Did you want to say something to me?"

"What?"

"I don't know, why else would you approach me? I felt like someone was watching me earlier, too."

"It's not for any bad reason." Lu Fei awkwardly wrung his hands together. "You just seemed, well, sad."

"Sad? Look at yourself, mister. You practically radiate sadness."

Lu Fei was surprised. "Does it really seem like it?"

"Yeah." And even though his face was serious, there was that semblance of Ren Guang that Lu Fei remembered. "Your face, it's tired, and you're looking at me like I remind you of someone from a long time ago. You seem listless, and even though the weather's nice, it might as well be cloudy for you."

So Ren Guang had always been good at reading people...

"It's okay. It's just life." Lu Fei picked at the grass. "But why are you sad?"

"It's nothing, really." Ren Guang put his book down and began pulling up the grass as well. "I got caught daydreaming again, and got a slap on the wrist and was forced to write lines. I don't know, I can't help it. It was so beautiful outside today, and that was all I could think about. And some of the other kids laughed, or were glad about it, because they hate me..."

"What about the outside were you thinking about?" Lu Fei asked, his voice quiet.

"Just..." Ren Guang paused, and Lu Fei sensed that he was teetering on the fence of how many personal thoughts he could share with a stranger he would never see again. "I thought of running away, of leaving this place, of taking a nap in a sunny field, of gazing at flowers that bloom in all sorts of colors that I don't know the names to, of seeing the ocean and wading through it, and of how cool and fresh it would be..."

"Have you ever seen the ocean before?"

"No, I haven't. Have you?"

"Many times..."

"Take me there, then!" And Ren Guang bit his lip, as if regretting his outburst. "I'm sorry, I don't know why I said that, I—"

"I will, if you want." Lu Fei cut him off. "I'm serious. If it's the ocean you want to see, I will take you there."

"Really?" And there was a spark ignited in Ren Guang's eyes.

The ocean, the place where he had... He was going to take him back to his death? Lead him to the place where he was buried? Lu Fei swallowed. "Yeah. If you want to. It'd be easy."

Ren Guang laughed a little, then sighed, dropping the clumps of grass between his fingers. "I have school, my parents would never agree, and it's so far from here... Some other day, maybe, if you're still around, mister, when I'm done with school and all that crap, and the weather is even more beautiful than it is now..."

"Okay." And Lu Fei was surprised at how readily he agreed to it. "If that all happens, it's a promise."

"I should go now." Ren Guang stood, taking his book and his drink with him. "I'm going to be reprimanded if I'm out any longer."

Lu Fei swallowed, feeling a tightness in his throat

that hadn't been there before. "Even if I'm not here, you can still go see the ocean, you know? One day. I'm sure you will."

Ren Guang smirked, tossing him a piece of a flower that he had torn up. "I don't even know you, mister. But whatever. Sorry to make you listen."

Lu Fei watched him swing onto his bike, and before he could say a word, the boy sped off, and Lu Fei was left alone. What could he have said? He was always happy to listen, right?

Ren Guang had always been happy to listen...

He looked back down at the half-ripped flower in his hand, and realized that something sparkling was inside it, and as he picked it out, he recognized it to be the same as the other shard from earlier. Another piece of the soul orb...

And, once again, everything changed.

He was standing outside of the apartment complex where Ren Guang lived. Shouting could be heard coming from an open upstairs window. Lu Fei winced at the vague fragments of sentences floating down, recognizing a couple of words here and there, and a few moments later, a door slammed, followed by the sound of running. Before he knew it, Ren Guang burst out from the front of the building, mounting his bicycle, and sped off. Lu Fei caught a quick glance of a dark bruise on his cheekbone as he passed by, and he followed, but the boy was already out of sight.

When he found him, Ren Guang was crouched behind a building by a small creek, talking to someone Lu Fei couldn't see. Lu Fei sat near the bicycle, staying in the shadows of the building.

"Yeah, it doesn't matter what I do! They're not happy!"

A pause for someone else in the conversation, but Lu Fei heard nothing.

"Well...no, I definitely could have done better. Yeah, maybe I was goofing off, like they said. But—"

Another pause. Then:

"But wait, what do you mean? Come on, don't you think I could have done better? I didn't—"

A brief moment of silence. Ren Guang started up again, still just as agitated as before.

"No, I didn't need to do all that! There was no reason for me to be wandering around after class instead of studying! No, no, listen, they were right, this was all my fault, I—" And he sounded like he was choking up.

Silence. And Lu Fei desperately wanted to look over and see who he was talking to.

"I-I guess you're right. No, yeah, I should go clear my head. I'm sorry. Yeah, no, they're going to—"

A shorter pause this time.

"No, maybe they'll have calmed down by then. No, you're right, I'll just...I'll just change my behavior for a few days, and it'll all blow over. No, yeah, I know, these are the college entrance exams, yeah, no, it's not gonna blow over. But they'll calm down, yeah? Anyways. Yeah. Thanks, I'll see you later."

Ren Guang came back around the building, but he didn't seem to notice Lu Fei as he mounted his bike again, checked his watch, and then rode off, this time at a slower pace. Lu Fei waited until he was out of sight, then quickly got up, and went behind the building to look, but there was nobody there. Just the small creek, the water flowing almost silently.

He found Ren Guang sitting under the tree where he had found him last, tuning a guitar. His bike was lying on its side, one of the wheels still rotating slightly in the breeze, and numerous pieces of paper were scattered on the grass.

"Hey." Lu Fei placed a hand on the tree and leaned slightly over, heart turning at seeing how livid the bruise was on Ren Guang's cheek.

Ren Guang barely glanced up. "Oh. It's you."

Lu Fei took a seat. "You look like you've had a... rough day. Who were you talking to earlier?"

"Oh, you heard?" Ren Guang scoffed. "Just a... friend..." He strummed a chord, then adjusted one of the knobs on the guitar. "He kinda comes and goes, like you. But I know where to find him."

"I see." Lu Fei resisted the urge to say anything else. "What song are you working on?"

Ren Guang handed him one of the papers, and Lu Fei recognized the title as a pop song that had come out when he had been a teenager. "I don't know, I'm just playing around. Nothing special."

"You like music?" Lu Fei remembered the keyboard in his room.

"Yeah, I guess you could say that." Ren Guang strummed another chord, and this time it was in tune. "I'm not very good though."

Lu Fei stayed silent, watching the boy play. He didn't recall Ren Guang ever saying anything about music during their time together in the workplace, but that made sense. It was probably just a personal hobby, and it wasn't like he had had any reason to mention it, it was—

Watching Ren Guang play, Lu Fei suddenly realized just how ridiculous and sad this situation was. How...not real, all of it was, even though it felt more real than anything he could remember in the past five, ten years. Here he was, sitting with his dead coworker as a young person, in a distant memory that probably meant a lot to him, learning more about Ren Guang than he ever had in real life. To this day, he still didn't know why Ren Guang had walked into the ocean, and he didn't know if he could ever ask. Ren Guang was gone, yet he was here, he had left him forever, but maybe, maybe he would stay...

"Would you really take me to see the ocean?" Ren Guang's clear voice broke the still of the air, his hand hesitating over the strings of his instruments. "You promised me that, years ago."

Lu Fei felt a pain in his heart, and he bit on his tongue, trying to replace one pain with another. "One day we will see the ocean together. I promise."

And it was like he could see Ren Guang sitting next to him on the sand, painted by the colors of the sunset, a grin on his face, his hair messy, the collar of his work suit unbuttoned, saying something that didn't matter now but probably had mattered a lot in the moment. Something that he didn't realize was important until it was far too late, something that he should have remembered and held onto and—

"I don't know if I'm going to make it." Ren Guang's voice was quiet, and his finger slipped. A stray note reverberated in the air. "My test scores are too low, I'm not going to be able to go somewhere good, or learn what I want. I'm not going to be able to leave here, I'll be stuck here all my life and—"

"Wait." Lu Fei couldn't stop the words from slipping from his mouth, and there was a sudden silence, like something had changed, and the air seemed cool to breathe. Because everything Ren Guang was saying reminded him far too much of himself, and it looked as if the boy was near tears. "Do you think you will be happy...if you were some place else?"

"What do you mean?" Ren Guang turned his gaze

towards him, and for the first time since Lu Fei had stepped into these memories, he felt as if he were catching a glimpse of the real Ren Guang.

"I mean...yes, everything will be different, and it will be refreshing, but in the end, there's just this sort of... hollowness, that sits in your heart. And you sit there, and you kind of forget your past life, because it was all the same..." He remembered his college days, quiet and unassuming, people passing and people going and never staying and never really mattering to him. He couldn't even recall their names. In all these years, there was only Ren Guang, who helped him remember that he was even alive.

"In the end, I don't really care if I'm happy or not. I just...want to be by the ocean."

"And I'm sure you'll get there," Lu Fei replied. "And what about...other people?"

"What do you mean, other people?"

"If you don't care about your own happiness, what about others' happiness?" It was a question that Lu Fei had long thought about after Ren Guang had disappeared. For if he had been so inclined to leave like that, why had he always seemed so focused on making other people's days brighter?

"I...don't know." Ren Guang furrowed his brow. "I haven't really thought about it."

"I don't think I've really seen you with your classmates before."

"They all have cram school, after school things. As do I. Not really any time for socialization."

"I'm sure that's not true. Even I had time for..." Lu Fei trailed off, remembering how his own days went. How he followed in others' shadows, barely able to hold a conversation or give an opinion that wasn't stolen from someone else. How he pretended to laugh, but no one even noticed that he did, how he would disappear some days to stare at the dark waters underneath a local bridge yet those who passed by only said hi, and nothing more. No questions asked, no warnings given, just him and that cold and crashing world.

Ren Guang was eyeing him with something less than callousness. "Yeah?"

"But just say, what if. What if you and your classmates were friends? What would happen then?"

Ren Guang gave a small laugh, a shrug and a roll of his eyes. "Sure, yeah, maybe. Maybe I might. Maybe I will. But they've never really cared about me in the first place."

"But maybe, if you reached out first, maybe then they would care."

Because Lu Fei himself, he had been lazy too, no? Always wishing, hoping, praying that someone would walk by and ask to be his friend. But it never happened. Well, not until he met Ren Guang.

"Who do you think you are to give me such advice, mister?" And Lu Fei couldn't tell if the boy was being rude.

"Well...maybe just think of it as life advice. Because I'm older." Lu Fei reached out and ruffled Ren Guang's hair. He couldn't help himself, there was something about this boy now, this person whom he thought he knew, that reminded him of himself, and he knew that he would never get another chance. Another chance, for...

Ren Guang stared at him, something unspeakable in his dark eyes, the bruise on his face seeming to pulse in the afternoon sunlight. Something glittered on his face, and Lu Fei brushed his fingers over it, and felt the piece of soul shard wrapped in the boy's tears. No, he wanted to say more, he didn't want to let go yet, he wasn't ready to—

The scene of sunlight melted away, yet Lu Fei still felt Ren Guang's gaze.

There was the familiar sound of the ocean, and Lu Fei found himself standing on a bridge, overlooking a shore lit up by the setting sun. Its beams melted into the large, never-ending waves. He closed his eyes and inhaled the salty air, taking in the cool breeze brushing through his hair and clothes. To be alive like this...

There was the sound of laughter and talking, and Lu Fei leaned against the railing as a group of people passed by. Ren Guang was near the forefront of the group, laughing about something with the others. They looked to be college students, bags slung over their shoulders after a long day of classes, perhaps off to eat a meal together. Though he was intimidated by the people, when Lu Fei saw that Ren Guang was happy, he, too, couldn't help but feel happy. After a moment, he started after them, trying to walk casually with his hands in his pockets because he wasn't sure if they had noticed him or not.

"So then he said—" And here Ren Guang had to stop to catch his breath from laughter. "So then he told me that maybe I was at the wrong store, you know, and—"

More laughter, and Lu Fei felt his feet fall behind. He had always been scared of groups like this, no? People who were such good friends with each other, and so many of them... But as he continued to observe their journey, he wondered if, maybe, they were all only good friends with Ren Guang, from the way they focused their attention on him.

They stopped at a place to get drinks, and Lu Fei waited outside, playing with the various pieces of the soul orb that he had collected. The cracked edges were sharp, but the material shone bright. Nothing like his own...

The group soon left the shop and Lu Fei followed them, although keeping his distance. He was reminded of when he had first seen Ren Guang at the company, surrounded by people, talking and laughing despite the cloudy atmosphere of the corporate environment. Lu Fei walked by, fully ready to be ignored, but Ren Guang had seen him, and called out his name.

Later, after night had completely fallen and they had gone to their dorm building, Ren Guang had come out alone, yawning, perhaps off to buy a quick convenience store dinner or something. Just as Lu Fei was about to approach him, one of the guys from the group earlier ran up behind Ren Guang, calling his name. Ren Guang forced a smile upon his tired face and began a conversation.

"Where are you off to?" His friend wore a black windbreaker, his eyes just as dark.

"Just off to get some dinner. What's up?"

"I just wanted to ask if you were doing okay."

"Of course I'm doing okay. I'm just tired."

"All right, all right, just checking...you know that you can talk to me about anything, right?"

There it was again. That invitation to open up.

"Of course. Thank you."

They stopped at the convenience store, and when they came out, the friend said, "I'm going down to the ocean for a bit, want to join?"

"I'm a bit tired, so I'll head back first. Stay safe, though. Text me when you're back."

"Suit yourself. Some other day?"

"Some other day."

The two parted, and Lu Fei quickly stepped up behind Ren Guang, matching his stride. Ren Guang noticed him almost immediately and gave a small grin, breaking apart the ice pop in his hand and gave him half.

"What?"

"Come on, it's melting." The rest of his dinner

swung from the plastic bag hanging from his wrist.

Lu Fei complied, and enjoyed the light taste of fruit on his tongue. "How have you been? I see that you've finally been to the ocean."

"Yep." Ren Guang bit off the end of his own ice pop, eyes vacant. "I have a small fear of the open water, though."

"Really?"

"Yeah. It's all so dark and...who knows what's under there. The shallow part's fine, though, right where the sand is."

Lu Fei wondered if he remembered his promise at all, and if he blamed him for never fulfilling it. Though, in actuality, that had never been the case at all...

"What have you been up to? You still look the same as usual."

"Not much...just work, school, you know."

"I see." Ren Guang finished the rest of his pop. "Interesting."

"You seem happier."

"Do I?"

It had just been a casual comment that meant almost nothing, but the way that Ren Guang looked at him, his shoulders sagging and eyebags dark, Lu Fei wondered if the Ren Guang he had seen earlier today had been nothing but a mask, a disguise, a façade that he had put up ever since they had had that conversation when Ren Guang was a teenager. But he didn't know how to ask, and didn't know if it would be right to do so.

"Who's that person you were with earlier? Back at the store?"

"Oh, him? Just a friend." Ren Guang sighed. "I like him because...he reminds me of someone I used to know, yet... I don't know, I feel tired of him, of everyone, of everything.

I'm not sure why."

"I see." Lu Fei had half a mind to ask, "Even me?" But it seemed as if his question was answered in the next moment.

Ren Guang glanced at him and gave a small smile. "You know, you always appear at the oddest times. Yet you, you feel like...a breath of fresh air. Yeah, something like that."

"I don't know if I really am, but thanks, I guess." And Lu Fei didn't know what to do. "How's school going?"

So they chatted and kept on walking, and Lu Fei felt like he was almost with the current Ren Guang, the one he knew, the one who had walked into the ocean, all those days ago. Although this Ren Guang was a little more reserved (perhaps because he was tired), and his eyes were sharp in a way that the other's were not, but his tone was still light and positive, his movements calm.

"But you, you know me pretty well, don't you?"

Lu Fei was caught off guard. Knowing him well? Certainly he knew him better than before, but if he thought about it, he wasn't sure just what he could say he knew about Ren Guang. Almost nothing.

"I'm not sure if I do." Lu Fei kept his voice quiet.

"Yet I feel like you do!" Ren Guang's eyes did not hold excitement, they held quietude, and maybe something akin to love. "I feel like I can tell you anything. You-you've always been here, no? You've just always been here for me. What can I say? Maybe it just turned out to be this way, I don't know. I'm not sure."

"You trust me so easily?"

"I don't trust anyone easily." Ren Guang turned his gaze back to him. "Not at all. Not even you. But right now... yes, I trust you. Should I? I'm not sure. Maybe it's the worst decision in the world. But tonight, right here, I trust you. So let it be."

"Why did you walk into the ocean?" That was what Lu Fei wanted to ask. "Why did you walk into the ocean, all those days ago? It's been two weeks, and you left me here alone. I have no one besides you, and now my days will return to those of gray and boredom, of gloom and despair. Ren Guang, I thought that you, of all people, wouldn't leave me, and yet, you were the first to go, and so blatantly, just leaving your shoes behind..."

No, he couldn't ask. He couldn't ask at all. For Ren Guang was right there before him, alive, smiling.

"You seem sad." Ren Guang's voice was quiet, but it broke through the mess of thoughts in Lu Fei's head. "You are, aren't you?"

It was less of a question and more of a statement. Ren Guang raised a hand to touch his cheek, brushing away tears that had fallen.

"How can I be sad? When you are here." Lu Fei tried to smile, but it was all a lie. Ren Guang wasn't here, he wasn't here, and he would never be here again. "How can I be sad? We're friends, aren't we?" And still, a lie. This was all fake, they were never friends, never had been, never would be, and soon he would be all alone again, and—

Ren Guang held a closed hand out to him, and turned it over, opening his palm to reveal a soul shard. "I found this in your tears," he whispered. "Must be yours, no?"

This time, Lu Fei hesitated to take it. He looked up at Ren Guang, meeting his eyes, but they were unreadable. But Ren Guang was waiting for him, so he closed his hand over his palm.

There was a blur of images, scenes and memories that passed by too fast for Lu Fei to count: Ren Guang was sitting on the beach, where the waves met the sand, barefoot as the waves lapped around him. He was talking to someone, making a promise, but Lu Fei couldn't hear what. He was crying, he was holding a knife, and Lu Fei wanted to yell at him to put it down. He was standing on the balcony of his apartment, staring at fireworks reflected over the ocean, the mess of his room behind him. Dust and neglect and another dream... Before he knew it, he sat in the familiar office of the company he worked at, Ren Guang next to him.

This Ren Guang looked around the age that Lu Fei knew, and he didn't seem to notice him. He chatted with a couple of guys around his cubicle, laughing, and Lu Fei wondered when had his workplace ever looked so bright, unlike the dreariness that usually came with it when he was there.

"I heard that there was a new hire today," one of the men said. "I think the manager's giving him a tour or something right now."

"Oh, are we in charge of orientation?" another asked.

"Probably. The manager said he's gonna be in our department. Dunno how he's like, though."

"I think that must be him." Ren Guang's eyes were on the door. "Come on, let's go give him a warm welcome!"

Lu Fei was about to follow when he noticed the shard left on Ren Guang's desk. But right before he took it, he looked up to see who the new hire was, and his breath caught in his throat.

Yes, of course it was himself. It always had been.

Ren Guang's smile had been infectious. His own smile had felt weak. And he knew, that since the beginning, Ren Guang had called him friend. They had always been.

Everything faded completely, and he found himself sitting on the cold floor of the Dragon King's throne room, a completed soul orb in his hand. No, it had been too soon, hadn't it? He felt as if there was a whole other life he could have lived in Ren Guang's memories, and yet...

Here he was, and there was Ren Guang, sitting, bound, on the floor near him. And he realized, no, he had wanted more. He had wanted to spend more time with him. But then he met Ren Guang's eyes, and realized that he already had.

He had spent a whole lifetime with him.

"Human? Are you there? Do you have the soul orb?"

Lu Fei tried desperately to reorient himself, trying to remember right from left. "Your Majesty, I have it, but please, allow me to place it back within its vessel, so that we can be sure I have the correct one..."

He didn't know what was going through his head. Hadn't Ren Guang promised that he would have a plan of escape for the two of them? He wasn't quite sure what it would involve, but if he could get close to him...

Much to his surprise, shrimp guards allowed Lu Fei to approach Ren Guang and he knelt. Right before he could plunge the orb back into his chest, Ren Guang grabbed hold of his wrist, pulling him close to his face.

"Let's run away, Coworker Lu! There's a whole ocean out there, waiting for us!"

Why was all of this, now, so much more dreamlike than any of the memories he had experienced before? Ren Guang had somehow broken free of his bonds, and was dragging Lu Fei along, laughing. The soul orb was tight in his palm, and the Dragon King shouted. The shrimp guards hurled their weapons towards them, yet they kept on running, faster and faster, until they had reached the edge of the palace...

Ren Guang pulled out two seeds from his pocket and handed one to Lu Fei. "Here. Keep it in your mouth for oxygen."

"What about your soul orb?"

"My soul orb?" Ren Guang's smile did not leave his face. "Thanks for collecting that for me, Coworker Lu. I'm not sure if I need one, though." With that, he pressed the seed between his lips and motioned for Lu Fei to do the same, as the guards were fast approaching behind them.

The two of them swam through the water towards the surface, Ren Guang dragging Lu Fei along. It was cold and dark and Lu Fei could barely hear anything except for the swirling of the waters around them, all the bubbles and shouts and the tight grip of Ren Guang's hand around his wrist. There was a sudden sharp pain in his foot, and he realized that he had been ensnared by one of the guards. Ren Guang pulled at him, then swam down and tried to kick the guard off, but with all the pulling and prying of everyone Lu Fei felt the soul orb slip through his fingers. All of them watched it sink down, deeper into the darkness of the ocean, shining like a light.

He wanted to cry out, but Ren Guang pulled him free, saying "Now!" He carried him along with such swiftness that before Lu Fei knew it the surface was in sight. Here Ren Guang slowed, and Lu Fei tried to pull him up, but in the light of the water he saw that...

"Come on! Ren Guang!" He wanted to scream, straining and pulling as hard as he could, but he could feel his coworker slipping away from him, dissolving into sand. Lu Fei screamed, the seed floating out from his mouth. His head broke through the surface of the water, and tears streamed down his face, as he was washed up onto shore, alone.

When he opened his eyes, he was lying in his own bed, as if he had never left. It was dark outside, but he was already dressed, so he got up and began preparing dinner for his grandmother.

Ren Guang was officially declared dead, and he went to his memorial service, the white flowers stark against his black suit. They removed the ones that they had placed on his desk, and soon there was someone else who worked there. When Lu Fei passed by, he could barely smell any of their rotting scent anymore. He said nothing to the new person, not of the person who used to sit there in his seat, talking and laughing with the rest of them. Not of how much Ren Guang would surely try to be his friend. When Lu Fei went on his water break, the fish in the tank still darted away at the sight of him, but this time his paper cup made the basket, yet he couldn't bring himself to care.

And yet, in his workplace, there was no more of that fog, that gloominess, that had constantly surrounded Lu Fei when he had been there. It was like someone had taken the curtains by the windows and opened them, and that the sky had cleared and the sun was shining again. The hollowness was not gone completely from his chest, yet he found himself there, again and again, working at his computer or carrying stacks of paper or eating lunch with his coworkers down by the beach. He could talk, and it didn't feel like someone was choking him.

And every time he passed by the ocean, on his way home from work, he would stare at the waves, and wonder if he dived deep enough, could he find the Dragon King's palace, where he lost the soul of Ren Guang.

About Linyang Zhang

Linyang Zhang enjoys writing speculative fiction, from fantasy to sci-fi to surrealism. When not writing she enjoys movies, reading, music, and spending time with friends. She currently resides in New England.

Once Upon a Stormy Sea

M. C. Kennedy

Karyna reclined in her throne—or at least, reclined as far as the straight-backed seat would allow. With all the carefully-carven swirls and motifs etched across its surface, this saltwood chair rivaled her solid pearl one in the audience chamber in terms of decor. However, it definitely lost points when it came to comfort. She drummed her fingers against the end of the armrest, her manicured nails clicking a steady rhythm across the wood.

"Are you sure about this, my lady?" Frode, the recently-appointed chief advisor to the queen, shifted closer to her, his voice barely above a murmur. "From what we have already learned of him, he would make an excellent king. Is it really necessary to subject him to these... difficult trials?"

"You know the rules, Frode." Karyna brushed aside his concern with a flick of her finger. She kept her attention on the field below, where a solitary man stood on the close-cropped seagrass lawn, a large bow in his hands. Before him waited a round target, anticipating the arrows the man would soon send into it.

"If he passes all three trials, he may have my hand." Karyna flexed her fingers, then curled them back around the armrest. "If he fails, then that honor is left open for the next suitor who comes along."

"Which seems like a fine idea, until we consider that you have already turned down every other eligible suitor who has dared your trials." Frode released a frustrated sigh, tugging at his short brown beard. Streaks of purple ran through it, matching the flecks in his silver eyes. "Might you consider making an exception at some point?"

"You seem quite convinced Latham here will fail the trials." Karyna lifted an eyebrow. "Have a little faith, Frode."

"Faith has nothing to do with it," Frode grumbled before lapsing into silence.

Karyna leaned forward a little to get a better view of Latham. The man had done quite well in the agility trial yesterday, he had answered the riddle posed to him, and he seemed in good spirits as he placed a silver-tipped arrow on the bowstring and drew it back to his cheek. Karyna held her breath, not daring to blink.

Latham sighted down the bow, and after several agonizing seconds, he released the string. The arrow zipped through the water and smacked into the target—a full handbreadth from the center.

Karyna released her breath, slumping back into her throne. She pulled herself quickly upright again and schooled her features into an expression of grave sympathy as Latham lowered the bow and turned to her, his eyes wide and pleading. He climbed the short flight of steps to her throne and knelt before her, holding the bow across his knee.

"Please, your majesty," he said, his voice quavering ever so slightly, "would you permit me to try again? I'm not sure what happened. My aim is always true. If you will allow me to try again, I can—"

"I'm sorry, Latham." The compassion in Karyna's voice wasn't entirely feigned. Her heart squeezed at the dejection in the man's stooped shoulders. He had tried so hard for this...

The ring hanging around her neck pressed against her skin, gently reminding her of its presence. She lifted her hand to her chest, feeling the thin circlet lying just under her dress. She exhaled slowly. *The rules exist for a reason.* Lowering her hand, she held it out to Latham. Hope flared in his eyes but died just as quickly at the sad smile she offered him.

"You have done well," she told him, keeping her voice gentle. "I am honored that you have attempted my trials. But the rules are clear. You have but one chance.

Failing to complete one task means failure of the trials as a whole."

Latham's head hung, his green-streaked brown hair falling across his eyes. "I understand, Your Majesty," he murmured. He stood slowly and looked from side to side, holding the bow awkwardly away from him.

Karyna lifted a finger, and a servant standing beside her throne stepped forward and took the bow from Latham, retreating back to her place. Latham turned to go, but Karyna stopped him.

"You have done well," she repeated once he looked back at her. She smiled. "Go home in honor. Find a lovely maid to be your wife. Anyone would be fortunate to have such a determined man for a husband."

"Except for you, it would seem." Latham ducked his head in a quick bow. Then he turned and strode from the field, leaving a heavy silence behind him.

Karyna stared at the empty spot where he had just stood. The water surrounding her brushed against her eyes, but she hardly noticed it. Her fingers again moved to the chain holding her ring, bunching the silver links into a small ball. *He* had stood right there the last time she'd seen him, the day before he went off to war, the day he'd given her this ring and she'd given him one in return to signify that she would wait for him no matter how long the war lasted, no matter how long it took for him to come back to her.

Could such a promise have a time limit?

"This is getting ridiculous." Frode stepped in front of the throne, a dangerous flash in his eyes. "You cannot continue turning down every single man who fails to pass your trials. You know they are impossible. That bow—" he gestured to the servant who held the weapon "—is enchanted. It is unfair to include it in the trials. These tests should be fair game, able to be completed by anyone who attempts them."

"Anyone can manage to make the bow shoot straight," Karyna reminded him. "It takes but a simple word, if one only knows that word."

"Ah, but how are they to prepare for that?" Frode shook his head. "Is that not your point? Who can know that word but the maker of the bow himself?"

"I did not ask for your opinion on this matter." Karyna allowed the regal frost she usually kept at bay to enter her tone, commanding her advisor's attention. "I appreciate and understand your concerns, but they are unwarranted. If I die unmarried, I have half a dozen nieces whom I can name as heir. The realm is in no danger of falling if I fail to choose a husband."

"But these trials make no sense!" Frode persisted. "Forgive me, but they border on the ridiculous. If I could but understand your reasoning behind them—"

"It is enough that I have decreed them." Karyna stood, her long skirt swishing around her in the sudden current her movement created. "The matter is settled. I will leave you now." She brushed past Frode with her head high and headed into the palace behind her.

Passing through the filmy, translucent substance that stretched between the doorposts, she stepped into the dryness of her home. Water coursed in gentle waves at the walls, but inside the protective coating of the doors and windows, no moisture could seep through. The bubble-like doors gently sucked away the water from her hair and clothes as she passed through them, leaving her as dry as if she were one of those strange overworlders who braved the snows of Rinnil and never knew what a paradise they were missing in her underwater realm of Loistoa.

She toyed with her ring chain again as she moved

from the antechamber into the left passageway, heading for her private chambers. It had been twelve years since the war. Twelve years since Steffen had left with her promise that she would wait for him. Twelve years that she had held stubbornly to that promise, refusing to accept any suitor who came for her hand.

Perhaps I am being a bit ridiculous. She sighed and let go of the chain.

***

The currents swirled fiercely around the palace walls, launching into the abalone stones and causing them to shudder ever so faintly. The underwater winds screamed with all the force of their overworld sisters, but their sound was muted by the filmy doors. Try as it might, the storm outside could not enter this dwelling place.

Still, the wind grated on Karyna's nerves as she sat at her dressing table, sliding her fingers through the remnants of her braid to work out the last few twists. Another especially loud shriek pummeled her wall, and she tensed. "Flooded storm," she hissed through clenched teeth. "I wish you would just go away."

"That's unkind, my lady." Eula, her handmaid, stepped into the room and pulled the door shut behind her. "I've only just arrived, after all."

"Not you." Karyna undid the last of the braid and tugged her hair into two separate strands. She tossed one over her shoulder and reached for her brush. "The storm. If it rages all night, I'll never get any sleep."

"It is quite loud," Eula agreed, peeking up at the window, where the black waters pressed angrily against the pane. "Though I never have understood why you detest storms so."

"I don't, either." Karyna pulled the brush through her hair, her muscles relaxing with each soothing stroke. She inhaled, held her breath for a moment, and let it out gently, her arm slowing as she continued her brushing. "I suppose it's just that they're so unpredictable. Something I can't control."

"Ah, there it is." Eula turned back the thin coverlet on the massive bed behind Karyna, then reached for the pillows. Fluffing the first one, she added over her shoulder, "It would do you good to relax your hold on some things. You don't have to be in control of *everything*, now do you?"

"I'm the queen." Karyna tugged the other strand of hair forward and began to brush it. "It's my duty to control it all." She stared at herself in the mirror as she spoke. Her face was looking so thin lately, and her eyes lacked their usual spark. She paused her brushing and fingered a blonde strand in her otherwise black, green-streaked hair. She was beginning to look positively *old*.

"Even queens need to rest." Eula crossed to her side and took hold of the brush. Karyna resisted at first, but her maid held on, and at last Karyna surrendered the brush to her. Eula ran it through her hair, and Karyna closed her eyes, savoring the gentle strokes against her scalp.

"I hear yet another man failed to complete your trials today," Eula said after a long moment. "How far did he get?"

"All the way to the archery test." Karyna grimaced at the memory of Latham's pained eyes. "He was trying so hard. So determined. He might make a good husband for you, actually."

"Unfair," Eula chided, though she chuckled. "Why should I settle for the ones you have rejected?"

"The council is growing weary of my rejections." Karyna sighed a little, toying with one of the dozens of hairpins strewn across the dressing table. "Frode told me plainly today that he finds this ridiculous." She met Eula's eyes in the mirror. "Do you think I'm ridiculous?"

Eula patted Karyna's hair down, then set the brush back onto the table. She paused to grasp Karyna's shoulders in a gentle squeeze. "I think you're doing what you believe is right."

"But does that make it right?" Karyna turned to face her handmaid. "Just because I have more power than anyone else in this realm, does that mean I should be allowed to do whatever I please?" Her fingers rose to the chain around her neck. She drew out the ring, the candlelight surrounding her dressing table catching on the silver band and the three black pearls set inside it.

"I refuse to marry because I cannot bear the thought of giving this up." She stared at the ring, caught in the mesmerizing glint of the pearls. Closing her fist around it, she returned her attention to Eula. Her maid stood silently in front of her, hands clasped at her waist, forehead creased in concentration. "Tell me, Eula," Karyna murmured, "am I justified?"

Eula was silent for a long while. The ring sat hard against Karyna's closed fist, and she lowered her head. *They're right. Of course they are. I can't keep doing this. It's time I just accepted that Steffen is gone.*

Then Eula touched her shoulder, and Karyna looked up again. Eula's smile was sad as she said, "You are faithful. I do not think anyone can ask for more than that."

Karyna let out her breath in a loud puff. "Tell that to the council members."

"You're the queen. Tell them yourself."

Karyna snorted. "I have. They don't take kindly to that, for some reason." She tucked the ring back into the collar of her nightgown. Its familiar presence was comforting against her skin. "For all their complaints, though, they haven't yet been clever enough to realize that there's really only one mer who can pass all three trials."

"We all hope that he will one day come." Eula's face softened, and she knelt beside Karyna. "I know you still miss him so terribly."

Karyna focused on the saltwood floor. Her throat ached with a sudden fierceness, and she swallowed hard to clear it. "If I could but have news of him, I could move on. But there has been nothing, no one to tell me with certainty if he yet lives or if he indeed fell in the war as all others have assumed. Without that knowledge, though, how *can* I forget him? I sometimes dream that I have given up and chosen a husband, and as soon as we are married, Steffen arrives. The hurt in his eyes... I wake up crying." Karyna rubbed at her forehead. Then she straightened. "Well. There is nothing more to worry about now. I have sent away my most recent suitor, and with any luck, we won't have another one to deal with anytime soon."

"Indeed." Eula rose and brushed the wrinkles from her skirt. "I will leave you to retire now. Sleep well, my lady."

"You as well, Eula."

The door closed softly behind her handmaid, and Karyna slumped back in her chair, rubbing at her temples. The ring lay like a cold lump against her heart. "If I could just be certain," she whispered. "If I could only know!" She folded her arms onto the table and rested her head on them. "Oh, Steffen... Where are you tonight?"

Outside, the storm continued to rage.

***

"My lady?"

Karyna stifled a groan and pushed her pillow away from where it covered her ears. Propping herself up on one hand, she yawned, leaving her face muscles somewhat sore. Wincing, she rubbed at her jaw. Her eyes felt puffy, which meant they were probably grey-rimmed and bloodshot. *I already have enough on my mind,* she grumbled as she kicked her covers away and dropped to the floor. The stones were cool against her bare feet, and she scampered across them to her dressing table, where she dropped into the chair. *The last thing I needed was a storm to keep me awake half the night.*

"My lady?" A gentle rap followed Eula's voice at the door. "Are you awake yet?"

"Yes." Karyna picked up her hairbrush and ran it briskly through her hair. The ends stuck out, following the brush bristles, but she tied it all at the back of her neck with a ribbon, securing it with a simple knot even as Eula opened the door and stepped into the room.

"In that much of a hurry today?" Eula cocked her head to the side, studying Karyna's hair with pursed lips. "I could make it look better, if you wanted."

"You insult my hair dressing skills." Karyna moved to her massive wardrobe, tugging open the doors and glaring at the array of brilliant colors awaiting her. "Why do I have so many clothes?"

"Because you're the queen, and you represent the nation's wealth in what you wear."

"Rubbish." Karyna reached into the wardrobe and selected a dark turquoise dress. She held it up, fingering the silver threads running through it, and snorted again. "I could double the nation's wealth by selling half of these." She tossed the dress onto her bed, then bent over and retrieved a pair of pearlescent slippers.

"Would you feel any better if I had some breakfast sent up for you?" Eula asked. A laugh hovered at the edge of her words.

"I'm fine. Just didn't sleep well." She carried the dress and shoes into the small room on the right-hand side of her bedchamber, where she struggled out of her nightgown and replaced it with the dress. The silk shimmered against her skin, and she sighed a little, her muscles relaxing ever so slightly. Her clothes might be a tremendous waste of resources, but they never failed to send a jolt of happiness through her.

Eula was folding the coverlet back over the bedsheets when Karyna returned to the room, her nightgown over her arm. She carried it to the bed and folded it neatly, slipping it under her freshly-fluffed pillow. Then she stepped back, exhaling. "Time for another day, I suppose."

"Anything special planned?" Eula patted the coverlet and straightened.

"Just the usual." Karyna moved back to her dressing table and fingered through her numerous jewels. Most of them she hadn't worn since the day she'd received them—indeed, some of them she'd never worn—but the pile continued to grow. Selecting a simple gold ring with a pearl set prominently in the center, she slipped it onto her finger and added a gold bracelet to complete the look. Her ring hung on its chain around her neck, as it always did.

"I'll spend several dull hours in the audience chamber." She turned back to face Eula. "Most likely, I'll be all alone, unless someone has an issue that needs to be resolved. I'm reviewing the guard this afternoon, which ought to be entertaining. They've been—"

A loud rap at the door interrupted her. She turned and raised an eyebrow. "You may enter."

The door opened, and a young man stepped hesitantly inside. His wide eyes settled on Karyna, and he clasped his hands in front of him in respect. "Your Majesty, please forgive this early intrusion, but you've been summoned to your audience chamber."

Karyna's other eyebrow went up. "Indeed? Whatever for? I've yet to eat breakfast."

"Lord Frode didn't say," the man stammered. His hands clasped tighter around themselves. "He said only that it was a matter of urgency."

"It's always amusing to see what Lord Frode considers to be urgent." Karyna smiled at the young messenger. He remained as stiff as ever, though, and Karyna suppressed a sigh. Why must being the queen come with the unfortunate side effect of striking terror into the hearts of her employees? "Tell him I am on my way," she said. "Thank you."

The man backed out of the room and, when he was far enough into the hall, turned and scampered away.

"Am I truly that terrifying?" Karyna glanced at herself in the mirror. Her dark skin was perhaps a bit pale, and her eyes were certainly as grey as she'd feared, but with the simple hairstyle, she looked just as normal as the next mer.

"Don't take it personally," Eula advised. "But you should be happy; the day is already proving more interesting than you'd feared."

"Ah, but is that actually cause for rejoicing?" Still, Karyna felt a bit lighter as she exited the room and headed down the long passageways between her private chambers and the large room where she held court. The tall windows lining the hallways revealed a calm, deep blue sea outside. The storm had spent itself during the night, and all was well again.

Karyna paused in front of the large iron doors leading

to the audience chamber, drawing in a deep breath. She closed her eyes for a moment, focusing on the stillness around her. *May your grace be upon me today,* she whispered to herself. *May your wisdom direct me. May your mercy guide me. May your justice decide me. In the name of the peerless Valoa, may it be so.* Such had she prayed every day since she had first ascended to the throne. Such had her mother prayed before her, and her mother before her. Tradition must never be overthrown. To do so would be to invite disaster.

Karyna pushed open the doors, stepping through them as they creaked into a wide passage for her. The chamber was empty, a breath of cold air rushing out to meet her. She shivered, then continued down the dark blue carpet leading to her throne. The magnificent chair, carved from a single pearl, always shone with its own gentle light, eliminating the need for further lighting structures in the room. The chamber was lined with windows, reaching from the ceiling to halfway down the wall, providing an unequalled view of the sea pulsating rhythmically against the filmy panes. Banners hung between each window, each representing one of the regions of Loistoa. Twelve years ago, there had been only seven banners. But after the war, another four regions had sworn allegiance to her crown, and their banners had been added to the ranks in the audience chamber.

Reaching the throne, Karyna settled into it, letting her hands drape across the armrests. She inhaled through her nose, exhaled through her mouth, and sat up straight. *And so we begin.* She reached for the tiny hammer that sat on a small table at the right side of her throne and rapped it against the equally tiny bell that hung above it. It gave one sweet, high-pitched note that rang across the room before falling silent.

The set of double doors just beside the ones Karyna had used to enter swung open, and Frode marched inside, the other ten council members trailing behind him. They each passed before Karyna, clasping their hands in front of them, before taking their seats around the room.

Karyna looked to Frode, who sat to the left of her throne. "I was told you had a matter of urgency to bring before the council. Do make it quick so we can hurry on to breakfast."

"As you wish." Frode inclined his head. "I am sure you are aware of the storm we experienced last night."

"As if anyone could miss it." Ingemar, the representative from the southernmost region, snorted and shook her head. "The wind was keening louder than a sea-wolf."

"Indeed." Karyna shifted in her throne. "What do you wish to tell us about it?"

"The storm caught a ship not far from our port," Frode explained. "It washed up in our harbor early this morning, more a shipwreck than a seaworthy vessel. They seek sanctuary while they make necessary repairs."

"Of course. They are welcome to any of our resources." Karyna frowned. "Surely you didn't summon a full council meeting to discuss this."

"Not exactly." Frode hesitated. "The ship's captain had another request."

"Indeed?" A small shiver ran up Karyna's spine at Frode's averted eyes. "What exactly is this other request?"

The doors to the chamber creaked open again. Karyna shot her gaze to them, irritation stirring in her chest. No one ought to be allowed in without permission. What were the guards thinking, to break such a simple protocol?

Two mermen entered, both dressed in the dark brown leather denoting a sailor. One also had a short black cape flung over his shoulder, naming him the captain. Karyna glanced from him to Frode, her frown deepening. "This, I presume, is the one with the request?"

"It is." Frode had the good grace to look guilty. "It seemed best for you to hear it from him. He names himself Lief."

"Very well, then."

The two mermen approached her throne and clasped their hands. While the one in the back kept his eyes on the floor, Lief met her gaze boldly. She returned it, refusing to blink. "I am sorry to hear of your misfortunes with the storm," she said. "Be assured that you may make use of any resources available here."

"Our thanks, Your Highness." Lief bowed his head. "We greatly appreciate your assistance. But as fate has brought us here, it would be remiss to not take full advantage of this opportunity."

"Opportunity?" Karyna leaned back, resting her chin on her fist. "Pray, what do you mean?"

"I have heard of your fruitless search for a husband." Lief's voice rang across the room, brazen in the sudden hush. "I request a chance to attempt your trials."

His words echoed against the stone walls, petering away into a heavy silence. Karyna stared at him, the full meaning slowly settling in on her. Then she laughed. "Indeed? You should like to exchange your ship for a crown?"

"I should like the chance to do so," Lief returned. He met her gaze unblinkingly.

Karyna shifted, uncomfortable beneath his gaze. There was a challenge there, an eagerness unlike that of her usual suitors. She hesitated. She ought to turn him down, to refuse to allow him to attempt her trials. But no; her own rules stated that anyone who wished could take them. She could not go back on her own word. She sighed to herself. *It will be all right. It's not as if he'll actually be able to complete them.* "Very well," she said. "Your request is granted. You may face the first trial this afternoon."

"I look forward to it." Lief swept into a low bow before spinning on his heel and marching to the doors.

The other sailor lifted his head then and met Karyna's eyes above the half-mask that covered the lower portion of his face. Her heart stuttered, and she half-lifted herself from her chair, a soft gasp escaping her. *Those eyes...*

Then the sailor turned away, and the moment passed as he followed his captain out of the chamber. Karyna slumped back against her throne, exhaling. Her pulse settled, though her thoughts continued to race. *Of course it's not him. It* can't *be. He would have said something. He wouldn't have just stood there.*

"This is a bad idea," Frode muttered. "He's just a common sailor."

"It's the rules," Karyna answered stiffly. "And let's not forget, you're the one who allowed him here." She stood. "This session is adjourned. We have much to prepare for."

***

The field was once again set up for the trials, hurdles, poles, and tubs of mud dotting the expanse of dark green seagrass. Karyna drummed her fingernails against the armrests of her wooden throne as she stared out over the field. It had been less than three days since she had last sat here, watching Latham make his way through the obstacle course. Having another suitor so soon afterwards had to be the record.

"How do you think he will do?" Eula stood behind Karyna, hands folded at her waist. She didn't always come to watch the trials, but this was an unusual case, and Karyna had thought she might be interested in it.

"I expect him to excel at this first one." Karyna rested her chin on her hand. "He's a sailor, after all, and so must be used to daring athletic feats. He will probably do well with the riddles, too. So overall, I expect he will do quite well."

"But he won't pass the final one?"

"Of course not." Karyna smirked. "Arrogant as he may be, he has no actual chance of winning."

"You take a sadistic kind of pleasure in presiding over these trials."

"I can neither confirm nor deny that." Karyna smoothed her skirt. "They are terribly amusing, though, aren't they?"

"If you say so."

A bell rang out, and Karyna directed her attention back to the field. Lief strode to the center, head held high. He had discarded his leather jacket and shoulder cape, the simple short-sleeved tunic underneath leaving most of his arms bare. His muscles flexed as he walked, and Karyna barely refrained from rolling her eyes. *Really, he needn't try* that *hard.*

Lief stopped in front of Karyna and clasped his hands, raising them to his forehead. She nodded at him, and he lowered his arms, meeting her gaze with that same impertinent audacity.

"Captain Lief," Karyna said, her voice sailing through the sea with practiced ease, "you have requested the honor of participating in my trials. The reward for completing all three of them is my hand in marriage."

Lief's eyes glinted at that.

Karyna continued, "The first trial is one of agility. You see before you an obstacle course. If you can complete it within the set time of three minutes, you may progress to the second trial."

"I look forward to seeing what the second trial holds in store for me." Lief bowed his head and sauntered to the beginning of the obstacle course, marked by a blue flag. Another man stood beside it, a sandglass in his hand. Lief stopped next to him and shook out his shoulders, jumping up and down in place a few times. Then he nodded to the timekeeper. He turned the glass over, and Lief shot away.

He sped across the seagrass to the first obstacle, a tall wooden tub filled with mud. He clambered up the ladder to the tub's rim and leapt over the side, landing on the upturned barrel bobbing up and down in the soupy mess. His hands splayed out on either side for balance, he rolled the barrel forward as he stood on it, making for the rope that swung in the current on the tub's far edge. Within seconds he had reached it. Leaping from the barrel, he latched onto the rope and swung across it to the thin wooden bridge stretched across an expanse of sharp rocks.

The rope carried him over the bridge, and when he was nearly halfway across, he released the rope and landed in a crouch on the wooden slats. As soon as his feet touched the bridge, two large hammers released from the supports and swung towards him. He ducked and rolled out of the way, then sprang up and dashed across the rest of the bridge.

From there, he jumped from the platform onto a thin pole, which he slid down to the ground. He raced across the seagrass towards the small trampoline sitting in front of a tower. He jumped up onto the trampoline and, as the net bounced him upwards, used the velocity to push himself through the water to the top of the tower. He slammed his hand against the bell sitting there, and it rang out in a loud peal across the field. A wide grin was on his face as he floated back to the ground and stood again, his chest heaving.

"One minute, fifty-four seconds!" The timekeeper

pronounced, holding up his sandglass. "A new record."

"Indeed." Karyna tapped her fingers together, one eyebrow lifted. She spoke softly so that only Eula could hear. "That was most impressive. I could almost wonder if he'd practiced the course before, if it weren't impossible to have done so." She leaned forward. "Well done, Lief," she said, her voice again carrying across the field. "You have exceeded my expectations for this first trial. You may now enter the second one."

Karyna gestured, and the timekeeper crossed the field to her throne, taking a scroll from inside his jacket. He handed it to her, and she unrolled it with deliberate slowness. "A riddle," she announced, glancing at Lief. That grin remained on his face, and he crossed his arms over his chest. Karyna's eyes narrowed. He was far too confident in his own abilities.

"'My first is deeper than the ocean,'" Karyna read. "'It owns the hearts of all, and many call it blessed, yet some there are who curse it. My second breaks the heart, is the enemy of seekers, and brings tears to the eyes of the strongest. Together, they destroy all. What am I?'" She rolled up the scroll and handed it back to the timekeeper, then leaned forward, her fingers steepled against her chin. "You have five minutes to deduce the answer." Beside her, sand swished against the glass as the timekeeper turned it over again.

"You needn't have bothered." Lief lifted his hand, his satisfied smirk reaching his eyes. "The answer is obvious. It's 'love lost.'"

Karyna sat back, her stomach twisting. It wasn't exactly the most difficult of riddles, but most of her would-be suitors took at least a minute to puzzle out the answer. The fact that Lief had answered it so quickly, so smoothly, without even the semblance of difficulty... She shifted in her throne.

Perhaps there was good reason for his conceit.

"You are correct," she said, keeping her tone even. No need for him to see that he had rattled her. "Congratulations. You may now proceed to the third and final trial. It will be held tomorrow afternoon in this field. You will receive a more specific time in the morning." She inclined her head. "The best of fortune go with you."

"I thank you." Lief bowed his head in turn, then crossed the field back to where he had entered it.

Another man stood there, waiting for him. Karyna peered across the field at him, soon recognizing the sailor from earlier that morning, the one with eyes that looked just like— She shook her head and looked away. No need to torture herself by dreaming someone's features onto another's face.

"I do believe it's high time I prepared for the evening meal." Karyna stood. "Come, Eula." She turned and strode back into the palace.

Inside the enclosed space, she let her shoulders slump, exhaling heavily. An ache was forming above her eyes, and she pressed her fingers to her forehead. "I don't like him," she murmured. "Something about him is just not right."

"I agree." Eula stood beside Karyna, a frown in her voice. "It's not just that he's so sure of himself. He has something planned beyond marrying you, I guarantee it."

"Which makes this whole thing so much more difficult." Karyna uttered a soft groan. "Confound my flooded trials! What if he does pass the third one?"

"You know that's impossible," Eula reminded her. "That's rather the point, isn't it?"

"Yes, but what if?" Karyna wrapped her arms around herself and leaned against the wall. "It's not a foolproof plan.

There is some possibility that he could have learned the word to control the bow. And if he has, what then?"

"You're the queen. Surely you can simply say that you don't want to marry him."

"But that would destroy the point of the trials." Karyna huffed out another breath, pushing away from the wall. "I need to think. I'm going for a walk in the garden. Could you please have some food sent to my chambers later?"

"Of course." Eula nodded and headed down the hallway.

Karyna moved in the opposite direction, ducking into a more secluded passageway that led to a small garden door. She pushed the wooden door open, wincing at the creak of the ancient hinges. Slipping through it, she shut the door quickly to prevent too much water from entering. The caretakers would be greatly displeased if a mini flood destroyed their meticulously arranged furniture. Then she stopped and spread her arms wide, drinking in the silent beauty of the garden.

The water was so clear here, such that the faintest shafts of moonlight from the overworld shimmered in the waves. Carefully-trimmed hedges lined the walkways, with tiny fish swimming in and out among the branches. It always smelled of salt and seagrass and the faintest hint of cinnamon.

Karyna's shoulders relaxed just a bit as she moved forward, trailing her fingers across the hedge leaves. It was always so good to be alone here.

Then she stopped, her heart skipping a beat. It seemed she wasn't alone, after all.

***

The man from the ship stood in front of a hedge sculpted into the image of a dolphin leaping over a crested wave. Leaves stretched away from the wave like water droplets, bobbing in the gentle current that surrounded them constantly. The man's hands were clasped behind his back as he gazed at the green sculpture.

Karyna's heart rate returned to normal, and she backed away. No need to talk to him. It would be easy enough to slip away and find another part of the garden to— Her foot crunched over a fallen twig, and it snapped loudly in the silence. She cringed as the sailor turned.

"Hello." She kicked the twig away and held herself straight. "I didn't mean to disturb you."

The sailor shook his head. His mask still covered the lower half of his face, and his eyes glittered beneath the waves of his blond-streaked dark hair falling over his forehead. Karyna couldn't look away from his eyes again. They were dark brown, with hints of green in the corners, the grey veins streaking the whites a bit more visible than was normal. Perhaps he wasn't getting much sleep, either.

Karyna took a step forward. "What's your name?"

The sailor didn't answer. He just stood there, hands at his sides, hardly moving.

Karyna squirmed, rubbing her hand briskly up and down her arm. "All right, don't tell me, then. So...do you like the garden?"

The sailor nodded, and the corners of his eyes crinkled, hinting at the smile that must be lurking behind his mask. He gestured to the dolphin sculpture behind him.

"I've always liked that one, too." Karyna took two more steps. She was now within arm's reach of him. She moved to the side and reached out to finger the leafy spray. "It looks like freedom to me. The dolphin is so happy. Nothing's inhibiting her from doing whatever she pleases. And what she pleases is to just exist, to soar above the waves and rejoice in the simple act of living. She's doing what she was made to do, and it's beautiful." Her voice had sunk to a whisper. She cleared her throat and shifted, dropping her hands to her sides. "Or at least, that's how I interpret it. What do you think?"

The sailor just stared at her, those brown eyes boring into her face. She held her breath as she returned his gaze. For a painful moment, she saw Steffen again standing before her. But then she shook her head. Steffen had green eyes, not brown. And if it were him, he wouldn't just stand there and not say a word to her. He wouldn't let someone else try to win her hand in these ridiculous trials. She sighed and looked away.

"You remind me of someone, you know," she murmured, then gave a small gasp when she realized she'd said it out loud. She glanced back at the sailor. He still stood there, stoic as ever, watching her with tender patience in his face. She found herself inching closer. "I once knew someone who looked so much like you," she said again, louder this time. "His name was Steffen." Did he stiffen at the name? "He went off to war twelve years ago to fight against the mer of Kova. He asked me to marry him the night before he left. We stood...right here." Karyna gestured to the ground in front of the dolphin sculpture, a smile quivering on her lips. "I told him I would. I promised to wait for him, no matter how long it took." She sighed again and focused on the hedge. "And here I am, still waiting. It seems rather pointless, doesn't it?"

As expected, the sailor was silent. Karyna toyed with a branch that had grown just a bit too far out of its carefully maintained boundaries. She ought to get the gardeners out here again to—

The sailor's hand brushed her arm, and she jumped,

pivoting to face him again. Her heart beat a strange rhythm as she stared up into his face. He shook his head once, eyes locked onto hers. His hand grazed hers again, and she trembled at his touch. She opened her mouth, her lips suddenly dry. "Who—"

"There you are." Lief's stringent voice shattered the silence, and Karyna winced, stepping away from the silent sailor. His eyes dropped to the ground as Lief emerged from one of the many walkways in the garden. He stopped beside his crewmate and scowled at him. "I need you back at the ship. Come on." He turned and stalked away again.

Karyna exhaled slowly. "I'm sorry," she whispered. "I don't know what's come over me. You didn't care about my story, I'm sure. Forgive me. Go return to your duties." She turned and stepped away from the sculpture.

"Karyna."

She stopped and spun around again, her heart pounding in her throat. The voice that had uttered her name had been tight, strangled, as if released from a mouth grown unaccustomed to the use of words. Her eyes flitted across the garden.

But there was no one there—only the same sailor, who still stood silently beside the sculpture, hands fisted at his sides. She caught his gaze once more. He stared back at her, depths of sadness welling in his face. Karyna's heart squeezed. Then he turned and followed his captain, leaving an even heavier silence behind him.

Karyna pressed a hand to her forehead, willing her pounding pulse to slow. "You've gone mad," she muttered. "You've been dwelling too long on your lost love. You must move on. You can't keep seeing him everywhere. That man is nothing more than a common sailor. He has perhaps known grief, but it is not your grief. You must come to your senses."

But still, her throat ached as she slowly made her way back to her palace. If only for a moment, her hope had once again arisen. It would be difficult to tamp it down again.

***

The next morning dawned with calm, clear waters, the pale light from the overworld shimmering down through the waves and supplementing the artificial lighting that provided near-constant illumination for the city. Scientists said the overworlders' light came from two moons that rose at opposite ends of the horizon and sailed towards one another for seven slow hours until they finally met in the middle. Then they would split ways and sink back beneath the earth, submerging the world in thirteen and a half hours of darkness before they again awoke to spill their light across the world.

Karyna stared up at the waves over her head, focusing on their gentle thrum as the current brushed past her. The moonlight had always fascinated her with its constant rhythm of rising and falling, of meeting and separating. In some ways, it made her sad. Did the moons long to be with one another, and thus pulled themselves back up day after day into their never-ending cycle? Or were they enemies, forced against their will to pass by one another and eagerly awaiting the moment when they could separate again?

Karyna smiled and shook her head, looking away from the light. *The moons are inanimate objects. They have no feelings to care if they are together or not.*

Unlike herself. The memory of last night's interaction with the strange, silent sailor had kept her awake half the night and haunted her dreams the rest, his piercing eyes staring out at her from the darkness of her bedchamber. If only she could have found out his name!

Sighing, she walked back into the palace and down the silent hallway past her audience chamber. Her usual presence there would have to wait until the afternoon. The final trial was scheduled for the morning, and she had to be on the field.

There's no way Lief can pass this one, she reminded herself as she went. *There's only one mer who knows the word to control it. Not even* I *know it. He will try, and he will fail, just like all the others.*

Still, her pulse beat at a faster pace than normal as she walked through the little door onto the field and took her seat on the wooden throne that awaited her. Eula was already there, standing like a statue behind the chair. She sent an encouraging smile Karyna's way, and Karyna did her best to return it. Then her face fell again. Really, there was no need to pretend with Eula. If anyone had a right to know how she was really feeling right now, it was her.

"It will be all right, my lady," Eula murmured. "This whole interesting adventure will be over in just a few minutes."

"Let us hope so." Karyna folded her fingers over the armrests of her throne. "Well then. No need to keep anyone waiting." She reached for the hammer and rang the bell.

As he had the day before, Lief emerged from the far side of the field, where he had been waiting for quite some time. An unofficial part of the trials was telling the attempters to arrive well before the actual event began, so as to test their patience. Karyna had had many a silent laugh at the frustrated faces of mermen who had, in their opinions, wasted a large part of their time.

Lief, however, seemed as unfazed as ever as he strode onto the field and stopped before Karyna. He made a show of clasping his hands, and then he crossed his arms. Irritation flared in Karyna at his disrespect, but she kept herself under control and nodded to him. "The day has come for the final trial," she declared. "Your task is simple: Shoot an arrow into the center of the target using the bow we have provided for you. Succeed, and you have won the right to ask for my hand. Fail, and you must leave with no reward... and no option for a second chance."

Lief inclined his head. "I understand."

"You may begin, then." Karyna sat back and waved her hand. The timekeeper from yesterday's trial stepped forward, the enchanted bow in hand, and held it out to Lief. Lief took it and ran his hand over the smooth wood, then fingered the string, drawing it back a hair to test it. He nodded once and selected an arrow from the quiver the timekeeper provided.

Lief strode across the field to the mark set out on the seagrass, fifty paces from the target. He took an expert stance —left foot pointed towards the target, right foot just behind it to balance him, shoulders straight. He set the arrow to the string and drew it back, pausing to take his aim.

Karyna tilted forward, holding her breath. He knew what he was doing with a regular bow, that was certain. How far off would his shot be this time? Would it come close to the center? Would it shoot far too wide? Her chest ached with the tension.

Lief released the string. The arrow tore through the waves, arcing slightly on its way down, and smacked into the target—dead in the center.

Karyna fell back against the throne, the blood draining from her face. Around her, astonished silence fell on the council members as Lief turned, gripping the bow in a tight fist, a triumphant grin on his lips. He looked straight at her, a wicked gleam in his eyes. The words coming from his mouth fell dully on her ears.

"I've won."

***

Karyna's breath caught in her throat. She stared wordlessly at Lief, standing so proudly in the center of the field. Everything else faded into a blur around her. Her pulse pounded in her ears, drowning out the clamor of her councilors rising up in astonishment. Frode's voice clashed with the roar of her heart, but his words wouldn't register. She just stared at Lief, her mouth half-open, her fingers curled around the wood of the armrests until they ached.

He shouldn't have been able to control the bow. He shouldn't have known the word. Yet somehow, he had. He'd done the impossible and made a perfect shot. He had, to use his own word, *won*. Nothing now could stop him from claiming her hand. She was bound to him now, trapped by her own rules.

Her throat burned, aching with a scream that longed to rip from it but that her lungs yet had no air to bring forth. She studied Lief's face, her chest tight. Was it somehow possible that this *was* Steffen, changed by some horrible magic? Stranger things had been rumored before. Perhaps he had come in disguise to test her and see if she truly remained loyal to him.

But that cruel flicker in Lief's hard brown eyes spoke of no affection. Never had she seen anything remotely resembling such an expression in Steffen's face. She shuddered and at last looked away.

"Your Majesty?" Frode was pleading, his voice high and strained. He leaned across his chair, holding out a beseeching hand to Karyna. "You must make a verdict. What is to be done about this?"

Karyna's gaze settled on him. His face was pinched, lined with worry. Her heart gave a dull thump in her chest. She couldn't reassure him, could only make those lines deeper. Slowly, she turned to face Lief again. She raised her hand and held it out to him.

Tense silence fell across the field. Lief's footsteps squelched across the wet seagrass as he crossed the short distance to Karyna. He took her hand in his, squeezing her fingers in a tight grip, and pressed a hard kiss to the back of her hand. She shuddered and drew her hand away, hiding it in the folds of her skirt.

"You have passed the trials," she said, her voice strange even to herself. "You have earned my hand as your reward. Do you choose to accept it?"

"I do." Lief didn't even bother trying to disguise his elation, a wicked grin sliding across his face. He crossed his arms over his chest again. "I will marry you, Queen of Loistoa," he proclaimed, his voice thundering in her ears. "I will take my place at your side as the rightful ruler of this realm." His grin disappeared, replaced by a stony expression as he murmured so that only Karyna could hear, "Such is my destiny."

"And so it shall be." Karyna sat straight, holding herself up with dignity. "As custom demands, we shall be married a week hence. I bid you go now to your ship and make what preparations are necessary. I shall do the same." She rose and stiffly inclined her head to him. "I bid you farewell for now." She turned and strode back into the palace.

Her feet carried her to her audience chamber, and she was pushing open the heavy doors before she realized where she was. Walking blindly down the long aisle to her throne, she sank into the pearlescent chair, dropping her head into her hands and pressing her thumbs against the ache in her temples. *What has happened?* she groaned to herself. *This cannot be real. It's a horrible dream; it must be.* If only the pounding in her head would cease and allow her to believe it.

The chamber doors swung open, and Frode stormed inside, his aquamarine robes billowing out behind him. "This is an outrage!" he sputtered, slamming to a halt in front of Karyna. He didn't bother clasping his hands, instead waving them wildly around his head. "You cannot marry a simple sailor! Hang the flooded trials! This is a fluke, a horrible mistake. You cannot doom the realm like this."

"You would have me break my word, then?" Karyna grasped the armrests until her knuckles turned white. "All the realm knows of the trials. When word spreads that someone has at last passed them and that I still refused to marry him, what then? What kind of respect would I command? How could I then expect anyone to obey my laws if I show myself to be in contempt of them?"

"There is such a thing as common sense," Frode snarled. "No one in his right mind would hold you to these rules you have created for yourself. You are the queen! You have the right to choose a husband as you see fit."

"This from you?" Karyna couldn't keep the bitter smirk from her lips. "You who not three days ago were insisting I cease my folly and marry as soon as possible?"

"To promote the wellbeing of our land, not to hasten its end!" Frode shoved a hand through his hair. "If you go through with this, if you marry this man, our land will soon perish. Surely you can see this. He has foul motives. You cannot be blind to that."

"And yet we have no proof of it. To accuse him of something entirely unfounded would set a dangerous precedent. It is a path I will not tread."

"So you would doom us all?"

"I would keep to my word." Karyna's jaw ached, but the muscles refused to relax. She raised her hand and waved it at Frode. "Leave me. I cannot listen to this any longer."

Frode opened his mouth, eyes flashing. Then he clasped his hands in front of him. "So be it, my queen." He marched from the chambers. The doors slammed shut behind him with an ominous boom.

Karyna sagged in her throne, her arms quivering. Her hand came up to her throat, her trembling fingers curling around the chain that still graced her neck. The ring seemed heavy at the end of it, a cold knot against her chest. She bit down on her lip, chin quivering. "Steffen," she breathed. "I'm so sorry."

She bowed her head and finally let herself weep.

***

Karyna sat stiffly in her chair in front of her dressing table, her unfocused gaze fixed on her reflection. Candlelight flickered in the background, casting shadowy rays around her face. Eula stood to the side, working the last few twists into Karyna's simple braid. She'd insisted on doing this for her tonight, and Karyna hadn't had the energy to tell her no.

"There." Eula let the braid fall. It swung against Karyna's back for a moment before stilling. Eula set a gentle hand on her shoulder. "My lady—"

"Please." Karyna swallowed and blinked. She lowered her gaze to her hands, folded in her lap. "I can't talk anymore. I just... want to be alone. Please."

"As you wish." Eula sighed, but she let go of Karyna and slipped out of the room.

Karyna sat as still as if she were frozen, staring at her

hands. In just a few days, those same hands would be set in Lief's, and the priestess of the seas would name them husband and wife. She would be bound to him then, bound by a vow that nothing could break.

She shuddered and wrapped her arms around herself. Her haunted eyes stared back at her from the mirror. How had this come to such a horrible end? It was never meant to be this way.

May your wisdom direct me.

The words of the ancient prayer darted into her mind. She closed her eyes and rubbed her fingers against her temples. If ever she needed guidance, it was now. "Valoa direct me," she whispered. "If ever you cared about us and our realm, then help us now."

She sat in silence for a long while, the burden of her situation pressing down on her shoulders. At last, she stood and crossed the room to her bed. She sank onto the mattress, fingering the filigreed coverlet. Just a few more days to have this to herself. The thought set her stomach to roiling, and she moaned, falling back onto her pillows. Her hand clutched at the ring lying against her chest. She would have to give it up... to *him.* Hot tears burned her eyes, and she dashed them away, rolling onto her stomach. Her head pounded, her stomach seethed. She tucked her arms under her pillow and buried her face in its fluffy whiteness. If only she could lose herself in it...

Something cold brushed against her fingertips. She stilled, groping for the object. It was small and round, and strangely thin. Her fingers curled around it, and she drew it out from under the pillow, holding it up to the failing candlelight.

She gasped, her heart pounding a strange new rhythm. A ring was in her hand, a thin silver band with three black pearls set in the top. Her other hand flew to her chest. Her ring was still there, right where it always was. So this one was its twin, the one she had given to...

"Steffen." Karyna swung out of bed, her feet smacking against the floor. She dashed to the door and flung it open, darting out into the hallway. Her pulse pounded wildly in her throat. Steffen was *here*! Somehow, somewhere, he was here. He couldn't be far away. She just had to find him, had to —

Strong arms came around her from the side, stilling her mad dash. She gasped and clawed at her captor, struggling to escape his grip. She opened her mouth to scream.

Then the arms released her, and she stumbled forward. Hands again settled onto her shoulders, but this time they were steadying, comforting. Karyna straightened and peered up at her unwanted companion, straining to see his face. Only his eyes were visible in the faint candlelight of the hallway, glittering as if they were filled with tears.

Karyna's heart stuttered. It was the silent sailor. He was looking at her with such intensity, such sorrow, such... love. Slowly, Karyna lifted her hand. She set it lightly against his cheek, the fabric of his mask rough against her palm. He closed his eyes, and she could feel him pulling in a deep breath. She couldn't breathe at all as she brushed her thumb against his cheekbone. Her fingers found the edge of his mask, and gently she lowered it.

"Steffen," she breathed, and her knees gave out.

Steffen caught her and gathered her to his chest. She clung to him, burying her face in his once-familiar shoulders. Her own shoulders shuddered as she choked back the tears that longed to come. Her ring was smashed against her chest, his ring was biting into her hand, both throbbing against her skin in time to the rapid beat of her heart. Steffen was here—

here! She was holding him again, and he was holding her, and suddenly though everything was wrong, everything was right. "Steffen," she said again. "How are you here? Why aren't you saying anything? What is going on?"

"I couldn't speak." Steffen's voice startled her, and she pulled away, gazing up at him. His words were strained, like a sword drawn from a rusted scabbard. "I was enchanted. He captured me and made me tell him everything. I was on my way home, and he found me. I'm so sorry."

"What's happening?" Karyna's voice shook, and she willed it to still. "I don't understand."

"It's Lief." Steffen's voice grew stronger with every word. Now he sounded almost as she remembered him—bold, ready to face any challenge that came his way. "Lief is the prince of Kova. Somehow he escaped when we destroyed the city. I had been captured shortly before the war ended, and they didn't honor their agreement to send back all the prisoners. I can only assume everyone thought I was dead. But I finally escaped, and I was on my way back. But then Lief found me, and he knew who I was. He's a master of dark magic, and he made me tell him how to pass your trials."

"But why bring you here? Why not just kill you once he found out what he needed to know?" Karyna's heart burned at the thought of what Lief had done. He would be executed as soon as the council could be assembled in the morning.

"I think he needed me near to keep the magic working. Otherwise, he would forget the word that would control my bow." Steffen swallowed. "I could sometimes slip away, though. That time in the garden? I could almost speak then. I called to you."

"I heard you." Karyna remembered that strangled voice speaking her name. Her hold tightened on Steffen's arms. "You looked so hopeless."

"He was winning." Steffen closed his eyes for a moment. "And then tonight, I got away again. I put my ring under your pillow. By some mercy, he never found that. I knew you would recognize it. And now I can speak again. He's not in control of me anymore. I don't know why. Perhaps it was enough that you found the ring."

"I keep yours with me all the time." Karyna drew out her necklace, holding up the twin rings side by side. "I've waited for you." Her voice broke, and she wrapped her arms around Steffen again, relishing his closeness. "I've waited so long for you."

"And now I'm home." Steffen stroked her hair, his touch sending soft tingles across her scalp. "I'm home, and I will never leave you again." His hand slid under her chin, tilting her face up to his. He bent his head, and Karyna closed her eyes in anticipation of his kiss.

"Please don't. Public displays of affection make others most uncomfortable."

***

Steffen whirled, throwing a protective arm in front of Karyna. Her eyes grew wide, a horrible shiver chilling her blood at the sound of Lief's evil voice echoing in the hallway. He stepped into view, pausing under a flickering candle. A drawn sword hung from his hand.

"You run a great risk in showing your face." Steffen took a step forward, his fists clenched. "I could kill you where you stand."

"You forget that I am the one with the weapon." Lief held up his sword, running a casual glance over it. "The odds are heavily in my favor."

"You will not survive another day." Karyna moved to Steffen's side, her shoulders straight and stiff. She narrowed her eyes at Lief. "You will be tried, and you will be found guilty, and you will be executed. I will see to that."

"And all I did was ask to marry you." Lief lowered his sword. "If you look so unfavorably upon marriage, I wonder why you ever held those silly trials at all."

"To keep mer like you from laying a wanton claim to my throne."

"There are no mer like me." All the humor fled from Lief's face, and he lifted the sword again, a dangerous light flickering in his eyes. "I am the prince of Kova, by right its king. That right you have stolen from me. You hold the throne of my kingdom, so I come now only to claim what is my own."

"We won the war," Steffen growled. "You are the prince of nowhere now."

"Only until I marry the one who usurped my throne."

"I'll die before I let that happen," Steffen spat.

"Precisely." Lief lunged, thrusting the sword at Steffen. Karyna gasped, throwing out her hand to Steffen. But he jumped aside and grabbed Lief's arm as it swung towards him. Lief tugged against him, but Steffen gripped the sword hilt and wrapped his fingers around it, straining as Lief fought against him.

The candles on the wall flickered in the wake of the fight. Karyna inhaled sharply and leapt for them, wrenching a candlestick free of its holder. She rounded on Lief and swung the candlestick at his head, a scream escaping her as she did.

The candlestick thumped into the back of Lief's head, and he lurched forward with a grunt. His grip loosened on the sword, and Steffen snatched it from him, pushing Lief back as he did. Lief stumbled backwards, and Karyna jumped out of the way to avoid him plowing into her. She held the candlestick over her head and started forward, but Steffen waved her back, pointing the sword at Lief.

"This is your only warning," he said, his voice colder than the blade in his hand. "Leave this realm now, and your life will be spared. You stay only for your execution."

Lief glared at Steffen with hate-filled eyes, then shifted his gaze to Karyna. She shuddered and gripped the candlestick harder. "You heard him," she muttered through clenched teeth. "Leave or die."

"I'm not the one who will die." From the folds of his cloak, Lief whipped out a dagger and lunged for Karyna. The blade gleamed wickedly in the candlelight as it arced towards Karyna.

Then metal clanged against metal, and the dagger hurtled through the air as the sword drove itself into Lief's heart. He gagged and stumbled forward, clutching at his chest. Steffen let go of the sword, and Lief dropped to his knees, his breathing labored. He forced his head up, venomous hate spilling from his eyes, and his mouth worked in one final effort to speak.

Then the hatred faded into nothingness, and he slumped over, falling onto his side. His breath left him in a faint puff. All was silent.

"I'm so sorry." Steffen pulled Karyna into his arms, turning her so that he stood between her and Lief's body.

She pressed her forehead against his shoulder, forcing herself to breathe. "He's dead," she murmured, squeezing her eyes shut. "He's gone."

"Yes," Steffen confirmed, his voice grim. "It's all right."

Karyna shuddered, her stomach churning. Then she

swallowed hard and pushed away from Steffen, willing her shoulders to stay straight. "It's over, then."

A fierce light entered Steffen's eyes as he gazed at her, and suddenly his arms were around her again. Her heart beat a wild rhythm as he whispered hoarsely, "I love you, Karyna. So much. I'm never going to leave you again."

"I never want you to." Karyna pushed back enough to hold up the ring she had given him so long ago. The black pearls gleamed in the candlelight. "I think this belongs to you?"

His hard kiss was answer enough.

About M. C. Kennedy

M. C. Kennedy fell in love with fantasy at nine years old after reading The Lord of the Rings. She now strives to reflect her Creator by dreaming up fictional realms that point readers to His truths in the real world. When she's not roaming through fanciful forests, struggling to understand Greek and Hebrew, or geeking out over one of her many fandoms, she loves to connect with readers on her website (mckenndyauthor.com) or on Instagram (@mckennedy.author).

The Storm's Surrender

Jessica B. Brown

"The battle is lost," is the storm's scream.
The captain stands at the wheel,
soaked to the skin,
a whispered plea on his lips.
The darkness is heavy,
the sky streaked with thunder.
The rain will not let up.
Tossed to and fro by angry waves,
his poor battered ship tries
to stay afloat in the fight.
"We cannot win," is the sailors' echo.
Wind tears at the ship's furled sails,
determined to rip her to pieces,
each swell carrying her closer to destruction.
The night has stretched on
and brought every crewman
begging for his own life on his knees.
They have come this far valiantly,
but now they have accepted
that they will go no further.
"Do not let it be over," is the captain's prayer.
He widens his stance,
his eyes searching the horizon
for any sign of deliverance.
His heart thuds in his chest
as water washes over his boots,
his plea coming ever the stronger.
He refuses to believe that God's plan
doesn't extend beyond;
that it should all end now.
"I have not forgotten you," is God's promise.
Through a lull in the storm,
something is spotted,

that brings a shout to the captain's lips.
For a radiant light
pierces the dark,
as the clouds part for the sun.
Tinging the horizon,
is the morning,
bringing with it new hope.
"The battle is won," is the dawn's song.

About Jessica B. Brown

Jessica B. Brown is a historical fiction author and poet, avid bookworm, and daughter of the King. She writes gentle, hope-filled poetry and character-driven stories that reach for your hand and touch your heart. A born South African, she currently lives in the picturesque North Island of New Zealand with her parents and two younger sisters. When not writing or reorganizing her bookshelves, she's trying out new gluten-free recipes or playing her favorite songs on her guitar. On any given day, you can find her feverishly typing away at a new story idea, holed up in her room reading, or unsuccessfully evading her very loved but talkative sisters.

The Vitalis

Jennifer G. Satnic

To my God, my family, and my mentor. "Thank you" doesn't even come close.

In a shipyard nestled at the edge of a seaside kingdom, a ship was born.

The process of being built took far longer than the ship expected, but it wasn't alone. As it began to take shape, plank by plank, a team of builders stood beside it every step of the way to guide it into existence. Some of them spent more time in the shipyard than others, but the ship soon knew them all to some extent. Listening in on their conversations, the ship began to learn about the world it had arrived in.

"What do you think of this idea?" one of the builders asked as he crouched beneath the ship's half-made hull propped up by stilts.

His companion—a man with graying hair—nailed the planks into their places as the other man assisted him. "What idea?" he asked, pausing to wipe the sweat from his brow.

The first man gestured to the half-formed skeleton of the ship. "Building a ship for exploring the world outside Mesa. I heard something about a search for allies, too. Figures that the admiral will pitch an idea like that to the king and then abandon us as we slave away to bring *his* dream to life." He scoffed, pushing back his brown hair that lay plastered to his cheeks. "He's just like the rest of his navy men—he doesn't care about the people who make the ships he sails."

The ship was...discouraged at this. Was this the man under whom it would serve? Was he truly as callous and flippant as this builder described him?

The older man smiled. "I think," he said, twinkle in his eye, "Elias Queen will surprise you."

A clamor sounded on the other side of the shipyard. At the entrance, a singular man ran through the throngs of workers. His black curls shook as he sprinted, booted feet slamming against the ground. He was set apart from the shipyard's workers—while they wore stained clothes of toil and sweat, this man wore a crisp uniform of deep green bordered by silver.

"Apologies for the *horrible* delay," the man called out as he neared. "I meant to come sooner, but I was away overseas and—" His sentence snapped in half as he froze in front of the ship. Face turned upward, eyes wide, he gazed at the skeleton of the ship as if it was the most beautiful thing he had ever seen.

"Is this it?" he asked, voice breathless.

"Yes, Admiral," the older man from before said, a grin on his face. He rose to his full height and joined the admiral—Elias—in gazing at the ship. "This is it."

Elias reached a hand up—gingerly, as if he were approaching an easily-frightened animal—and laid it on the ship's bow. The ship dwarfed him in size, but as it looked down at that man in his green uniform, the ship saw something in his eyes it had never seen before.

Wonder.

"It's perfect," Elias whispered. He turned to the men around him and shrugged off his uniform jacket, rolling his white shirt sleeves up to his elbows. "Show me how to help bring it to life."

That was the moment the ship knew Elias Queen was a good man.

***

On the day the ship was finally completed—three long years

after the undertaking had begun—the building crew threw a celebration. People from all over the kingdom of Mesa converged upon the shipyard and the port beyond it, eager to catch sight of the creation. The ship found it strange to be surrounded by so many unfamiliar faces, but the moment it caught wind of their words, the strangeness faded.

Everyone spoke of the ship's beauty. Everyone commented on its regal majesty—its golden-kissed oak and crisp white sails that billowed in the breeze. While the ship had been afraid of being stared at by unkind eyes, all it found in the gazes of the people below it was wonder. Now, the ship felt proud—an emotion that tied back to its new leader. Now, everyone else could see what a benevolent man Elias truly was.

The admiral himself was praised heavily for his efforts. The building crew lifted him on their shoulders, cheering out his name as Elias got the recognition he deserved. After all, it was his leadership that had led to the ship being built. That *deserved* praise.

At a point during the celebration when morale was at an all-time high, Elias climbed on a stack of supply boxes near the dock where the ship was anchored. The crowd fell silent, all holding their breath as they looked to him.

Elias motioned toward the ship. "There it is," he called out, bearing a smile that seemed to shine light on the entire port. "The beauty that our team has assembled plank by plank—there it is in all its glory."

A round of cheers went up from the crowd again.

"And now," Elias continued once the crowd had quieted, "I will give my second in command the honor of revealing our chosen name."

A name? The ship was confused. Did it need a name? Names were for humans, after all.

Was it *worthy* of a name?

Elias motioned to a shorter man standing near the front of the crowd. He was one of the more prevalent faces among Elias's navy men. If the ship thought back to the months when it was being built, it could also recall a name to go along with the face: Captain Morgan Trent. Like Elias, he was skilled with his hands and had worked on the ship along with his admiral. There were very few navy men who had done the same.

Morgan detached himself from the crowd and stood next to Elias on the boxes. A small boy—his son, Jesse—followed him, and Morgan helped him onto his shoulders so he could sit far above the rest of the crowd. In one hand, Morgan held what appeared to be a metallic plaque, possibly constructed from the same type of material that had gone into the ship's creation.

Morgan held the plaque up to Jesse, who took it in his small hands to proudly show the crowd. The ship could now clearly see what was written on it.

The Vitalis.

"The *Vitalis,*" Morgan called out to the crowd, beaming with the force of the sun itself. "Admiral Queen has chosen that it will be named the *Vitalis.*"

And the crowd erupted into cheers.

The Vitalis. The ship pondered the name. It seemed far too high and mighty for a ship such as itself. This would take getting used to.

Elias clapped Morgan on the back, matching his friend's smile with one of his own. "The *Vitalis,*" he repeated, a sparkle in his eye. "Because it will be the ship to exemplify this time of peace and prosperity we live in. It will be the ship to discover what else exists beyond our kingdom. It will see the entire world our Creator has gifted to us from one edge of the sea to the other." Elias looked at the ship and smiled so brightly that the ship found it difficult to look at anything else. "It will be the ship to truly experience life."

Once more, the crowd showed their resounding approval. This time, however, both men climbed down and reentered the crowd, receiving the cheers and claps on the back they were due. Jesse in particular looked quite joyful as he continued to sit on his father's shoulders, beaming.

But all the while, the ship sat in the port, quietly thinking over what had occurred. Elias's words were imbued with admiration and pride, but the ship felt as if it wasn't worthy of such a thing, least of all the name. After all, a ship—a mere creation of metal and wood—didn't have life. Not in the way its builders did. How could it *experience* it?

But Elias thought it was worthy of the name. Perhaps that meant it truly was.

***

The first time the *Vitalis* was let out to sea came a few days after the celebration marking its completion. From what the navy men said as they walked on the deck for the first time, Elias had assembled a crew to spearhead the journeys the *Vitalis* would make overseas. Many of the faces were unfamiliar, which was a saddening discovery. The *Vitalis* knew the crew who had assembled it plank by plank wouldn't be the same crew that would later call it home, but it had hoped to see more familiar faces.

However, Elias and Morgan were there, being the only men who were on both the building crew and the navy crew. Given that information, the *Vitalis* was comforted. If Elias was there, the *Vitalis* would be able to find its way through the new chapter of life ahead—of that, it was certain.

On the day the *Vitalis* was first let out to sea, a

myriad of people pressed together on the streets around the port, eager to witness that new chapter. There were many faces the *Vitalis* couldn't recognize and that it knew it might never see again. In the crowd, the *Vitalis* could see a crowned figure—flanked by a considerable number of guards—exchanging some last words with Elias. This must be the Mesan king—the man who had given Elias his blessing to begin this journey. He and all those faces in the crowd were there to watch the *Vitalis* as it sailed out to sea.

That was something the *Vitalis* couldn't understand. None of those people in the crowd would know a single thing about what happened until the *Vitalis* came home. Why were they all so eager to witness the beginning of the journey when they would only hear tales of it long after it ended?

Just before the embarkation was supposed to take place, Elias left the crowd and climbed onto the *Vitalis*'s deck. He towered several feet above the masses waiting below. The *Vitalis* thought that was fitting.

Elias held up his hands to indicate he requested silence from the crowd, which the people were quick to give him.

"Today marks a historic day," Elias called over their heads. "Today is the day our people will no longer be confined to this land we've lived on for so long. Today is the day the Mesans explore the sea!"

The cheers that rose in response were deafening. The air was full with the sound of them—cheers of pride and happiness, of excitement for what the future could hold.

"With this ship," Elias said, gesturing to the deck of the *Vitalis*, "we will embark into the world. We will journey to places that none of us have ever dreamed of. We will witness the true expanse of the world and what awaits us in it." Elias threw his hands out to either side as if to encompass the entirety of that world in his mere arms. "When we come back, we won't be the same. Wait for us, Mesa—we *will* return!"

The crowd dissolved into all-encompassing cheers once again, and the *Vitalis* was left to wonder about Elias's words as it pulled out of the port and into the open sea. When Elias turned from the quickly-disappearing crowds and intermingled with the crew instead, wide-eyed excitement was plain on his face.

The *Vitalis* had no idea what lingered beyond the shipyard where it was born, but now it realized that neither did its benevolent leader. All of them were embarking into completely unknown waters—into uncharted sea never before crossed by their people.

But the *Vitalis* wasn't alone. It would have Elias and the rest of the crew there. None of them knew what lurked out in the sea, but Elias would guide them all as best he could.

After all, that was what a leader was supposed to do.

***

With the uncharted sea spreading before it, the *Vitalis* thrived under the direction of Elias and his crew.

As the hours blended into days, the ship cut through the sea while birds soared far above its deck. Being able to course through the wide open blue after a short life spent within the boundaries of shipyard and port was exhilarating. The sea was unlike anything the *Vitalis* had ever experienced before. It was terrifying, but it was fulfilling. The *Vitalis* knew *this* was where it belonged: under the direction of a noble crew and sailing freely through the waves. This was where its meaning lay.

And so, the journey truly began.

The *Vitalis* quickly found that the sea was far larger

than it imagined. The days spent seeing nothing but endless waters passed easily enough, what with the number of stories from the crew to pass the time, but it was still a shock to the *Vitalis* that the world could be so large. That fact made itself seem small in comparison—so insignificant in the face of such unbelievable size.

But still, it proved to the *Vitalis* how much of that world had yet to be explored. With the entire sea before them, there were immeasurable discoveries to be made, and the *Vitalis* would be a witness to them all.

As the days bled into weeks, one morning brought with it a yell from the man stationed in the crow's nest.

"*Land!*" shouted the ecstatic navy man. "Off the starboard side!"

Instantly, every soul on the deck of the *Vitalis* flocked to the rail. All of them crowded over each other, desperate to be part of the first glimpse of the land across the sea.

The *Vitalis* looked as well. The distance was so great that it was hard to even ascertain, but still—there was undeniably *something* there. Amid the neverending blue, there was now a break from the endless, rhythmic monotony that the sea offered. *Land*. The *Vitalis* couldn't even *begin* to think about what might await its crew in that place, but they all seemed to be excited.

Elias seemed especially overcome with emotion. While the rest of his men sent up hoots of joy and clapped each other on the back, Elias stood there, gazing out at what lay in the distance with nothing but a smile on his face and tears in his eyes.

As the land grew ever nearer, the *Vitalis* and its crew could now make out the details. Even before they docked, the city that sprawled on the shore was clearly visible. Strangely, it reminded the *Vitalis* of Mesa: an island kingdom set apart from any other form of civilization. Maybe that meant they would find allies here.

Once the *Vitalis* drew near enough to what appeared to be a port, it could see the men lingering on the docks, shielding their eyes from the sun.

"Greetings!" Elias shouted over the small distance of sea that separated them. "We come in peace from across the sea!"

"For what purpose?" the man nearest the end of the dock shouted back. The *Vitalis* made note of the firearm he held in his hands and the identical ones the men behind him held.

"We set out from our home kingdom to explore the world," Elias called. "We are a peaceful people who wish to establish a friendship if your leaders would be so inclined to see us."

For a second, there was nothing but silence as the man considered Elias's words. Everyone on board the deck of the *Vitalis* seemed terrified that the answer would be shots. After a torturous period of silence, the man returned his firearm to its holster on his back, the men behind him following suit. Without a smile, the man raised his hand and beckoned them toward the port.

Elias beamed. The *Vitalis* continued sailing on until it came to a stop in the port, its anchor dropped soon after.

Elias, as the leader, was the first off the gangplank to meet the crowd.

Now that they weren't separated by the sea, the *Vitalis* studied the man at the front of the group—the same one who had spoken earlier. He was also dressed in a uniform, but his was pure white and covered with rich golden embellishments. His blond hair fell into neat ringlets on his head, and his cold blue eyes looked over Elias and his crew with an observing stare—one that cut through the *Vitalis*. Even though the man appeared much younger than Elias, the men on the dock lined up in strict formation behind him as he approached the *Vitalis*.

This was a man of power here.

"Byron Coss, prince of Selis," the man said, but didn't extend a hand for a shake. "Welcome to our kingdom, Sir..." Byron trailed off after that, and it was clear he expected Elias to offer his name.

Elias dropped into a deep bow, his men following suit. "Admiral Elias Queen, Your Highness," he said. "A pleasure to be welcomed into your kingdom."

Byron smiled at that. "It isn't mine, exactly," he said. "But my mother will be very interested to see you. We have never hosted visitors from across the sea before. I believe she'll enjoy it."

At the news that their arrival would be well-received, all the men seemed to relax. This was especially true of Elias, who now looked as if a considerable weight had been lifted off his shoulders.

"I assure you, Your Highness, the news that your people were willing to receive us will be celebrated back home," Elias said with a smile.

Byron motioned to the path before them that led into the city beyond, where a palace of marble and gold glittered in the morning sun. "Please follow me, Admiral—Selis has much to show."

***

Unfortunately for the *Vitalis*, it remained alone in the port for the entirety of the crew's stay in Selis. With only the occasional guards in the port for company, it made for a lonely few days. However, eventually, Elias and the crew returned. The sky was clear and blue, the sun was warm and bright, and the world around the *Vitalis* was full of life. It was a day for sailing.

As the group neared the *Vitalis*'s dock, it was happy to find that Elias and his crew weren't alone. Elias walked in the front alongside Byron, but a woman lingered on Elias's right. Her blonde hair, cold blue eyes, and similar dress of white and gold made it evident that this was Byron's mother —the queen of Selis.

And she laughed as she spoke to Elias.

The navy men once again boarded onto the *Vitalis*'s deck, but Elias remained on the dock next to the queen, Byron, and Selisan guards.

"What an immeasurable pleasure it has been to have you and your men here," the queen said. "Express to your king our sincere desire to pursue this alliance. One day, I hope Byron and I will come to visit Mesa for ourselves."

Elias beamed. "It would be a pleasure to accommodate people such as yourselves, Your Majesty."

The queen chuckled. "Please—just Rowena." She stepped forward and placed a kiss on his cheek. "Come back soon, Admiral. We'll be waiting."

Elias, face visibly flushed, bowed before following his men onto the deck of the *Vitalis*. With a shout from him, the ship quickly sailed out of the port and into the open sea.

The *Vitalis* noted that Elias looked back for as long as he could before Selis and the people lingering in that port faded into obscurity.

Morgan came up to Elias, smiling devilishly. "Have a sweetheart across the sea now, do you?"

Elias turned away with a dismissive wave of his hand, but the grin on his face shone across the deck. "Back to your station, my friend. Home awaits us."

Yes—Mesa awaited them. Though it loved the sea, the *Vitalis* was eager to return to its place of birth. After all, no trip was complete without the return journey. They all had much to tell those in Mesa, and the *Vitalis* knew that Elias couldn't wait to relay the good news to the king.

However, it soon seemed as if their journey home wouldn't be as smooth as they hoped. A few days into the return voyage, Elias was struck with a vicious cough. As the days bled by, it morphed into a raging fever paired with hacked-up blood. Soon, the once-capable admiral was reduced to his bed below deck—a pale and trembling shell of the man he once was. Much to their grief, the crew had no remedy. They were prepared to treat injuries, but they had no cure for mysterious illnesses. They could only watch and pray as Elias wasted away into a pale ghost.

The *Vitalis* was no better. It could do nothing but witness as its leader fell apart, cracking and breaking until his last breath echoed through the ship's quiet rooms.

On the day Elias Queen died, the *Vitalis* longed to cry. How it *yearned* to raise its voice in grief along with its crew, but it couldn't. It could only continue on the path set before it—the path toward a home that Elias, his body having since been left to the sea he so loved, would never see again.

Eventually, the *Vitalis* returned to Mesa. The crowds there joyously awaited their return, but when they saw that the *Vitalis*'s crew returned with grim faces and one figure noticeably missing, that joy faded away.

The *Vitalis*, remaining in the Mesan port much as it had in Selis, wasn't privy to the news Morgan and the rest of the crew gave the king, but it heard enough from the talk of the few navy men that passed by. The king was told of their budding alliance in Selis, but with Elias gone, none of the crew had any will to journey across the sea again. The *Vitalis* heard rumors that Morgan had resigned from the navy that very moment. He reportedly begged the king to let the *Vitalis* rest in the shipyard in honor of Elias's memory, saying that no man would long to discover the world as much as Elias had.

The *Vitalis* knew all the rumors were true when it was pulled from the sea by the shipyard's machinery and laid to rest among the remaining half-formed ships with little fanfare. After all, a ship that no longer held any purpose had no need to sit in the port, waiting for a day that would never come.

After that declaration, the *Vitalis* soon stopped counting the days that passed. As it sat in that shipyard, day after week after month after year, it fell into disrepair. Small upkeeps were overlooked as it lay forgotten in a corner of the shipyard. No one had the strength to let it see the sea again—that was the truth the *Vitalis* needed to come to terms with.

But how could it? How could it come to terms with the fact that it no longer had meaning?

Still, the world continued turning. Morgan was a familiar face in the shipyard. The *Vitalis* heard that he bought the shipyard after his resignation, longing to still do something with his hands. He never spent much time around the *Vitalis*, though. Whenever he looked at the ship, deep-rooted pain lingered behind his gaze. He spent his time with the other things that drew his attention—namely, his son Jesse, whom the *Vitalis* remembered from its assembling days.

Everyone had things to move on to, things to help heal their grief, but not the *Vitalis*. The *Vitalis* could only sit, watch, and remember.

Still, the world continued turning. The years passed by, eventually taking Morgan with them. Jesse filled his father's shoes and governed the shipyard, remaining in the occupation long enough to reach the young age Elias had been at his death. However, even with the change of hands, the *Vitalis* was still forgotten. It was still nothing more than a painful heirloom—a memory of a past dream that no longer had any meaning.

And so, the *Vitalis* accepted its fate: eternal hibernation, plagued by the grief that haunted it and the knowledge that no one wanted it anymore. If the people of Mesa wished for it to collect dust, then that was what the *Vitalis* would do. If that was what it took for them to move on and heal, so be it.

***

The day the *Vitalis* woke from its long hibernation started like any other. A warm wind blew through the forgotten landscape. Summer was beginning to take hold again, and the sun was already relentless as it rose over the shipyard and the group that stumbled their way inside.

The *Vitalis* stirred.

This group was unlike anyone the *Vitalis* had spent time with. While Elias and his navy men had been refined and proper, these people were nothing but rough edges and sea-worn clothes. However, though they looked like rugged messes, the light in their eyes suggested some sort of rustic hope underneath their exteriors.

In spite of itself, the *Vitalis* studied them intently. Just who *were* these people?

There were three of them: two men and a pregnant woman. Both of the men had long and rather unkempt golden-brown hair that they swept back into ponytails. One sported a scraggly beard as well, making him seem the perfect picture of a seafaring man.

The woman stood at equal height to them, but while the two men seemed to share the same features, there was nothing in the woman that mirrored that sort of relation. Given how similar the two men looked, the *Vitalis* assumed they were likely brothers, but the woman stood apart from them with her fox-like features and jet-black hair pulled into a hasty updo. She had an inquisitive eye, too. While the men focused only on what lay before them, she looked everywhere she could, observing everything.

All three of them entered the barely-occupied shipyard with little fanfare. Jesse and his workers were the only ones around, either tinkering away at their projects or making the rounds and ensuring that everything else was in order. Jesse himself, who had been working on something elsewhere in the yard where the *Vitalis* couldn't see, was the one who approached the trio.

"Greetings, friends!" Jesse called as he wiped his hands free of sawdust. "I'm Jesse—I'm more or less the man who runs this place. How can I help you three?"

As if to take charge of the group, the bearded man stepped forward. This one was likely the oldest.

"Esben," the man said in reply, extending a hand that Jesse quickly took in a firm shake. "This is my brother, Willem, and my wife, Isla. We're part of a group of fishermen who recently lost our only ship at sea. We're interested in looking for a suitable replacement."

Jesse's face visibly brightened at that. This was a chance for business, after all. He motioned to the expanse of the shipyard and nearby port. "Well, I regret to say we're not often in the business of creating ships nowadays—more centralized around upkeep, you see—but I do have a few unclaimed options on hand. Would you care to look around?"

Isla was the one who broke off first. While Willem

and Esben remained with Jesse, content to be led around the shipyard and shown the recommended choices, Isla searched on her own. She walked to and fro between the lines of ships, craning her head to look at each of them in turn. No matter how many options she studied, though, her expression never changed. There was never a single moment when she looked interested or captivated. She seemed to know what she was looking for, and it was clear that none of the ships she had seen fell into that category.

The *Vitalis,* overshadowed by the more suitable ships around it, couldn't understand why. The other ships were new, whole, and ready to be sent out to the sea at a moment's notice. The *Vitalis* was nothing but a painful ghost of the past longing for the days when it had felt useful. Why wasn't Isla letting her glance linger on any of the better options?

In the distance, Jesse showed the brothers all the ships Isla had passed over. While she had shown no lasting interest in them, the brothers seemed to be intrigued and carefully deliberated.

But the *Vitalis* didn't listen to that conversation. Isla now stood before the *Vitalis* itself.

As Isla looked at the *Vitalis* with a calm eye, her face morphed into a pleased smile, and the *Vitalis* was shocked to realize that it recognized that expression. It was an echo of the one Elias had worn the day they reached land—the smile of witnessing one's dreams become reality.

The *Vitalis* didn't understand. How could it be the fulfillment of someone's dream? The only time it achieved that was in an age long past, under the leadership of a man who had long since left the world. In its broken form, it couldn't be the fulfillment of anyone's dream.

So why did Isla look at the *Vitalis* as if it was hers?

"Boys!" Isla called over her shoulder, her voice as

wisp-like and fleeting as an animal running through the forest. "I think I've found the one."

Esben, Willem, and Jesse all turned at her call. Isla still hadn't looked away from the *Vitalis,* so the trio was forced to walk to her to get a better look at what had caught her attention.

As they neared, Jesse's face visibly fell, but the *Vitalis* didn't blame him. It was no longer the same sight to behold that it had been in its younger days.

"Why has no one bought this one?" Isla asked Jesse.

Jesse sighed. "This ship hasn't seen the open sea for many long years. Not since the days of my father."

"Why not?" Willem asked, running his hand along the ship's hull. "It seems like a fine ship." The *Vitalis* was struck by how quiet his voice sounded in comparison to his older brother. While Esben seemed to be the solid, outspoken leader, these two were the inquisitive ones, content to remain out of the spotlight to ascertain as much of others as they could.

Jesse looked grieved. "Can't you see the extensive damage rendered to it?" He pointed toward the time-inflicted wounds that littered the *Vitalis*. "It's *far* from being a seaworthy vessel."

Isla looked at the *Vitalis* with a newfound sense of appreciation, her eyes observing every part of it—from its sails that had gone so long without feeling the wind to its body that had gone so long without feeling the sea. She gazed over every part of its broken and abandoned form, and yet...

What the *Vitalis* saw in Isla's gaze felt like love.

"Is our value to be found merely in our wounds?" Isla asked, giving Jesse a pointed look.

The words stunned the *Vitalis*. Was Isla right? Was its value more than its uselessness and role as a painful memory of the past? Was its value ingrained in something else?

Jesse seemed to be as stunned as the *Vitalis*. He absentmindedly ran a hand through his hair, casting another look at the broken ship. "This ship was built to be a ship of exploration," he said quietly. "But after the admiral who led it passed away, Mesa turned from the sea and chose to focus on building itself up instead. The age of exploration has long since passed, and no one found it worthwhile to fix a ship that will serve no purpose." Jesse sighed. "It's a tragedy, truly. My shipyard has long focused on constructing and repairing smaller fishing ships—ships of this magnitude haven't been used in decades."

"But most fishing groups are small," Isla countered. She earnestly grabbed onto Esben's arm. "A group our size could use a ship like this, Esben."

Esben, for his part, appeared deep in thought. It seemed that Isla's words had struck home. If everything was truly as she said, perhaps the *Vitalis* would find a new purpose. But what about the damage that had been rendered to it? That was a factor Isla wasn't fully considering. Who would want it now that it was so ruined?

"But the damage, Isla." Esben studied the *Vitalis* with the trained eye of someone who had grown up around ships and knew their ins and outs perfectly. "Would it be worth the price?"

"Wouldn't it be worth the chance to have such a vast space at our disposal?" Willem put in. "Think of the possibilities, Esben—think of the work we could get done with it on our side."

"But would it be worth the price?" Esben asked again, quieter this time. The pain of indecision lingered behind his frown.

Jesse stepped back into the conversation. "Never mind the price," he said with a dismissive wave of his hand. "If you three truly want it, you can have it for no charge, and I'll have my men help you with the repairs. The ship will never be used for anything else—it's the least I can do to honor the legacy that my father and the admiral left behind."

The trio gawked at the words. Immediately, Isla and Willem beamed, each talking over the other as they attempted to fully pull Esben to their side.

The effort on their part didn't seem to be necessary. Before long, Esben turned to Jesse and smiled. "We'll take it."

The *Vitalis* couldn't believe the words. Would it truly have a new crew after so many years spent forgotten by the world?

Based on the looks they all wore, it was clear that was the case.

"Thank you," Esben said, shaking Jesse's hand once again. "You've saved my family's generations-long business."

"Don't thank me," Jesse said. "I'm the one who was unable to spare the men to repair it since there would be no crew to command it. You've brought a sense of purpose here. I can now pay homage to the heirloom my past has left me—I'm the one who should be thanking you."

Isla turned back to the *Vitalis*. "What is its name? The plaque is old and faded."

Jesse smiled. If the *Vitalis* could, it would smile back. "The *Vitalis*," he said.

"The *Vitalis*," Isla repeated. She beamed bright enough to illuminate the entire sea.

Hearing its name after so many long years infused the *Vitalis* with hope again—hope that its story was far from over. This was only another chapter. Though the *Vitalis* didn't know what this new chapter would hold, it was once again comforted by the idea that it wouldn't be alone.

"Fitting," Willem responded with a grin, "since we'll be the ones to give it new life."

"Fitting indeed," Esben remarked, studying the *Vitalis* with a sparkle in his eye.

***

The process of making the *Vitalis* seaworthy again took a great many days and the combined efforts of all the fishermen and the shipyard crew, but eventually the *Vitalis* was brought back to life and lowered into the sea once more.

And the *Vitalis* was happy.

After one last goodbye between Jesse and the trio, the entirety of the fishing group loaded their supplies on board the *Vitalis*, assembled on its deck, and set out.

Life soon fell into a predictable pattern again. Much as with Elias and the first crew, the *Vitalis* found that it slowly began to learn more about its new passengers as the days went on. While the days spent with Elias and his crew had been characterized by refined tales and conversations, these fishermen were nothing but rugged smiles and loud hoots of glee. Being together on the deck of the *Vitalis* seemed to imbue them with a renewed sense of hope—hope that was unlike anything the *Vitalis* had ever seen. As they sailed, there was nothing but happiness to be found. In between casting nets over the side, the fishermen would sing and dance and spend the days laughing as if they had no troubles in the world.

These people were nothing like the *Vitalis*'s crew of days long past, but that wasn't necessarily unwelcome. The *Vitalis* just couldn't help but compare what now was to what once had been. Even if those around it had all forgotten about the past, the *Vitalis* could never forget.

However, though there were many differences between these fishermen and the navy men, they were united across the years by a common thread: hope, dreams, and excitement for what the future might hold.

If they could all harbor that hope, the *Vitalis* could as well.

A few months into their journeys, Isla gave birth to a boy—an occasion that sparked an increase in the already-present joy. After Esben came onto the deck to announce the wonderful news—Isla and the child resting below—the fishermen broke into shouts of happiness, surging forward to clap him on the back. The *Vitalis* soon learned the name of the child: Caspian, first announced by the beaming Esben as all the crew hurried to ask him.

Caspian—the child born on the sea. If he grew up to be anything like his parents, the *Vitalis* was sure it would enjoy serving under him.

As the weeks went by and Isla recovered enough to come out on deck with the child, the *Vitalis* adored him more and more. Caspian had inherited both his mother's black hair and her inquisitive eye. Instead of crying in the midst of the hot sun and the smell of saltwater, he simply stared at the world around him.

The *Vitalis* always gazed back.

There were a multitude of other things to capture the *Vitalis*'s attention. Throughout all those weeks, it sailed to many places it never knew existed—small towns and larger cities on islands, all for the sake of selling the crew's catch—but it never came across another kingdom.

This was intriguing. As far as the *Vitalis* could tell, it seemed that Mesa and Selis were the only two kingdoms in the world—the two superpowers separated by the sea. Perhaps that large distance separating them was for the best. That would make the journey there worth even more.

The *Vitalis* hoped it could return to Selis soon.

During a docking period at a small town, yet another joyous occasion occurred: two of the crew decided to get married. However, there was no space large enough in the town to hold both the crew and the townspeople who were starved of happy occasions. The church was a small thing, and the preacher was grieved that the humble town couldn't give the happy couple the space they required.

That was when Isla, holding the two-year-old Caspian in her arms, said, "Why not have it on board?"

Things fell into place immediately. The couple welcomed the idea readily, the woman—a distant relation of Isla's—wondering how she and her fiancé hadn't thought of it themselves. The next day, given that there wasn't much to do other than finding a location, the wedding took place. The *Vitalis* was happy to be used for such a joyous thing, even when that had never been its intended purpose.

After the wedding itself, the celebration was extraordinary. The crew and townspeople alike danced far into the night, eating and laughing and bringing a little bit of light to the space around them. Caspian, who had realized by then that he possessed two legs—much to the chagrin of his tired parents—walked back and forth over the deck as the party went on, holding onto Isla's fingers for support.

The *Vitalis* could scarcely believe how quickly the years were flying by.

After that happy day, life settled back into routine. The days were still spent sailing wherever the wind took them, following the currents and catching copious amounts of fish to be sold in whatever small town the group could find.

Caspian quickly grew into a child who loved the sea more than anything. On the days when his parents were busy or away on business in whatever town they were currently docked at, Caspian could usually be found at his uncle Willem's side. The pair became kindred spirits as the years went on and Caspian entered his teen years. In the late hours when others on board were sound asleep, the pair often lingered on the deck, repairing the crew's broken fishing nets by lantern light.

On one of those nights, it seemed that something was weighing on Caspian's mind. He set down the section of the net he held in his already callused hands and looked out toward the sea.

Willem paused. The years hadn't been kind to him—a few months back, he had purchased a pair of spectacles from one of the markets they visited to help manage his ailing eyesight. Now that Caspian had paused, Willem took the opportunity to rest as well, setting down his side of the net and swiping his spectacles off his nose.

"Something bothering you?" Willem asked.

Caspian sighed. "Why don't we ever dock at the two kingdoms?" he asked. "Wouldn't we get better trade there than we do at these seaside towns?"

Willem gazed out toward the quiet sea beyond the deck's rail. "In the days when your parents and I washed up in the kingdom of Mesa after our old ship was lost at sea, that place was a blessing." He smiled as he looked back on the memory. "There were good people there—people who helped us procure the ship we now stand on." Willem's smile faded, replaced by a grieved expression. "But there are very few good people in that kingdom now. The old king's son is a different man from his father. He rules unjustly and thinks nothing of his subjects. Your parents don't want to support such a king with their catch. As for Selis, we supposedly had an alliance with them, but even if that was true, it's believed to have fallen into obscurity years ago. Now, some people don't think they exist at all. Your parents don't see the point in an extensive journey to search for a kingdom that's more legend than fact, especially when we have so many other small towns that are more in need of food."

The *Vitalis* hated to hear this talk again. In the last few months, it had been discussed among the elders in the crew, and the *Vitalis* labored to ignore it each time. It seemed the world was still turning, and the *Vitalis* could do nothing to slow it. It could only sit and try to preserve the sense of home it still had here.

But oh, how the *Vitalis* longed to cry out that the legend was true.

Caspian looked floored. "And why haven't I heard of this?"

"Your parents knew that, when the time was right and you had matured enough, you would ask and they would explain. Until then, they wanted to let you grow up knowing only the sea—not what poison lay on the land."

Caspian grew silent. After a few moments spent with only the sounds of the sea for company, he asked, "And what happens when we need more income? Income that only Mesa's subjects could provide?"

"Pray that day never comes," Willem said quietly. "That's all I can tell you."

***

A few weeks after Caspian and Willem's discussion, tragedy struck the crew of the *Vitalis*. The same sickness that had taken the life of Elias came onto the *Vitalis* once again after its crew stopped to sell. The sickness ripped through the unsuspecting fishermen, targeting young and old alike. Weeks were spent below deck, coughing and heaving and searching for relief from a fever that wouldn't break while the ones who were healthy enough to work toiled upstairs.

Those weeks claimed the lives of too many of the crew. More than fifty bound bodies were soon laid out on the deck and tossed into the sea. Caspian's dear parents and his beloved uncle were among the dead—a fact that grieved the *Vitalis* more than anything else.

Caspian was now eighteen—that age where childhood had been left behind, but adulthood had yet to be entered. Those deaths propelled him to step forward. The crew now looked to Caspian as the inheritor of his family's business, and he couldn't let them down. The moment it was required of him, Caspian took charge, stepping into the shoes of his family as easily as if they had been his own.

The *Vitalis*, torn by terrible grief once more, tried to find the same strength that Caspian now wielded.

As the years passed, however, one thing became clear. Though Caspian was a benevolent leader and brought the remaining crew together, there were so few of them compared to the numbers they once possessed. They weren't able to bring in as much fish as they once had, and that meant their income was steadily dwindling.

Now, Caspian was in his early twenties. The years had turned him into a callused man, but he was still someone who tried to hold on to hope as best he could. In the face of such desperate need, though, there was no other path for them to take. In order to have enough income to keep up their way of life and all the materials it required, they needed to trade in Mesa.

Caspian's decision was swift and backed by much of

the crew. None of them seemed quite excited to journey there, given all they had heard, but Selis—the other kingdom across the sea—was considerably far away, even if it truly did exist. Mesa was their last chance.

The *Vitalis*, of course, was unable to offer any input. However, it was overjoyed at the idea of going home again.

It was only after another week spent sailing and consulting tattered maps that the *Vitalis* and crew finally reached Mesa. From the outside, it was still the kingdom the *Vitalis* remembered—the sea lapping against the port, the shipyard nearby, the glistening palace in the distance.

After decades spent away, the *Vitalis* was home.

As they drew nearer and began the process of docking, however, it was clear that something was different. For one, the ships in the port around them were smaller and sleeker than the *Vitalis* remembered. Navy men ran to and fro, loading weapons and cargo onto them faster than the *Vitalis* could keep track of. Those ships didn't look like the merchant and fishing ships of old—they looked like ships of war.

For another, the colors hanging from those ships were different. The colors of Mesa had once been greens and silvers entwined, but now they were replaced with red and black.

Caspian's face darkened as he undoubtedly recalled the stories of his parents and uncle. However, he didn't show that to his men. Instead, he turned from the helm and called out, "Ready the cargo!"

The *Vitalis* was soon docked. The crew filed below deck to bring up the barrels of fish they had stored over the weeks. They all needed the additional income *desperately*.

However, it soon appeared that Mesa had other plans for the *Vitalis* and its crew.

The *Vitalis* saw the group as they approached the port. The men were decked out in those colors the *Vitalis* couldn't recognize. A whole throng of them sped to the *Vitalis*, where Caspian and crew labored to unload the supplies as fast as they could in order to go sell.

It was Caspian who first saw the navy men. Brows furrowed and eyes narrowed, he left his barrel and walked down the gangplank to greet them.

"Gentlemen?" he called out, voice wary.

The *Vitalis* hadn't seen the navy men of Mesa in at least two decades, but it didn't remember them looking so grim—so devoid of hope.

And the man at their front—if the *Vitalis* could physically shy away from something, it would shy away from him. He carried himself with an aura of intimidation around his very being. The salt and pepper hair that fell to his shoulders did nothing to hide the dark glints in his eyes. At merely a glance, the *Vitalis* knew this was a man who led by fear.

The leader, followed by his navy men, came to a stop on the dock right beside the *Vitalis*'s hull. The leader held up a hand, and his men stopped short behind him. He gazed at the *Vitalis*, studying every inch of it as if searching for something he had long been chasing.

Finally, the leader spoke. "Is this the *Vitalis*?"

Caspian looked surprised at the mention of the ship's name but nodded. "Yes sir," he said hesitantly, as if unsure what confirming the question would bring upon them.

The leader smiled, but it was a cruel smile. Whatever this man was searching for, he had found it.

"The *Vitalis*—the ship that was abandoned after the death of its admiral and later sold off, never to be seen again?" he continued. The *Vitalis* was pained at the mere allusion to

Elias, especially with the decades that separated it from its leader.

"Yes," Caspian said again, using that same hesitant tone. "This ship has been my family's home for decades, sir. It's ours by all rights."

The leader looked rather irritated at that. "While that might be true, it cannot remain that way any longer. We believed this ship was lost to the sea, but now that it has returned to us, we'll put it to good use." He cast another smile at Caspian, and the latter almost recoiled at the sight of it. "It will help us win this war."

Caspian's eyes grew wide. "War?" he cried. "War with whom?

"With the kingdom across the sea, of course," the leader said, as if insulted by the question. "Truly, where have you people been?"

Caspian looked stunned. The *Vitalis*, in turn, was wrecked with grief. Why would Mesa be at war with Selis? Elias had sparked the fires of an alliance between them. Even if the waves of time had dulled that relationship, they weren't *enemies*. What had happened to damage that legacy?

"Why are you at war with them?" Caspian asked.

The leader cast him off as if he were of little importance. "Mesa has long since been confined to this island. His Majesty is looking to...expand our horizons. Our alliance with Selis was nothing more than a tall tale, given that no one bothered to journey there since that admiral sank to the bottom of the sea, but we've confirmed their existence after many long years and are fighting with them for control of the land."

Oh, how the *Vitalis* was angered! Who was this man to think he could torch Elias's legacy?

With that, the leader turned to the navy men,

nodding. "Remove the passengers and commandeer the ship in the name of the king of Mesa."

At those words, the navy men surged forward, roughly pushing past Caspian and flooding onto the deck of the *Vitalis*.

"That is my *home!*" Caspian cried. He attempted to run onto the deck, but was held back by a few of the navy men. Caspian struggled against the men's grips, but it was in vain. All around him, the navy men grabbed onto nearby members of his crew, and the *Vitalis* longed to cry out at the sight.

The leader ignored Caspian like he was an ant beneath his shoe.

"You would take my home—my *family's* home—and turn it into a beast of war?" Caspian cried. "Who are you to do such a vile thing?"

The man smiled again, and as the navy men flooded onto the *Vitalis* and forcibly removed all the people lingering below deck, the *Vitalis* realized it was right. This was a man who ruled by fear, not by grace. This man was Elias's antithesis.

"Admiral Fabian Kalnar," the leader said with a sneer. "And I'm taking over this ship because this ship will turn the tide."

Tears lingered in Caspian's eyes. The rest of his family and crew were roughly shoved down the gangplank and fell to heaps beside him. All of them stared at the *Vitalis* with wide, tear-filled eyes, but each of them was held back by the navy men.

"You can't take away our home," Caspian called out in a broken voice as Fabian climbed onto the deck of the *Vitalis*. "That is our livelihood, our means of income—you *can't* take that away."

"Oh, but I can," Fabian said. "And I will." He looked

away, seeming as if he was barely interested at that point. "Take them out of here," he called out to the navy men. "If they resist further, arrest them for obstructing the will of the crown."

"This kingdom used to be kind!" Caspian cried as they dragged him away. "You've all poisoned it—*you've poisoned*—"

The dull thump of pistol against cheek cut off Caspian's words. The rest of the navy men crowded around Caspian's weak form, pulling his crew to their feet as they dragged every one of them into the streets beyond.

How the *Vitalis* longed for a voice to cry out in protest with. How the *Vitalis* longed to join them and stand by their side. How the *Vitalis* longed to do anything other than sit in the port and watch as yet another of its crews was ripped from it. But it was nothing but a ship. Ships couldn't cry, nor could they scream—they could only sit and watch as the world turned around them.

Just before the guards dragged Caspian out of view, he managed to snatch one last look at the *Vitalis*. All the *Vitalis* could see was the tears in his eyes and his bloody mouth open in one last yell of defiance before he was gone. The guards dragged him around the corner and out of the streets adjacent to the port, and that was the last the *Vitalis* ever saw of him.

All the *Vitalis* now knew was the group of navy men standing on its deck and their leader by the helm, looking out over the sea as if he ached to conquer every inch of it.

How the *Vitalis* longed for a voice.

***

Under Fabian's thumb, the *Vitalis* was turned into something it never imagined itself becoming. After Fabian assumed command of the ship, Mesan morale was reportedly through the roof—that was the news the navy men discussed among themselves as they prepared the *Vitalis* for war. Now, with the *Vitalis* on their side, they actually had a chance at claiming the sea.

Through it all, the *Vitalis* was aghast. As the navy men ran back and forth to the port over the next few days, polishing its barely-used cannons and loading up on ammunition and other various supplies, the *Vitalis* ached to lash out in protest. All it could think of was Caspian and the rest of its old crew.

How many more people would it lose?

The day the *Vitalis* finally set out for war, several smaller ships sailed in tow behind it. The *Vitalis* could barely recognize them. Though they were of similar makes and designs, the other ships were smaller and sleeker. They wore colors the *Vitalis* didn't know, sporting those deep reds and blacks that symbolized Mesa's change in heart. Gone were the green and silver threads that had mirrored the beautiful life of the world—now, there was only darkness and blood.

It took weeks for the *Vitalis* to reach its destination. It had to rely on the talk of the navy men on board to infer what the general plan was, and even then it was difficult to understand. From what the *Vitalis* could surmise, there were already Mesan ships fighting with the Selisans, but they were in sore need of more support. Fabian intended for the *Vitalis* to be that support—to be the boost the Mesans needed to win the war and gain the Selisan territory for their own.

Never had the *Vitalis* wanted to be used for such a purpose. It was meant to be a ship of exploration—a ship meant for discovering the world, not destroying it. It was never meant to be placed under the thumb of a greedy king and a black-hearted admiral. It had never wanted *any* of this.

But when had anyone cared what the *Vitalis* wanted?

Before long, the *Vitalis* finally reached the war front and was met with nothing but destruction. Ships stretched out in the distance, all firing at each other with vengeful fury. Multiple ships were in flames, and the *Vitalis* could spot sword fights happening on a few of the decks as both Mesan and Selisan ships were boarded by the opposing side.

Fabian commanded the men to continue forward, and the *Vitalis* sailed onward into the death.

Everything blended into one mass of violence. As its cannons were fired at Selisan ships, the *Vitalis* tried not to remember the faces of the Selisan soldiers when they jumped from their flaming vessels. The *Vitalis* fought to keep those images at bay, but it remembered them anyway—just like it remembered every single soul who had stepped foot on its deck.

The *Vitalis* remembered them all.

But, even though the Mesan side seemed to be propelled by the arrival of the *Vitalis,* the tide turned back to Selis as the fighting waged on for the next few days. The Mesans were simply outnumbered. The *Vitalis*'s arrival couldn't help when they were fighting on Selis's native waters. The Selisans were like prey backed into a corner, but they were numerous and fought with bared claws and teeth. Mesa didn't stand a chance, and they never had.

That was the realization echoing through the thoughts of the *Vitalis* as it saw the Selisan warship coming straight for it, cannons blazing. Its own crew was too late to return fire.

With three hits directly to the hull, the *Vitalis* slowly sank beneath the waves.

All around the *Vitalis,* there was nothing but death.

As it sank, unable to do a single thing to stop the slow passage of the waves as they claimed its hull, there was nothing but destruction. Its crew jumped from the deck left and right, desperate to get off and escape before the sea completely overtook it.

But where would they go? The enemy ship was no more than a few feet away, barely separated by a few waves. It was either death by the unrelenting sea or death by their unrelenting enemies.

Once the surface of the sea finally closed over the tallest mast on its deck, the *Vitalis* lost sight of them all. Now, it was struck by the silence. Of course, nothing could ever truly muffle the sounds of screams and cannon fire from the surface, but hearing them through the sea's haze of calm offered the *Vitalis* some form of peace.

Eventually, after a fall that seemed to add years to the *Vitalis*'s memory, it finally hit the bottom of the sea. It was an agonizingly slow fall, as if it glided its way down on the gentlest of air currents like the birds it had once seen in the sky.

It would never see those birds again.

The sandy sea floor was such a different surface compared to the rhythmic waves of the sea. The *Vitalis* found it terribly strange to hit something it couldn't pass through—something hard and unrelenting as opposed to the gentle waves that had cradled it on the surface. But, as the wreckage and debris finally settled, the *Vitalis* found that the idea of resting against a steady foundation wasn't unwelcome.

Rest. The *Vitalis* had never known what rest meant. Its entire life had been spent fulfilling the expectations others had placed upon it, drawn from the hand of one human to another. It had seen kingdoms rise and kingdoms fall, humans both good and evil, and the whims of humanity and every form they took. Through all that, it had been content because it had never known anything else. Those things had given it meaning.

And what was the *Vitalis* now? Nothing but a useless wreck at the bottom of the sea—a mere echo of what Elias had hoped it would be. It had no meaning. Now, it was nothing but a painful picture of the past—an ode to a humanity it couldn't reconcile itself with.

The *Vitalis* looked up. The surface was so far above its deck that it couldn't make out where the water ended. Maybe this grave was what it deserved. Maybe this loneliness was what it had always been destined for. There would never be meaning for the *Vitalis* anymore.

And so, the *Vitalis* settled in for a sleep that would be long and deep. However, its preparation for the monotonous end was stopped short by something unexpected: the movement of water currents, echoes of someone or something darting forward through the waves.

Soon, the *Vitalis* was faced with an entire school of fish lingering in the water before it, staring at it with wide eyes.

It wasn't as if the *Vitalis* didn't know what fish were. It had seen plenty of them during its days as a fishing ship, ferrying their dead bodies far and wide to different cities across the sea. But these were alive, and they looked at the *Vitalis* with an expression that it had first seen on the face of Elias.

Wonder.

Slowly, one of the fish near the front swam forward. It was a small thing—barely larger than the forearm of a human—and parts of it emitted a low, glowing light. The fish swam until it nearly touched the hull. Once it was clear the strange construction that had fallen from the sky wouldn't attack them, the rest of the fish followed suit. Soon, the entire school crowded as close to the hull as they dared, staring at the *Vitalis*. Though no words were spoken—at least, not in the way that humans spoke—the *Vitalis* heard the voices clear as day.

Tell us a story from the world above.

And so, the *Vitalis* obliged them. It told them stories about the benevolent admiral who helped create it and all the adventures it went through under his direction. It told them stories about the trio of fishermen who found it after it had been abandoned in a shipyard and who transformed it into their home. It told them about the weddings, births, and lives that were lived on its deck. It told them stories about being taken over by a vile admiral and forced to fight in a war it didn't agree with. The *Vitalis* told them stories about each one, recalling all the memories as if they were still fresh.

As the *Vitalis* recounted these things, it was surprised to see the fish were no longer its only audience. Other sea animals of all shapes and colors—the *Vitalis* had no hope of recognizing most of them—crowded around, lingering in the water beyond the *Vitalis* as well as swimming through its broken hull. Every inch of the *Vitalis* was full of them, imbuing it with a new sense of life.

Slowly, as the days bled into weeks and months into years, the stories never stopped.

Before long, the *Vitalis* began to gain a new sense of meaning.

The *Vitalis* had been thrown about by waves far greater than it for its entire life. It had been propelled by winds far more powerful than it for the entirety of its journey across the sea. The *Vitalis* had always thought those things—and what it could accomplish because of them—were what gave it meaning.

That wasn't true. That had never been true, not once in the decades it had been on the sea. The waves and the wind had never given the *Vitalis* meaning. They merely gave the *Vitalis* a sense of duty. Its purpose and meaning had always been greater.

The purpose of the *Vitalis* was to sail through the waves of life and tell stories about what had befallen it. Its purpose was to be a vessel for all the memories others had forgotten—to remember the lessons that came with a long and full life. And its meaning? Its meaning was never defined by its circumstances. It went deeper than even its physical body, now riddled with wounds and decay. From the moment the idea for the ship's creation had been sparked in Elias's mind by a Creator far greater than he, the *Vitalis*'s meaning was inherent.

The people it had met, the journeys it had taken, the love it had felt—thanks to them all, the *Vitalis* now knew what life meant.

The *Vitalis* wished it could tell Elias it had lived up to its name. But, somehow, it sensed that Elias—and the rest of the people it dearly loved—already knew. In the meantime, there were plenty of other visitors who were eager to hear stories from the surface—to hear what it meant to live.

And the *Vitalis* would share that tale time after time with any soul willing to listen.

About Jennifer G. Satnic

Jennifer G. Satnic started writing at thirteen years old and never stopped. She's a God-driven storyteller who seeks to honor the first Author in all that she writes. In 2024, Jenni graduated Summa Cum Laude from Cuyahoga Community College with an AA in English. She's currently in school at Liberty University to complete her Bachelor's in English and Writing with a specialization in Creative Writing. Presently, she's working on a pirate fantasy novel about forgiveness and coming home, which will be part of an interconnected series of stories set in the same world. When she's not writing, you can find Jenni with Pippin (the family cat), playing the violin, reading Sanderson's novels, or staring out at any large body of water and thinking of her pirate characters. To get a taste of her fantasy world and keep up with her novel's progress, follow her on Instagram at @musingsandlore.

And Neither Can the Floods Drown It

Grace King-Matchett

For B.W. Call me when the world looks bleak. Our summer never ends.

The first time I met Dal, it was August, the month when all things begin to end. He was standing down at the shore, and his nose was bleeding. He watched, hands stuck in the pockets of his shorts, as a little divot of dark red grew in the wet sand. The sand was like brown sugar, sweetened twice as much by the late-summer air.

Piff.

Piff.

Piff.

That was the sound the blood made when it hit the sand.

It was a very quiet sound, but there nonetheless.

He did nothing about it. Head down, watching the sugar-sand go red.

I wonder what he was thinking about on the shore? Dal, why would you stand there and let your nose bleed? Aren't you going to do something? Are you just going to stand forever, bleed forever, stare at that one divot of red sand forever, until the world spins out of control or the sun blows up?

Maybe he thought that if he stood there long enough, his body'd make up all the blood he was losing in the time he spent standing there.

(Isn't that always the way it goes? Time takes things away from us, and our bodies fight to keep up.)

Regardless if this was what he was thinking about or not, he stood there and stood there, watching the drops slowly fall into the dark red spot in the sand like a little bloody thumbprint.

Later I wondered if that was all he wanted—for what he kept inside him to finally come out into the world and make a mark.

Maybe that's what held him there by the shore as his nose was bleeding.

He must've stood that way for at least ten minutes before he looked up and saw me across the sand.

"Oh, hey."

He wiped his nose, making no regard of the crimson smear that appeared across the back of his hand. Grinned a little, like he hadn't just been standing there watching his nose bleed into the sand for heaven only knew how long.

He looked at me.

"How long you been standing there?" he called, still grinning. As if I was the one deserving the question.

"Oh...a bit, I guess," I said, taking a few awkward steps forward.

"That's cool." He nodded, wiped his nose again, stepped up. "You new 'round here? Haven't seen your face before."

"Yeah. I just moved here."

"Cool." He nodded again.

"Your nose is bleeding," I blurted, for lack of anything else to say.

Dal grinned. "Yeah, I know it."

He enthralled me with his feverish existence, and he deleted from my mouth any hope of intelligent speech. He was clearly a summertime being. His eyes were like the sun-stained sea, it turned out, and his hair was fluffy and also sun-stained. Some boys turn ethereal in summer, like they're not even solid beings, not quite tethered to the world. They've been out in the sun so long that their very existence is just a little feverishly warm at the edges, and after summer fades and everything goes back to normal, you wonder if it was all real...

"What's your name?" he asked, and it was then that I realized I'd been silent for too long, a great swath of a pause between us.

I told it to him.

Dal repeated it back and then said, "That's a nice name."

"Thank you. What's yours?"

"Dal. It sure is nice to meet you." He stuck out his hand for me to shake, the one with blood on the back of it—it seemed he didn't notice the crimson smear. He laughed, a real casual, easy-going laugh. Like it was commonplace to shake bloody hands with strangers without thinking twice.

Just another few seconds out of his day, something he probably wouldn't think back on in the future. Or maybe he would. It was hard to tell.

I took his hand and shook it.

It was solid, sun-warmed.

He grinned at me.

And that was the first time I met Dal.

***

Dal, Dal, I should've thrown my arms around you at our first meeting.

If only I'd known, if only I had known.

The next time we met, I was sitting in the front yard —doing what, I don't really know. Pulling up grass blades, picking rocks out of the dry, sandy lawn, thinking about everything and nothing at all.

Summer evenings have that certain sort of restlessness; it's hard to ascertain what causes it. Maybe the hot air, maybe the song of the crickets changing slightly—but it's a restless feeling. The faint awareness that with every moment that goes by, we get older. That in the future we will never be able to visit exactly where we are now, because it won't ever be quite the same again.

I was thinking on these things when Dal puttered up the lane, gaze focused on a pebble as he kicked it up and up, taking his time with it. A prayer for a soccer ball, perhaps.

"Oh, hey," his voice reached my ears. "It's you."

I looked up.

He was grinning.

"Hey."

He came over and stood on the lawn across from me. "Whatcha up to?"

"Not much...just thinking."

"'Bout what?" he asked, and then he sat down next to me, like we'd really been friends our whole lives. My face burned—partly him, partly the day's dying heat.

"Well...soon summer will be over, and I'm a little scared of that." I pulled apart a piece of grass.

"Scared? What for? The fall don't bite." He laughed.

I studied him.

He just kept on grinning at me.

"Why're you scared?" he asked again, and I could sense his eyes searching mine, curiously picking up pieces of a shattered answer.

"I don't like that time passes so quickly. I'm not ready." Why was I baring myself to him like this when we'd only seen each other once? I don't know, I don't know, but there was something about him that made me talk. He was hot —not in the sense of the word everyone would think, but his very self, his very body and existence burned hot with brimming aliveness.

"Well, time *has* to pass, or else the whole world'd all

be stuck in one big long day, wouldn't we?" he said.

"I guess." I didn't feel like explaining myself. Not to someone I barely knew.

"Hey, we wouldn't have the tides if time didn't pass."

"I suppose so..."

He looked at me a moment longer, and then stood. "C'mon, I wanna show you something. It'll be good, I promise." He winked.

"O-okay," I managed, getting to my feet.

He beckoned for me to follow. If it weren't that we were just strangers who knew each other's names, I think he would've taken my hand to lead me along, too.

That was Dal, all right. Always so *existent* and in the world, with no time to waste on small talk or getting to know someone. It was always straight to the big points. Life, in his eyes, was too short to spend on anything else but moments that would make your eyes glimmer with summer evenings, with the relishing feeling of being teenage and alive.
In fact, being teenage and alive seemed to be his greatest achievement; now, it wasn't that he *hadn't* achieved anything else, but that he *made* this his greatest achievement. It was evident he ravished life—he was full of it.

And so I followed along, and he led me a street or two over, and there was the beach, unapologetically lying there for all to see.

"The beach?" I asked.

"Yeah!"

"What about it?"

"What *not* about it?"

"I mean...it's nice."

"Come on, that's all you have to say? Nice? Look at that sky! Perfect! Awesome!" He pointed at the sunset and laughed, that real easy, nice-on-the-ears laugh that made my blood rush.

"I really like summer evenings," I said, all awkward like I was.

"Yeah, me too! They make me feel alive!" And he laughed again. Nothing about it was inherently funny, he just wanted to laugh, and suddenly, the sky seemed more vibrant.

Laughter is a memory-sound—when you hear it, a real good laugh, you know you'll remember it, and when you remember it, the memory is thrice as bittersweet and thick and saturated and intense in the mouth of the mind.

The taste of the summer dusk is tangible; the light is brighter than it really is; the sunset remains an ingrained constant throughout summertime memory. Was every evening really like this? Was it always this good?

"Hey!" And he said my name.

I looked up.

"They say the ocean tastes like tears!" He laughed again, and he ran into the water without a second thought, and before I had time to process *that*, he scooped said ocean into his hands and drank it down like his life at that very moment depended on it.

A laugh burst past my lips, and he whirled around and grinned, his eyes bright.

"Well? Does it?" I said, still laughing.

"Yeah!" He laughed, too. "Yeah, it sure does!" He ran out of the water and grabbed my hand, and then I was just stumbling into the water right along with him, splashing and making my shorts all wet and making him all wet and he was just laughing and laughing.

And there was a touch of melancholy to it—how did he know what tears taste like, to draw such a comparison to the ocean? I suppose everyone has tasted tears—but why would he draw such a metaphor, this summertime boy? why speak in sad words?

I supposed he had noticed my silence, because his grin faded a little. “Sorry, I don’t always think before I do stuff. Hope you’re not mad.”

“I’m not mad,” I promised.

And he turned towards the open water, and the golden beams of dusk caught in his eyes, and suddenly the sun was setting in two worlds—the one before him and the one within him.

I stepped in next to him and scooped up water, though with far less vigour than he had, and I drank the ocean from the palms of my cupped hands.

I tried not to gag as I spat it out. Regret. It tasted like tears—or, rather, it was sure salty and murky and disgusting enough to warrant them.

“Very salty,” I said, to elucidate the obvious, because I had no idea what to say in front of someone like him when I was trying to get that taste out of my mouth.

“Yeah, it sure is.”

“Anyway.”

He looked at me and said my name. “Do you like the ocean?”

I nodded.

“Why?”

I blinked. “What do you mean?”

“Why do you like it?”

“Oh...well, sometimes the tide goes out and the water gets farther away, but it always comes back. It’s always there, I guess.”

He studied me, blue eyes curiously tracking my face.

“I like that,” he announced eventually. “I hadn’t thought about that before.”

I nodded. “What about you? Do you like the ocean?”

The waves brushed past our legs, and the water was cold, but it was good.

"Yeah, I like it." He stuck his hands in his pockets and nodded.

"Why do *you* like it?"

"Well, I used to hate it. But I kinda like it more now."

"Why did you hate it?"

And he looked at me and just smiled, as if that in itself was a response.

He didn't say anything.

"Can you swim?" I asked him.

"Sure I can."

"Oh. Okay." Maybe he just hated it for the sake of hating it? Some boys could be like that. I'd hoped he wasn't one of them, but maybe he was?

"Yeah."

He made no further explanation. It was clearly something that could not be talked about—there was a time for everything, but that time, it seemed, was not now.

"It's funny, huh?" he said suddenly.

"Funny? What is?"

"How we all need water to survive, but water can kill us. If you drink too much, or get it in your lungs, or if it just flat-out crushes you 'cause of pressure."

"Um..."

He kept on smiling, and a breeze came and tousled his fluffy hair.

I folded my hands behind my back, suddenly slightly out of place, though I wasn't sure why.

"You kinda look familiar, you know," he said to me.

"Oh?"

He said nothing more.

My gaze fell to the water. I couldn't decode him, his language of grins and brightness. I couldn't get anything out of him.

As it turned out, Dal was Dal, and no one else quite understood him. He was a shining figure, yet shrouded in a certain kind of loneliness, I could tell—like a young mountain kissed by clouds. I recognized the loneliness, but I didn't know what it was saying.

I looked up again.

He was staring at me.

My face went hot. He was so unapologetically...out there. No qualms about staring or telling me I looked familiar. He just *was*, and didn't let anybody contest his existence.

Perhaps I needed to learn from him.

"Shoot, if the water ain't just the right temperature right now. I reckon we might could go for a swim."

"But—but it's gonna be dark out soon. And we have no bathing suits." Not to mention he was still a nascent friend, I didn't know him very well; he seemed well-meaning, but even golden things can turn out abominable.

I expected him to pester me, but he didn't.

His eye on the water—it changed, almost a little critical somehow. "Yeah, it was a bad idea anyway."

"Well—not a *bad* one, maybe just another time..."

"Another time," he echoed, voice distant.

His smile came back.

"Are you all right?"

He nodded, hair all fluffing around. Then he padded onto the sand, sitting down.

I did the same and sat next to him.

"Are you sure?"

"Yeah. I'm good." He nodded. "Thanks for asking."

"All right." I nodded back at him and smiled.

He just stared at the water.

I thought back to him talking about how he had once hated the water. Maybe he wasn't quite over that yet... maybe that was what this was all about.

"Hey," I said, just to start a conversation, "what's your favourite colour?"

"Red," he told me. "And yellow."

"Yellow is a very nice colour. I like blue."

"Blue's good too." He nodded, curling his knees up to his chest, his toes digging into the sand.

"Dal?"

"Mm-hmm?"

"Is your name short for something?"

"Sure is."

"What is it? If, well, if you don't mind me asking?"

"Dallas, as in Texas, and as in the Cowboys."

That name had sun in it, a certain portion of light. It was very much *his* name—teenage, alive, a little reckless. Dallas. Bright, wild-eyed, running through the summer.

"That's a nice name," I told him.

"Thanks. Yours is too." He winked.

"Hey...do you want to get ice cream before it gets dark?"

He looked at me, nodded, and a tiny hint of his smile came back. "That'd be nice."

"Sounds good, then." I got to my feet and he did the same, and we walked up onto the lane, the bare shore behind us. I took off my sandals and shook them onto the road, put them back on, but of course there was still sand between my toes anyway—that was how summer was, it stuck in the crevices of your body and you could never quite get it out.

"Sand bothering you?"

"A little. It itches my feet when it gets in my shoes."

"Just take off your shoes."

"The gravel around here hurts too much to do that."

"Shoot, a little gravel never killed nobody." He shrugged. "C'mon, I know a shortcut to the ice-cream stand."

I followed along dutifully, and the setting sun outlined his existence with a sleepy orange.

The shortcut took us through some bushes and back alleys. All of it was tired—the town was small, the buildings ever-so-slightly crooked, the streets were dusty and barely asphalted. The toads hopped in the grass along their designated fringes where town-land and toad-land sometimes bled together. Mosquitoes' thin proboscises sank into our sun-warmed flesh as the air grew a little chilly, and we slapped them away absentmindedly, as is the way in summertime.

"Here we are," Dal announced once we'd made it across another alley behind a deserted street lined with weary houses. And there it sat: on the one good road in town, the ice-cream stand was next to the park, with no one manning it.

"Looks like we got here too late." I sighed.

"Nah, not too late." He shook his head.

"But there's no one there."

"So?" He walked over.

"Are you gonna steal?" My eyebrows drew upward with concern.

He shook his head. "I know the guy who works the stand. He'll get it. 'Sides, sometimes I work here too. I'll leave the money in the cash jar."

"All right." I nodded.

"Whatcha want?" He hopped over the counter that was padlocked with a banged-up lock, got behind the stand and looked at me expectantly.

"Hm...what flavours are there?" I couldn't help a

smile in spite of myself—there he stood, behind that counter, looking at me, serving me.

"Let's see." He turned around and bent down to the coolers, opening them up. "Chocolate, vanilla, strawberry, mint chip. Banana. Rocky road. Bubble gum—yech. Chocolate peanut butter."

"Hm...strawberry sounds nice right about now." I nodded.

"Let's make it double." He hopped up with the tub and a scoop and two waffle ice-cream cones, winked at me, and set it all on the counter.

I laughed and leaned over onto the plywood, splinters digging into my arms, but I didn't care.

He wrestled with the lid of the tub for a moment, and then got it off, digging in with the banged-up metal scoop. "How many scoops d'ya want?"

"Oh...well...how much are they?"

"Don't worry about it. I'll pay. How many do you want?"

"Are you sure? I can—"

"How. Many. Do. You. Want?"

"Three?" I couldn't help my smile.

He nodded and got in there with the scoop like it was his life's mission, and a few moments later, he held out my three-scoop cone to me, grinning proudly.

"Thank you, Dal." I smiled and took it from him, and our fingers brushed together. It was only a moment, but enough to feel the constant warmth that emanated from him.

"'Course." He winked.

The sun, by now, had almost fully slipped away; we were enveloped in the indigo dusk, with dustings of orange motes falling here and there. My ice cream hardly even looked pink; at night-time, the world loses its saturation, and things that were once distinct fall into line with other values and hues until it is all blue (with, yes, the lingering of that orange on one's palate) and the air smells like memories.

Surely it wasn't already August? Days hot, nights less so, a liminal threshold between what was and what was to come? The increasing awareness that time walks on regardless of us? As if blinders hamper its vision and it only walks on in an unaware, steady continuum? Because August is the tragic herald of summer's end; no, not quite the one who waves the flag at the finish line, but the last rest station before the race is done. August is the month when everything begins to end. Though not the biological center of the year, it is the unlikely lynchpin, the axis around which the year somehow, if even unknowingly, unwittingly, revolves. August is the culmination of the year, the moment when water remains in cupped hands before it all begins to slip through the fingers. August is the high point of the Ferris wheel before its acquiescence to gravity, the still point of the turning world, truly.

"The summers here are the best you'll find anywhere."

I believed him.

We walked home, through the brush, across the dusty, sandy streets. One lone streetlight flickered on a few streets over on the main road, and the bullfrogs started up from wherever they were.   Soon enough my ice cream was gone, with all that was left of it being the sweetness on my back teeth and the stickiness on my hands.

"Guess it's dark now, huh? I'll walk you home." He slapped at a mosquito.

"You don't have to. It's not that far."

"Nah, I will. You just got here—I'm sure your folks don't want you getting lost."

I softened. "I appreciate it."

"'Course." He wiped his sticky hands on his shorts.

"Do you know where my house is?"

"I know this town by heart." And though the dusk had stolen both the saturation and the daytime, I could see his grin.

"Have you lived here your whole life?"

"Yup, long as I can remember."

I nodded.

"C'mon, let's get you home. It's late." He put his hand on my shoulder for a moment, and it was pleasantly warm against the cold world.

"Where do you live?" I asked him as we walked down the road.

"On the other side of town from you, which doesn't mean a lot." He laughed, and it echoed in the dusk. The grass by the side of the road rustled. "Like five or six streets away or something. My place's the one with a basketball hoop in front."

"Oh, I think I might've seen it when I first got here."

"Uh-huh. This place's so small we don't even have numbers hangin' on our houses, everyone knows where everyone else lives."

"So then I guess it was a big thing when I moved here?"

"E'rybody knew right away."

"Did anyone...talk about me? My family?"

"'Course they did. E'rybody's clamouring to get to know you guys, but I got to be the first."

"Oh..."

"Don't worry, I'll tell everyone that you're a good person. And they'll know it. E'ryone knows me." He stuck his hands in his pockets, head tilted back to look at the sky.

"Hey," he said. "Look. Them there's the stars."

And when I looked up, there they were—it was still not quite late enough for them to have become prevalent over the sky, but there they were, beginning to peek through the holes in the curtain, like little children playing hide-and-seek in a time-worn house. Though the stars have been around for such a long time, they have always seemed so young, full of life, vibrancy.

"Do you know the constellations?" he asked.

"A little bit, but not very well."

"Hey–I'll teach you the constellations tomorrow night."

"Okay," I whispered. "I will."

He was too good. He was so feverishly good, like the heat in the head that accompanies illness—did I make him up?

"Dal?" I said into the night, maybe just to prove to some part of myself that he was real.

He paused, looked at me, said my name in return.

And I'm not sure what came over me right then and there, but I asked him, I really did ask him: "Are you real?"

And right after I asked it I clapped a hand to my mouth. No, no, one's idiotic delusional thoughts should be kept to oneself, shouldn't they? Why would I say that out loud? He would laugh, and think I was terribly stupid. "Sorry. I dunno what I meant by that. Forget I said that."

"I'm real as anything else, I reckon," is what he said instead, and he stood next to me.

I could hear him breathe.

We walked home together, and perhaps the night was less humid, sad, than I'd thought.

***

The next morning, I went outside, up the lane, through the bushes and over to the ice-cream stand. The morning was already proving itself hot, the sky clear and burning and blue. I had a feeling that he might be there.

And there he was, standing behind the counter, closely picking at a splinter on the wood.

"Hey." He grinned and said my name.

"Hi."

"Sure is a hot morning already, huh?" He grabbed at the collar of his tank top, fanning himself. "Sheesh."

I nodded.

"Want any ice cream?"

"I didn't bring any money, but I don't want you to pay for it again. That's not fair to you."

"Nah. It'll be on the house."

"Dal..."

"Hey, I help work this stand, so what I say goes." He jerked a thumb towards himself. "It's on the house."

"You don't h—"

"On the house!" he declared loudly. "Now, what flavour do you want?"

I knew there was no use arguing, and so I sighed. "Rocky road?"

"Good choice." He gave a triumphant grin.

"You really don't have to..." One last attempt, maybe?

"Hey, no more arguing. I said what I said. Got it?" Accompanied by a wink. "How many scoops?"

"Well...two?"

"Perfect." Moments later, he was holding out my rocky road cone to me.

"Thank you, Dal."

"'Course."

The ice cream was thick and sweet, but it was awkward to stand there licking it while he was behind the counter, so I stood next to the ice-cream stand instead.

"I'll get the guy who normally works this thing to take over, so we can hang out." He grinned, eyes intently on me, curious but trained.

"Okay."

"Yuh. It'll be a good day today." He stretched his arms over his head, revealing pale underarms patched with hair.

"Hey, Dal?"

"Uh-huh?"

"You said you'd teach me the constellations, right?"

"Yup."

"Will you still do that tonight?"

"'Course. I don't break my promises."

I licked my ice cream, focusing on the drips, *not* his winks and easy-going stances and strong arms and sun-bleached hair. The boy was not afraid to take up space, that was sure.

"All right," I even dared to tell him, "I'm looking forward to it."

"Me too." He grinned. "Now, you wait here." Then, he walked a few paces into the park and yelled, "HEY, RAYSON! COME GET YOUR ICE CREAM STAND! I'M DONE WITH IT!"

Promptly, a dark-haired guy who looked only a few years older jumped up from a bench across the park and chewed him out. "You can't claim you're no employee if you only workin' fifteen minutes a day, *Dallas*."

"Aw, c'mon, man, I have plans."

"Plans for what?" Rayson snorted. "To go stare at the ocean? To beg free blueberry candy off Miss Johnson with the pretty face at the general store? Or today will it be to ride your bike up and down every street in town singin' "Take On Me" at the top of your voice so everyone can hear like you did that one time...you know, when he was around." He trailed into a mutter.

Dal's smile faltered for an unbearably long moment, and then he quipped, "Hey, at least I'm not a bad singer."

"Oh, mm-hmm, sure, boy."

Dal's smile came back, and after a moment a grin spread itself on Rayson's face too.

Then Rayson's eyes landed on me, as I was standing small-ly and awkwardly, as if hoping that perhaps, by some chance, I might be mistaken for a very, very short streetlight.

"You know her?" His eyes flicked to Dal.

Dal threw an enthusiastic glance over his shoulder, and he said my name, turning back to Rayson. "That's my friend! She just moved here," he said, not quietly at all. No, unapologetically loud, loud enough to pierce my chest and tear it open, lodging in my heart like the blue sky of a person that he was.

Friend.

My ice cream was melting in my hands, but I didn't care. My hair was plastered against my temples, but I didn't care. I didn't care that I had rocks in my sandals and that I was standing about awkwardly, because I had made a friend.

"You got plans today?"

"Yuh-huh! We're gonna hang out."

"Nice. Gonna smooch each other on the beach at sunset?"

He laughed. "We'll see." And he did not say *that* quietly either.

The sun was suddenly thousands of times hotter, beating down on me with full unrequited force, a light-year's worth, pummelling me with bright, laughing beams, and my heart flipped in my chest, again, again, up, down, again, again.

Dal, Dal, Dal...

Now that the image was in my head, it was hard to get it out. Fresh and unpredictable, I could already taste the salt on his lips, the ocean, the sweet sky, all of it—

"Your ice cream's melting. Better eat that quick. It's hot out."

I nodded, my face burning.

"C'mon, let's go on an adventure." He grinned at me, threw a glance at Rayson, and then beckoned for me to follow him.

"Okay." And a silly smile spread itself over my face as I walked after him.

I caught up with him a few moments later. Right off the bat, he said, "I have a surprise for you."

"What kind of surprise?" I licked my ice cream.

"A good one." He grinned.

"That's all you got for me?" But inside my head, the words *we'll see* were sky-bright and pounding with life; throbbing, even.

"Uh-huh. Wait and see." He looked at me, gave me a quick smile and a touch on the shoulder, and then he was off.

We walked down dusty roads, deeper into the perimeter of the town that was rich with verdant, prime summer vegetation. He pushed branches and briars aside to let me through, making sure none of them sprung back and hit me. Evidently he was well-versed in the brush; his feet—which were dirty and bare—knew exactly where to step so that he wouldn't be hurt, his legs knew how to avoid most of the scratches from all the thorns and briars. And he made it seem so effortless—though I supposed it was years of life, really, summer after summer after summer that constituted his existence, that had taught him the paths like this, that had taught him to live like this.

"Well," his voice floated over eventually, "here we are! This is the surprise!" He turned around and grinned at me, gesturing at a large patch of raspberry bushes, bursting with vibrantly red fruits, like stars.

"Raspberries?" I looked to him, feeling as bright as the little fruits before us.

"You ain't lived until you've tasted real raspberries off the bush. I know you ain't from here, so, you know, thought I'd share them with you. Like a welcome present."

"Wow...thank you, Dal. I've only ever had ones from the store."

"'Course! It'll be great. Now. Before you pick 'em, I have a couple tips for you. A quick little raspberry-picking masterclass, if you will." Dal nodded, cleared his throat, put a hand to his chest. "Tip number one: the teeny-tiny green and white ones aren't ripe yet and they taste sour, so don't bother with them. Only pick the bright red ones."

I nodded.

"Tip number two: always check them for bugs. Sometimes silly little critters get in there, and you don't want to eat 'em. Just be careful."

I nodded again.

"And finally, tip number three: the ones that are *too* red, dark and burgundy-ish, taste like wine, so maybe don't bother with them either, unless you're into that—but they taste pretty bad." He laughed. "Otherwise, have at it! You'll never be able to eat a store-bought raspberry again after this!"

I wandered over to the bush and tentatively pulled off a raspberry. It slid off easily, leaving behind a whitish lump on the bud where it had been attached.

Inspecting the berry, I held it up, letting the sunlight

hit it. No 'critters', thankfully, and so I popped it in my mouth.

My eyes widened.

This—*this* was summer.

The warmth this held—the taste of sunlight, bursting into my mouth, running over my back teeth—*this* was summer.

Dal was shoving a handful of them into his mouth. His face was already sticky with raspberry juice, sunshine juice, red stains around his mouth like boiling blood. "Sure is good, ainnit?"

"It's incredible," I managed. "I know this will sound silly, but—it tastes like the sunlight."

"It does. I love 'em. All warm and sunny."

I reached for another, and moments later the warmth burst through over my lips again, sunshine staining my mouth.

Right then and there, as my fingers slipped another berry from the bush, I held summer in my hands. It was a coalescence of sunlight and sweetness and the heat of the day, and the slight sour aftertaste was like days going by faster than I could keep up with. The berries were a summation of August in themselves—sweet, yet also sour; sun-warm and bright. All too ephemeral, all too quickly devoured and swallowed, leaving behind only a faint taste on my tongue and the seeds stuck in my teeth, the seeds of a summer yet to come.

When August comes, I do not count the days, in the faint hopes that, perhaps, as a watched pot does not come to a boil, perhaps the days of the month will stick in my teeth longer if I do not number them, perhaps the month itself will hang in a state of never coming to an end...

But all of these things are only hopes. I swallowed the

raspberries so quickly, and similarly, the seeds are eventually worked out from between the teeth. The nights grow longer before anyone's ever ready, the sun goes down on someone's anger out there before they say sorry. There always has been and always will be twenty-four hours in a day; not looking at the calendar does nothing to lengthen time—but it's the thought that counts.

So there I stood in the heat, picking raspberries, juice staining my hands and face, getting my fill of summer. Yes, I would consume it, fill my body with it, so that I would never be able to forget these moments ever again.

"They sure are good," Dal said softly, and his arm brushed against mine for a moment.

"Thank you for bringing me here, Dal." I didn't bother to wipe the juice dripping down my chin.

"Sure thing. We can come here as often as you like."

"I'm trying my best to not forget this summer," I blurted. "My grandpa died a while ago and I miss my old house and I want to go home but I'm trying to be all right with this whole summer."

"Oh—well—shucks, I'm awful sorry to hear about your grandpaw," he started, "but, you know, summer always comes back around. It never really even leaves. Not in a place like here. You can always try again every year. All year."

"You know, Alabama's growing on me, I guess." I pulled a dark red raspberry off the bush, just to see how it would taste.

Dal was right: it tasted like wine; not that I had ever had it before, but how I thought it would taste. Summery imagination-wine, hot and thick with the air's warmth, dark like molasses.

I reached for raspberry after raspberry with him, enjoying every single one of them, revelling in the juices staining my existence.

And the awareness struck me then, like a slap to the cheek:

I would miss this. I couldn't pick raspberries forever, no matter how much I wanted to; eventually the raspberries would all dry up and fall off and the bush would be as good as dead, and I would be older, standing there looking at a dead bush, as I, myself, died more with every second going by.

All earthly things come to an end.

But I *would* pick these raspberries while I could, I *would* spend my summer with Dal and enjoy every moment, because if I did not take the time to intentionally cultivate moments and experiences, if I did not make it my goal to *live* more with every second going by—it would all be gone before I knew it.

It would all be gone before I knew it.

***

We ended up at his house some time later, and it was exactly the sort of house that I pictured Dal coming from. Buttery yellow clapboard, a crooked wooden porch with white paint peeling off of it, and a white screen door in a similar state of affairs. Toys and various flotsam and jetsam were strewn about the porch, an old basketball hoop standing sentry on the cracked driveway. The lawn was yellowed out in some places, and in the garden in front of the porch, there were dehydrated pink begonias and white hydrangeas planted, their petals browning at the tips. But it was a good old house—dependable, accepting. It was exactly Dal's house.

He stepped up onto the porch and opened the screen door, holding it for me. "Ladies first."

I smiled and stepped over the threshold onto a faded

colourful rug, and a moment later he was alongside me, letting the door bang shut behind us. There was another, more proper front door in the entranceway—when closed, it would sit just behind the screen one, to protect from too much weather or bugs, and it too was chipped and worn down with time.

"Dal? That you?" called a voice from deep within the home, presumably his mother.

"Yes ma'am," he called back. "I've got my friend with me, too."

"Why don't you two come to the kitchen, so I can meet her?"

"Yes ma'am," he yelled again. "We'll be right there." Then he turned to me. "Sorry if any of my siblings bother you, by the way. There's a few of them around."

The house was full: trinkets on the surfaces, artwork on the walls, blankets and clothes lying haphazard, dolls and trucks on the floor, noise from an unseen television and from other rooms, and a dish here and there. It all felt foreign to me, as my own house was usually in decent order, but I didn't mind it. This was his familiar terrain, not mine, and it would have somehow been wrong should his house have been neat and tidy.

"Brought your girlfriend over, Dal?" A young man—I assumed an older brother—surfaced from the living room, grinning.

Dal just laughed, throwing a glance at me, not even denying the obvious. "Sorry 'bout him."

"It sure is nice to meet you," said Dal's brother, sticking out his hand to shake. "I'm Curtis."

"Nice to meet you too, Curtis." I shook his hand and told him my name.

"C'mon, don't bother with him. My mama wants to

meet you." Dal grabbed my hand and pulled me along.

I laughed, letting him lead me to the kitchen.

"Well, you must be the new girl Dal's been telling me about!" Dal's mother turned to me from where she stood at the counter, a big smile on her face.

Dal introduced me to her. "This is my friend." He told her my name, and I couldn't help but notice his smile as he did.

"Pleasure to meet you." I smiled and shook her hand. She was blonde, like Dal, and looked very much the same manner as the house she lived in, pleasant and careworn and inviting.

"Would you like to stay for supper? We've got quite the array tonight, and I'd love to get to know you more. Dal has told me lots of nice things about you." She gave a friendly wink, and in that moment, it suddenly hit me that they really did share the same blood. That wink was genetic, and when Dal did it, it was magnetic.

"I'd love to. Thank you very much." I beamed at her.

"Well, good! We've got fried chicken and collard greens and butter beans and tuna casserole and mac n' cheese, and rolls, of course, and peach cobbler and ice cream for dessert." She beamed back. It was impossible not to immediately like her, this welcoming woman, round and friendly at the edges.

"That sounds lovely!" I said at the same time Dal interjected with "Fried chicken? Oh boy!" And we shared a glance and laughed.

"Has Dal been minding himself with you?" His mother reached over and gave a friendly swat with a spatula, which Dal ducked. "Been using his manners like a big boy should?"

"He's been just fine." I couldn't help a laugh, stealing

a glance at said big boy. He rolled his eyes, but he was smiling.

"Mama, she moved from Montana," Dal informed her. "I reckon this is her first real, authentic Southern dinner."

"All the way from Montana, now? That's pretty far, ainnit?" Dal's mother threw me a kindly glance over her shoulder as she worked something on the counter—looked like the makings of pie crust. "Well, I'm honoured for tonight to be the first Southern dinner you get to put in your belly."

"Yes ma'am," I said to her. I wasn't born Southern, but something about her, this household—it felt wrong to address it all without respect.

"Lots of nice mountains there in Montana?"

"Yes ma'am," I said again. "I didn't live in the mountain part of the state, I lived up closer to the Canadian border, so it was mostly prairie, but I visited the mountains a few times."

"Hey, close to Canada? You ever been to Canada?" Dal asked, eyes curious.

"Two times."

"What's it like there?"

"Well, everyone's very nice and polite."

He laughed and nodded. "Just like e'rybody says. Them Canadians sure seem pretty nice."

"They are."

He grinned, leaning against the kitchen doorway and crossing his arms.

"So, what were you two up to today? Hangin' out together?" asked his mom.

"Yes ma'am, I took her raspberry picking. She said she only ever had the store ones and so I told her she ain't ever need to eat a store one again."

"Amen to that." She laughed and looked at me. "Did

you enjoy them?"

"Very much so." I nodded. "Dal really knows lots of nice places around town."

"He sure does. This boy is outside pretty much all the time. He's had sixteen years to explore." His mom nodded as well.

"What do you do for school, then?" I wondered.

"I'm homeschooled," he told me. "Being outside is a big part of my education. And, you know, I cook, I do woodworking, I read my Jane Austen."

I couldn't help a laugh. Something about him...

The remaining minutes until supper were passed in friendly conversation. Dal's mother was inquisitive and easy to talk to, and I was introduced also to his father and to his two younger brothers and his sister; Dal being there made things much more comfortable.

It was as we sat around the dinner table that I realized —Dal cared, he really did care. I was juxtaposed against those whom he knew and loved, the people populating his memories, his innermost circle. But he wanted *them* to know *me*, the outsider, the juxtaposed one. He *welcomed* me.

And I could tell by the way his family spoke with me, as we sat around the dinner table eating together, that I was somehow regarded as important. Dal's older brother spoke to me with respect, and his younger siblings were inquisitive and curious, but never rejecting me. I had no idea what things Dal had said to them, but I was grateful.

The food was gone all too soon, and I was left incredulous. In the South, it seemed, people did what needed to be done, and everything was done with love. It was tangible; the food tasted more decadent, the desserts sweeter and richer, the time spent supping around the table made more valuable by conversation and togetherness.

As I waited in the entranceway for Dal—he was upstairs to find a sweater—his father came over to me, surveying me with worn, lined eyes. "Thank you for being good to my boy," he said after a moment, voice low and quiet. "He's been pretty happy these past few days."

My brow furrowed, and the unspoken question must have been written on my face, because he went on to say, "He's had a rough go of things for the last little while. Thank you for being good to him."

"Of course, sir," I managed to get out, steadying the shake in my voice. Maybe it wasn't the world, but just my head that was spinning, with the near-vertigo of the words setting in. "It's my pleasure."

Dal's father gave a somber nod, just as his son came sprinting down the stairs. "Okay, I'm ready to go!" he declared.

I smiled, but when I looked at Dal, he was suddenly placed into context.

They say the ocean tastes like tears.

So he did know that salt, that fear.

Out of all the things Dal knew about, I wouldn't have expected that to be one. He was such a sunshine boy, a summertime boy, a fever-dream-fever-heat-fever-sun boy.

"You two have fun together," Dal's father said to us. "And don't be out there too late."

"Yes sir." Dal saluted him, grinning mischievously.

"At ease, soldier. Now go teach your friend the constellations."

"Roger, sir!" And he laughed, pulling me out the door.

"Thank you for the wonderful dinner!" I called before it closed.

Dal laughed again, so joyous and alive and in the

world, and I wondered at how *this boy* was supposedly so sad.

When I pictured him crying... No. Not Dal. Not the sunshine, not the clear blue sky. He didn't cry, did he? But the ocean tastes like tears, doesn't it? And Dal knew that, didn't he?

Why should Dal, of all people, have to know that the ocean tastes like tears? Why not someone like me instead?

Why him?

***

We made our way across the streets of the tiny town. The hour was waning, the dusk waxing. Mosquitoes lined up on our arms like tourists on a prime meridian, and the air smelled like ocean-salt and nostalgia.

"Good, the night is clear," Dal declared from next to me. "Perfect conditions to learn constellations."

I smiled. "I've always wanted to learn them."

I could see him grin, even in the night. "Then I'm honoured to be the guy who gets to teach you."

We made our way to the shore, and when we got there, all was silent but for the waves, ever-lapping at the shore, ever wearing at the sand.

He sat down. "This is the best place to watch stars. Nothing in the way of 'em, just sea and sky for as many miles as you care to look at, and if you lie down, it's only sky."

I sat next to him, pulling my knees up to my chest. There was a breeze, and the summer was late enough that even the Alabama nights weren't as warm as they used to be, the heat departing from the months in the hardest way to bear, like a close friend growing distant.

"You cold?"

"A little."

He yanked off his sweater, just like that, and held it out to me.

"But, Dal...you'll get cold."

"No I won't. Take it."

"Are you—"

"Yeah." He grinned. "I am."

I was glad that the remnants of daylight had fully slipped away by now, else he would have seen me blushing as I pulled his Alabama Crimson Tide crewneck over my head.

It smelled like him: sea, sky, the good outside air, warmth, and a little bit of sweat, but that didn't bother me.

"Any warmer now?" he asked, digging his toes into the sand.

"Yeah. Thank you." I smiled softly.

"Of course. Keep it if you want."

My face grew brightly hot, like the sun, like him. "Are you—are you sure?"

"'Course. Looks better on you than on me, anyway."

"Are you flirting with me?" I blurted out, half-joking, half-curious, and my gaze flicked up to his face, painted indigo-grey by the darkness.

He shrugged. "Who knows?" And before I had barely pieced together that he meant "yes", he went on: "Hey, c'mon, if you lie down, you can see the whole sky."

So I laid down on the sand there with him, and once we were staring up at the sky, he didn't let go of my hand.

I didn't mind.

Before us was an entire world, a world of pinprick lights, stars sewn vibrantly into the cloth of the universe—each one exactly where it needed to be.

"Pretty special, ainnit?" His voice had dropped to a whisper, as if now afraid to disturb the peace of the moment.

"Yeah," I whispered back. "I think it's one of the

most special things we humans get to see."

"Shame people don't look at the stars more often... why hit the drink or get all high on them gosh darn drugs when we have something so much better? Something that won't destroy us, but will just, y'know, heal the soul a little more?"

"Yeah...that's exactly right."

He was silent for a little bit, allowing the sound of the waves to close the space.

Here and there, ocean spray would spatter my legs, and I was reminded that the world still goes on beyond our own selves. The water still flows even when we aren't watching it, the waves still wear tirelessly at the shore, the tree still falls regardless of if no one is around to hear it, the sun still rises and sets. The earth still dances and is destined to until it is destroyed and made new—but in the meantime, it turns steadily on its established axis, irrespective of if we know it does or not. These things require little of us; they will simply exist, go on and on, regardless of if we are thinking of them or aware of them or not, and there is a certain amount of comfort to be found in that.

Sea and sky surrounded the two of us, and it was as if we were alone in the world. No one in existence but me and Dal and the waves and the stars.

"There's the Southern Cross, down there in the bottom of the sky. That's my favourite constellation." He lifted a hand and pointed, carefully guiding my eyes to the right patch of stars. And my eyes eventually alit on it—there was a small cross in the bottom of the sky, just as he'd said.

"I've never heard of that one before."

"It's my favourite."

"Why's it your favourite?"

"It reminds me about the Crucifixion, you know, there's all those Greek gods and stuff up there that people invented, sure, and everybody knows those. But I like the cross."

He was still holding my hand, so I gave it a gentle squeeze. "Yeah."

"I thought I ought to teach you that one first. Nobody ever talks about that one, but I like it."

The ode to the cross in the sky, held dear down here on earth in the heart of one Southern boy. "Oh, Dal...thank you." I looked over at him, and he was smiling. "Thanks for teaching me, anyhow."

"Sure thing. They're special. E'rybody ought to know the stars."

The sand under us was cool, but his hand was warm, and my world was filled with the scent of him and the waves and the night-time air.

"Do you know where the North Star is?"

"Show me?"

With his other hand, he pointed into the sky, tracing a certain constellation. "See the Big Dipper? D'ya know that one?"

"Yeah, I see it." The ladle in the night, scooping up dripping indigo, swishing dark matter.

"At the tip of the Dipper—if you look straight up, then there's a real bright star. That's the North Star. Polaris." His finger pointed it out.

I looked.

"See it?"

"It's bright."

"Uh-huh. As long as you can see Polaris, you'll never get lost. Sailors navigate by it. For thousands of years, people's lives have depended on that one star."

"Quite thoughtful that it got put right there, then."

"Yup, exactly."

The cool wind on our faces; the sky stretching out from east to west, as wide as love; the waves like lullabies; Dal beside me, holding my hand; I memorized it all.

"Hey," he said my name, "you know something?"

"Hm?"

"I'm going to remember this forever," he whispered, and he interlaced his fingers with mine.

"Dal..." He was so sincere, he was so *alive*. He was really living. He said what he longed to say, he didn't seem afraid of meaning it—a dying art.

It all made me believe death was worlds away. That life was long, and that happiness could be found in something like a football crewneck, and that the heat of the summer wasn't overwhelming, and that everything really would last forever. That maybe it was time to let go of the end, and focus on the means, focus on the life that I had to live before I was too obsessed with it being over one day, before my existence was released to the sky to live among those same stars, freed from mortal hands, the sticky hands of a child who did not know what she was doing.

"Can I hug you?" I whispered.

"Go for it."

I sat up, and he did the same, and I wrapped my arms around him.

"Thank you, Dal," I mumbled into his T-shirt.

"'Course."

The smell of him was so overwhelming, making me lose the little rationality I possessed. My head, spinning like a car in a highway accident late at night—my tongue, thickly laden with unsaid words.

The rest of our time together was spent in co-created

warmth, and he taught me the stars little by little until after an hour or two I could trace most of them, name them, turn them over in my mind to peruse as I wished.

"Good night," he said my name as he stood outside my house. "You sleep well, and I'll come see you tomorrow morning. I have somewhere I want to take you."

"All right." I stood on the step, my heart doing funny things. It always happened whenever he talked.

"Have good dreams." He nodded at me. "It was nice getting to hang out with you."

Before he walked away, I ran down and gave him one last hug, my tired thoughts spurring me on.

I heard it—a surprised hitch of his breath, but he didn't hesitate a moment. His arms were around me again.

"Good night, Dal," I murmured, and pulled away after a few seconds, before I stood there forever, before I stood there like he had that day on the shore, unable to move, standing and standing and destined to stand until my body grew weak and decayed in his arms and my heartbeat fell perfectly into sync with his and every piano on earth went out of tune and the world spun out of control and the sun blew up.

"I'll see you in the morning." His eyes were soft in the dark.

He walked down the dusty dirt road, and I stared after him until he rounded the corner and was gone, gone, gone.

***

The next morning, I went outside, and there was Dal, rounding the corner, blond as anything, bright as the sun, skin radiant with evidence of summer.

Looking up, he noticed me and quickened his step,

hands stuck in the pockets of his shorts.

"Hey." I smiled at him when he was close.

"Hey." He winked back. "Ready to go on an adventure?"

"Always."

"Good," he declared. "I have a real nice place I wanna show you."

I thought of how I had held his hand. It was too good. We had known each other for what was, objectively, just a few grains of sand on a beach's worth of time—but it was almost natural. Dal was the sky, the golden beams of light found scattered throughout late summer, the simultaneous saturation and fadedness of memories that made me wonder if the grass really had been that green, the decision that I didn't want to let go of any of it.

Maybe that was why I didn't want to let go of his hand. The knowledge I held, having now held his hand. I knew what it felt like. I knew what having him at my side, what having his hand in mine, the tangibility of summer wrapped up into a body and holding my hand, felt like. Maybe that was why.

No, I wouldn't let go, not of the boy who drank the ocean and went for ice cream and picked raspberries with me and taught me stars.

Dal led me along, his golden cross necklace gleaming in the sweltering sun, and I remembered the Southern Cross.

"It sure is a good day out," he said, an uncontrollable smile on his face.

"You seem pretty happy today."

"Yeah." He looked at me, still grinning, and I could tell from his eyes that he really was happy. Clear and summer-blue, not just his eyes but the whole of him, and it all made a thousand white cranes take flight in my chest, wings beating, straining to be set free into those tender heavens.

"Did something good happen?" I smiled at him.

"I just—oh, boy, I got a good surprise for you." His hand brushed mine. "Gosh darn it, my face hurts from all this smilin' you're making me do."

That in itself is the most beautiful pain one can experience, to be so happy that it hurts, to be so happy that your body physically cannot contain it—like biting into an apple that tastes terrible, but you don't even care, because the skin was so truly and perfectly red, the reddest red there ever was, so vibrant, so intense, like it wasn't even true, and it excuses the discomfort. To smile so much that it hurts, but it's more than all right, because you were smiling.

The tiniest signs of stubble poked through on the side of his face and on his chin, practically invisible but for the bright sunlight, slivers of an adulthood that was still yet to come.

And, ordinarily, I would have made this a tragedy within myself. Noting the all-too-familiar pattern: we get older before we are ready, and even our bodies know it, and the once-distant future was actually far nearer at hand before any of us thought it would be, before any of us were prepared...

But, perhaps, it was all right to take things one moment at a time.

Yes, I wouldn't get ahead of myself, my life, any more. I would take things slow, stop to drink in the sun, the summer, the nectar that was these hot, sweet months, and not think of their end—one beautiful moment at a time.

"Dal?"

He looked at me, eyes bright, still smiling.

"Thank you," I told him.

"What for?"

"Well—I—you know, I've seen that you really seem to just, I don't know...you treasure every moment, and make it all like an adventure. I really like that."

When he was silent, I blundered on: "I know it's only been a couple days, but...yeah."

"It's only been a couple days..." he trailed off. "Huh. That sure is weird. It felt right away when I met you like I already knew you."

"Exactly." I looked down at the ground. My sandals were dusty, and Dal wasn't wearing any. I didn't know how his feet weren't killing him from all the rocks and pebbles, but Dal was Dal.

"I hope you feel a little better since your move and everything that happened before you came here." He looked at me, face illumined with the high morning sunlight, tracing his face, his hair, making him golden.

"I do."

I could only imagine the way his mother smiled at him on the day he was born.

The walk passed in easy conversation, until soon enough, I realized we'd passed the town limits and the tiny blue-painted sign was in our wake of dust and words.

"Dal...we're outside the limits," I blurted.

"Don't worry, it ain't much farther than this. It's very safe around these parts. Plus, I wouldn't letcha come into harm's way, anyhow. Don't you worry."

I nodded, trusting him, throwing a glance back over my shoulder at the faded blue sign.

I'd always wondered—where did the town end, and the countryside begin? Was there some sort of invisible line that proclaimed a full stop to the town, announcing in that sort of announcer-y voice, "FULL STOP", when you got to the tiny invisible line that marked town's end? Or did they merge, and at some very thin point, there was a sort of no man's land, an intersection between town and countryside? Did the two just melt together, like two different ice-cream flavours after having sat out a little too long while you laughed with someone you loved and forgot all about your ice-cream bowl in front of you? Or was there really a line that distinctly demarcated the town and the rest of the state, that people trod upon without even knowing it was there?

"Well, here we are!"

Somehow, when I looked up, we were standing in the cool shade of a tree now, leaves and fruits hanging down over us.

"I come here all the time. You can see the ocean." He looked out at the sea that lay past the dusty road, where the grass on the other side eventually faded to sand, and the sand faded to water, glimmering brightly in the sun.

"Dal...this is really, really nice." I looked up at him.

"Ainnit?" He grabbed a fruit off the tree, and then sat down against its trunk, beckoning me to sit down as well.

"What are they?" I asked after I'd sat, glancing at the fruits, and then back to him.

"Nectarines. Related to peaches, but they ain't got no fuzz, so your mouth doesn't get all itchy-like. This time of year, they're all pretty sweet." He dug in the pocket of his shorts, and a moment later, produced a pocketknife. "Nothin' quite like a good summer-ripe nectarine."

He scored into the sunset-coloured fruit with the blade of his pocketknife, cutting a thick slice, dripping with juice, off the stone. A moment later, he offered it to me, our fingers brushing as I took it.

"Now, these things're pretty messy, but the taste is all worth it, don't worry." He nodded at the piece he'd given me. The flesh was thick and raw-honey-coloured, almost orange. "Go on. It's good."

I didn't hesitate, popping the fruit into my mouth.

Warmth and summer and juice exploded on my tongue, bright juices, the flavour of the sun, of the summer, all greeting me like friends.

If the raspberries had been summer—then *this* was a thousand times more so, every day of those long, hot months unfolding in my mouth, as sweet and bright as the future, as Dal's words, as summer itself, and I knew that as long as I ate nectarines, summer really would never end. The South, the stars, the breeze, the blue sky, the wonderfully sweltering heat, all of it could be found here. It glided down my throat like milk and honey, and not even the finest wines of David or Solomon could have come close to this, this ineffable light, warmth, nectar.

"It sure is good, huh?" Dal laughed. "You've got this look on your face. Ever had a nectarine before?"

"No," I mumbled, sticky and dish-eyed.

"Shucks. Here. You take it." He handed me the rest of the fruit and jumped up to grab one for himself.

I bit into it, rivulets of vivid juices running down my chin, not even caring as it dripped onto my shirt.

When he sat down again, he was close to me, and our arms were touching as we both ate of the fruit in the fever-chill shade of the fever-hot day, every moment as blissful as a dream.

"Oh, Dal... it's like some kind of dream," I murmured between bites, not even caring that I probably looked ridiculous, with my shirt all stained and my smile dripping with juice.

"It sure is good," he said again quietly. "It sure is good."

I smiled at him, hoping he knew what I meant when I

hid behind simpler words, just praying that he would know how I felt.

He moved a little closer, and put his arm around me.

"I hope that's okay," he said after a moment, voice still soft.

"It's okay," I whispered, face warm. Dal's arm was around me and we were eating nectarines together and the heavens were blue and tender and the sea was bright and the day was hot and it was light and it was good.

He smiled, too, and his face was pink.

"Hey, Dal?" I whispered.

"Hm?"

No, I couldn't ask.

"I'm lissenin'," he said after a moment.

"Are you—okay?" I glanced out at the sea, making sure to keep my tone gentle, so as not to ruin it all.

He hesitated, and I feared that he might take his arm away and the world would spin itself to ruin.

"Your dad said you were having a rough go of things."

"Yeah," he said.

"You don't have to tell me. I just...I was just wondering. I'm sorry, I shouldn't have asked."

"That's all right." He went quiet.

"I'm sorry if I made you upset..."

"It's okay." His eyes were soft, tone calm, but I could tell he was distant. "It woulda come up one way or another. But...yeah. My old best friend—he drowned."

"Oh, Dal...I'm so sorry..." I whispered, and I hugged him.

"Nothing anybody can do 'bout it." He hugged back, and his arms around me were a little tighter than usual.

"Still...I'm sorry..."

“Time has passed. I’m getting better. Ever since you got here, I’ve felt a lot better.”

I hugged him even more tightly.

All of a sudden, even more pieces of Dal made sense.

They say the ocean tastes like tears.

“Being here helps.”

I sat there with him, quiet, calm, sticky with nectarine juice.

Time passed.

“Thanks for staying with me,” he said eventually. “I’m sorry. I’m not being any fun.”

“It’s okay, Dal. I know how death feels.”

A soft smile came over his face, and we sat for a while longer.

He took a bite out of his nectarine.

“It sure is good,” he echoed quietly to himself.

“Tastes like summer, right?” I smiled a little, looking into his eyes.

He nodded.

“Summer never leaves a place like here,” I told him, remembering when he’d told me the same.

His smile grew, and he looked into my eyes.

“Hey,” he said my name, suddenly soft and quiet again, “can I—can I tell you something?”

“Of course.” I smiled back at him, but the way he was looking at me...my heart began to race.

His cheeks were flushed, and after a moment his gaze fell. He took a deep breath, his eyes going back to mine.

I watched: he nervously tracked from freckle to freckle, finally settling, clenching his jaw, determining himself for what he was about to say.

My heart beat against my chest, and out of the blue, the day was so very hot, the sky so very blue and clear, like his eyes, his eyes...

"I...I don't know, I, I think..."

I was wide-eyed and hung up like an idiot, staring into his face, desperately hoping that he was saying what I thought he was saying.

"I really like you," he whispered. "I think I kinda love you."

My breath caught, and ten thousand white-winged cranes burst through my chest, into the skies that were his eyes, as his nectarine-tasting mouth met my own, lingered there.

Sweetness and summer were on his lips, all tragedies fading, time slowing to the velocity of two heartbeats coalescing, the moment neverending, like the nectarines, the raspberries, the bright and vibrant and light-crying sun, the joyful, vivid heavens, *him*.

Dal's touch was as soft as I'd ever felt it, and his hand was pleasantly anchored against the side of my face as he kissed me, loved me, filled me with the bright blue sky and his golden beams, all of it gentle.

My hand found his shoulder, sun-warmed, something solid to hold onto, someone who loved me. I wanted to weep, for he was so lovely.

He was first to pull back, his mouth just inches from mine, cheeks flushed and hot and eyes young, like a child.

Dal.

***

We sat there under the tree by the shore late into the afternoon, eating those wild nectarines and telling each other things we would likely never have said before a kiss. I think both him and I were bewildered at what it felt like, what it felt like to love someone else, kiss someone else. We kept telling each other what we loved about it, but neither of us kissed the other again, for fear that we might ruin it, might take away from how special it was if we did it too much.

We were pulled apart from each other by the notion of dinnertime, and eventually, both of us went home with ridiculous smiles on our faces, and the whole evening, my thoughts were on him, remembering the care in his touch, his lips tasting sweetly of nectarines, and I knew I would go back again and again for that memory, again and again to him.

***

The next morning, I decided I wanted to be the one to surprise Dal with a visit, and so I was out early to make my way to his house.

The sky was bright, the sun hot, as always—but there was a strong, vivid breeze in the air, and as I walked there I smiled, remembering his lips on mine, over and over and over again.

I walked up his driveway, smiled at the yellow clapboard house, smiled at the toys on the porch, smiled at the screen door. The door behind it was closed, too, so I opened the screen door and gave a knock on the white wooden one that lay behind it.

I waited, not minding as seconds went by, because I would get to see his grin, get to see him, Dal...

The door opened.

Dal's brother Curtis stood there, his eyes red-rimmed.

"You're here to see Dal, aren't you?" he said, voice trembling, the words bitter.

"Yeah..." My smile faded as I took in the dishevelled

young man.

Curtis opened his mouth, and then closed it, and then finally opened it again after a long, long moment.

"Do you know that it was very windy last night?"

"What?"

"The ocean was choppy and white."

I stared at Curtis.

"Dal hadn't swam in months," he choked. "Not since his friend died."

Trees and brush rustled in the distance. A pang weighed down my stomach.

"Dal went swimming last night for the first time in a long time, you know. Said he was just feeling so good that he would give it a go. That he felt better about it now."

I stared at Curtis's eyes, redder and redder now.

"There was a big wave."

My breath caught. "Is he o—"

"He's dead. He got water in his lungs and he choked and drowned and none of us got to him in time. Dal's dead."

I stared at Curtis for a very, very, very long time.

I couldn't speak, couldn't think, couldn't do.

I turned and walked off the porch, walked and walked until I walked straight into the sea. In my mind I might as well have scrambled to the water's edge—the time floated by in a strange rapid stasis, and suddenly I was there, standing in the water.

I stood there. Cement might as well have kept me there, blocked into the sand. It all paraded before my eyes. Couldn't stop it.

Surely, he would come out of the water, and hug me. Surely, he would tell me we should go get ice cream. Surely, we would keep talking about our kiss, and maybe we would even kiss again.

It wasn't supposed to have been him. Dal wasn't supposed to die—

I choked, an inaugurating sob pulling my ribcage tight.

Water cut at my knees. Sand bristled between my toes.

My chest ripped open. It all spilled out.

They say the ocean tastes like tears.

He wasn't dead, he wasn't, he wasn't, Dal wasn't dead, Dal wasn't dead, Dal wasn't dead, wasn't he? The waves were cutting at my knees, not even sorry for what they had done, no, and I couldn't take it anymore, and suddenly I was prostrate in the sand, I couldn't be in that water any more, beating the sand, he wasn't dead, wasn't dead, wasn't dead, wasn't dead!

Why the boy who, himself, had lost a friend to drowning? Why the boy who taught me the stars, who kissed me with nectarine lips, who showed me the summer? He wasn't dead, wasn't dead, oh, God, why take him?

His nosebleed. The sunset. *They say the ocean tastes like tears.* The ice-cream stand. He was real. The raspberry patch. Dinner at his house. The constellations. The nectarines. His kiss. Him. All of it gold to me. All of it I had held so carefully in my hands, and now it flashed before my eyes in searing sequences.

I would never get to see him again.

I don't know if it was ocean spray or tears on my face —likely both.

They say the ocean tastes like tears. The summers here are the best you'll find anywhere. I'm real as anything else, I reckon. Summer always comes back around. It never really even leaves. As long as you can see Polaris, you'll never get lost.

I really like you. I think I kinda love you.

I suddenly knew:

It was my duty to stand by the shore, to man the ice-cream stand every once in a while, to pick raspberries, to invite people over for supper, to admire the stars and remember the Southern Cross, to eat nectarines in the shade, to care, to learn, to live, to love.

No matter how much it would hurt, no matter how my body would feel empty, aching for him, it was my duty.

Maybe twelve long months would pass, and we'd all be a little more fine, maybe, I would be able to endure summer next year, knowing I still had his love. I still had his memories, I did, I had his laugh, his touch, his kiss, I still had his love, even if his body might be gone.

His body might be gone and I might not forgive the water. I might not ever set foot in the ocean again.

But if nothing else, at least many waters could not quench love, and neither could the floods drown it.

Acknowledgements

Right off the bat, I will boldly admit that this story would not have been possible without the elephant in the room, the guy I had a crush on when I was like fifteen. So, here's to you, D.H., I guess you got me published. Yee-haw. (Readers, do with this information what you will.)

G.J., my lovely friend, editor, and publisher: THANK YOU! The support and encouragement and patience you had (and still have!) for me about everything means the world. You are wonderful and I'm so blessed to have you as one of my best friends. I think about sitting in the kitchen of the Chesteen with you, and peeling oranges, and shelling those good fresh pecans, and watching Cars 2 (what a fever dream). You mean so very much to me. Thank you for providing me the opportunity to realize my writing dreams (and sorry it took me like a year to edit this story). Love you to the ends of the earth, king of Bashan!

The Peasants (G.J., L.Z., E.S., J.W., L.B., & L.P.): You guys are forever my support system! I'm so glad Kingdom Pen brought us together, I really and truly love you all more than words can describe. Twelve-year-old me could never have imagined that all of this would have led to me being published. Three cheers for the Peasants! I'm so grateful to have you guys. (In addition, a special thanks to L.Z. and J.W. for allowing me to go on and on about OMB in your DMs.) Thank you all for doing life with me and always being here for me—you mean so much to me and have shaped my life in ways beyond any of our wildest imaginings. I wouldn't be where I am now without you.

L.S.: You have been my favourite teacher, and thank you for always supporting my writing! I remember me asking once, half-joking, if you were proud of me. You told me that you're always proud of me—to this day, that still means a lot, and I am touched to know my writing has impacted you.

Thank you for everything you've done for me. I hope I've been a good student.

C.R.: Look! I got published! Yippee! Us trading writing back and forth always brightens my day. Thank you for being a brother to me--I'm so grateful to have you. You are such an amazing friend and I miss you all the time. Can we keep having conversations about baseball? I'd like that.

Vansire, my favourite band: Should you ever read this by some bizarre chance, you ought to know that this story would have been quite literally impossible without your music. Reflections & Reveries was a crucial album for me when I wrote this novelette (and, in all honesty, it still is. I love R&R). Songs like "Montana Girl", "Postal Codes" and "Love You Too" are at the very core of this story—especially "Montana Girl". Your soundscapes helped to create the world and imagery that my writing lives in, and your music has shaped my personal canon to a degree I can barely explain. I'm still living off having seen you guys in Toronto in 2025! One of the most special nights of my life. Thank you for making music that I go back to again and again. I learn something new about myself every time.

A.M.: I know, I know, it's not OMB, but I got published and that's a start! YAY!! Thank you for putting up with my craziness, and thank you for always encouraging me to write, for always listening to me, loving me. You mean so much to me and you are one of the dearest friends I never expected to make. Your fingerprints are on my heart and I think that's really showed up in my writing. Thank you for always cheering me up when I'm down and for laughing with me in various locker rooms. Despite all jokes, this guy is most certainly not a letdown. I love you forever. You mean the world to me and I hope you always remember that.

B.H.W.: Besides the fact that my author photo is not a picture of a certain Nathan Squire, what about this story isn't for you? Even though we got close after I had written this, it's yours now. I'm so glad it could inspire aspects of SE. You saw the potential in this story even when it was purely just potential. You are a colourful and bright puffin, you are the steady blinking beacon light of a cell tower so that airplanes don't crash into it, you are hands that hold me and peel me oranges, you are a giving tree, you are the satisfying warmth found in a good bowl of soup and the tone of a nice Telecaster, you are the cup to my droplet, you are worms that make the soil good and fertile and you are a golden tortoise beetle that is bright and resplendent and you are why I alter my words out of love. Call me when the world looks bleak. Our summer never ends.

L.K.M., G.M., S.A., my family: Thank you for always supporting me! I would never be able to realize any of my dreams without you. I know that me going on and on about writing surely gets old, but your willingness to listen and to support my passions is what makes things like this possible. I love you guys beyond words and I cannot express enough my gratitude for having such a wonderful and loving family. Thank you, thank you, thank you always. I hope that this story will be the first of many things I get published someday!

God: For everything ever, everything beyond articulation. You know my heart. Here is my effort and everything, all of it, is all Yours. I love You.

About Grace King-Matchett

Grace King-Matchett is a writer, lifelong student, and lover of all things whimsical and silly. She enjoys writing literary fiction saturated with emotion and metaphor. Besides writing, Grace loves spending time with friends, listening to music, making art, going on walks, and playing video games (albeit poorly). She lives in beautiful Canada, but pieces of many places take up space in her heart. You can find her odds and ends online at aliveinaugust.substack.com.

Shattered Shells

Molly McTernan

Silently, she walked on the sandy shore,
Quickly, she stepped in the frothy waves,
Longingly, she held out a pale hand,
But no one took it.

Barefoot, deep blue dress flowing behind,
Lafina jogged lightly across the sand.
She stopped to look at the beckoning sea,
Repeatedly wishing she weren't on land.

As her lungs gasped for more air
And her worn feet began to ache,
The young woman decided to turn around,
Knowing that her desires were at stake.

Looking up first, peering at her lighthouse home,
Lafina gently pushed open the wooden door.
Immediately, she was met by savory smells
And the face of her father as he crossed the floor.

After a meal full of oysters, bread, and laughs,
The two went outside on the beach to sit.
They spoke softly, watching the waves,
Then her father took shards from his pocket.

Hesitantly, Lafina asked why he
Always carried broken shells around.
Her father only sadly smiled and said,
"Someday, your answer will be found."

Feeling an urge, the girl quietly admitted,
"I want to leave, being here brings me chafe."
The old man placed a hand on her shoulder,

"Daughter, I want you here to keep you safe."

The slow weeks passed; the months went on,
And Lafina started to take on a bitter tone.
While her father worked the lighthouse,
The young woman was left on her own.

Why shouldn't she do things a different way?
Why shouldn't she be free to explore?
And so, one dark, shadowy night,
Lafina packed, left her home, and shut the door.

The red-haired, pale-faced, barefoot young woman
Walked away, hoisting a bag on her bony shoulders.
She grimaced as her feet and memories were pricked
By thoughts of times gone, shells and small boulders.

In two hours, she saw a building's distant light,
Knew her journey was about to begin.
Getting closer to the town, wondering if she should stay,
Lafina traveled a bit farther, then took room at an inn.

Before the rise of an early, morning sun,
The young lady had already woken and stood in line
At an old, wooden shop called 'The Conch Shell'
Which looked like a good place to dine.

Her short hair fell in restless, bed-made tangles
And she slowly fingered them while she waited.
But as she tried to pass the time, she turned because
"You're looking for an adventure," had been stated.

Lafina was confused, cocked her fire-adorned head,

For a tall, weather-worn man stood there
With a hand on the top of a wooden cane
And a smiling face framed by wavy black hair.

He limped over and offered to buy her some warm soup
And then she sat at a nearby table, he over by the door
As he told tales of his past, daring sailings abroad,
Which may have been truthful; she wasn't quite sure.

All too soon, Lafina and the sailor had decided that
The young woman would come aboard the next sail
To find what she had been so looking for
And to be able to share her own tale.

In just a few days, she stood on the dock,
Staring at a ship named the *World*.
With a gulp, Lafina walked up the plank,
Whilst all the while her little heart unfurled.

She told herself it would be all right,
Her father probably wouldn't notice her absence.
So, she made herself quite comfortable
As they traveled into the morning's brilliance.

For the first week, Lafina enjoyed it all,
With sea shanties and fish stew galore.
But soon she began to wonder about
When she would start to find more.

One starry night, she sat out on the deck
While most of the sailors slept in hammocks below,
And just rocked gently and cautiously listened
To the ocean's lull and the wind's blow.

Suddenly, the ship came alive with men,
Each one seemed ready to throw a fit,
And when Lafina looked in the horizon,
She saw something terrible: pirates!

They sailed in swiftly, flying a black flag,
And before the girl knew, came to her vessel.
Planks were laid, swords were drawn,
And the ship was taken without a tussle.

The once-thought "brave" sailors
Now lumbered aboard the opposing craft.
The ones Lafina had assumed would save her,
Didn't have or offer a getaway raft.

Her small hands were soon bound tight,
And she was then seen to a chair
Where she was told to wait until dealt with,
Just her and the breeze's salty air.

It was in this moment, so dire and fearsome,
That she began to think on her father's words.
He had said that staying would keep her safe,
Now she was trapped, regretting afterwards.

The next morning, the pirates announced
That the crew was to become members of their clan.
But as Lafina was no use to them,
She was to walk the plank with tied hands.

Of course, she begged and protested,
But it all fell on deaf ears,

For the girl was shown to a wooden board
While her vision was blurred by tears.

"This is the end," she thought with remorse
As she jumped and let out a shriek.
She then hit the water and started to kick,
But as she thrashed harder, she saw a green streak.

As it whizzed past her once again,
Lafina's eyes widened in the salty sea
While she stared into the haunted eyes
Of the one thing that couldn't possibly be.

Its whiskered snout was long and toothy,
Its body was leathery, sleek and blue-green,
But worst of all was its horrible smile
Which was the evilest thing she had ever seen.

The sea monster reached out its claws,
And began to drag her farther into the deep.
Just when she thought her breath would run out,
She was taken to a surface rock and started to weep.

The creature opened its hungry jaws,
And Lafina knew this truly was her end,
When from afar, there came a voice,
Sweeter than even a dearest friend's.

"Stop!" it shouted, and a boat appeared,
Carrying a single man. "She is my own."
He continued, threateningly and with truth.
"You are to give her to me, I am to take her home."

The monster cackled, menacing eyes alit,
But before he could start his horrid croon,
Lafina hurriedly scrambled back
As his fate was met by a flying harpoon.

Very soon, she was wrapped in her father's arms,
Even sooner, she was back at her own home,
And the two of them sat on the beach,
Heads leaned on each other, watching the waves foam.

The man reached into his pocket and took out a necklace.
Made of shattered shells and skill thereof.
"This is why I keep them and you with me," he said.
"Because there is beauty in the broken. My child, whom I love."

Silently, she walked on the sandy shore,
Quickly, she stepped in the frothy waves,
Longingly, she held out a pale hand,
And Someone took it.

About Molly McTernan

Molly McTernan is a daughter of the King who loves good books, folk music, and being outside. She writes sweet and soulful stories and poetry and loves connecting with fellow creatives. When Molly isn't writing, she can usually be found reading, playing her violin, or spending time with her family and many pets. If you'd like to learn more, you can find her online at mollymcternan.com.

Acknowledgements

To each of the authors and poets who have contributed to this epic collection, thank you. Your creativity, talent, patience, and hard work are appreciated beyond words. I love you ladies and am so proud of how this anthology has turned out. Your stories and poems couldn't be more perfect.

To our readers, ARC reviewers, Kickstarter backers, family, friends, and everyone who has supported this project, we're so grateful for you and all the ways you've helped us bring these stories to life.

Issabelle, Joy, and Grace—thank you for helping me select, edit, and polish these stories and poems. Y'all's insight, feedback, and friendship is invaluable.

Em, your art has given this collection another layer of depth and another spark of life that truly completes it. Thank you for putting a piece of yourself into this project.

To you, reader, thank you for picking up this book and showing some love to these fantastic authors. We hope you enjoyed this epic adventure and look forward to having many more with you as we continue bringing more God-given stories to life!

- Grace A. Johnson
Founder of Sky's the Limit Press

www.ingramcontent.com/pod-product-compliance
Lightning Source LLC
LaVergne TN
LVHW090547110826
845146LV00001B/55

* 9 7 9 8 9 9 5 3 6 8 3 0 4 *